fake
boyfriend

Also by

KATE BRIAN

The Princess & the Pauper

The Virginity Club

Sweet 16

Lucky T

*Megan Meade's Guide to
the McGowan Boys*

The Private series

And don't miss
Kate Brian's new series:

Privilege

by
KATE BRIAN

SIMON PULSE

New York London Toronto Sydney

alloyentertainment

Produced by Alloy Entertainment
151 West 26th Street, New York, NY 10001

SIMON PULSE
An imprint of Simon & Schuster Children's Publishing Division
1230 Avenue of the Americas, New York, NY 10020
Copyright © 2007 by Alloy Entertainment
All rights reserved, including the right of
reproduction in whole or in part in any form.
SIMON PULSE and colophon are registered
trademarks of Simon & Schuster, Inc.
Also available in a Simon & Schuster
Books for Young Readers hardcover edition.
Designed by Andrea C. Uva
The text of this book was set in Minion.
Manufactured in the United States of America
First Simon Pulse edition February 2009
2 4 6 8 10 9 7 5 3 1
The Library of Congress has cataloged the hardcover edition as follows:
Brian, Kate, 1974–
Fake boyfriend / Kate Brian. — 1st ed.
p. cm.
Summary: When Lane and Vivi's best friend Isabelle has her heart broken by
her unreliable boyfriend, they decide to save her by inventing a new boy on the
internet to ask Isabelle to the prom, but the scheme quickly
becomes complicated, and the results surprise them all.
ISBN-13: 978-1-4169-1367-2 (hc)
ISBN-10: 1-4169-1367-X (hc)
[1. Interpersonal relations—Fiction. 2. Dating (Social customs)—Fiction.
3. Mistaken Identity—Fiction. 4. High schools—Fiction.
5. Schools—Fiction. 6. Friendship—Fiction.] I. Title.
PZ7.B75875Fak 2007
[Fic]—dc22
2007024328
ISBN-13: 978-1-4169-1368-9 (pbk)
ISBN-10: 1-4169-1368-8 (pbk)

For Matt, my forever boyfriend

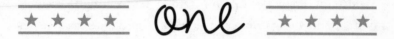

★ ★ ★ ★ *one* ★ ★ ★ ★

"Who would *ever* buy something like that?" Vivi Swayne grabbed the *Lucky* magazine her friend Lane Morris was holding. It was open to a page full of hideous black-and-white dresses that looked like they'd walked out of an *Alice in Wonderland* nightmare—all checkerboard patterns and ridiculously poufy skirts. It was only one month until their prom, and neither of them had a dress yet. But if this was the junk the fashion world was offering, Vivi thought she might be better off without one. "I wouldn't even wear one of those on a dare."

"Please. You've never taken a dare in your life," Lane pointed out, leaning back in the green vinyl booth at Lonnie's Bagels and Coffee Shop, sipping her chai. All around them, groups of kids from Westmont High chatted, sipped their coffees, and noshed on Lonnie's famous chocolate desserts. The brightly lit family-owned place was all chrome accents, fluorescent lights, and old-school counters and booths, yet somehow it managed to maintain a cozy appeal. During the morning rush it catered to frenzied commuters and their caffeine addictions before they hopped the train to New York City. During lunch it was *the* local destination for deli sandwiches. But in the evening it was a favorite hangout for the Westmont High population, and it had enough designer coffees and sweets on the menu to keep their sugar rushes rushing all night long.

"It's true," Curtis Miles added from across the table, gesturing with a decadent-looking forkful of chocolate cake.

Lane blushed fiercely under her freckles and pulled her long red hair over her shoulder so she could busy herself with tugging at it. Vivi had come to recognize it as a nervous gesture—one that was most often inspired by Curtis. Even though the two of them had been neighbors since they were on tricycles, Lane had been harboring a huge crush on Curtis for the past couple of years. Curtis, however, was totally and completely clueless that he inspired it.

"I've taken a dare!" Vivi protested, snatching the fork from Curtis's hand. She took a huge bite of the cake and pushed the plate back across the table. "What about the time I ate that entire carton of Chubby Hubby in ten minutes?"

"Yeah, but you wanted to do that anyway," Lane said.

Vivi deflated slightly. "Okay, fine. So I don't like it when other people tell me what to do. That's not news." Vivi pulled her long legs up underneath her on the bench. She tossed the mag aside and picked up her black-and-white cookie, taking a bite out of the white side. Slumping down, she settled back next to Lane and moved her head around until she found a comfortable position—one that kept the rubber band holding her thick blond ponytail from jabbing into the back of her head. "Where the hell is Isabelle already?" Isabelle and Vivi had been best friends since they shared a desk pod together in first grade, and when they met Lane and Curtis in middle school, the four melded together in a perfect little foursome. Even though Curtis didn't always chill with them now, they were still all really close and had promised Izzy they would meet to talk about prom, since, naturally, they were all going together. "You told her Lonnie's, right? Not Starbucks?"

"Why would we tell her Starbucks? We never go to Starbucks. It's evil," Curtis said, glaring out the window at the new shop that had gone up across the street last winter.

"Please. You're addicted to their Frappuccinos," Vivi scoffed.

"They do make a mean Frappuccino," Curtis agreed, staring into his plain coffee.

"Curtis! God!" Vivi whacked his arm. "Lonnie's right *there*."

They all glanced over at the elderly proprietor behind the counter, who seemed to live in her shop. She was currently counting out change for Kim Wolfe, one of their classmates. Normally loud and totally obnoxious, Kim waited patiently, snapping her gum, as Lonnie sifted out her pennies one by one. Everyone was patient for Lonnie. The woman was an institution.

"It's not like she can hear us," Lane said, lowering her voice.

"She turns her hearing aid down when the place is this

JP'd" Curtis added, shoving his long brown bangs away from his big brown eyes.

"JP'd?" Vivi asked impatiently.

"Jam-packed," Curtis said with a shrug.

"Okay, the whole initializing everything is getting beyond annoying," Vivi told him.

"Tell me how you really feel," Curtis shot back, smoothing his bangs back again.

Just then, the front door opened and in walked their significant fourth, Isabelle Hunter. Tonight, Izzy looked as perfect as ever in a pink turtleneck sweater, skinny jeans, and black ankle boots. Her cocoa-colored skin was blemish-free, her straight hair pulled back in a white headband, and tiny diamonds sparkled in her ears.

"Omigod! You guys are so gonna love me!" Isabelle squealed, rushing over to their table. She slapped a pink binder down on the table with the word PROM spelled across the cover in big glitter letters.

"Uh, you really sure you want to bring that thing out in public?" Vivi asked as Izzy scooted in next to Curtis. It was Isabelle's infamous Prom Planner, which she'd been working on since ninth grade.

"Uh, yeah, I do. Since it has inside . . ." Isabelle rifled through the many colorful, dog-eared pages filled with dresses, flowers, limos, jewelry, shoes, bags, and other random photos she'd cut out of magazines over the years, and she yanked out a yellow sheet from the back. "Ta-da!" she announced, holding it up with a huge grin. "One receipt for a white Mercedes stretch limo!"

"What!?" Vivi gasped, grabbing the page.

"I booked it this afternoon. It's perfect and it's all ours," Isabelle said giddily. "It fits four couples, so we're all in!"

"Iz, this is so OTH!" Curtis said.

"Off the hook?" Isabelle guessed.

Vivi saw the rental fee total at the bottom of the page and whistled under her breath. "Uh, Iz? This is, like, Mount Everest steep."

"It's already paid for," Isabelle said, waving a hand. "I got graduation money from my grandparents, and it was about four times as much as I thought it was going to be."

"You're kidding," Lane said. Isabelle's grandfather, a former NBA superstar, was always bestowing insane gifts on his grandkids. "Isabelle, that's incredible."

"In that case, wanna pay for my tux, too?" Curtis joked, gulping down his coffee.

"Why not? I paid for Shawn's," Isabelle said, grabbing Lane's unused fork and digging into Curtis's cake.

Lane, Vivi, and Curtis exchanged a look of doom. "You didn't," Vivi said.

Isabelle shrugged. "This is what people do when they're in a mature relationship, Vivi," she replied, taking on the tone of a kindergarten teacher.

"Yeah, or when they're in a relationship where one person is totally taking advantage of the other," Vivi muttered. A comment that Isabelle ignored, as usual.

Vivi, however, was officially irritated. Isabelle was valedictorian of their class, captain of the girls' varsity basketball team; she never drank, smoked, or cursed, and had recently received a commendation from the mayor of their small New Jersey town for her volunteer work with Meals on Wheels. She'd been accepted early admission to Stanford University. She was the class's crown jewel. Her boyfriend, Shawn Littig, however, was the class screwup. Shawn was constantly rolling in late, cutting class to sneak cigarettes, and talking back to teachers just to show that he could. Everyone knew he was a total jerk, but Isabelle maintained that he was just misunderstood and that no one knew Shawn the way she did. Unfortunately, Vivi had a feeling it was the other way around: Everyone in the world could read Shawn Littig like a book—a seriously trashy, bargain-bin novel, to be exact— but he had Isabelle completely and totally snowed.

"He just spent all that money on his car, so he was totally tapped out," Isabelle explained. "And my date is not going to prom in jeans and a T-shirt."

"Well, he should have saved. Everyone knows how important prom is to you," Vivi said. "Or is he the only one who's never been taken on a page-by-page tour of that?" she asked, nodding at the prom book.

"Hey. Do not dis the book," Isabelle scolded, placing a protective hand on the cover. "And yes, he has seen it. In fact, he got the exact tuxedo I picked out for him from the sophomore year *Teen Vogue* prom issue," she added proudly. "Speaking of which, has Jeffrey rented his tux yet?"

Vivi took a deep breath. She had been hoping to avoid this conversation, but she should have known better. "Um . . . Jeffrey and I kind of broke up." Vivi picked at a random crusty stain on the green vinyl.

"What? When?" Isabelle demanded.

"Did you know?" Lane asked Curtis, reaching across the table to smack his arm.

"Uh . . . I talked to Jeff this morning," Curtis replied, rubbing his arm and looking snagged.

"Why didn't you tell me?" Lane demanded.

"Hello, I'm a guy. We have a code." Curtis rolled his eyes.

"Vivi, what happened?" Isabelle interrupted. "I thought—"

Vivi held up her hands, and her friends all fell silent. "We broke up last night. No big. It had to happen eventually."

She cracked off the black half of her cookie, folded it, and shoved the whole thing into her mouth, looking out the window in hopes of putting a quick end to the subject. Across the street, Starbucks was overflowing with freshmen and sophomores who weren't cool enough yet to get the understated allure of Lonnie's.

"Vivi, what happened? Why didn't you call?" Lane asked.

"Are you okay?" Isabelle put in.

"I'm fine," Vivi said through her mouthful of cookie. "We only went out for, like, three weeks. It's not the end of the world."

It wasn't like she could actually tell them the truth. Jeffrey had told her he liked her, but said that it was pretty clear that she didn't actually like him. Every guy Vivi had ever gone out with since middle school had said pretty much the same thing—or some variation of it.

"He broke up with you, didn't he?" Lane said softly. Then, when Vivi didn't answer, she groaned. "Viv, I told you that if you kept picking on him like that—"

7

Vivi sighed. They had had this conversation ten million times before. Daniel Lin had been Vivi's eighth-grade boyfriend. They had gone out for months, and Vivi had been crazy for him. He was smart, funny, hot, athletic, and totally attentive for an eighth-grade boy. Everything she could ever have imagined wanting in a boyfriend. And then, out of nowhere, he'd broken up with her for another girl, and Vivi had been crushed. But she had gotten over it and Daniel had moved away and that was that. Vivi thought it was mildly ridiculous that her friends thought that this one thing affected every relationship she'd had since. Vivi never even thought about Daniel except when Lane and Izzy brought him up. Well, almost never.

"Can we *please* change the subject?" Vivi asked, staring out the window again. Instantly, her heart dropped and she dropped her cookie. She could not be seeing what she was seeing. No way. No . . . freaking . . . way. She kicked Curtis under the table and nodded toward Starbucks.

Curtis looked out the window, and his eyes grew wide. "Oh my God," he said.

"What?" Isabelle asked, looking over.

"Isabelle! Don't!" Vivi said automatically. Vivi thought she was going to hyperventilate. Shawn Littig, the guy Isabelle had been dating on and off since freshman year, the guy she was so in love with that she was somehow blinded to the fact he was a total sleezeball, had just walked out of Starbucks with his arm around Tricia Blank—a sophomore who took her imitation of trashy celebutante fashion way too far. And now, he was pressing her up against the brick wall of the

8

building, shoving his tongue so far down her throat, she was gonna need the Heimlich.

And Izzy had seen the whole thing. Her face paled, and she made a choking sound in the back of her throat.

"Oh my God," Lane said, finally catching on. She looked fretfully at Isabelle. "Iz, it's—"

"No. No, no, no, no, no, no, no," Isabelle rambled.

She shoved herself out of the booth and ran outside. For a split second, Vivi was too stunned to move. Then, she, Lane, and Curtis all jumped up and followed. Isabelle stormed to the corner, where the evening traffic was lazily making its way down the road.

"Shawn!" Isabelle yelled at the top of her lungs.

Across the street, Shawn sprang away from Tricia. Isabelle quickly looked both ways, somehow judged that the oncoming Jeep Wrangler was not going to hit her, and dived into the street.

"Isabelle!" Vivi screeched, shoving her hands into the pockets of her green zip-up and running after her friend.

Curtis ran out ahead of Vivi and threw his hands up to stop traffic. The Jeep slammed on its brakes and squealed to a stop.

"What the hell are you doing?" the driver shouted.

"Sorry! Crisis in the making here," Curtis said. He waved Vivi and Lane across the street, then quickly followed.

"What are you doing!?" Isabelle cried as all the kids on the sidewalk stopped to stare.

Shawn backed away from Tricia as if she were on fire and gaped at Isabelle. His light blue eyes darted around as if looking for an escape route. Vivi only hoped he would try to get past her. That way she could punch him right in his infuriatingly hot face.

"Isabelle!" Shawn said, stunned.

"Oh, please. Half the school is here," Vivi blurted, her hands curled into fists. "Did you really think you wouldn't get caught?"

"Back off," Shawn snapped at Vivi. "This is none of your business."

Vivi gritted her teeth and fumed.

"What's going on?" Isabelle asked shakily.

Shawn looked imploringly at Isabelle. "Baby . . . can we just go someplace and talk . . . on our own?"

"Hey!" Tricia protested, crossing her skinny arms over her barely-there tank top. "You told me you broke up with her."

Vivi's heart plummeted as Izzy's eyes filled with tears. "What? Shawn . . . you're breaking up with me?"

Shawn glanced around and seemed to realize there was no way out of this. He looked at the ground, his dark hair falling over his face, and shook his head. "I'm sorry, Iz . . . I'm with Tricia now."

"With her? *With* her?" Isabelle blurted. "For how long?"

"About a month," Tricia said smugly, sliding her arm around Shawn's waist and snuggling into his side.

"The last—" Isabelle buckled slightly, as if she'd been kicked in the knees. All the air went right out of Vivi's lungs. She stepped over and put her arm around Izzy. Her friend started convulsing, tears streaming down her face.

"Iz, please . . . ," Shawn said, extricating himself from Tricia's grasp. "I didn't mean to hurt you. I—"

Vivi glared up at Shawn. "Walk away. Right now," she said through her teeth.

Shawn snorted a laugh. "You can't tell me what to do."

"I think we just did," Curtis said, stepping up between Shawn and the girls and getting right in Shawn's face.

Shawn had four inches and approximately twenty pounds on Curtis, but he was showing no fear. Shawn raised his hands and backed off. Coward. Vivi knew he welcomed the excuse to bail, not to have to deal. Just like all the other times he'd broken up with Izzy—via note, e-mail, text, a message on her voice mail. It was always in the most cowardly way possible. And yet, Isabelle always took him back. Every time. No matter what.

Well, maybe that was all about to change. Izzy couldn't forgive him this time. This time he'd *actually* cheated on her. And half the school had witnessed it.

"Isabelle, are you okay?" Lane asked as Shawn and Tricia headed for his vintage Vette, parked down the street.

"He's been cheating on me for a month!" Isabelle blurted, hugging Lane and clinging to her light blue sweater. "A month! How is that even possible?"

"I know, Iz. I'm sorry," Lane said, stroking her hair.

Vivi glanced around at the freshmen and sophomores, who were still looking on quietly, eavesdropping as hard as they could. Vivi glared around at the onlookers and gently pulled Izzy away and back toward the street.

"And with Tricia Blank!" Isabelle ranted. "She's a . . . a . . ."

Skank? Cheesebomb? Easy McSlutty? Vivi thought.

"... sophomore!" Isabelle wailed.

Lane frowned sympathetically. "We know, Iz."

"It's gonna be okay." Vivi put her hand on her friend's back. Her heart felt sick. Worse than it had when Jeffrey had dumped her last night. This was Isabelle. Her best friend since grade school. Izzy's heartache had more of an effect on Vivi than her own did. "Come on. Let's get out of here," Vivi said.

"I'll go get our stuff and meet up with you guys," Curtis said, jogging over to Lonnie's.

"We'll go back to my house and ... I don't know ... come up with a revenge plan," Vivi said comfortingly. "Between us we should definitely be able to whip up a voodoo doll," she joked, trying to lighten the mood.

Isabelle choked a laugh and nodded through a fresh wave of tears. "Okay." Vivi had a feeling the girl would agree to anything right then.

"Don't worry, Iz," Lane said as they headed down the street toward the municipal parking lot and Vivi's car. "Everything's gonna be okay."

"Yeah, it is, because if the voodoo doll doesn't work, I'm going to go over there and kick his ass. Believe me," Vivi said, determined. "That idiot has broken your heart for the last time."

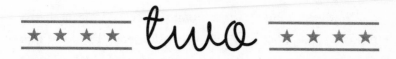

★ ★ ★ ★ two ★ ★ ★ ★

Pick up tray with both hands. Place change on tray. Do not drop change. Do not . . . drop . . .

Lane managed to transfer the coins and bills from her sweaty palm onto the side of her plastic lunch tray without overturning the whole thing. She breathed a sigh of relief and smiled in triumph at the cafeteria worker. The woman looked like she was about to phone the school shrink.

Lane managed an apologetic smile and stepped aside.

"And then, out of nowhere, my dad's like, 'If you don't get all A's and B's on your final report card, you're not going to camp,'" Curtis babbled to her as he stepped up to the register. "I mean, how wrong is that? I'm a head counselor this year."

As always, he was totally oblivious of Lane's extreme stress—all of which was caused by him. Lane pretty much lived not to do anything embarrassing in front of Curtis. As long as she didn't, she figured that one day her fantasy of him waking up and realizing she was his one true love might actually come true. She knew it was a thin thread of logic, but she had to cling to something.

"Don't you think?" Curtis asked.

"What? Oh yeah," Lane replied, not really knowing what she was agreeing to.

"So then I'm, like, I am so totally screwed. I mean, there's no way I can pull a B in Calc. Lazinsky sucks, giving us that much homework," Curtis continued. He paid for his lunch, pocketed the change, and picked up his tray with one hand. He clearly had no problem. "We're graduating in a month. Is he some kind of sadist?"

"You could just not do it," Lane suggested.

"Were you not listening to me? I have to get a B or no camp this summer. I have to do it," Curtis told her as they started down the center aisle of the cafeteria. Lane glanced at him from the corner of her eye and smiled. As silly as it was, she loved the way he looked in this light. The gold flecks in his brown eyes seemed brighter, and the sun brought out the red highlights in his floppy brown hair. What she wouldn't give to be able to paint him in the middle of the cafeteria. It would totally be her masterpiece. The best thing she'd done all year, hands down. If only she could get him to . . .

"So will you?"

Lane stopped walking abruptly, and her soda almost slid off the edge of her tray. Luckily, Curtis caught it in time.

"Whoops. That was close," he said with a grin. There was the tiniest little chip in his front tooth from a skateboarding accident he'd had earlier that year. He always touched his tongue to it when he was concentrating really hard. It was totally adorable.

"Will I what?" Lane asked, balancing the tray against her hip. She nervously pulled her hair over her shoulder.

"Help me. With Calc. After school," Curtis said in a voice that made it perfectly clear he'd said all of it already.

Lane had planned on spending her afternoon in the art studio finishing up her senior project. She'd been looking forward to it, actually. She had even created a new playlist on her iPod for inspiration. But Curtis was looking at her with big, puppy dog eyes, and she could never turn down that face.

"Sure. Want to meet up in the library after eighth?" she said, tugging at her hair again.

Curtis grinned. "What would I do without you?"

I don't know. But right now you should kiss me, she thought. Then she blushed and turned around, heading for their prime cafeteria spot.

They always sat in the same place, right next to the glass doors to the courtyard, which were always open on a beautiful spring day like this one, letting in the warm sweet-smelling air. Lane's knees were quaking a bit after her space-out, and she couldn't have been more relieved when she slid safely into a chair. Unfortunately, the vibe at the table was not a happy one. Isabelle was slumped in her seat as she had been all week, listlessly toying with her fork, while Vivi eyed her sadly. This had to stop. Lane had never seen her friend so depressed for so many days in a row. Usually, she and Shawn would have kissed and made up by now—not that Lane wanted *that* to happen. She just wished she could figure out some other way to cheer Isabelle up.

"Hi, guys!" Lane said brightly.

"Hey." Isabelle's voice was barely a whisper.

"What's up?" Curtis asked, shaking his chocolate milk. He looked around at the girls hopefully, as he'd been doing all week long. Lane knew he was just waiting for them all to snap out of it already. Curtis was a good friend to them, but he knew nothing about the required female mourning period after the end of an intense relationship.

"Nothing," Isabelle replied in another near whisper, staring listlessly out the window.

Curtis sighed, shrugged, and grabbed a fry. Lane saw him look at Isabelle out of the corner of his eye, and she knew he was trying to think of a way to cheer her up. Which only made her love him more.

The door to the cafeteria opened, and Lane and Vivi both looked up automatically, as anyone facing the door did when there was a latecomer. It was Tricia Blank, and she was wearing a very familiar black sweater. Lane's face prickled with heat, and she looked over at Vivi. Instantly she knew Vivi recognized it, too. They had, after all, spent an hour in the hot, crowded, Christmastime mall helping Isabelle pick it out. And another half an hour helping her select the perfect manly wrapping paper for it.

"Oh, I don't believe this . . . ," Vivi snarled through gritted teeth.

"What?" Isabelle asked, turning around. Lane wouldn't have thought it possible, but Izzy's skin actually grew sallower before her eyes. "Wait. Is that the—?"

"The sweater you bought Shawn for Christmas?" Vivi fumed, shaking her head.

Isabelle looked over at Shawn's table, where he sat with the rest of his friends—kids who thought that wearing offensive T-shirts and keeping packs of cigarettes in the back pockets of their jeans made them anarchists. Shawn instantly locked eyes with Isabelle, as if he had Izzy radar, then glanced over at Tricia, who was busy smiling and chatting with some of her girlfriends near the wall. He was out of his chair like a shot and walked right over to Isabelle's side.

"Belle," he said, his blue eyes pained.

"You gave her my sweater?" Isabelle said, her voice thick.

"No. I swear. She must have taken it out of my dresser," Shawn said pleadingly. As if he cared about Isabelle's feelings. As if he had any conscience at all.

"She was in your room?" Isabelle half whimpered.

Shawn pushed his hands into the front pockets of his jeans and looked around at the others. "Belle, can we please just talk for a second?"

"Don't call me Belle," Isabelle said sadly.

"Fine. I'm sorry. You're right. Can we just . . . please?"

"Fine," Isabelle said, standing.

She and Shawn walked to the other end of the table near the open doors.

"Unbelievable," Vivi said, shaking her head so furiously that her messy blond bun tumbled into a ponytail. "I can't believe she's actually talking to him."

She got up quietly and walked around the table, headed for the vending machines near the wall—about three feet from where Izzy and Shawn were now standing.

"Vivi!" Lane hissed.

Vivi turned around and shot her a wide-eyed look, telling her to shut up. Lane deflated and turned back to her food. It wasn't like she was going to argue. Vivi was going to do what Vivi wanted to do anyway.

Over at the vending machines, Vivi made a good show of it, pulling some change out of her pocket and pretending like she was totally baffled by the myriad candy choices. Meanwhile, Shawn and Izzy just kept talking, too engrossed in their conversation to notice the eavesdropper. Finally Vivi aggressively punched in a number, grabbed her Twix bar, and stormed back to the table. She yanked out her chair and dropped into it with a huff.

"Okay, that guy should be a politician," Vivi said. "He is all slime."

"Why? What's going on?" Curtis asked, finally buying into the soap opera.

"First of all, he said he still cares about her and always will," Vivi grumbled. "And that he'd never give the sweater she gave him to another girl."

"Well, that's good, right?" Curtis asked before chugging his milk.

Vivi rolled her eyes. "Then he told her that she should move on. That he thinks she's too good for him and she can do better," she whispered furiously.

Lane snorted. "Well, he's got that right."

"Yeah, but to him it's a total joke. He knew she was going to disagree, which of course she totally did. 'I don't understand why you're so hard on yourself. I love you. You know that,'" she said, doing a perfect imitation of Isabelle's voice. "He's totally keeping her hanging. I swear I could just—" She curled her hands into fists and grunted in frustration.

"Okay, okay. Calm down," Lane said, putting her hand over Vivi's.

"She can't take him back," Vivi said, shaking her head. "She can't be second to Tricia Skank-Ho Blank. We need to stage an intervention. Threaten her with something."

Lane rolled an empty straw wrapper in her fingers and laughed. "Like what?"

"I don't know . . . maybe we should tell her we won't be friends with her anymore! Freeze her out," Vivi announced. "Tough love, like in that DVD we watched in health class sophomore year."

"Um . . . Isabelle's not a crack addict," Lane pointed out.

"No. But she is a Shawn addict," Vivi shot back.

Lane's heart dropped. Vivi couldn't be serious. At least, Lane hoped she wasn't. Because usually, when Vivi came up with a plan, she stuck to it. And she made everyone around her stick to it as well.

"We can't do that," Curtis said, crumpling up the empty milk container. "It's way too mean. And besides, none of us could actually go through with it."

Vivi's face dropped and she slumped. "You're right. But we have to do something to make her realize she doesn't need this jerk," Vivi said, glancing over at them. Lane saw Isabelle nod at something Shawn was saying, and the very sight made her tense.

Lane shook her head. "Isabelle is *way* too good for him. If she goes back to him, it'll be a total disaster."

Curtis nodded, his mouth full.

"Good. At least we all see it," Vivi said, setting her jaw in a determined way. She pulled her sneaker-clad feet up on the chair and rested her chin on her knees. "Now we just have to come up with a way to make *her* see it."

"Do you really think empowerment-movie night is going to help?" Lane asked, sifting through the pile of DVDs Vivi had rented.

"It's just a preliminary plan. Until I come up with the real one," Vivi said, setting a huge bowl of popcorn down on the table in her basement.

The basement door opened. "Hi, honey! I'm home!" Vivi's mother trilled jokingly as she tromped down the stairs.

She was wearing one of her more colorful head scarves, with her curly blond hair sticking out in two perfect triangles on either side of her head from her ears to her shoulders. Huge wooden monstrosities dangled from her earlobes, and her makeup was even more elaborate than usual. As always, Vivi's mom had gone all-out for her work party that evening. It was one of the hazards of working at the regional theater, the Starlight Playhouse. There was, apparently, a lot of pressure to look as boho kooky as possible.

"I just thought you girls might want some snacks!" She lifted a grease-stained brown bag. "Leftovers from the cast party!"

"Oooh! I knew I loved you for a reason." Vivi grabbed the bag from her mother. Inside was a stack of white takeout plates with clear covers. Mini hot dogs, mini quiches, mini spring rolls. She tore off the lids and started laying the food out on the table.

"Hi, Ms. Swayne," Lane said, standing up. She walked around the table and hugged Vivi's mom.

"Hello, dear!" Vivi's mother exclaimed, high on life. "What are you girls doing? Movie night? Got anything good?" She inspected the array of films. "Oh! Kate Winslet? I just love her. The actress who starred in my production of *Twelfth Night* last month reminded me so much of her."

"Cool, Mom. And we'd love to hear all about it. Really. But Isabelle's gonna be here any second so . . ." Vivi advanced on her mother, steering her back toward the stairs.

"Oh. Okay. Well, if you girls need anything—"

"We won't," Vivi said, patting her mother on the back. "But thanks for the snacks."

Her mother's shoulders drooped, and her hundreds of plastic bracelets clicked together. "Okay. Well. I'll be upstairs."

"Bye!" Vivi smiled until her mother was gone, then turned around and rolled her eyes. She shoved her hands into the pockets of her oversized track hoodie and slumped down onto the couch.

"I don't know why you're so mean to her," Lane said with a sigh, munching on one of the mini hot dogs.

"Lane, you know that she'd stay down here all night if I didn't kick her out," Vivi said, grabbing a quiche from one of the plates. "She thinks she's one of us."

"Well, she's cooler than my mom," Lane said, pulling her long hair into a high ponytail.

Vivi laughed. "I'd give *anything* to have your mom."

Lane's mother worked as an image consultant at a huge media conglomerate in New York. She was stylish, sophisticated, and unmeddling. In other words, the exact opposite of drama queen Sylvia Swayne.

"Yeah, well, if I ever see her, I'll tell her you said that," Lane deadpanned.

The doorbell rang, and Vivi and Lane both jumped up. "Finally!"

"I got it!" Vivi shouted.

She barreled up the stairs with Lane on her heels and slid across the hallway in her socks. But when she got there, her younger brother, Marshall, was already talking to Isabelle, who was eyeing him uncertainly from the front step, as most people eyed Vivi's book-loving, pasty-faced brother. His blond hair was, as always, slicked back from his face with some thick gel, and he was wearing a T-shirt that read LOVE ME, LOVE MY MAC. Vivi wanted to groan just looking at him. The kid could have been somewhat cute and maybe halfway cool if he wasn't so intent on being a dork.

"I got it, loser," Vivi told him, hip-checking him out of the way.

"Shut up," Marshall grumbled, blushing slightly. "See you later, guys. I'll be in the living room," he told them.

"Don't care," Vivi shot back. Marshall narrowed his green eyes—exactly the same shade as Vivi's—and went.

"Bye, Marshall," Isabelle said, polite as ever.

She stepped inside, and Vivi closed the door. "Okay, what do you want to watch first? *The Holiday*? *She's the Man*? *Erin Brockovich*?"

"Iz?" Lane said uncertainly. "Are you all right?"

Vivi's heart clenched, and she turned around. Tears were streaming down Isabelle's face. She dropped her Kate Spade overnight bag on the floor and wailed, "He's going to the prom with her!"

"Omigod, Izzy!" Lane said. "How did you . . . Who told you?"

"She did! I ran into her at the mall, and she was all showing off about it!" Isabelle cried. "He's taking her to the prom in the tux I picked out. The one that I paid for!"

"What an asshole," Vivi said through her teeth. The prom meant everything to Izzy. They all knew this, especially Shawn. It wasn't like Vivi wanted Isabelle to go with him, but for him to ask someone else, and for her to find out this way, was devastating. "Am I allowed to kill him yet?" Vivi asked.

"I hate him," Isabelle said as she gasped for air. "I hate him so much!"

As Lane hugged Isabelle, Vivi saw something move from the corner of her eye. Her brother was standing just on the other side of the open doorway to the living room, listening to every word that was said. She shot him a look that could have melted steel and put her arm around Isabelle's shoulder.

"Come on. Let's go downstairs," Vivi said.

"'Kay," Isabelle replied, her voice all watery.

After about ten minutes of incoherence and sobbing, Isabelle finally calmed down. She looked around the wood-paneled basement with heavy-lidded eyes and sniffled.

"What movies did you guys get?" she asked, pulling her hands into the sleeves of her fuzzy sweater.

"We don't have to watch anything if you don't want to," Lane said.

"Yes, we do! She needs the distraction," Vivi put in, reaching for the DVDs.

"True," Isabelle said weakly.

Vivi got up and popped *The Holiday* into the DVD player. Just as the previews were starting up, the door to the basement opened and Vivi saw her brother's dorky brown shoes on the stairs.

"Did we invite you down here?" Vivi shouted.

"I'm just bringing you guys some soda," Marshall replied. He stopped at the bottom of the stairs with a bottle of Mug root beer and three plastic cups. "Seemed like you could maybe use something to drink."

"Thanks, Marshall," Lane said, cutting off the insult Vivi was about to spew.

"I love root beer," Isabelle said blankly.

"Well, there you go." Marshall placed everything on the table and backed up. "I'll be upstairs."

"Again, don't care," Vivi replied.

Marshall shot her an irritated look, but turned around and retreated.

"Vivi, he was just trying to be nice," Isabelle said.

"No. He just has nothing better to do on a Friday night," Vivi said.

She got up, took the stairs two at a time, and latched the old-school lock on the door. On her way back down, she turned off the lights, then settled back on the huge leather sectional between her friends. It was time to put Operation Distract and Empower Izzy into motion. No more diversions.

Vivi tossed a few kernels of popcorn into her mouth as Kate Winslet slammed the door on her idiot ex-boyfriend's face and threw her arms in the air. Vivi couldn't have picked a more perfect post-breakup movie than *The Holiday*. Cameron Diaz and Kate both think their lives are over after breaking up with their respective jerks, and then they both find real happiness. It was an inspired choice, if she did think so herself. She glanced over at Isabelle, half-expecting to see her grinning with romantic inspiration. Isabelle, however, was staring at the floor, chewing on her thumbnail.

"What's the matter?" Vivi said, grabbing the remote to pause the movie. "You're not even watching!"

"I know," Isabelle said. She pulled her knees up and sat back. "I can't stop thinking about Shawn. What do you think he's doing tonight?"

Uh, getting dirty with a certain skank? Vivi thought.

"I don't know, Iz," Lane said.

Isabelle bit her lip. "Do you think we could still get back together?"

Vivi sat up so fast, she dumped half the bowl of popcorn on the cold cement floor. "What?"

"Vivi," Lane said in a warning tone.

"You just told us he asked Tricia to the prom. What are you thinking?" Vivi asked.

"I know," Isabelle said. She ran her hands up into her hair. "I know. It's just . . . I love him so much. Tricia's not going to make him happy. And the prom is still a few weeks away. . . ."

"Omigod, do you even hear yourself?" Vivi blurted, gripping the couch cushions at her sides. "You're worried that *he's* not gonna be happy? You're the one who's miserable!"

"You don't have to attack her," Lane said, zipping her fleece hoodie all the way up as if for protection.

"I was just . . . talking," Isabelle added, averting her gaze.

"You're talking about getting back together with him after he cheated on you. After he asked someone else to the prom," Vivi pointed out. She shoved herself out of her seat and started pacing in front of the TV, where Kate was paused in midcelebration. "I mean, come on. When does it end? Forget all the *little* breakups." She raised her hand to tick off the big ones. "You took him back after he skipped the play last year. You took him back after the sweet sixteen debacle. You took him back after he dumped you on the day of your Stanford interview. Remember how freaked you were? You might not have gotten in because of him! And now he cheats on you and rubs it in your face and you *still* want him? When are you going to see that you deserve much better than Shawn *Slut*tig?"

"Oh, that's very mature," Isabelle sniffed, crossing her arms over her chest.

"Calm down, Viv," Lane said, scooting forward and grabbing a mini quiche off the table.

"Why should I?" Vivi said. "Seriously. It's time for an intervention."

"Don't say something you'll regret," Lane said in her schoolteacher tone. "I mean, if you rip him to shreds and then they get back together—"

"They are not getting back together!" Vivi protested, her hands on her hips.

"Uh, I'm right here." Isabelle raised her hand, sounding frustrated. "And you can't tell me what to do, Viv."

"Well, I should be able to," Vivi replied, her blood boiling. "Clearly you're incapable of making your own decisions. I want you to be happy, and all Shawn does is make you miserable. Your relationship with him is all one-sided."

Isabelle's face screwed up in consternation, and she stood, facing off with Vivi over the coffee table. "Oh, please. What do you know about relationships? You haven't had one that's lasted more than a month since Daniel! Shawn and I have been together for four years!"

"Probably more like two if you factor in all the times you've broken up," Vivi shot back.

"You guys—," Lane said.

"Well, at least I'm not always reeling guys in and then torturing them until they dump me!" Isabelle replied.

Vivi felt as if she'd been slapped. "What?"

"Oh God, Viv. I'm sorry," Isabelle said. She briefly covered her mouth with her hand. "I didn't mean that."

Vivi had to sit down again. Was that really what her friends thought she did? Systematically tortured guys?

"I'm sorry, Vivi," Isabelle repeated. "Really."

Lane looked at Vivi hopefully. Vivi took a deep breath and combed her fingers through her thick ponytail. She was a champion at the uncalled-for word bomb. There was no way she could hold it against Isabelle without being a huge hypocrite. Especially in Izzy's current state.

"It's okay," Vivi said, grabbing Izzy's hand and squeezing it.

Isabelle took a deep breath and turned to fold up the afghan she'd been huddled under all night long. "I should just go."

"What? We haven't even gotten to the ice cream yet," Lane protested.

"I'm really not in the mood for ice cream," Isabelle said apologetically.

Vivi suddenly felt desperate. This whole night had been intended to distract Isabelle and help her get over Shawn, and it hadn't worked in the slightest.

"Don't go, Iz," Vivi said. "I'm sorry. I didn't mean to attack you. I just . . . I don't want you to go backward. I mean, you're gonna be at Stanford next year. It's gonna be a whole new world, you know? New people, new *guys*. . . . Why would you want to go backward?"

Isabelle's eyes watered as she shrugged. "I love him. I'm sorry I can't just turn that off."

She took a step past Vivi and grabbed her pink Nine West raincoat and Kate Spade overnight bag off the floor. "Thanks for trying, guys. I do appreciate it. I just kind of want my own bed right now, you know?"

Vivi and Lane exchanged a defeated look. "We know."

They walked Isabelle upstairs, and Vivi gave her a hug before sending her off to her car. When Vivi closed the door, her shoulders sagged.

"How are we ever going to get her over him if she doesn't want to?" she asked.

Lane shook her head. "I don't know."

Vivi stared at the tiled floor of the foyer. "You know, I could have a long relationship if I wanted one. It's just that the guys at school can't handle me."

"I know."

Lane put her arm around Vivi's back and Vivi rested the side of her head atop Lane's. Together they shuffled toward the kitchen with its 1970s avocado countertops and yellow Formica table. Vivi's mother loved kitch, and therefore hadn't changed one thing in their kitchen since buying the house from an elderly couple when Vivi was still in kindergarten. Vivi yanked open the ancient freezer and took out a few pints of ice cream while Lane went for spoons and bowls and toppings. Within two minutes they had put together a pair of towering sundaes. Vivi took a huge bite, dripping chocolate sauce down over her hand. She grabbed a napkin from the ceramic cow holder at the center of the kitchen table and sighed.

"All right. That's it," she said, sitting up straight.

"What's it?" Lane asked warily, nearly losing some of her ice cream out the side of her mouth.

"We are going to come up with a way to keep Isabelle away from Sluttig," Vivi said, determined.

"Like what? Kidnapping?" Lane asked.

Vivi narrowed her eyes, imagining Shawn tied up in a rat-infested basement somewhere, wearing nothing but dirty rags and begging for mercy. "Nothing that drastic," she said. She grabbed her bowl and spoon and a few more napkins. "Come on. Let's go up to my room and brainstorm."

"But what about the movie?" Lane asked, stalling.

"Screw the movie," Vivi said, shoving another huge wad of ice cream into her mouth. "This is much more important. We have to save Izzy."

✳ ✳ ✳

"Maybe we could find her a therapist, you know?" Vivi babbled, pacing back and forth behind Lane, who was sitting at the computer in Vivi's bedroom. She had to step over the piles of clothes, books, and random crap all over the floor, and she kept kicking stuff out of her way. "Or a hypnotist! Someone who could deprogram her. Google that!"

"Yeah, sure. I'm on it," Lane lied, typing her password into the MySpace login page.

"Not that she'd go, because apparently she doesn't see this

whole thing as a problem, which is totally OOC," Vivi said, looking at the ceiling.

Lane smirked. "You sound like Curtis."

"Oh, crap! I do," Vivi said, holding her head. "Your little love bug has totally infiltrated my brain," she teased.

"He is not my love bug," Lane said, pulling her ponytail over her shoulder to toy with it.

"Whatever you say," Vivi replied, sitting down on the edge of her unmade bed. She crossed her legs and bounced the top leg around as if she were stirring something. "I don't know why you don't just ask him to the prom already. I mean, you're just as bad as Isabelle except you can't get up the guts to *get* the guy and she can't get up the guts to *lose* the guy. Why won't you just ask him to the prom? What's the worst that could happen?"

"Umm . . . he could run screaming in the other direction and never speak to me again, which would break up our entire group and change our lives forever," Lane recited automatically.

"Oh. Yeah. That would suck," Vivi replied, looking irritated that Lane actually made some sense. "Whatever—back to Isabelle. What are we going to do?"

"I don't know," Lane said lightly. She knew better than to encourage Vivi. If she did, this rant might sooner or later become an actual plan, and Lane knew from experience that Vivi's plans rarely worked out for the best. But sometimes, if she was lucky, Vivi would just babble with no direction until she tired herself out and the whole thing would come to nothing.

Lane had already navigated to her in-box and was psyched to see a message from SurfBoy07 at the top of the list. He was supposed to be critiquing her last painting. SurfBoy07 was an art student from California whom she'd met months ago on the site. After a few IM conversations, they had realized they both harbored a love of art and a need for unbiased feedback from someone outside their regular classes. They had started sending jpegs of their work back and forth. and Lane felt that her painting had much improved, thanks to his comments. She crossed her fingers for luck and clicked his message.

"Oh! Maybe we could find a way to make Shawn totally unappealing to her," Vivi continued, pushing herself off her bed to start pacing again. "I mean, the guy *is* hot—I'll give him that. Maybe that's how Izzy sees past all the other crap, right? Maybe we should break into his house and shave his head!"

"I draw the line at breaking and entering," Lane said as she read through SurfBoy07's message.

> Hey Penny Lane,
> This painting is amazing. Your use of shading and shadow has improved dramatically. Really. Your best work yet. Would it be lame to admit I'm jealous?
> ☺
> SB07

Lane's heart expanded, and she could barely contain a grin. This was exactly the message she'd been hoping for. Her best work yet. SurfBoy07 was in a real art program at a great school. If he loved it, then it would have to earn an A.

"Whoa. Who's that?" Vivi stopped and stared over Lane's shoulder. Lane glanced at SurfBoy07's picture. With his sun-kissed good looks and friendly smile, he *was* rather Oakley-icious.

"He's just a MySpace friend of mine," Lane said, trying to contain her critique-related glee so that Vivi wouldn't grill her about it. "He's an artist. We chat sometimes."

"Omigod. There's no way that's his real picture," Vivi said. She reached around Lane's back and grabbed the mouse, scrolling quickly down SurfBoy's page. "He totally stole that off the Hollister website or something."

"No, he didn't. I asked about the picture. That's totally him," Lane protested.

"No way." Vivi stood up straight. "No real guy is that hot."

"Do you have any idea how insane you sound? Some-body *is* that hot because that picture is of somebody," Lane told her.

"Well, it's not SurfBoy07. No one that gorgeous has time to be on MySpace," Vivi said. "Sorry to tell you this, Lane, but he has to be a fake."

Vivi scoffed, like Lane was ridiculous, and paced away. Lane's heart hurt. Why did Vivi have to tear her down like that? Couldn't Lane ever be right about anything?

"Wait a minute! That's it!" Vivi announced suddenly.

All the tiny hairs on the back of Lane's neck stood on end. "What? What's it?"

"A fake!" Vivi whirled around, her eyes bright. She grabbed the arms of the chair and twirled Lane toward her. "We'll make up a guy for Isabelle on MySpace! Someone who will totally take her mind off that skeezoid Sluttig."

Lane's skin tightened as her entire body filled with dread. Crap. Crappity crap crap. "What?"

"Come on! Who knows Isabelle better than we do? We can make up her perfect guy," Vivi said, clasping her hands together. "We can make him a little bit dangerous, you know, because we know she likes that. But we can also give him a life! Make him interesting! Shawn's only interests are smoking, playing three chords on his guitar, and being a jackass. We can do *so* much better than that. And MySpace is the perfect place to do it. We can make him as incredible as we want him to be!"

Lane squirmed in the chair. "Please tell me you're kidding."

"Do I look like I'm kidding?" Vivi asked, putting her hands in the front pocket of her hoodie.

Lane stared into her friend's excited green eyes. "Unfortunately, no."

"Good," Vivi said with a grin. "Now get out of my chair."

three

"Unbelievable," Vivi said, leaning back in her chair and crooking her arms behind her neck. She checked her Nike sports watch. "Less than an hour to make up a whole person."

"You sure you don't want to give him a cool screen name?" Lane asked from the rickety old kitchen chair next to Vivi. "Most people have them."

"That's all right, *Penny Lane*," Vivi said facetiously. "Brandon is too cool for that."

Lane rolled her eyes at the dig.

"What? Come on. You're the one who said he should be a man of few words—which was totally perfect, by the way," Vivi said, trying to appease Lane with a compliment. She reached for the mouse and scrolled up. "Would a guy whose 'About me' reads only, 'Drums. Summer. Books. Coffee—black,' really make up a doofy name for himself?"

Lane considered this with a thoughtful frown. "Okay. Good point."

They both leaned back again to admire their work. The cool black-and-brown background had been cribbed from one of Lane's other male friends—she seemed to have a lot, which surprised Vivi—but then maybe her friend was better at talking to guys online than in person. Lane had also constructed some killer favorites lists. They were spare, but they included a few of Isabelle's faves, and had been rounded out by choices that were convincingly guy stuff like *The Art of War, Junk Brothers,* and select Adam Sandler movies.

Then, the pièce de résistance: his profile picture. A photo of a black-and-white boxer dog they had lifted from some other guy's page. Isabelle loved dogs. Brandon having his pup as his picture might even distract Izzy from the fact that she didn't actually know what the guy looked like. They'd even put "My dog Henley" in his "Heroes" section. Vivi's most inspired idea of the night.

"It's perfect," Vivi said, satisfied.

"Not quite," Lane told her, reaching for the mouse. "He needs some friends."

"What do you mean?" Vivi asked.

"We can't just have him add Isabelle first. He'll look like a loser stalker," Lane pointed out. She navigated to her own page and went to her friend space. "Here. We'll find some people that are online right now and send them friend requests."

"Lane, I think you might be good at this deception thing," Vivi said, impressed.

"I won't let it go to my head," Lane replied with a touch

of sarcasm. She hadn't let Vivi forget for one moment that she disapproved of this whole plan, but she blushed slightly anyway.

Within fifteen minutes, Brandon had eleven new friends and two comments about how cool his dog was.

"I can't believe how many people have nothing better to do on a Friday night than this," Vivi said, shaking her head.

"Including us," Lane replied.

"Yes, but we're on a mission," Vivi pointed out. She dropped forward and put her feet on the ground, pulling the keyboard to her. "Okay. Let's do this."

"Now? You're gonna message her now?" Lane was panicked.

"Why wait?" Vivi asked.

"Let's just think about this a sec," Lane said, getting up. "I mean, yeah, creating Mr. Perfect has been fun, but do we want to mess with her like this?"

"We're not messing with her," Vivi protested. "We're helping her see the light at the end of the tunnel. She needs to know there are other options out there."

"Yeah, but—"

"Lane. It's totally harmless," Vivi told her, tilting her head. "I mean, any real guy could add her on here at any second and serve the exact same purpose. We just can't wait that long. Don't be a wuss."

Lane took a deep breath, and Vivi knew she had her. Her eyes trailed to the computer screen, open to Isabelle's pretty white-and-pink page. The photo of Isabelle from Lane's bowling birthday party last February grinned back at them.

Lane squeezed her eyes closed. "All right, fine. Let's get this over with."

"Yes! What should I write?" Vivi asked, her fingers hovering over the keyboard. She started to type. "Hey. You're hot. Where do you—?"

"Vivi!" Lane blurted.

"What?"

"You're hot? You've gotta be kidding me," Lane said.

"What? I'm trying to sound like a guy," Vivi replied, eyes wide. She turned her hands palm up over the keyboard. "Think you can do better?"

Lane shrugged. "Maybe . . ."

"Fine," Vivi said, standing up in a huff. "Go ahead."

Lane cleared her throat. Tentatively, she stepped up to the keyboard. Vivi stood and looked over her shoulder while she typed.

> Hey,
> Your dog looks exactly like my uncle Franklin. It's very weird.
> Does he smell like coffee and cigarettes, too?
> —Brandon

For a long moment, Vivi stared at the message, completely baffled. "His uncle Franklin? What are you—?" Then, it hit her, and she started to think that Lane really might be an evil genius. "Oh! Because she always says she thinks Buster is part dog, part old man!"

"Exactly," Lane said, crossing her arms over her chest.

"It's perfect." Vivi reached over and hit SEND.

"Wait!" Lane blurted.

"Too late," Vivi said, slapping her hands together. She navigated back to Brandon's page and preened. "Operation Skewer Sluttig is now in motion."

"But I didn't read it over!" Lane cried.

"So? I did. It was perfect," Vivi replied.

"What if she writes back?" Lane asked.

Vivi put her hands on Lane's bony shoulders and looked her in the eye. "Dial down the drama, okay? It's fine."

Lane took a deep breath and nodded shakily. "Okay."

"Besides, look at her page. She's not even online." Vivi released Lane and grabbed a towel off her floor, heading for the bathroom. "She said she was going to bed when she got home. She probably won't even get it until the morning."

"Right. Right," Lane said, crouching down next to her bag and unzipping it. "She's gotta be sleeping by now." She yanked her blue Paul Frank toiletries bag out and stood, but after one glance at the computer, she completely froze. "Uh. Vivi?"

"Yeah?"

"She wrote back," Lane said.

Vivi's heart stopped for a full five seconds. "Already? But she's not—"

"You can cover up the fact that you're online," Lane said, her voice growing shrill. "Something we probably should have done since right now she can tell that we—that Brandon—is on."

Vivi's eyes widened, and she walked over to the desk. "Wait, so she's waiting for us to reply?"

"Maybe! I mean, she knows we're . . . he's . . . oh God!" Lane cried, collapsing onto the end of Vivi's bed. She

39

clutched her toiletries bag with both hands, shaking up the contents like a rattle. "I thought she was going to bed!"

"Well, that was a big lie," Vivi said, putting her hands on her hips.

"What're we gonna do? What're we gonna do?" Lane asked. She dropped the bag as if the monkeys all over it had come to life and bitten her fingers. She shook her hands in front of her as her face grew beet red.

"Calm down," Vivi said, rolling her eyes. "Let's just read the message and see what she says."

She sat down at the computer and opened Isabelle's message.

> OMG! That is TOO funny. I've always thought that Buster had an
> old man trapped inside of him. Nice to know someone else sees
> it, too. New to MySpace, huh? Welcome. Hope you'll accept my
> friend request. So what are you doing home on a Friday night?
> WB!
> Izzy

"She totally loves him," Vivi said, feeling giddy.

"She totally knows we're here!" Lane said through her teeth, pressing her hands into the back of Vivi's chair. "I mean, *he's* here!"

Suddenly an IM popped up on the screen, and Lane screamed, grabbing Vivi like some psycho killer had just broken in.

> **IzzyBelly:** I'm not a stalker. Just bored. Are you there?

"Oh my God. Oh my God. What do we say?" Lane cried,

pressing down hard on the back of Vivi's chair.

Vivi's blood rushed in her ears, and everything felt suddenly shaky. "Will you calm down? You're freaking me out!"

"Well, what's she doing? This isn't like her!"

"Maybe she's taking our advice. Trying to move on?" Vivi said hopefully, pushing back her sweatshirt sleeves.

"We have to write back," Lane told her. "She's waiting. If we don't write back, she's gonna feel rejected all over again."

"Okay." Vivi put her fingers on the keyboard. They were trembling. Lane's psychotic tension was rubbing off on her. If she screwed up, this plan would be over before it ever got off the ground. But if she said the *right* thing—whatever it was Isabelle needed to hear—everything could change for the better. "What do I say?"

"What would a *guy* say?" Lane asked, her hands clasped.

"I don't know," Vivi replied. "Contrary to some people's asinine jokes, I'm not one."

The clock at the bottom right corner of her screen clicked over from 11:31 to 11:32. Vivi's heart rate ratcheted up a notch. On the other side of town, Isabelle was staring at her computer screen, waiting for the perfect response.

"I can't take it!" Vivi blurted, backing away from the computer. "This is too intense!"

"Vivi! We have to do something!" Lane turned around in a circle like a dog looking for a spot to lie down, wringing her hands the whole way. Down the hall, Death Cab for Cutie blared out from tinny speakers. Lane suddenly stopped, facing the door. "Marshall!" she announced.

"What?" Vivi demanded.

"Marshall's a guy!" Lane flew out of the room and down the hallway.

"That's debatable!" Vivi called, following her to the hall.

Lane walked right through the open door to Marshall's room and came back two seconds later, steering a pajama-clad Marshall toward Vivi by his shoulders.

"This is never gonna work," Vivi said, raising her hands— even though she had no alternative in mind.

"Um, what's never gonna work?" Marshall asked warily.

Lane stopped him next to the desk and pulled out the chair. "Sit," she ordered.

"Why?" Marshall was understandably concerned.

"Lane. Marshall has more estrogen in his veins than I do," Vivi said.

"Estrogen isn't in your veins," Marshall corrected, rolling his eyes. "And I do not."

"And see? He's a complete brain! He's not Brandon," Vivi said.

"Brandon *is* a brain," Lane replied. "Smart guys are sexy."

"They are?" Marshall asked, brightening slightly.

"Not this one," Vivi muttered.

"Marshall, please just sit?" Lane begged.

Marshall did as he was asked, though he still looked concerned. He kept his butt near the edge of the chair as if ready to bolt at any second. Like he could really make it out the door if Vivi wanted to stop him.

"We don't need him," Vivi said.

"Yes, we do. We need a guy to talk to her. We are not guys.

Marshall, however, is," Lane explained calmly and logically, her hands on her hips.

Vivi opened her mouth, but Marshall reached up and slapped his hand over it. "Don't say whatever you're thinking of saying."

Vivi rolled her eyes and turned away—her method of consenting to involving Marshall, however ill-fated the idea was.

Lane pressed her hands into the arms of the chair and looked Marshall in the eye. "Okay, here's the deal. We just made up a fake guy for Isabelle on MySpace and now she's IMing him. You have to talk to her for us," Lane said.

What little color there was in Marshall's face drained out of it. He glanced at the computer screen in fear, as if it were scrolling satanic messages. "Wait, if I type back, I'm typing to Isabelle?"

"Yes! And she's waiting," Vivi said, leaning in close to Marshall's face for emphasis.

"Are you guys out of your minds?" Marshall asked, scooting back and looking back and forth between them.

"I think that's obvious, don't you?" Lane said. "Now please! Type!"

"Well . . . I . . . who is this guy?" Marshall asked, sinking down into the chair slightly.

"He's a drummer. Very cool. Kind of monosyllabic and, you know, hot," Lane said.

"So your complete opposite," Vivi put in, cocking her head to the side.

"Vivi!" Lane said through her teeth. "But he's also smart,

and well read. Just like you." Lane told him. "Please, Marshall? Pretty please?"

Behind her, Vivi scoffed. She couldn't believe she was letting this happen. But she knew that if she tried to IM with Isabelle, she would say something personal that would give her away, and she couldn't let that happen. Marshall was as good a choice as any. He'd barely ever said a word to Isabelle, anyway, so there was no way he could reveal himself.

"Fine," Marshall said finally, though he looked ready to hurl. "Monosyllabic, huh?"

"Yes!" Lane said.

Marshall cleared his throat and wiped his palms on his black sweatpants. He typed and hit SEND.

Brandon: I'm here.

"Well, I could have come up with that!" Vivi chided.

"Shhhh!" Lane said.

IzzyBelly: Nothing to do in Connecticut on Fridays?

"Connecticut?" Marshall asked, looking at Lane for guidance.

"That's where he's from," Lane replied.

She sat down on the extra chair and pulled it closer to the desk. Vivi picked up her purple beanbag chair and dropped it next to Marshall, settling in on his other side. Marshall's fingers trembled as they hovered over the keys.

Brandon: Probably about as much as there is to do in Jersey.
IzzyBelly: Touche. ☺

Vivi laughed and clapped her hands together. "She likes it!"

Both Marshall and Lane visibly relaxed.

"Still think this was a bad idea?" Vivi asked Lane, peeking around Marshall.

"We'll see," Lane said, trying to stifle a smile.

"Oh, please. Operation Skewer Sluttig is in full effect, and it was all me," Vivi said with a sniff, crossing her arms over her chest. "Geniuses are never appreciated in their own time."

four

Lane pressed her lips together and checked out her gloss in her locker mirror, then smoothed the front of her new floaty, baby blue blouse from Anthropologie. Normally she wouldn't wear something so special to school, but today, she had a date with Curtis. Well, not a date, exactly. They were studying for their Calc exam the next day. But they were going to walk home from school together and hang out until dinner, which was a nice chunk of one-on-one Curtis in one day. Her heart went all fluttery just thinking about it, and she had no idea how she was supposed to get through eight whole class periods. She felt like she might not actually be able to wait. Like she might spontaneously combust in the process.

"Lane!"

She flinched, feeling as if she'd been caught at something, then realized all she'd been doing was standing at her locker. Vivi barreled toward her, all bright eyes and smiles, paying no attention to the pack of freshmen who had to dodge out of her way to avoid being trampled. She was wearing her jeans and a fitted blue American Eagle hoodie, and her hair was smoothed back in a headband and brushed to a gloss. This was a good-mood outfit for Vivi. She never spent more than five minutes in front of a mirror unless she was in a very happy place.

"Hey! So, did you talk to Isabelle yet?" Vivi asked, leaning against the locker next to Lane's.

Lane smiled slightly. When Vivi was in the midst of a plan, it was pretty much all she talked about. All she thought about. Basically, the plan became her life.

"I talked to her last night," Lane told her blithely. Because she knew that being blithe and vague would drive Vivi crazy.

"Well? How did she sound? Did she mention Brandon?" Vivi whispered, glancing over her shoulder.

"Nope," Lane said, slowly taking her books out of her upper locker.

"No? Come on. You've got to be kidding. She and Marshall IM'd all freaking weekend. I barely left my room, keeping an eye on him," Vivi said, turning around to kick her heel back against the lockers. "She's never going to get over that jackass, is she?"

Lane decided to take pity on her friend. "I haven't told you the good news yet, Viv."

Vivi's eyebrows shot up, and she turned and huddled toward Lane. "Good news? What good news?"

Lane leaned in, savoring the moment. "She didn't talk about Shawn either. Not one single word. No 'Will we get back together?' No 'Why hasn't he called me?' No 'Do you think he's with Tricia right now?' Nothing. And we were on the phone for at least an hour."

The news had its desired affect. Vivi's entire face lit up. "Not one word?"

"Not one word."

Vivi laid her hand out to be slapped, and Lane slid her palm across it with a smirk. At first she had thought that Vivi's MySpace plan was ridiculous and fraught with potential disaster. But Isabelle had sounded good on the phone last night. Almost happy. And after more than a week of self-doubt and misery, hearing her friend laugh was enough to get Lane behind the Brandon plan. At least for now.

"Hey, girls!"

Lane and Vivi looked up to find Isabelle striding toward them. Her hair was neatly brushed, her makeup was in place, and she was wearing her favorite red top and cute floral skirt. Lane went giddy at the very sight of her.

"She's ba-ack," Vivi sang under her breath.

"She *so* is," Lane agreed.

"Come on," Isabelle said as she passed them by. "I need a bathroom run before homeroom."

Lane happily slammed her locker shut, and she and Vivi flanked Isabelle on their way down the hallway. They were almost to the bathroom door when Shawn Littig himself came around the corner, looking as bad-boy hot as ever, all unshaven and messy hair, wearing a beat-up long-sleeved thermal T-shirt. Lane's heart caught with nervousness at the sight of him, so she could only imagine what Isabelle's heart was doing. Vivi cursed under her breath.

"Hey, Belle," Shawn said, leaning against the wall and giving her his puppy dog eyes. This was how he always sucked Isabelle in. Playing the bad boy who was bad only because he was all tortured and needy.

This is it. This is where the whole plan goes to crap, Lane thought.

But Isabelle didn't stop. She simply breezed right by him, shoved open the bathroom door, and disappeared. Lane paused for a second, completely stunned, and glanced at Shawn over her shoulder. He looked as baffled as she was.

"That, my friend, is the Brandon Effect," Vivi said quietly.

"Impressive," Lane said.

"I know," Vivi said. "Maybe you'll start listening to my Curtis advice now."

Lane rolled her eyes as Vivi walked into the bathroom, but she was starting to wonder. Maybe Vivi *was* right about the Curtis situation. Maybe . . . it was time to start listening to her best friend.

* * *

Lane walked toward the bleachers after school, her heart pounding against her rib cage, trying to get out. All day she'd been thinking about Vivi and Isabelle and Shawn and Brandon. All day she'd been psyching herself up to do the deed. To follow Vivi's advice. To open her mouth and just say it:

"Wanna go to the prom with me?" About five minutes earlier, she'd been ready. She'd been absolutely, positively sure that she could do it. But now, seeing Curtis up ahead chatting with some of the guys, she knew the exact opposite was true.

There was no way she could do this. No way in hell.

But at least then you'll know, she told herself. *At least then you can stop feeling so nauseated all the time.*

Curtis spotted her and grinned, lifting a hand in greeting. Lane's heart soared.

"Just do it," she said under her breath. "You can do it."

"Hey, Lane!" Curtis said when she finally got close enough.

"Hey," she replied, smoothing a piece of her hair over her shoulder.

She was out of breath, and not from the walk. Behind him, a few of his friends bounced a basketball around on the outdoor court.

"You ready to go?" she asked, consciously trying not to jump up and down.

Curtis pressed his teeth together and cocked his head to the side. His floppy hair fell adorably across his eyes, and he smoothed it out of the way. "Actually, I can't."

Lane went hot with disappointment. "What do you mean?"

"I totally forgot I promised the guys I'd play three on three today," Curtis said, gesturing over his shoulder. "If I don't stay, they've got uneven teams."

"But what about the exam?" Lane said, feeling lame even as she said it.

"We still have tomorrow to study," he said. "I can cram."

Lane felt tears prickling behind her eyes, which made her feel like a total loser. And that just made her want to cry more. She'd been looking forward to this all day long. It was all she'd thought about. But clearly, Curtis didn't care about being with her one bit.

"Oh. Okay," she said finally, putting her hair behind her ears.

"Listen, I have a kind of huge favor to ask," he said.

"What's up?" Lane asked. Maybe the favor at least involved spending some time with him at some point this week.

"Can you ride my bike home for me?" Curtis asked, biting his lip winsomely. "Jeff's gonna drive me home later, and he just has his Mustang."

Lane glanced at his mountain bike, which was lying in the dirt nearby. Getting it home wouldn't be a major deal, considering they lived right next door to each other, but it wasn't exactly romantic.

"Lane?" Curtis prompted, bending a little to look her in the eyes.

"Oh, uh, sure," she said.

"I mean, unless you want to stick around and watch," Curtis suggested, grinning. "I could always use another cheerleader."

For a split second, Lane considered it. If he wanted her to stay, maybe she should. But then she looked over his shoulder and saw that Kim Wolfe and a few other girls from her class were already kicked back in the bleachers, chatting on cell phones and half-watching the guys. It wasn't like it was a special invitation. Apparently, lots of girls were involved.

"Nah. That's okay," Lane said. "I should probably just go home and study."

"You're gonna make me feel guilty," Curtis joked. He knocked her shoulder with his fist, and she smiled. Even when she was upset, he could so easily make her smile. "So you'll take the bike?"

"Yeah. Have fun," Lane said.

"Thanks! I'll call ya later, okay?"

"Yep."

Curtis turned and jogged toward the court, where the girls in the stands greeted him with hoots and hollers. Lane crouched down and lifted Curtis's bike out of the dirt. As she stood up, the handlebar dragged across the front of her blouse, leaving a big brown smear.

"Perfect," Lane said under her breath as cheers erupted behind her. "Just perfect."

★ ★ ★   *five*   ★ ★ ★

Vivi walked into her room after track practice to find her brother already sitting at her computer.

"God! You scared the crap outta me," she said, throwing her bags down on the floor.

"Sorry. History paper," Marshall replied without looking up. Of course. That was her brother. He hadn't even changed after school—he was still wearing the ridiculously preppy polo shirt and khakis he'd worn that day. He'd probably come through the door, had a healthy snack of apples and water, and come right upstairs to work. How they were from the same gene pool, Vivi had no idea.

"I can't wait until I get my new computer." Vivi threw her duffel bag onto her unmade bed and sat down to peel off her sneakers. "Then you can have this one and leave me alone."

Marshall tipped his head back in frustration, and his blond bangs fell back from his forehead.

"Hey! Your hair isn't gelled into a helmet today," Vivi noticed. "What gives?"

Marshall's face grew blotchy, and it was clearly taking an effort for him to keep from looking at her. "Just . . . trying something new."

Vivi stood up and leaned back against her desk next to him to check it out. "It looks nice."

His blotchiness deepened. "Thanks."

"So, is Isabelle online?" Vivi asked, gesturing at the screen.

"How would I know?" Marshall replied.

"Uhh . . . because you've got the MySpace window minimized right there," Vivi replied. "Why don't you check?"

Marshall blinked. "Oh, yeah. I forgot that was there."

He clicked on the bar, and the MySpace screen popped up. Brandon's MySpace screen, to be exact.

"What were you doing on Brandon's MySpace page?" she asked. "And how did you get the password?"

"First of all, your password has been 'double-v' since the beginning of time," Marshall said. "And second, I wasn't doing anything. I was just checking it out. Seeing what you and Lane think a guy's page should be like. I didn't really get much of a chance over the weekend with you ordering me around and breathing down my neck."

"Oh," Vivi said. She pulled her second chair over, turned it around, and straddled. "So? How'd we do?" she asked, resting her arms on the back of the chair.

"Actually, he seems pretty cool," Marshall conceded, clicking on VIEW: MY PROFILE.

"Good," Vivi replied. She noticed that the ONLINE NOW

icon was flashing next to Isabelle's name on Brandon's top friends. A rush of excitement shot through her. "Look! She's on. Let's IM her."

"Right now?" Marshall said, looking at Lane with wide eyes.

"No. Next Wednesday," Vivi said, rolling her eyes. "Just ask her what she's up to."

Marshall took a deep breath and cleared his throat. "Fine. But only for a few minutes. I have to get back to my paper."

"I promise I will get you back to your precious homework before you know it."

He ignored her and opened the IM window.

> **Brandon:** Hey. What's up?
> **IzzyBelly:** Hi! Not much. How are you?
> **Brandon:** Fine. What're you doing?
> **IzzyBelly:** Stressing actually.

Vivi and Marshall exchanged a glance. "About what?" Vivi asked.

Marshall typed.

> **Brandon:** About what?
> **IzzyBelly:** Prom. Everyone's talking about it and I don't have a date. Too bad you live so far . . . LOL I don't know. It just feels like there's no one to go with.

"This is perfect!" Vivi said, getting up and turning the chair around so she could lean toward the screen. "Tell her you're sure she's going to find a date. Tell her she's so amazing there are probably hundreds of guys who want to go with her."

Brandon: Please. I bet a lot of guys would kill to go with you.

"Nice edit," Vivi said, impressed, leaning her elbow on the desk.

Marshall blushed and shrugged.

IzzyBelly: I wish. There's no one good in my class. At least no one that doesn't have a date already.

Vivi opened her mouth to make a suggestion, but Marshall was already typing.

Brandon: What about other classes? Juniors, maybe?

He hit SEND before Vivi could stop him, so instead, she whacked him across the back of his blond head.

"Hey! Ow!" Marshall protested, rubbing the spot Vivi hit.

"Don't send her stuff without my approval!" Vivi said.

"Why not? You liked the last thing I wrote!" Marshall pointed out.

Vivi pressed her lips together. "All right, fine. But at least let me read it first."

Marshall huffed a sigh. "Whatever."

They both stared at the screen. It was taking Isabelle a while to type back.

"Where'd she go?" Vivi demanded. "Dammit, Marshall. You scared her away! Why the hell did you have to mention the juniors? Your class is like a walking horror movie. She probably thinks you're an idiot now."

"I'm sorry, I just—"

Suddenly another message popped up. Vivi and Marshall fell silent.

> **IzzyBelly:** Maybe. I don't know. It's just . . . my ex has been texting me all day today. Just got another one from him. I think he might want to get back together. And I always imagined we'd go to the prom. . . .

"Oh, no! No, no, no!" Vivi jumped up and dug through her cluttered bag for her cell phone. When she finally unearthed it, she hit speed-dial three for Isabelle and clutched the phone to her ear. She was going to save this girl from herself if it killed her.

"What're you doing?" Marshall gasped, now standing as well.

"I'm calling her," Vivi replied, pacing in front of her bed. "She can't be talking to Sluttig. There's no way."

"But you're not supposed to *know* that!" Marshall pointed out.

Vivi's heart dropped just as Isabelle picked up the phone. She stared at Marshall, eyes wide, like she'd just been called on in class and had no idea what the question was. What was she going to say? What the hell was she *thinking*?

"Hey, Vivi," Isabelle said. "What's up?"

"Uh, nothing," Vivi replied, heart pounding. "What's up with you?"

There was a pause. "Nothing . . . You called me."

"Oh, right. I did, didn't I?" Vivi improvised. Marshall tipped his head back and covered his face with his hands. "Uh . . . whatcha doing?"

"Not much," Isabelle replied. In the background, Vivi could hear Isabelle typing. Two seconds later, another IM popped up on her computer screen. She and Marshall both stared at it like it was about to explode.

IzzyBelly: Still there?

Vivi waved at Marshall to sit down and type back. Marshall looked like he was in the midst of an extremely premature heart attack, but he did as he was told. He typed something quickly, and the keyboard sounded like a jackhammer. Cursing to herself, Vivi got on her bed and curled into the far corner of the room.

"Not much, huh?" she said loudly, trying to cover the sound of typing. "Sounds like you're on the computer. Are you IMing someone?"

Instantly Marshall stopped typing and shot her an exasperated look. On the other end of the line, Isabelle was silent. Vivi closed her eyes and held her breath. What was she thinking?

"Actually . . . yeah," Isabelle said finally. "And I kind of have to go. Unless . . . was there something you wanted to talk about?"

"No. Not really," Vivi replied. "I'll talk to you later, okay? Bye!"

She turned off the phone without waiting for a reply and collapsed back on her bed, where a pillow promptly hit her in the face.

"Hey!" she shouted, sitting up and throwing the pillow back at Marshall.

"So much for you being a genius!" Marshall blurted, catching the pillow easily. "You almost gave us away! She could have been e-mailing someone or working on a paper. What're you supposed to be, psychic now?"

"God. Chill out, Marshall. She doesn't suspect anything," Vivi said grouchily, lying down on her side, facing Marshall. "Besides, this was my idea. I can give it away if I want to."

"Well? What did she say about Shawn?" Marshall asked. He put the pillow down and crossed his arms over his chest. His biceps bulged slightly. Apparently he had been working out behind her back. Weird. "Are they getting back together?"

"She didn't say anything. Brandon probably has a better chance of finding out the truth than I do," she said, glaring at the computer. "She knows I hate the guy."

"That's great, Viv. It's nice to know you've alienated your friends so much, they won't even talk to you about life-altering decisions," Marshall said, swiveling from left to right in the desk chair.

"What do you know about having friends?" Vivi shot back.

Marshall's jaw dropped slightly. "I have friends!"

"The people you work with at Barnes and Noble don't count," Vivi replied.

"You suck, Viv, you know that?" Marshall said. He got up, grabbed his books, and closed the MySpace screen. "I'll finish my paper later."

"See ya!" Vivi said, following him to the door so she could slam it.

Alone in her room, she realized that on some level, Marshall was right. She couldn't help if Izzy refused to talk to her about Shawn *or* Brandon. Tomorrow she was going to have to get the girl to open up, and she was going to have to talk her out of getting back together with Shawn, once and for all.

✶ ✶ ✶

"I think I might ask Shawn to the prom," Isabelle announced, standing in the center of her pink-and-white Laura Ashley bedroom.

"What? No!" Vivi cried, sitting up straight on the floral window seat.

"I thought he was going with Tricia," Lane offered. She put the basketball trophy she was toying with back on the jam-packed award shelf on the wall.

"I think she lied. He said they've talked about it, but he hasn't actually asked her," Isabelle said, making a face.

"So you guys are talking again," Vivi said flatly. She turned sideways, bringing her feet up on the pristine cushion. "Great."

"Just e-mailing and texting . . . mostly," Isabelle replied, walking over to knock Vivi's feet down again, which Vivi had been fully expecting. "We're working our way up to actual talking."

"I'm working my way up to not vomiting," Vivi said, glaring up at her friend.

"That's nice. Very supportive," Isabelle shot back.

Frustrated, Vivi put her head in her hands and looked over at Lane, who sat on the canopied bed with her tongue tied, as usual. If Isabelle went to the prom with Shawn, she would be completely sucked back in, and they would spend the entire summer breaking up and getting back together. For all Vivi knew, Shawn could convince Isabelle not to go away to school next year because it would destroy their star-crossed love. He had that kind of power over her.

Isabelle paced over to her big wooden desk and leaned back against it, twisting her silver ring around and around her finger.

"I know you guys don't like Shawn. Obviously," she began. "But I can't help how I feel. Besides, you don't know him like I do."

Vivi had to grip the cushion under her butt to keep from rolling her eyes. How many times had she heard this exact speech?

"His parents are, like, evil. Like *Oliver Twist* evil. They're so mean to him, you have no idea. I'm all he's got, you know? I'm the only person in the world who really cares about him," Isabelle rambled, still twisting her ring around her finger. "I don't know . . . maybe this thing with Tricia is just, like, separation anxiety because I'm going away next year."

"You're gonna use your psych class to make excuses for him?" Vivi blurted.

Isabelle leveled her with a stare. "I'm not making excuses. I'm just trying to understand. He apologized. And I know I shouldn't take him back." Isabelle stopped pacing and dropped her hands. "You guys, I really think he might have changed this time."

Vivi scoffed and looked away. How could the smartest person in the entire school be so ridiculously stupid when it came to guys?

"It's just that I've always imagined going to the prom with him," Isabelle said, slumping down next to Vivi on the window seat. "Getting all dressed up and dancing with him—"

"Just because you imagined it that way, that doesn't mean it's how it's *supposed* to be," Vivi said firmly, turning to face Isabelle. "You're supposed to be with a guy who loves you. A guy who *respects* you."

Isabelle's face fell. "I *know* he loves me."

"But he doesn't respect you," Lane piped in quietly from the bed.

Vivi and Isabelle looked over at her. She'd been so silent for the past few minutes, Vivi had practically forgotten she was there.

"I'm sorry, Iz, but a guy who really respects you and cares about you isn't going to hook up with some girl behind your back," Lane said calmly. "And he wasn't even discreet about it. But even if he was, it wouldn't make it okay."

"You guys—"

"She's right, Iz," Vivi said, buoyed by Lane's backup. "There are other guys out there. Great guys. Guys who won't cheat on you and just expect you to take them back. Guys like—"

Lane's eyes widened, and Vivi snapped her mouth shut. She couldn't believe the word that was on the tip of her tongue. Had she really been about to mention Brandon?

"Guys like who?" Isabelle asked.

"I don't know! Like—"

Something in the room beeped. Isabelle got up and walked closer to her computer. There was an IM screen dead in the center. Vivi, Lane, and Isabelle all leaned toward it to see. Vivi's heart caught in her throat when she read the message.

Brandon: Hey, Izzy. What's up?

Vivi looked at Lane, livid. What the hell was Marshall doing? What if he flipped into his default dork setting and started going on about how Batman is the only true superhero or something?

Oh, Marshmallow, you are so very dead, Vivi thought, fuming.

"Uh . . . who's that?" Lane asked finally, with a too-calm voice.

"Oh . . . uh . . . no one," Isabelle said quickly, bringing up her New York Liberty screen saver. "Just someone I met online." Her cheeks turned a little pink, and she bit her lip to keep from grinning. Vivi's heart started to pitter-patter in her chest. It was working!

"No one, huh? Then why are you blushing?" Vivi teased, nudging Isabelle with her arm. As irritated as she was at Marshall right then, she was ecstatic to see Isabelle's reaction to Brandon firsthand.

"I don't know. He's . . . he's sweet. But it's nothing. I mean, it's ridiculous," Isabelle said, lifting her hair off the back of her neck as if she were overheating just thinking about it. "We've just been talking. That's all."

"Flirting, you mean," Vivi said, moving to take charge of the mouse, as if she wanted to check out Brandon for herself.

"Well, maybe," Isabelle admitted with a shrug, letting the grin finally come through. In the same move, she swooped in and stood between the computer and Vivi.

"You're totally crushing on him!" Lane announced, looking amazed.

"That's insane. We met on*line*." There was another beep, and Isabelle flinched. "I'd better write back. Give me a sec."

She pulled out her chair and sat down, forcing Vivi to back up a step, but she managed to hover close enough to be able to see what Izzy and Marshall were typing.

IzzyBelly: Busy just now. Sorry. Can I IM you later?
Brandon: Definitely. Just wanted to ask how the prom stuff is progressing. Found anyone worthy?

Isabelle giggled before replying. Vivi held her breath to see what she would say.

IzzyBelly: Still working on it. Will keep you posted.

No mention of Shawn. That had to mean something— Isabelle wasn't telling her online crush about her potential date with her ex. It had to mean that part of her was still hoping for something better—that there was still a possibility they could fix this. But how?

Isabelle brought up her screen saver again and stood. "What were we talking about?" she asked, all goofy.

"The prom," Lane supplied, with a huge grin.

"Oh. Right," Isabelle shook her head and looked toward the window, still smiling. She was still giddy over just four lines between her and Brandon. The last thing Vivi wanted to do now was steer the conversation back to prom and Shawn and away from Izzy's new crush.

"Look at you. I haven't seen you like this since you got Dwayne Wade's autograph," Vivi said happily. "This Brandon kid makes you as giddy as Dwayne does."

Isabelle laughed and crossed her arms over her chest. "Ha-ha. Too bad I can't take *him* to the prom."

Vivi felt as if someone had just dumped a bucket of ice water over her head. Every single nerve in her body tingled. How had she not thought of this before?

"Hey, Iz? I'm kinda hungry. Can Lane and I go raid the fridge?" Vivi blurted, her voice unusually loud. Lane looked at Vivi quizzically and then quickly covered it up when Izzy looked at her.

"Sure," Izzy said with a shrug. "I think there's still some sandwiches left over from the fund-raiser my parents hosted the other night."

"Perfect!" Vivi said with a grin, yanking on Lane's arm.

The second they were through the door, Vivi pulled Lane's arm hard and dragged her down the hallway.

"Ow! Vivi! What the heck?" Lane said, wrenching free from Vivi's grip.

"I just had the most brilliant idea!" Vivi whispered furtively.

Lane took one look at her, and her shoulders slumped. "Why do I have a bad feeling about this?"

"Don't! I'm telling you! It's the most genius, brilliant, perfect idea I have ever had!" Vivi promised her. "Even you are not going to be able to deny my genius."

Lane took a deep breath. "All right," she said reluctantly. "Lay it on me."

★ ★ ★ ★ *six* ★ ★ ★ ★

"You have *got* to be kidding me!" Lane cried an hour later, sitting in the passenger's seat of Vivi's convertible Jetta. It was a beautiful, sunny spring afternoon. Kids played hopscotch in their driveways, moms speed-walked along the sidewalks, a pack of middle school boys did tricks on their dirt bikes in the deserted parking lot of the old roller rink. It was the kind of day on which Lane would have normally enjoyed tooling around with the top down, reveling in the quaintness of her town. Unfortunately, Vivi and her insanity were making that virtually impossible. "You really want to hire some guy to play Brandon and take Isabelle to the prom?"

"Why not? It's perfect!" Vivi replied, her blond hair whipping around her head as she drove. "Brandon is perfect for her. What better way to get her mind off Shawn than to set her up with her perfect guy?"

Lane stared at her Vivi. Had she finally cracked? One too many schemes, and she'd crossed the line into total delusion.

"Yeah. One problem. Brandon doesn't actually exist!" Lane's voice rose with each word as she held her own hair back from her head so that it would stop hitting her in the eye.

"So? We didn't post a picture. We could get anyone to play him!" Vivi said easily.

"Right. And where are we going to find a guy our age who'd be willing to go to our prom? Oh, and who Isabelle has never met?" Lane asked as Vivi turned onto her tree-lined street.

"At another school," Vivi replied, lifting a hand off the wheel. Like it was so obvious.

"And how, exactly, are we going to get him to pretend he's some fictional guy named Brandon?" Lane asked, using one hand to hold her hair back and the other to shield the glare of the afternoon sun.

"We'll pay him!" Vivi said.

"With what?"

"I still have money left over from lifeguarding last summer," Vivi told her. "It's gotta be enough to buy one prom date."

"Come on. What kind of guy would do this for a little money?" Lane asked.

Vivi gave her a sidelong glance. "Please. Look at Curtis! What would that boy *not* do for some extra Xbox cash?"

Lane sighed in consternation. Curtis had once babysat his next-door neighbor's twin two-year-old girls for an entire

Saturday just so he could get the new Tony Hawk game. He'd come home with a chunk cut out of his hair, applesauce up his nose, and permanent purple marker slashes all over his arms, but had claimed it was totally worth it.

"Okay, but once we find a guy, he's going to have to learn everything we made up about Brandon," Lane said as Vivi stopped her car in front of Lane's house. "How are we going to teach him all that?"

"Please. The prom is almost three weeks away!" Vivi said happily, turning to face Lane as the car idled. "We have plenty of time. Besides, Curtis can help. It might be good to spend as much time with him as possible right now," Vivi wheedled, looking sly. "Maybe plant some seeds about what a perfect prom date you'd make . . . ?"

Lane leaned her head back on the leather seat and groaned. Why did Vivi have to be so damn persistent? And why, why, why did she always have to suck Lane into her plans? As if Lane didn't have enough to deal with in her own life. Although, the idea of bringing Curtis in did make it slightly more appealing . . .

"Come on, Laney," Vivi pleaded. "We can*not* let Isabelle go to the prom with Shawn. It'll be her sweet sixteen all over again!"

A lump formed in Lane's throat at the very memory. Isabelle's sweet sixteen was supposed to be the party of the year, and Shawn was supposed to play an integral role. Back then, when Izzy's parents weren't as familiar with Shawn as they were now, they had left Isabelle's new car with him, and he was supposed to drive it to the hall where the party was taking place. Unfortunately, Shawn had decided to take the auto for a joyride first and, while flipping stations on the satellite radio, had driven the thing right into the rear bumper of a student driver. Then he proceeded to tell the driving instructor off until he noticed the guy taking down the license plate number and ran off, abandoning Izzy's car in a parking lot like a coward. In the end, Shawn never showed up, the car was impounded before Isabelle ever got to see it, the police had come to the party to inform Isabelle's parents, and Izzy had ended the night in tears.

"I still can't believe she forgave him for that," Lane said, her heart heavy.

"Yeah, well, it was an 'accident'!" Vivi said facetiously, throwing in some air quotes. "All he had to do was make himself the victim and, presto, instant forgiveness."

Lane looked down at her hands. As insane as Vivi's plan was, it was preferable to seeing Isabelle that heartbroken all over again.

Lane sighed and looked at Vivi. "Okay, now let's just say I said yes—"

"Yes!" Vivi cheered, slapping her hands together.

"I haven't said it yet!" Lane blurted, avoiding Vivi's eyes and looking out the windshield. "But say that I did. Where are we going to find some perfect hottie to be Brandon?"

Vivi smiled slowly and Lane's heart sank. She should have known the girl would have an answer for everything.

"Where do all the most perfect boys in the tri-state area go to school?"

Lane, suddenly, found herself smiling as well. Vivi *was* brilliant.

"Saint Paul's Prep."

Vivi slammed open her bedroom door. Marshall was so startled, he jumped up from her computer and knocked over her chair.

"Omigod! Are you *still* talking to her?" Vivi demanded, walking across to the computer screen. Marshall reached for the mouse to try to close the window, but Vivi was too fast. She snatched it away, and he backed up a few steps. Sure enough, there was an IM window open, and Isabelle was typing a response. "You are unbelievable!" Vivi shouted at Marshall. "You can't write to her when I'm not here!"

Marshall's mouth opened and closed a few times as he struggled for words. "How did you—?"

"We were at her house when a message from Brandon suddenly popped up," Vivi said, pulling her Rutgers sweatshirt off over her head as she tugged down on the black T-shirt underneath. "I was so surprised, I almost freaked out and gave the whole thing away."

Marshall shoved his hands into his armpits. "Did you . . . uh . . . see what we were writing?"

"That is not the point! I'm *supposed* to see what you're writing," Vivi blurted. She crouched down to set her chair up again. "You cannot write to her without me here!"

"Why not?" Marshall asked.

"Because! What if you . . . I don't know . . . said something that contradicted what we made up?" Vivi asked, yanking her ponytail out and then smoothing her hair back to retie it.

Marshall followed her with his eyes as she paced across the room, his expression doubtful. "It's not that much, and it's all on his page," he said. "I think I can figure it out."

"Don't you have anything better to do than talk to my best friend as a fictional character?" Vivi asked, whirling on him. Then she thought about it for half a second. "Never mind—I know the answer."

"You're the one who asked for my help with this thing," Marshall said, indignant. He grabbed his soda can from her desk and headed for the door. "If you don't like the way I do it, then maybe I'll just not do it anymore."

"No!" Vivi blurted, panicking. "You can't quit now."

Marshall paused and looked at her, eyebrows raised. "Why not?"

"Well, we don't want her to think you've lost interest," Vivi said, cursing herself for having to plead with Marshall. "You have to keep it up—at least until we find somebody to play Brandon."

"Play Brandon?" Marshall asked, suddenly looking a little pale.

"Yeah. We're gonna hire someone to pretend he's him and take Isabelle to the prom," Vivi explained quickly, grabbing a brush from her dresser and pulling it quickly though her hair. "You know, so she doesn't go with Sluttig."

Marshall's jaw dropped, and he walked over to Vivi's

dresser. "Are you out of your mind? You're going to set your best friend up with a fake prom date?"

"He's gonna be a real guy," Vivi retorted, swinging her hair to her other shoulder to brush out the ends. "It's not like I'm building a robot or something."

"You may as well be!" Marshall said, putting his soda down on the wood. "Where are you going to find this person?"

Vivi's nerves started to sizzle, and she slammed the brush back down. "Coaster, loser?" She practically tossed the soda can back to Marshall and quickly checked for a water stain. "I don't know. Around," she replied. "We're thinking about going to Saint Paul's Prep, actually."

Marshall let out an indignant noise that only irritated her more. "So you're just gonna pick up some guy off the street? What if he turns out to be a psycho killer or something?"

"Dude, you've read too many Hannibal Lecter novels," Vivi replied, tying her hair back again. "You don't think I'm smart enough not to hire some crazy person?"

"No. No way." Marshall turned and walked out the door. "I can't do this. Helping her get over a breakup is one thing, but hiring guys to take her out? That's way too pimplike for me."

Vivi jogged out her door and followed him down the hall to his room. On the way, she couldn't help noticing his jeans. His brand-new, dark-wash, kind-of-distressed, and totally cool jeans.

"Hey, where did you get those?" Vivi asked, pointing as she leaned into his doorjamb.

Marshall looked down. "The mall," he said. "Now would you please leave me alone?"

Part of Vivi wanted to grill Marshall a bit more about all these random changes. The new hair, the new jeans, the toned arms. But she had more important details to focus on.

"No. I won't," Vivi protested. "Come on, Marshall. You can't quit now! What're you gonna do? Break up with her?"

Marshall flung himself down on his bed and raised his hands to his temples like he had a splitting headache. "I don't have to break up with her. You can talk to her from now on."

Vivi considered this a moment, but knew it would never work. She could never sound like Marshall if she tried.

"No I can't. You've already set up a whole relationship with her. I don't know what you guys talk about. What if she references something you said and I have no clue? Besides, I don't have time now. I have to find a guy and teach him to be Brandon!"

"Vivi—"

"Marshall, you're the one who's got her all gooey over there. You can't just quit on us now," Vivi begged, leaning one hand against the doorjamb.

"I do?" Marshall asked, lifting his head.

"You do what?" Vivi asked, confused.

"Have her all gooey?" he asked. "It's actually working?"

Vivi rolled her eyes and threw her hands up. "Yeah. Congratulations! You're a virtual Romeo. And if you bail now, she'll be heartbroken all over again. Not that you care."

Marshall sat up straight, crossing his legs. He knocked his fist against his knee a few times and smiled. "Fine. I'll do it," he said finally, looking a little nervous.

"Yes!" Vivi cheered, dancing around a little in the door-way. "Thank you."

She ran over to the bed and hugged him quickly, but he pushed her back to look her in the eye. "But in thirty years when I'm forced to commit you to a mental asylum, I don't want a hard time," he said.

Vivi laughed and then raised her right hand. "I promise."

# seven

"I'm in," Curtis said with a nod, standing outside Westmont High the next day.

Lane's jaw dropped slightly. "You're in. Just like that. You have no problem with this totally insane plan, and you want to come with us to Saint Paul's right now to pick up guys."

"Why not? It's for Isabelle, right?" Curtis asked with a shrug. He slipped his Oakleys on and started down the hill toward the parking lot. Lane and Vivi exchanged a surprised and amused look.

"Curtis, are you gay?" Vivi asked, as they jogged to catch up with him.

"Vivi!" Lane said with a laugh.

"Um, no. But out of curiosity, why do you ask?" Curtis said.

"What? It would just explain so much," Vivi explained. "Your willingness to come with us to scope guys, the fact that you've never had a girlfriend, the fact that you don't yet have a *prom date*," she said pointedly.

Lane blushed and looked at the ground. Could Vivi be any less subtle?

"One, I'm just helping you with your plan," Curtis said, holding up a finger. "Two, I've never had a girlfriend because I have very high standards, and three, I don't see either one of you guys rocking a prom date either."

Vivi frowned quickly. "Hmm. True."

They arrived at Vivi's Jetta, and Curtis jumped over the side into the backseat. "Ow. Damn. Could you keep any more crap back here, Vivi?"

He pulled a bottle of gel out from under his butt and tossed it on the floor at his feet.

"Back off, Mr. High Standards. I don't tell you how to keep your car," Vivi said, getting in behind the wheel and tossing her blond hair over her shoulder.

"That's because I don't have a car. But if I did, you would," Curtis pointed out, taking a long swig from his water bottle.

Lane laughed as she handed him the blank canvas she was bringing home for a new painting, and he placed it carefully next to him in the backseat.

"So, what's the plan again?" Lane asked as she got in the car. Her chest felt tight, and her palms were already starting to sweat. She could hardly get up the guts to talk to the guys at her own school—guys she'd known since kindergarten— let alone the thought of all the perfect Saint Paul's Prep boys and their perfection.

"It'll take about twenty minutes to get there, so we should

catch a bunch of them on their way out of practices and club meetings," Vivi said, starting the car. "Grab the first cute guy you see, tell him you have an incredible proposition for him, and then just sell it."

Lane nodded and took a deep breath. "Just sell it."

"You okay?" Vivi asked, looking over at Lane as she buckled her seat belt. "You look a little pale."

"I'm fine." Lane propped her elbow up on the top of the car door. "Let's just get this over with."

"You got it!"

Vivi whipped her car out of its space. They sat in the bottleneck of traffic near the parking lot exit for a few minutes, and Curtis started drumming his hands on the backs of their seats. Lane saw Vivi's hands tightening on the steering wheel and knew her friend was about five seconds from totally flipping out on him.

"So no basketball today?" Lane asked Curtis, turning around in her seat to look at him. She had to shade her eyes from the glare of the sun.

"They're playing, but I'm sick of it. Jeff's way too competitive. Did you see that black eye Lewis Richards had today?" Curtis asked, sitting forward and propping his forearms on his knees.

"Yeah. So nasty," Lane said.

"That was all Jeff and his flagrant fouls," Curtis replied, leaning back suddenly as if exasperated. "I like my face the way it is, thank you very much."

So do I, Lane thought, pulling her hair over her shoulder and facing front again so Curtis couldn't see her blush.

"So, Curtis, really. Why haven't you asked anyone to the prom yet?" Vivi asked out of nowhere.

"God! TFP!" Curtis groaned.

"Curtis!" Vivi scolded.

"Sorry! The freaking prom!" Curtis amended. "It's all anyone's talking about. Like there's nothing else going on in the world. What I wouldn't give for one good conversation about global warming," he joked. He crossed his arms and looked out the side of the car. "Do either of you know who you want to go with?"

"No," Lane said. Her heart was going to give up on her. It had to. It could not keep up this insane rhythm.

"I'm thinking about going stag," Vivi said.

"Really?" Lane asked, looking over at Vivi. That was news to her.

"That's brave," Curtis added.

"Yeah, well, our school is devoid of datable guys," Vivi said, turning onto Essex Road, the wide thoroughfare that connected Westmont to the next few towns. "And I definitely don't want to babysit some random setup date all night."

"Exactly! I want to go with someone cool, you know? Someone who'll just be able to kick back and have fun and not take the whole thing so seriously," Curtis said.

What about me? Lane thought, her heart pounding. *I can kick back and have fun!*

"Anyone in mind?" Vivi asked, looking at Lane out of the corner of her eye. Lane squirmed, wishing she could be anywhere but here right now. Why couldn't Vivi just leave it alone?

"Well, there's this one girl . . . ," Curtis said. "But I don't know. I doubt she'd ever go with me."

Vivi looked uncertainly, pityingly, at Lane. Lane felt like the whole world had just stopped as the trees and mailboxes continued to whip past her. Like she wasn't even really there. Curtis had a date in mind. He liked someone. Someone he saw as unattainable. In other words, not her. Not Lane. Of course he wasn't thinking of Lane. Why would he? She was his friend. His neighbor. Literally, the girl next door. The girl who walked his bike home from school. Why did she ever let herself think for even a second that he might see her as anything more?

"Who is she?" Vivi demanded.

"No one you know," Curtis replied.

I'm going to throw up, Lane thought, checking the junk near her feet for something that could double as a barf bag.

"Come on. Who is she?" Vivi wheedled, probably figuring Lane would want to know. Well, Vivi was wrong about that. Lane would rather tear her eardrums out than talk about Curtis's dream date.

"Vivi, he doesn't want to tell us. Drop it," Lane said quietly.

Vivi took one look at Lane's pallor and bit her tongue. "Fine," she grumbled.

"Okay! So! New topic!" Curtis announced, oblivious. "So what, exactly, are we looking for in a Brandon?"

Vivi filled Curtis in, babbling on and on about hotness factor and smoldering qualities. Lane, meanwhile, stared out the window, trying to get control of her breathing.

It's over. He doesn't want you, she told herself, trying to accept it. *At least now you know, and you can move on.* But her logic didn't make her heart hurt any less, and it didn't make the unshed tears recede from her eyes.

Somehow, the not knowing had been a whole lot better.

✳ ✳ ✳

"Eh. She's not that hot," Toothy Blond Dude said to Vivi, giving Isabelle's picture a cursory glance. He wore the standard Saint Paul's Prep uniform—light blue shirt, burgundy-and-blue plaid tie, and burgundy jacket over tan pants. But since it was after hours, the tie was loosened and the shirt was untucked. Vivi had thought he looked pretty sexy, until he blew off her perfectly gorgeous best friend as if she were a troll. "Now *you* on the other hand . . . ," he added, looking Vivi up and down.

Vivi rolled her eyes impatiently. What was it about attending an ancient school with all-brick buildings and no estrogen to speak of that turned guys into egomaniacs? She saw over his shoulder that Curtis and Lane had reconvened on a bench in the center of the sun-drenched quad. Neither of them looked particularly happy.

"*I*, on the other hand, have a black belt in karate," Vivi lied, stepping slightly away from the swiftly advancing guy. "So if you have any interest in retaining your ability to procreate, you'll walk away right now."

Toothy Blond Dude made a disgusted face and walked away. "Freak."

"Loser," she called out loudly. Then she pocketed her

Isabelle picture and walked off to join her friends. "No luck?" she asked, dropping down on Curtis's right.

"Nothing. All the guys I talked to either thought I was in some cult or thought I was punking them or something," Lane said, slouching far down onto the bench.

"I figured her picture would seal the deal, but they all thought I was showing them a fake. Like there's no way a girl as pretty as Isabelle can't get a date to the prom." Curtis sighed, dejected. "Which, of course, makes sense."

"This is ridiculous," Vivi said, scuffing her sneakers into the dirt at the base of the bench. "We have to find somebody." She spotted a pair of tall basketball-player types strolling along the path toward the parking lot and nodded in their direction. "What about them?"

"Too scrawny," Curtis replied. "Shawn's a big guy."

"Him?" Lane asked, pointing to a kid who was bobbing his head to his iPod as he walked.

"No chin," Curtis put in.

"Wait a minute! I think we have a winner!" Vivi announced, straightening up a little.

Coming toward them on the pathway was a tall, broad guy with shaggy blond hair—just like Shawn's. He was rocking a killer tan early in the season, so he was probably one of those privileged guys who got to vacation with his parents in the Caribbean all the time. Or skiing in Aspen. He was chatting with a teacher as they walked together, and he carried himself with total confidence.

"Now *he's* hot," Curtis said, sitting up straight.

Vivi and Lane both looked at Curtis in amusement.

"What? I'm just totally secure with my sexuality," he said. "Secure enough to be able to say that guy is physically worthy of Isabelle."

Lane and Vivi cracked up laughing. The boy in question was getting closer.

"All right. I'm on it," Vivi said, standing up.

God, he was even hotter up close. His eyes were like aquamarines. She was just about to reach out and interrupt the conversation when the guy laughed at something the teacher had said. Cackled, actually. Exploding all over the place like a rabid hyena. He doubled over at the waist right in front of Lane and sucked in air with wheezing gasps. Vivi backed up a step, worried he might have a seizure or something. It was the most awful noise she had ever heard.

When he finally stood up again and started walking, still struggling for air, Vivi was still too stunned to speak. But as he passed her by, she got a very up close and personal look at his "Caribbean tan." It was practically orange. She looked at her friends, baffled.

"Was he wearing makeup?" Curtis asked gleefully.

"I think it was a spray-on tan," Lane replied. "How superficial can you be?"

"Okay, that was scary," Vivi said, picking up her messenger bag. "Let's get the heck out of here. This school sucks. I have lost all respect for the Saint Paul's Prep mystique."

"Yeah. These guys are not that hot," Lane agreed, standing as well.

"Well, they are hot, but they still suck," Vivi amended. "Come on. Let's go get something to eat and regroup."

✳ ✳ ✳

"This is good pizza," Marshall said brightly, gnawing away on his third slice of pepperoni.

"Glad you like it. You owe us six bucks," Vivi grumbled. She crumpled her napkin and tossed it into the open pizza box on the kitchen table. Upstairs, Vivi heard her mother corner Curtis on his way back from the bathroom, chatting with him about the open call the Starlight was holding for their production of *Bye Bye Birdie*.

"Mom! Leave him alone! He doesn't want to be in your musical!" Vivi shouted, tipping her head back.

"We're just talking, sweetie!" Vivi's mother trilled.

She did, however, release poor Curtis, who rejoined them seconds later. "Your mother is TTF."

"Yeah, right," Vivi replied, taking a sip of Pepsi. At least she knew that TTF was "totally too funny." She was getting more and more accustomed to Curtis's strange language. "Sorry about that."

"She's just being Mom," Marshall said lightly, chewing his slice.

"Why are you in such a good mood?" she asked her brother.

Marshall shrugged, smiling as he chewed. "No reason. Good pizza. Good day. That's about it."

Vivi glanced at Lane across the table. Her brother was acting like he was on something. Something a bit more powerful than pepperoni and Pepsi.

"So. No Brandons at Saint Paul's Prep, huh?" Marshall

asked, reaching for his soda. "That's too bad. I mean, if you can't find a willing guy there . . ."

"He has a point, Viv," Lane said, sitting forward in her vinyl chair. "Saint Paul's is the hot guy mecca of the tri-state area. Maybe it's time to—"

Vivi threw her hand up. "Do not finish that sentence. We are not giving up. We've just had a minor setback."

Lane's posture crumbled, and she rested the side of her head in her hand. "I had a feeling you were going to say that."

"Come on, guys. Think!" Vivi said, standing up. She paced over to the shelf on the wall that held all her mother's kitschy salt and pepper shakers and toyed with them. Ceramic cacti from Arizona, a pair of glass owls, the Eiffel Tower and Notre Dame. "Where else can we find cute boys that Isabelle's never met? There has to be somewhere."

"We could try a different school," Lane suggested half-heartedly.

"Nah. If we learned anything today, it's that strangers approaching high school guys with a proposition like this is way too weird," Curtis said, gnawing on a piece of pizza crust.

"Exactly." Vivi paced at the end of the table, racking her brain. "We have to think outside the box. How else do people find dates?"

"Match-dot-com?" Marshall suggested.

"No time for that," Vivi replied. "What we need is to find a guy who would be up for anything. Someone who needs to make a quick buck. Someone who doesn't mind the idea of potentially making a fool of himself."

"Too bad we can't ask my mom for help," Lane said. "Whenever one of her famous clients needs an image boost, she just holds a go-see and picks out some hot model for him to go out with and be photographed with. She'd be able to find us a Brandon in less than an hour."

"What's a go-see?" Vivi asked, leaning back on the kitchen counter.

"It's like an audition," Lane said. "Except the models just come in and show their portfolios and strut around. It sounds totally shallow to me, but—"

"Wait a minute, what did you just say?" Vivi asked, her skin prickling with heat.

Lane stared at her. "I said it sounds totally shallow to me, but—"

"No! Not that part. An audition! That's perfect!" Vivi cried, slapping Notre Dame back on the shelf.

"You want to hold an audition," Lane said flatly. "Are you kidding me? How would we get people to come without Isabelle hearing about it?"

"We don't have to get people to come," Curtis said, pushing himself away from the wall, his brown eyes sparkling. "We already know someone who's holding an open call."

Vivi grinned at Curtis.

"You guys," Marshall said warily. "You're not thinking what I think you're thinking, are you?"

"Mom!" Vivi shouted at the top of her lungs. She turned and jogged to the bottom of the stairs.

"Omigod! It's perfect!" Lane said, finally catching on. She

got up and she, Curtis, and Marshall followed Vivi, crowding around her in the entryway.

"Vivi! What in the world?" her mother asked, appearing at the top of the steps.

"Sorry!" Vivi said, bounding up the stairs. She took her mother's arm and practically dragged her back down to the foyer. "I'm just so excited about your auditions. You're doing *Bye Bye Birdie*, right?"

"Right . . . ," her mother said, confused. She looked around at all the eager faces and seemed slightly disturbed.

"There's a lot of teenagers in that, right?" Curtis leaned on the stair railing.

"We are looking for some younger cast members," Vivi's mom said. Then her eyes sparkled with excitement. "Have you changed your mind about auditioning, Curtis? Because that would be—"

"No, Mom. We were just wondering . . . can we come to the auditions with you on Monday? Me and Lane and Curtis? Just to watch."

Vivi's mother was stunned. "Come with me? Why?"

"I don't know. I'm just . . . I'm just dying to see how the whole thing works," Vivi improvised, grasping her mother's hand and walking back into the kitchen. "I mean, it's your job! Your passion! I want to share it with you!"

Marshall shook his head, dropping back into his chair at the table.

"But, Vivi. You've never expressed an interest in musical theater before!" Vivi's mother pointed out, breathless with surprise.

"Oh, please! You are so wrong!" Vivi protested. "Mom, theater is my life!"

Marshall crossed his arms on the table and dropped his head down.

"Oh, Vivi! You have no idea how much it means to me to hear you say that!" her mother said, tears springing to her eyes.

Vivi flashed Lane and Curtis a thumbs-up as her mother hugged her happily. At the table, Marshall groaned.

"I'm going to call the casting director right now!" Vivi's mother announced. "She's going to be so excited you kids are coming!"

She floated out of the room, and Vivi basked in her triumph. "Theater geeks! Why didn't we think of this before?"

"It's too perfect," Curtis said, beaming.

"And we don't even have to go up to any of them," Lane put in, obviously relieved. "They'll be up on stage auditioning for us."

"For Mom," Marshall said, looking a little green. "They're going to be auditioning for Mom. Who, by the way, you just completely snowed," he said to Vivi.

"Dude. Chill out. She's happy—I'm happy. It's a win–win!" Vivi said, grabbing another slice of pepperoni off the counter. "By this time next week, we'll have our Brandon."

"I just wish we didn't have to wait until Monday," Lane said. "What if Shawn convinces Isabelle to go to the prom with him before then?"

"We'll just have to keep her away from him until then. Marshall will step up the lovey-dovey talk online, and we'll keep her occupied," Vivi said. "If she hasn't said yes to him yet, it has to be because of Brandon. We just have to keep it going."

"So you're using our mother—by toying with her fondest dream, by the way—so that you can hire a fake prom date for your best friend, who has no idea any of this is going on," Marshall said, staring up at her. "You're going to hell, you know that, don't you?"

Vivi smiled. "Yeah, but it's gonna be a fun ride."

eight

Lane stared at herself in the full-length mirror of her dressing room. This was it. This was the dress. After trying on two dozen different gowns, she had thought she would never find it, but this was definitely the one. The light blue color brought out her eyes, but didn't make her skin look too pink, as so many other dresses had. And she loved the way the lace scalloped at the top. With the little ribbon belt and the full tea-length skirt, it was both pretty and trendy. Perfect.

"You guys! Come out already!" Vivi shouted from the little sitting room outside. "What's taking so long?"

"All right! I'm coming," Lane replied.

"Me too!" Isabelle added.

Lane stepped into the common area of the dressing room, and Vivi and her mother both stood up. Vivi was still wearing the dress she had picked—a sophisticated floor-length black gown with a halter top that tied behind her neck—and both she and her mom covered their mouths with their hands when they saw Lane.

"Honey. That dress is perfect on you," Vivi's mother said.

Lane beamed. "I know. Now I just have to call my mom and get her to agree to spend double what she said." The very thought took the smile right off her face.

"Let me call her. I can be very convincing," Vivi's mother offered. She pulled out her cell and stepped out of the room.

"I love it," Vivi told Lane. "Seriously. It's perfect."

"Thanks." They both turned to look for Isabelle, who had yet to emerge from her dressing room. "Iz?" Lane called.

Silence. Vivi's brow creased in concern, and she walked over to the room. "Isabelle? Are you okay?"

"M'fine," Isabelle replied tearily.

"Oh God." Vivi shoved open the door, and there stood Isabelle in what could only be described as her dream dress. It was her signature powder pink with a skinny waist and a slim skirt—just like the dresses she had been admiring in magazines for years. Lane could just imagine her standing up on stage, beaming with pride as the prom queen crown everyone knew she was going to win was placed atop her perfect hair. But right then, Izzy was staring at her reflection with miserable tears in her eyes.

"Isabelle! It's beautiful!" Lane searched around for something Izzy could use as a tissue. "What's wrong?"

"I don't have a date!" Isabelle cried. She collapsed onto the little upholstered seat in her dressing room. "It's a perfect, beautiful dress and I have no one to wear it for!"

"So wear it for yourself!" Vivi said.

"No. This is wrong. I'm calling Shawn." Isabelle dove for her purse and started digging though it. "We have to go together. He knows we have to go together."

"No!" Lane blurted. Before she even knew what she was doing, she had grabbed the strap of Isabelle's purse and yanked it away.

"Lane! Give it back! It's my decision," Isabelle said, advancing on her.

Lane shoved the bag at Vivi, who was much stronger and faster than she was. "Isabelle, no," Lane said, holding out a hand. "You are not thinking clearly right now. You are under the influence of the dress."

"No, I'm not! In fact, I'm thinking clearly for the first time!" Isabelle ranted. "I mean, what am I waiting for? Some guy on the Internet to tell me that he loves our conversations so much, he's going to drive two and a half hours to take me to the prom? Ha! Like that's ever going to happen."

Lane looked at Vivi, nonplussed. So the plan really was working. She really did want to go to the prom with Brandon. She just didn't think it was a possibility.

"Besides, I love Shawn. I know he's not perfect, but I love him. I can't help it. Why shouldn't I go to the prom with him?" Isabelle asked, twirling her little silver ring around on her finger. She suddenly made a grab for her purse, but Vivi held it out of her reach.

"Because he'll ruin it!" Lane blurted. "Just like he ruins everything for you!"

Isabelle looked at Lane, her bottom lip trembling.

"I'm sorry, Iz, but it's true. Look at yourself." She turned Isabelle so she could see herself in the mirror. "You look beautiful even without the makeup and the hair and the jewelry. Now imagine yourself all done up, waiting at your house all excited. And waiting. And waiting. Because he never shows up. Or he shows up drunk and acts like a jerk the whole night. Just imagine how you'll feel then."

Isabelle took a deep breath. Lane held on to her arms from behind. She and Vivi stared at each other in the mirror, hoping that this would work. For the first time, Lane truly thought that a fake Brandon was the best alternative for her friend. It had to be better than Shawn.

"Fine," Isabelle said finally, slumping.

"Good. Good decision," Lane said, releasing Izzy.

Isabelle smoothed down the front of her dress and squared her shoulders. "I didn't say I was definitely not going with him, though. I'm just not calling him right now," she cautioned.

"But Isabelle," Vivi said. "I—"

"I don't want to talk about it anymore," Isabelle said determinedly, standing up and advancing toward Vivi and Lane. "I'm getting changed."

Izzy closed the door on her friends, and Lane took a deep breath. Vivi pulled her aside, far enough away from Isabelle's cubicle to go unheard.

"What are we going to do? She's about to crack!" Vivi whispered.

"At least we stopped her for now. One step at a time," Lane told her. "And tomorrow, we'll find our Brandon. No matter how many bad renditions of 'Put on a Happy Face' we have to sit through."

Vivi's brow creased. "'Put on a Happy Face'?"

"It's from *Bye Bye Birdie*. I did my research," Lane told her, slapping her hand down on Vivi's bare shoulder. "We are *so* in for it."

★ ★ ★ ★ *nine* ★ ★ ★ ★

"Okay, now I know why your mom was so desperate to have me audition for this thing," Curtis said, putting his feet up on the seat in front of him. On the stage, a man with salt-and-pepper hair crooned his way through "Put on a Happy Face," which, as Lane predicted, Vivi had already heard *way* too many times today. "I thought this show was about teenagers. This guy is, like, geriatric."

"There are some older roles in the show," Lane whispered. "Mr. MacAfee . . . Albert Peterson . . . Ed Sullivan . . ."

Curtis looked at her, and then at Vivi, who rolled her eyes. "She did research," Vivi said facetiously.

"Hey! I like to be prepared!" Lane sulked.

Curtis patted her on the head. "We know. It's what we love about you."

And, of course, Lane blushed like a madwoman.

Mr. Geriatric finally finished his song and walked off stage.

Vivi took a deep, calming breath and adjusted her position in her seriously uncomfortable theater seat. The Starlight Playhouse, where her mother spent most of her waking hours, was an old, airy theater with gilded box seats and a huge balcony that seemed like it hadn't been renovated since the dawn of time. Although the décor was beautifully old school, with its carvings and elaborate tapestries, there were loose springs in every seat and the distinct scent of rotting wood in the air. Still, they put on some of the most acclaimed regional shows in all of New Jersey each year. Or so her mother was always telling her.

"Oooh. What about him?" Lane asked suddenly, sitting up straight.

A tall guy with broad shoulders and dark hair strode out on stage. He wore a black T-shirt and jeans and looked to be two or three years older than Isabelle, but that wasn't too bad. "Possibly . . . ," Vivi said.

Then he sniffed back some phlegm, reached down and adjusted himself, and spoke. "Yeah. I'm auditionin' for da parda—" He looked down at his script. "—Conrad? That's a main part, right? 'Cuz I don' take no bit roles no more."

"Or not!" Vivi blurted as Lane slapped her hand over her mouth.

"Unless you want Isabelle to get whacked on prom night," Curtis joked.

"Ugh. I guess the end of *The Sopranos* put a lot of people out of work," Vivi said with a grimace.

"Ew. Ew!" Lane said, turning her face away as he sucked back more phlegm. "That is just so wrong."

As the guy performed his solo—sounding like a bad Elvis impersonator—Vivi tried to think happy thoughts. They were going to find a Brandon. Isabelle was going to be happy. The prom was going to be tons and tons of fun. . . .

"Thank you, Rocco!" Vivi's mother called out from a few rows ahead, where she was sitting with Jeannie, the director.

"He's done. You guys can open your eyes," Curtis told them.

Vivi did as she was told, but ten minutes later, she wished she hadn't. Rocco was followed by Paul of the three chins.

"He looks like he swallowed an accordion," Lane said, which sent Vivi into laughter convulsions and earned her an admonishing look from her mother.

Paul was followed by a guy named Rajeesh who cartwheeled his way on and off stage.

"We need to make a pact right now: no circus performers," Vivi said, putting her feet up on the back of the seat in front of her.

"Unless it's a bearded lady. 'Cuz that would just be fun," Curtis put in.

And Rajeesh was followed by Danny, who looked to be about twelve. He had blond hair, a pair of candy apples for cheeks, and a neck like a pencil. Vivi tipped her head back and groaned at the cracked ceiling above. "This is not working."

"Name, please?" Vivi's mother asked.

"Uh . . . Danny Hess?" the kid said, his voice cracking.

"He's kind of cute," Lane said hopefully, scooting closer to Vivi and crossing her arms over her chest.

"Yeah, for a kindergartner," Vivi put in.

"They're too young . . . they're too old. . . . There's no pleasing you people!" Curtis joked.

"I'm auditioning for the part of Randolph?" Danny said shakily.

"The little brother," Lane explained.

"Go ahead with your song, Danny," Vivi's mother said.

Danny cleared his throat and started to sing "A Whole New World" from *Aladdin*. He started out shaky, but was actually really good. Still, the whole time he was singing, Vivi's foot was bouncing up and down.

"Okay, okay. Get the kid offstage so we can get on with this!" she hissed.

Finally, Danny finished his verse and someone in the theater started to hoot and applaud. "Yeah, Danny! Whoooo!"

Startled, Vivi turned around, along with every other person in the auditorium. Standing in the very back, clapping his hands loudly, was a guy who must have been Danny's brother. He had to be, because he was basically an older, taller, broader version of Danny himself. Instantly, Vivi sat up. This guy was hot. Blond hair. Perfectly chiseled face. He was a bit preppy to be Brandon, in his rugby shirt and clean jeans, but that could be rectified. All Vivi cared about was the fact that looking at this guy was making her heart pound, and it was the first time that had happened all day.

"Well. What do we have here?" she said under her breath.

"Sorry." The guy stopped clapping and raised an apologetic hand toward Vivi's mom and her colleague. "Just . . .

trying to be supportive." He grinned in a totally endearing way. "I'll just go backstage now and wait." Then he grabbed a blue-and-yellow varsity jacket off the chair in front of him and fled.

"Sorry," Danny said from the stage, purple from neck to temple. "My brother's kind of . . . um . . . loud."

"That's all right, Danny," Vivi's mother said, smiling warmly at the boy. "We'll let you know about callbacks."

"Come on!" Vivi said, jumping out of her seat, which smacked back loudly. Her adrenaline was rushing through her veins so fast, she actually felt a bit faint.

"Where are we going?" Lane asked. She started grabbing their stuff up from the floor. "There's still an hour left."

"Not for us," Vivi hissed. "We just found our Brandon!"

✳ ✳ ✳

Vivi speed-walked along a hallway full of guys warming up their voices and going over their lines. Old guys, fat guys, skinny guys, seriously pale guys. None of them even compared to Danny Hess's brother. At least she knew that she wasn't going to be missing anything in the upcoming auditions.

"Vivi! This guy's not even an actor," Lane whispered, side-stepping a ballet dude who was stretching in a way no guy should ever stretch. "What if he can't pull it off?"

"Shut up, Lane. He's perfect," Vivi shot back.

"Wow. That was real nice," Curtis said sarcastically.

"I'm sorry, all right?" Vivi replied, glancing at them over

her shoulder. "I just don't want to miss him!"

She was just about to turn the corner toward the wings when the man himself shoved open the door to the men's bathroom and nearly took her out.

"Whoa! Watch where you're going, there!" Vivi joked.

"Sorry," the guy blurted. He started past her, but looked up as he went and paused. "Sorry," he said again.

Vivi blushed. Was that a double take he'd just done there?

Older Brother Hess was way hotter up close. His eyes were the gray blue of the Atlantic Ocean on a cloudy day, and his smile took all the air right out of her. He had a tiny white scar on the middle of his chin, and he already had a bit of a tan—not a fake one—and it was only May, which meant he was an outdoors-loving guy.

"Vivi?" Lane said as she and Curtis caught up to them.

Vivi blinked, snapping out of her trance. "You're Danny's brother, right?"

"Uh, yeah. Jonathan," he said, pulling his varsity jacket on. She wished he would turn around so she could see what school he was from and what sport he played. "Is there a problem?"

"What? Oh. No. He was great," Vivi improvised.

He smiled, and it sent shivers right through Vivi. Isabelle was going to freak for this guy.

"Great. Do you guys work here?" he asked. "Because if you do, I just want you to know if he gets the part, he'll work really hard and he'll always be on time. My parents work, but I'll drive him wherever. He really wants to be an actor for some unknown reason," he said with a laugh.

Even his laugh was sexy.

"Oh, no. We don't work here. My mother does. She's the casting director. I'm Vivi Swayne. This is Lane Morris and Curtis Miles. We're just here for . . . uh . . . fun," she said, raising her shoulders.

"Oh. Well, tell your mother I'm sorry about the outburst," Jonathan said. "I'm just proud of him, you know?" He looked around at the busy hallway, shouldering his backpack. "Where is he, anyway?"

"Oh, Curtis will go find him . . . right, Curtis?" Vivi said, turning around to beg him with her eyes.

Curtis sighed. "Yeah, yeah. I'm going." He turned and walked into the wings in search of Danny.

"So, where do you go to school?" Vivi asked Jonathan.

"Cranston Prep," Jonathan replied, turning slightly so that Vivi could see the back of his jacket. Which was, it turned out, a lacrosse jacket. She should have known. "You guys from around here?"

"We go to Westmont," Vivi replied. "Amazing, huh? We probably live fifteen minutes away from each other and have never met before. There are just way too many people in this state. Right, Lane?"

What am I saying? Vivi thought.

"Uh . . . right." Lane gave Vivi a confused look.

"So, Jonathan," Vivi said, getting ready to make her pitch. "We just—"

"Here he is!" Curtis announced, returning with Danny at his heels, all ready to go. Vivi could have strangled them both.

"Hey, thanks," Jonathan said. "Hey, great job out there!" Jonathan clasped his hand on Danny's bony little shoulder.

Danny shrugged modestly. "I did okay. They said they'd call in a couple days."

"You'll totally get it." Jonathan ruffled Danny's hair. "Well, it's been nice talking to you guys, but we should be getting back. I have an exam to study for, so . . ."

Vivi's heart pounded as he shoved open the exit door. There was absolutely no way she was letting this guy out of her sight.

"Wait! You can't go," Vivi said, running over to the exit.

Jonathan and Danny paused. "Ooookay. Why not?" Jonathan asked.

"Because . . . uh . . . we have a proposition for you," Lane said.

Jonathan looked at them, intrigued. Vivi was nearly drunk with relief. "What kind of proposition?"

"Come on. There's a diner across the street," Vivi said, pushing through the door ahead of them. "We'll buy you guys some fries and explain."

✶ ✶ ✶

Jonathan rested his wrists against the table—no elbows anywhere near the surface—and stared at Lane and Vivi. A few booths away, Curtis and Danny were wrapped up in a very serious Xbox versus PlayStation conversation that Lane knew could very well take hours. She had suggested they take their own table so that Vivi and Lane could really lay out the plan without Danny asking tons of questions—and being totally corrupted by their deviousness.

"So you want me to pretend to be some guy you made up on the Internet and take your best friend to prom so that she won't go with her boyfriend," Jonathan said flatly.

He is so *out of here,* Lane thought, glancing quickly at Vivi.

"Her *ex*-boyfriend." Vivi took a sip of her chocolate shake and placed it down on the table. "So you in?"

Jonathan sighed and leaned back into the creaky booth. "I knew I should have kept my brother away from this acting thing. Everyone in the theater business is out of their mind."

"First of all, we're not *in* the theater business," Vivi pointed out, playing with her empty straw wrapper. "And secondly, we're not crazy. If you knew what this guy was like—"

"Let me ask you this, does she want to go with him?" Jonathan said.

Vivi fell silent and huffed as she looked out the window.

"Yeah. Kind of," Lane admitted, earning a look of death from her friend.

"So why not just let her?" Jonathan asked. He grabbed a cherry tomato from his salad and popped it in his mouth. "You've gotta let people make their own mistakes, you know? You can't control your friends. If you try, it's just gonna put a strain on all your relationships."

Lane hid a laugh by shoving a French fry into her mouth. Jonathan had decoded Vivi in less time than it took for them to finish their food.

"What's with the analyzing?" Vivi said, letting her arm drop down on the table with a *smack*. "Are you a junior shrink?"

"Nah. Just taking a psych elective at school," Jonathan said with a grin. "I kind of wish my teacher were here right now, 'cuz she might bump my C to a B if she heard that little speech," he joked.

"You're getting a C and you're trying to lecture us?" Vivi shot back. "Nice try."

"Insults! Good tactic! Do you want me to help you out with this thing or not?" Jonathan asked.

Vivi glowered at him, and Lane tried not to smile. She liked this guy. It was the rare person who could actually render Vivi speechless. Still, the silence dragged on, and Lane suddenly sensed that if she didn't step in soon, Jonathan was going to bail and they'd be back to square one. And with prom less than two weeks away, square one was not an option.

"The thing is, Isabelle *has* made this mistake before. A bunch of times," Lane said calmly. "I totally understand where you're coming from. I wasn't all that psyched about this plan in the beginning either—"

Vivi mumbled something under her breath and took another long drink of her shake. She wiped her mouth with the back of her hand and glared at Lane.

"But now I think it really might be the best thing for Isabelle," Lane added. "Shawn is not a good guy, and if he keeps this up? I honestly think he might ruin her life."

Vivi glanced over at Jonathan to gauge his reaction. He seemed to be mulling it over for the first time since they'd sat down. Lane felt a little thrill inside her chest. Had she actually convinced him?

"I don't know," he said finally, playing around with the remnants of the salad with his fork. "It just seems so dishonest."

"We'll pay you," Vivi blurted.

Jonathan's eyebrows shot up, and he dropped his fork. "You're kidding."

"I've got three hundred dollars that says I'm not," Vivi told him. "Plus all expenses will be paid for. Tux, corsage, limo. Everything."

"Everything?" Lane gulped.

"Everything," Vivi replied, never taking her eyes off Jonathan. "You're gonna be driving your brother to the theater every other day for rehearsal if he gets the part, right? Three hundred dollars is a lot of gas money."

Lane smirked. Ever since Vivi had gotten her own car, she'd been complaining that all her allowance went right into the tank, and half the kids at school had part-time jobs just to pay for gas. Girl knew how to make a convincing argument.

"Yeah, but I don't know," Jonathan said. "I mean, have you guys really thought this through? What if Isabelle figures it out? Or what if someone from your school brings someone from my school to the prom and we get caught? This could be *really* messy."

Vivi sat back and crossed her arms over her chest. "You know what, Lane? I think we should bag this. This guy has no guts. There's no way this guy could be a badass like Brandon anyway." Vivi made as if to slide out of the booth.

Lane's heart skipped a surprised beat. "Vivi! What are you—?"

"Forget it, Lane. I'm done," Vivi said pointedly. She grabbed her suede jacket from the coat hook on the outside of the booth.

"Wait! I can be a badass!" Jonathan protested. "That is so not the issue. If you wanted me to be badass, I could be badass."

He pushed up the sleeves on his jacket and cracked his neck back and forth, all tough. Lane grinned. Suddenly she understood what Vivi was doing.

"See? That's not bad," Lane said.

"Oh, please. All prepped out with your lacrosse and your high moral standards and your *salad*. This is a diner, for God's sake. Who gets the garden salad?" Vivi said, zipping up her jacket like she was still going to bail. "I bet the most dangerous thing you've ever done is part your hair on the wrong side."

"Hey! I've done dangerous stuff," Jonathan replied.

"Like what?" Vivi countered. She stood next to the table with her hands on her hips.

"I snowboard," he said. "And I'm saving up for a motor-cycle."

"No way," Vivi said.

"So you *do* need money," Lane added.

Jonathan glanced away, his foot bouncing up and down under the table. He looked Lane and Vivi over, as if consider-ing whether or not they were pathological, then sighed in a resigned way. Vivi winked at Lane from the end of the table.

"All right, fine. I'll do it," he said finally.

"Yes!" Lane and Vivi cheered and Vivi sat back down.

"But right now, I do have to get my brother home." He whipped out a notebook from his backpack and scribbled something down, then tore out the page and handed it to Lane. "Here's my information. Call me and we'll figure out a time to meet."

"Thanks. We really appreciate this," Lane said, grinning widely.

"No problem. You, at least, seem like a nice girl," he said pointedly to Lane. Then he looked at Vivi and narrowed his eyes. "Jury's still out on you," he joked.

"Ha-ha," Vivi said, giving him a little smirk.

Jonathan started past the table to get his brother, but paused. "And, by the way, my hair is not parted on the wrong side."

The second he was gone, Lane and Vivi cracked up. "We did it! We found our Brandon!" Lane cheered, giving Vivi a high five.

"Isabelle is going to *love* him!" Vivi said proudly, grabbing one of Lane's fries. "Shawn Sluttig is history. Thanks to my brilliant maneuver."

"Oh my God. I can't believe he fell for that! Reverse psychology is the oldest trick in the book!" Lane said. She got up and moved to the other side of the booth, dragging her plate of food with her. Considering how wary she'd been about this plan from the start, she was surprised to find that her heart was pounding with excitement. But why not? Jonathan was gorgeous and funny and, with a little work, could definitely be Isabelle's perfect guy. Maybe Vivi had been right all along. Maybe this plan was really going to work. The very idea of Isabelle being happy and Shawn Littig–free made Lane's skin tingle.

"Well he *does* have a C in psych," Vivi joked, munching on the fries.

"So, ladies. Is Operation Skewer Sluttig a go?" Curtis asked, standing at the end of the table and rubbing his hands together. The girls cracked up.

"It's a go!" Lane cheered.

"Sweet!" Curtis slapped both their hands, then groaned when his cell phone beeped. He yanked it out of his pocket. "Third message from my dad. We'd better go."

Vivi started to get up, but Lane grabbed her hand. She was too high on life to let this moment pass just yet. "Wait! Don't you guys think we should, like, soak in the moment? We just found our Brandon!"

"Totally! A toast!" Vivi said, picking up her chocolate shake. "Here's to helping Isabelle be Sluttig-free. To Brandon!"

Lane lifted her soda glass, and Curtis grabbed one of the untouched ice waters. "To Brandon!"

★ ★ ★ ★   *ten*   ★ ★ ★ ★

"What if he's never read any of the books that Brandon's supposed to like?" Lane asked as they walked back into Vivi's house later that night. "Or seen the movies? Oh my God. What if he doesn't watch *Extreme Makeover: Home Edition* like we said? Isabelle has every episode practically memorized! If he's never seen one, she's gonna know."

Vivi bit the inside of her cheek and tried not to snap. Lane was so putting a damper on Vivi's victory buzz.

"Okay, what happened to you between the diner and here?" Vivi asked. She whipped her suede jacket off and threw it toward the hooks next to the door. It missed by a mile and hit the floor, where she left it. "You were loving Jonathan half an hour ago."

"I know. And I still am. It's just . . . how are we going to turn a preppy boy with manners into a bad boy who plays the drums?" Lane paused on her way up the stairs. "Oh God! He's supposed to play the drums!"

"It doesn't matter!" Vivi said, frustrated. She charged ahead up the stairs and down the hallway. "They're just going to the prom! Do you think Isabelle's going to bring a drum set with her and demand that he play?"

Vivi pushed open the door to her bedroom and, as always seemed to be the case these days, there was Marshall, sitting at her computer. Over a plain burgundy T-shirt and those new jeans of his, he was wearing a trendy army green military-style jacket. It was the first time in her life Vivi had ever seen her brother sporting a totally unboring and semi-badass outfit.

"Nice jacket," Vivi said, tossing her bag on her bed. "Maybe you should, like, wear it outside the house where there are people. Instead of, you know, sitting in here where no one will ever see you."

"She's right, Marshall. You've been spending an unhealthy amount of time in front of the computer lately." Lane dropped onto the beanbag chair and forced all the air to wheeze out.

"I was bored and I happened to notice that Isabelle was online, so I just figured I'd chat," Marshall replied. He glanced at Vivi and tugged at his cuffs. "You really like it?"

"Yeah. It actually rocks," Vivi said offhandedly. She was too busy jumping three moves ahead in her mind. She leaned toward the computer, and Marshall quickly minimized the window he had been typing in. "You're on with Izzy right now?"

"Yeah. We were just talking about what we're doing this

summer and—" He paused, looking up at Vivi with sudden concern in his eyes. "Why do you look so happy?"

He glanced at Lane, who, Vivi noticed, looked rather green. What was wrong with her? They'd found a Brandon. And yet Lane looked more uncertain than ever.

"Why is she so happy?" Marshall repeated to Lane.

"We kind of found a guy," Lane explained, sounding like she was announcing an execution.

"Yeah, and she was all giddy about it half an hour ago before she started overthinking it, as always," Vivi groused.

Marshall's face was blank. "You found a guy."

"For Isabelle! To be Brandon," Vivi announced, refusing to let their negative vibe get to her. "IM her and tell her you want to take her to the prom."

"Wait a minute," Marshall said, standing up. He pushed the desk chair in with his butt, preventing Vivi from getting anywhere near her own computer. "You found a guy? Who is he?"

"His name is Jonathan Hess, and he is amazingly hot," Vivi explained, clasping her hands together as her heart fluttered at the very thought of him. "Isabelle is going to die when she sees him."

"How hot?" Marshall asked, gripping the top of the chair behind him.

"Why? Do *you* want to date him?" Vivi shot back.

"You know, after seventeen years, the gay jokes are getting tired, Viv," Marshall replied.

Vivi rolled her eyes. "Fine. I'm just saying. What do you care how hot he is? Just IM the girl." She reached past him, grabbed the mouse, and opened the window again. Marshall, just as quickly, reached over and closed it.

"No, Vivi. Hang on a sec," Marshall said, pushing his newly floppy bangs away from his head, where they flopped right back down. "I mean, where's this guy from? Are you sure he's not some deviant or something? Did you get references?"

"From who? His ex-girlfriends? God, Marshall, have a little faith," Vivi said. "Lane and I are not going to pick some guy out of a police lineup to take our best friend to the prom. He's a good guy. Now would you *please* just do your job?"

She reached for the chair and yanked it out, nearly knocking her brother over in the process. Marshall's shoulders slumped, but he sat down and pulled the keyboard tray toward him. His fingers were just about to touch the keys when Lane shoved herself up.

"Wait," Lane said, wringing her hands.

"What now?" Vivi asked, ready to burst from excitement and frustration. "This is no time to be squeamish. For all we know, she could be on the phone with Shawn right now telling him what color corsage will go with her dress. Which, by the way, he will totally ignore."

"I just want to be sure we're doing the right thing," Lane said, her forehead wrinkled with worry. "Are we totally positive we can change Mr. Prep into Brandon the Bad Boy? We only have two weeks, and he has to be totally believable."

Vivi wanted to scream. What did Lane think they were doing, brain surgery? All Jonathan needed was a little stubble, a leather jacket, and a fake tattoo, and they were in business. "Yes. We're totally sure," she said firmly. "Marshall, let's do this."

* * *

"I left him a message last night, but he hasn't gotten back to me yet," Lane told Vivi. She paused outside her art classroom and sighed. "I hope he's not backing out."

Even though she did sort of hope that Jonathan was backing out. If he backed out now, it would definitely be too late to find someone else, and they could go ahead and bag the whole plan.

Lane took a deep breath and sighed. She had to remember why they were doing this. Isabelle was her best friend. All she was doing here was protecting her from Shawn.

"I knew I should have been the one to call him," Vivi grumbled.

"Why? What would you have said that would have been so different from what I said?" Lane asked, irritated.

"Nothing! I don't know," Vivi replied. She unzipped her yellow Nike hoodie and slipped it off to tie it around her waist. "It's just . . . I'm more forceful than you are, you know?" she said, yanking on the sleeves.

"Yeah. I'm aware." Lane looked around to make sure the coast was clear and lowered her voice. "That's why we decided I should call him. Since you're the one who almost scared him off."

"Whatever," Vivi said with a scoff.

Lane's fingers curled into fists, and she held her breath to keep from screaming. If Vivi wanted to do everything by herself so badly, why had she sucked Lane into this mess in the first place? It wasn't like she enjoyed scheming and lying and sneaking around.

"Hey, guys," Curtis said, coming up behind Lane.

Her heart stopped at the sound of his voice. But when she turned around to greet him, he looked morose. "What's wrong?"

"I'm out," Curtis said, shoving his hand into the pocket of his baggy jeans. "My dad found out I got a C on that Calc test, and he grounded me. No unapproved outings for the rest of the year. So I can't help you train Jonathan or whatever."

"You're kidding!" Vivi said, wilting visibly.

Lane's eyes stung unexpectedly, and she looked at the floor. She was already way too emotional to hear that Curtis was going to be MIA for this whole thing. Spending time with him was one of the arguments Vivi had used to talk her into the plan in the first place. And now she'd be spending *less* time with him.

"I'm really sorry," Curtis said, nudging Lane's elbow with his own.

Lane sucked it up and raised her eyes. "It's okay."

Then, behind Curtis, Lane saw Isabelle practically skipping toward them, a huge smile on her face. Lane's heart skipped an excited beat, even as her stomach turned. She had a feeling she knew what Isabelle was so happy about.

"Shhh. She's coming," Lane said.

Vivi's green eyes widened. "Hey, Iz!"

"You guys are never going to believe what happened!" Isabelle announced, jumping up and down in front of them. "Brandon talked to his parents, and they said he could come down for the prom! I'm going to prom with Brandon!"

"Oh my God, Izzy! That's awesome!" Vivi said, hugging Isabelle. "Congratulations."

She's good. I'd never know that she knew what was going on, Lane thought. Her heart pounded wildly, wondering if she could be half so convincing.

"Brandon? Who's Brandon?" Curtis asked, just as smoothly.

"He's this *incredible* guy Isabelle met on MySpace," Vivi said with a self-satisfied grin.

"Oh. Sweet, Iz," Curtis said.

"Yeah. That is *so* cool," Lane said calmly. She glanced at Vivi warily. "But do you really think that's a good idea? I mean, making a date with someone you met on the Internet?"

Vivi's eyes turned into tiny black dots. Lane knew that if the girl could have eviscerated her on the spot, she would have.

"What? I'm just worried about her," Lane said innocently. "What kind of friend just lets another friend go out with some random guy she met online? He might not even be a guy. He could be an old man. Or a woman! Or—"

"Okay, Lane, we get your point," Vivi said through her teeth.

Lane bit her tongue. She was only trying to say what she would have said if she had no clue that Brandon was actually Marshall.

"I knew you were going to say that!" Isabelle said, swatting Lane's arm. "And you're totally right. I already decided I'm going to e-mail him tonight and ask him to meet up somewhere this weekend so we can make sure we're both, you know, normal."

"This weekend? Really?" Vivi said, her voice tight. "That's so soon."

Lane gulped, knowing exactly what Vivi was thinking. If this pre-date went down the way Isabelle wanted it to, then they had only four days to get Jonathan up to believable Brandon standards. Four. Measly. Days.

At that moment, Lane's cell phone beeped. She whipped it out of her pocket and turned toward the wall. Technically students were not supposed to have their cell phones turned on during school hours, so she, her friends, and everyone else in school had become quite adept at hiding them from clear sight. She had one new text message, which she quickly opened and read.

Can meet 2day. My house. 4pm Call l8r & get detes. C u then.
—J

"Who is it?" Isabelle asked.

"Oh . . . uh . . . no one," Lane replied, quickly shielding the screen from her friends. "Just my mom saying she won't be home for dinner. Guess Dad and I are on our own again."

"Oh. Sorry, Lane. That sucks," Isabelle said, shuffling her books from one arm to the other.

Lane felt like she was going to burst into flames. Here Isabelle was commiserating for poor Lane and her subpar home life. Meanwhile Lane was lying to Izzy's face and plotting behind her back all at the same time.

"Yeah, well." Lane shrugged and quickly texted back.

OK. Thnx. Btw no shave 2day. Will xplain l8r
—L

She pocketed the phone and touched the sleeve of her sweater to her forehead, which was itchy with sweat.

"Everything okay?" Curtis asked pointedly.

"Fine. Dad and I are gonna go out. Around four?" she said, looking directly at Vivi. "Maybe someplace in Cranston?"

"Sounds like a plan!" Vivi said happily, winking at Lane for good measure.

Lane smiled, relieved that Vivi had so clearly gotten the message. Isabelle, meanwhile, looked at them like they were speaking in tongues. Which, in a way, they were.

"Um, isn't four kind of early for dinner?" Isabelle asked. "Doesn't your dad have to work?"

Lane's mind went completely blank. "He has the afternoon off, right?" Vivi said loudly, grabbing Lane's arm.

"Yeah. Didn't you mention that yesterday?" Curtis put in.

"What? Oh. Yeah. So we're gonna . . . go shopping first and then, you know, eat. Dinner. Together. After four."

Isabelle blinked. "Oh."

The bell rang. Ten seconds too late.

"See ya!" Lane blurted. She darted into class and grabbed the stool in the far back corner, hiding behind the easel that held her senior project. Her nerves didn't stop sizzling until the second bell rang and the door was closed. Thank God prom was less than two weeks away. This was not a lifestyle she could maintain for very long.

✳ ✳ ✳

Lane was at her locker at the end of the day, rummaging through her things for her history notebook, when she felt someone watching her. She looked up to see Curtis's brown eyes hovering around the side of the locker door, and she yelped.

"God! You scared me," Lane said, blushing.

Curtis laughed and popped his gum as he came around the open door. "I've been there for, like, two minutes," he said. "You were deep in concentration."

"I can't find my history notebook, and we have an exam tomorrow," Lane said, tucking her red hair behind her ear as she crouched down to check the books on the floor of her locker. "I must have left it in class."

"You want me to go get it for you?" Curtis asked, pointing over his shoulder.

Lane's blush deepened at the chivalrous offer. "Really? Thanks."

"No problem. As long as you agree to go to the mall with me right now," Curtis said with a grin.

Right. Of course. He couldn't just be offering to something nice for her just to offer.

"I thought you were basically grounded," Lane sighed, hoisting her messenger bag onto her shoulder.

"Yeah, but even my dad knows a guy can't go to the prom without a tux," Curtis said.

Lane suddenly felt as if she were moving through mud. The prom. He was getting a tux for the prom. So that must mean he had a date. He had asked someone. And that someone had said yes. He wouldn't be dropping eighty bucks on a tux unless he was planning on using it.

"And you know I have, like, zero style, so . . . ," Curtis said, rubbing a hackey sack ball between his palms. Lane glanced at him. His ripped-in-seven-places jeans, the layered T-shirts, the watch she'd given him for his sixteenth birthday, which he wore every day. Had he been wearing it when he'd asked this random girl to the prom? The very idea made her ill. "What do you say? Will you come? I don't want to look like a tool."

For her. You don't want to look like a tool for her. Whoever she is, Lane thought.

"Hey, guys!" Vivi said, showing up at the exact perfect moment. Her cheeks were ruddy from eighth-period gym, and she was breathless from jogging all the way across the school. "Here. You left this in class," she said, slapping Lane's history notebook against Lane's chest. "Ready to go?"

"Yeah." Lane shoved the book in her bag and zipped it up. "We have plans, remember?" she said to Curtis. "Vivi and I are going to meet Jonathan."

"Oh, right," Curtis said, pushing his hands into his pockets. "Well, can't you, like, postpone it for an hour or something?"

"For what?" Vivi demanded.

"He wants to go to the mall," Lane explained.

"Uh, no," Vivi said, slamming Lane's locker for her. "This is Operation Skewer Sluttig, remember? This is way more important than shopping."

Curtis's eyebrows knitted. "But I—"

"You said you were out, and that's fine, but it doesn't mean you can bogart my main ally," Vivi said, slinging her arm over Lane's shoulders. "Besides, I thought you were grounded."

Then Vivi pulled Lane around a stunned Curtis and strolled off down the hall. "We'll call you and let you know how it goes!" Vivi shouted to him.

In her entire life, Lane had never been so grateful for Vivi's tendency to take charge and make decisions for her.

"You totally saved me back there," Lane said gratefully.

Vivi shrugged. "Don't I always?"

★ ★ ★ **eleven** ★ ★ ★

Waiting outside the front door of Jonathan's brick Tudor-style house, Vivi couldn't seem to make her knees stop bouncing. She held the box of books and movies Lane had put together in front of her, and the stuff inside kept knocking around.

"What's up with you?" Lane finally asked.

"Nothing. Just psyched to get started," Vivi replied, staring at the slats of the wooden door, the iron number *22* in the center. It was a big house, but not that big. And they'd rung the bell a good minute ago already.

"Yeah. Me too. Psyched," Lane said flatly. "But that doesn't explain why you're wearing that top. You're all . . . dressy."

Vivi's face reddened. Snagged. She had put on and taken off the trendy purple top her mother had bought for her birthday about ten times and eventually left it on. It had been hanging in her closet untouched for four months.

Not that she was trying to impress anyone, of course. Certainly not Jonathan. "It's not *that* dressy," Vivi said innocently, balancing the box of stuff on her hip.

"Yeah, but you're a T-shirt person," Lane said.

"And tank tops," Vivi pointed out.

"Yeah, but not—"

"Can we drop this, please?" Vivi snapped. "God, sometimes your whole 'I'm so observant' thing is a little annoying."

Lane's face crumbled, and Vivi instantly felt guilty. But just then the door opened and Jonathan stood before them in a worn gray Cranston Prep sweatshirt and distressed khaki shorts. He had somehow gotten even hotter overnight.

"Finally!" Vivi grumbled, striding by him.

"Come on in," he said wryly. "Sorry it took me so long. I was on the phone with work."

"You work?" Lane asked, stepping inside and looking around.

"Yeah. At the Cranston movie theater," Jonathan said, sticking close to Lane, Vivi noticed. "If you ever come by, I can get you free popcorn."

"Mmm . . . I *love* movie theater popcorn," Lane gushed.

"Are we doing this or what?" Vivi asked impatiently.

"Well, I can get *you* free popcorn, anyway," Jonathan said to Lane.

Vivi's face heated up. "You're hilarious, you know that?" she said, hovering near the foot of the wide staircase. She lifted the box slightly. "Where do you want this?"

"I guess up in my room," he said. "Second door on the right."

Vivi stomped up the wooden stairs and into Jonathan's room. It was a wide, airy space with a huge bay window overlooking the front yard, and it was neater than Vivi's room could ever hope to be. The sports photographs—a signed Derek Jeter, an old-school Ruth and Gehrig, a panorama of Yankee Stadium—were framed and spaced evenly apart from one another on the walls. The bed was made with plain blue sheets. The rattan throw rug was perfectly angled on the floor. The sweaters on the shelves in the open closet were folded, and the hanging clothes organized into sections of shirts, pants, and jackets. Even his shoes were lined up.

"Wow," Vivi said, marveling at the organization. "Anal much?"

"I just cleaned it," Jonathan said as he walked in.

"Oh, just for us?" Vivi tilted her head and let her long blond hair tumble over her shoulder.

Jonathan blushed slightly. "Do you guys, uh, want anything? Soda? Snacks? Anything?"

"You're such a good little host!" Vivi teased, sitting down on his bed. "But we're fine. Let's just get to work."

At that moment, Vivi's cell phone rang. Her heart all but stopped when she saw Isabelle's name on the caller ID.

"Crap. It's Izzy," she said, standing. "Where do I tell her I am?"

"I don't know," Lane said. "Make something up."

Vivi's mind was a complete void. "I can't say I'm at Lonnie's, because she might already be there. And I can't say I'm home, because she might want to stop by."

The phone trilled again.

"I can't take it! You answer it." Vivi tossed the phone at Lane.

"I can't! It's your phone, and I'm supposed to be out with my dad!" Lane threw the phone, and Jonathan picked it right out of the air.

"*If* she asks, just tell her you're out shopping. But only if she asks. The less detail, the better," he said calmly, handing the phone back to Vivi.

Vivi grabbed it, annoyed. If there was one thing she hated, it was when she lost her cool and someone else got to play the calm and collected one. But still, Jonathan was right. She swallowed hard and opened the phone. "Hey, Iz!" she said brightly.

"Oh my God, Vivi! Brandon is, seriously, *the* most amazing guy ever," Isabelle gushed.

Vivi's heart relaxed. "Really?" she said happily. "What happened?"

"He went on some florist's website and just sent me an attachment of five different corsages to choose from," Isabelle said. "He wants to make sure he gets it exactly right. Isn't that just the sweetest thing *ever*?"

"That's so sweet," Vivi said, flashing a thumbs-up at her cohorts. "This guy is going to be your perfect prom date."

"I know! Plus he said he'd be more than happy to come all the way down here this weekend so I don't have to drive," Isabelle added. "We're gonna meet at Lonnie's."

Vivi smiled. Marshall was doing his job so well. "That's great."

"I'm so happy I didn't call Shawn this weekend," Isabelle replied. "You guys totally saved me. And now all we have to do is get Curtis to ask Lane and find your perfect guy and we're good to go!"

Vivi glanced at Jonathan, who was watching her intently. "Yeah. Totally. We have to get on that," she babbled.

"Oops! I gotta go. He's IMing me right now," Isabelle said. "Talk to you later."

"Later!" Vivi snapped the phone closed. "She is totally in love with him."

"With who?" Jonathan sat down at his desk, pulled up his feet, and locked his elbows around his knees.

"With you!" Vivi said. "Well, Brandon. The guy we're going to make you into."

"Well, that's good, I guess," Jonathan said. "And see? She didn't even ask where you were."

"Yeah, yeah. You're very smart," Vivi said.

Jonathan grinned flirtatiously at her. "You know, I'm not the goody-goody you want to think I am."

Vivi smirked as he held her gaze. She had to concentrate to look away. "Okay. Are we going to do this, or what?"

"Yeah. What'd you bring me?" Jonathan asked Lane, peeking into the box.

"Just a bunch of stuff Brandon is supposed to like." Lane pulled a few books out of the box and handed them to him.

"Yeah. I checked out his page. He's into literature, huh?" He sifted through the novels, and then tossed them onto the bed near his pillow. "There's no way I can read all that."

Lane's jaw dropped. "You have to."

"I'm sorry. I'm a slow reader. Especially with novels.

Fiction is so annoying. You have to keep track of all these characters, you know? Remember how they look—"

"And who they know and what they like and where they're from," Vivi agreed. "I know exactly what you mean! I hate . . . imagining stuff."

"Wow. We finally agree on something," Jonathan said. He leaned back against his desk chair and crossed her arms over his chest. "If I'm gonna read something, I'd much rather read a historical book or a biography. Something that actually happened."

"Exactly!" Vivi cried.

"You guys," Lane said.

"If I could take two history classes and skip English entirely, I would totally do it," Vivi said.

"I know! And don't half the books they make you read just make no sense at all? Like *As I Lay Dying*. What the hell was that gibberish about?" Jonathan said.

"I *hated* that book!" Vivi agreed. "I actually threw it at my brother. He had a bruise on his arm for a week."

Jonathan looked at her quizzically. "Why at your brother?"

Vivi shrugged. "He kept telling me what a great piece of literature it was. He had to be stopped."

Jonathan laughed, and Vivi grinned. There it was again. That sexy laugh.

"You guys!" Lane shouted, standing up.

Vivi looked at her friend. For a second she'd actually forgotten where they were and why.

"We're kind of in a time crunch here," Lane said, ripping her jacket off. She looked at Jonathan. "I'm sorry if you hate fiction, but Isabelle loves to read. We hired you to do a job and part of that job is knowing these books. So you will read them."

She plucked *A Separate Peace* out of the box and handed it to him.

"And by the way, if you read history books and biographies, you still have to 'imagine stuff,'" she said, throwing in some air quotes. "It's not like you were actually there."

She sat down in a huff, and Vivi met Jonathan's gaze.

"Wow. I thought you were the tough one," he said.

"I've never seen her use air quotes before," Vivi replied. "You'd better take her seriously."

"Hello? I'm right here," Lane said, yanking out a printout of Brandon's MySpace page. "Now let's get to work."

✳ ✳ ✳

"This is a total disaster. We should just call it off. I'm serious. This is never going to work," Lane rambled as Vivi pulled up in front of her house. It was a cool evening, and she shivered in her jacket as a stiff breeze rustled the leaves of the oak in the center of her front lawn.

"Wow, you have a fabulously positive attitude," Vivi said, resting her hands on the steering wheel. "You should have been a cheerleader."

"I'm not kidding! He hasn't even read *Catcher in the Rye*!" Lane blurted. "Who hasn't read *Catcher in the Rye*?"

Vivi pulled a face and raised her hand. "Uh . . . me?"

Lane blinked. "Then how did you pass the paper?"

"It's this little thing called the Internet? Maybe you've heard of it. They have whole plots online," Vivi told her.

"Well, that's just great. Nice to know you're a cheater," Lane said, reaching for the door handle. She seriously felt as if she were going to explode. This had been a bad day even before Curtis and his tuxedo proposition, what with having to lie to Isabelle at every turn. But at Jonathan's house it had only gotten worse. Not only had he never read a single book on Brandon's list, he'd seen only a couple of the movies. Plus they had gone through his entire closet and hadn't found one thing that a guy like Brandon would ever wear, so now they had to spend the following afternoon walking Jonathan through the mall. And to top it all off, it was already past nine and Lane hadn't even begun to study for her history test tomorrow.

"You have to chill out," Vivi said, lowering her chin as she stared Lane in the eye. "You're taking this whole thing way too seriously."

"Yeah, well, somebody has to," Lane said. "If you could just take a step back from your evil hand-wringing for five seconds, you would see that this is never going to work."

"Evil hand-wringing?" Vivi said.

"Yeah! And by the way, in case you've forgotten, we have a history exam tomorrow. An exam which neither one of us had a chance to study for thanks to this project of yours," Lane said. "Unless you're just planning on cheating on that, too."

"Okay, first of all, enough with the personal attacks," Vivi said. Lane sat back, clenching her teeth in impatience.

"Secondly, we're seniors. You have a straight-A average. One bad test is not going to kill you. Besides, you could probably pull a C without even studying."

"I don't want to get a C," Lane said, throwing the door open. "And if I do, it's on you."

"Hey! Don't act like this is all my fault!" Vivi called after her. "We're doing this for Izzy, remember?"

Lane ignored her and speed-walked up to her house. Inside, she slammed the door behind her. This was *never* going to work.

twelve

"Remind me again why we need to shop," Jonathan said, following a couple of paces behind Lane and Vivi as they cut across the center of the Mall at Short Hills. He was looking around, head tipped back to take in the skylights, as if he'd never been in a mall before.

"Because Brandon is supposed to be a badass," Vivi said, quickly power walking. "And you are not."

"I told you. I can be a badass," Jonathan protested.

A toddler in a stroller dropped a rattle on the floor as her mother pushed her by, and Jonathan stopped to retrieve it, then jogged to catch up with them. He chatted with the mom for a couple of seconds, and Vivi couldn't help noticing how the sun pouring through the windows seemed to follow him. Ridiculous. When he returned, he was smiling over his good deed until he noticed Vivi and Lane staring him down and his face fell.

"What?"

"Oh, yeah. That was totally badass," Vivi said with a snort. "Come on. We have to get to work."

Vivi made a beeline for Hollister and headed straight for the back, where they kept the sale racks. She started pulling out distressed T-shirts and chose a couple of jackets off the wall. Immediately she recognized the army-green number her brother had been sporting the other day and grabbed it. If Marshall could make it look good, then Jonathan would make it hot.

When she turned around, Jonathan was standing in front of a mirror, wearing a pair of aviator sunglasses off the rack and checking himself out. Vivi's heart skipped a beat. This guy could model. Seriously.

"What's the matter?" Lane asked.

Vivi jumped. She hadn't noticed her friend standing at a rack of distressed button-down shirts just to her left. Lane glanced at Jonathan, then back at Vivi, as if she were trying to put two and two together and coming up with zero. Vivi crossed the crowded store and shoved the clothes at Jonathan.

"Here. Try these on."

Jonathan took off the sunglasses, and the very movement was sexy. Like he'd practiced doing it a thousand times, even though she knew he hadn't. And naturally, that made it even hotter. He grimaced at her armful of items.

"I would never wear this stuff," he said.

Vivi rolled her eyes. "That's kind of the point."

He shot her a sarcastic look, but took the clothes and

headed into the dressing room. Vivi casually leaned against the wall while he changed. When he folded his sweater over the top of the door, her breath quickened.

"So, are you really going to the prom stag?" Lane asked, inspecting a sweater with a faux-torn collar and frayed sleeves.

Vivi stood up straight. Could Jonathan hear them in there? And if so, what would he think of a girl who was going to her own senior prom without a date?

You don't care, she told herself. *It doesn't matter what he thinks, because he's Isabelle's date.*

"Yeah. No one worth going with, so why not?" Vivi said rather loudly.

Lane bit her lower lip and looked thoughtful for a moment. "Maybe I will, too."

"Really?" Vivi felt a dash of hope at the idea that she might not be the only one. On any given day, she could be as individualistic as she wanted to be, but prom night was a huge deal. It might be nice to have a wingman. Except— "Wait, Lane, I thought you were going to ask Curtis."

"Well, that was before he had a date," Lane said nonchalantly as she moseyed over to a sales rack filled with girls' clothes.

Vivi balked. "Curtis has a date?"

"Well, not definitely. He just—"

At that moment, the door to the dressing room opened and Vivi and Lane were cut short. Jonathan stood there, wearing the clothes Vivi had picked out for him, looking like a total tool.

"You didn't actually roll up your jacket sleeves," Vivi balked.

"What? It looked all messy," he replied. "And why would anyone buy a T-shirt that already had a hole in it?"

He held out the collar of the T-shirt—which was tucked into the waistband of his jeans—like it was covered in dog poo.

"You're such a dork," Vivi said, shaking her head at the sight of him.

A blush crept across Jonathan's face. "If I'm a dork because I don't understand this universal need to look like you just rolled out of bed, then I guess I'm hopeless," he said, rolling his eyes. "Hang on."

He closed the door, and the clothes he'd been wearing were once again flung over the top.

"Vivi? Uh . . . maybe you should try to not be so hyper-critical," Lane whispered. "He *is* doing us a favor."

"What did I say?" Vivi started to flip through the other shirts on the sales racks, just in case they had to go back to square one.

"You just called him a dork to his face," Lane pointed out, coming back over the men's racks.

"Oh, please. He's fine," Vivi said.

"Maybe. For now. But if you don't watch out, your critical side is going to scare him off, and then Izzy will be dateless," Lane hissed.

Vivi's heart squeezed. That was pretty much the last thing she wanted to have happen. And she didn't want to hurt Jonathan's feelings either. But had she already done it? Was he in there right now, wondering why the heck he'd agreed to this?

The door opened. Jonathan had changed into a gray T-shirt and short blue jacket.

Once again, he had rolled up his sleeves. He turned to the mirror, then to the side to check himself out.

"There. How's this?"

Lane groaned, folded her arms atop the clothing rack, and collapsed her head against them. Vivi sighed. This was going to be harder than she thought. You could take the kid out of prep school, but you couldn't take prep school out of the kid.

"Awful," she said, walking over to Jonathan. Time to take charge of the situation. She grabbed his arm and yanked the fold out of the sleeve, then did the same with the other. Then she knelt down and yanked down on the jeans so that they weren't sitting so high, and uncuffed the hems, leaving the fraying edges to cover the back of his shoes. When she stood up again, she yanked the T-shirt out of the waistband and reached for his hair.

"Whoa! What're you doing?" Jonathan asked, holding up a hand.

"Just trust me," Vivi said.

She shoved her hands into his hair and yanked up, then ruffled the back with her fingers. From the bench in the dressing room, she grabbed the aviator sunglasses and handed them to him. He paused for a second before putting them on. Together, Vivi and Jonathan faced the mirror.

Dear Lord, I am a miracle worker.

"Huh," Jonathan said, turning to the side. "That's not bad."

"Nope. Not bad at all," Lane said, joining them.

"So, this is the kind of guy your friend likes?" Jonathan asked, shuffling around to see himself from different angles.

"We're getting there," Vivi told him. "Now if you'd just let us do our job . . ."

Jonathan sighed and took the sunglasses off again. "All right, then," he said. "I give. You paid me. So you should make the decisions."

"So you'll read the books?" Lane asked hopefully, clasping her hands in front of her in excitement.

"As many as I can," Jonathan conceded.

"And you'll let us take you to the salon?" Vivi asked.

Jonathan checked his look in the mirror again and frowned in thought. When he turned back to Vivi again, his smile was heart-stopping.

He's Isabelle's date. Isabelle's date, Vivi told herself.

"I'm all yours."

Vivi's knees nearly buckled at the words. This was going to be trouble.

✴ ✴ ✴

"Okay, so I'm going to skim *Catcher in the Rye* and *Farewell to Arms,*" Jonathan said, consulting the list he'd made at the food court. "Those are the two most important, right?"

"That should do it," Vivi said, the warm wind in her hair

as she drove Jonathan back home. "Now what are you wearing on your date this weekend?"

Jonathan smirked. "The T-shirt with the hole, the jacket with the frayed cuffs, the jeans with the fake dirt on them, and the black boots that look like they lived through World War Two."

"Good boy," Vivi said with a sly smile.

"Oh, and I can't forget the fake tattoo." He whipped out the black, twisted bicep cuff from the bag.

"Not that she'll see it, but it'll be good for your attitude," Vivi said. "It'll make you feel dangerous."

"I feel dangerous just looking at it," Jonathan joked.

"Don't forget to practice your monotone," Vivi reminded him. "And you'll want to keep the talking to a minimum. Cool guys answer with one syllable. Got it?"

"Cool," he said, lowering his voice.

Vivi laughed again. Date or not, she was having more fun than she'd had with the last three guys she'd gone out with combined.

"This guy your friend is in love with must be a real tool," he said, back to his normal voice. "I feel like I'm playing to the very worst in male stereotypical behavior."

"Yeah. That's Shawn for you," Vivi said darkly. "If I never see that jackass again, it'll be too soon."

"You know, when I first met you I thought you were just an insane control freak—"

"Wow. Blunt much?" Vivi said.

Jonathan laughed. "But now that I've spent some time with you," he continued. "It's pretty clear that you really are doing this to help out a friend. Which is cool. Slightly crazy, but cool."

Vivi blushed. She turned her head, pretending to check the next lane as she switched, so that he couldn't tell. Okay. This was very not good. Between the sweating palms, the pounding heart, and the easy blushing, there was no more denying that she had a crush on Jonathan. A guy she could definitely *not* have. Vivi was starting to wish she hadn't dropped Lane off on the way to Cranston. She wasn't sure she could trust herself alone with him. Vivi had never been big on self-control when there was something she wanted in her sights.

"So, you're going to your prom alone?" Jonathan asked. He took out the pair of sunglasses, which he'd bought for himself, and picked at the little UV protection sticker on one of the lenses.

Vivi cleared her throat. So he *had* overheard. How very humiliating. "Looks that way." She turned off at his exit and headed for his street, suddenly wanting more than anything to get him out of her car. The posh houses and lush lawns of Cranston zoomed by her without her so much as noticing them.

"Huh," Jonathan said.

Vivi turned on her blinker by whacking the control as hard as she could. "What?"

"Nothing," Jonathan said. He finally freed the sticker and shoved it into one of the bags at his feet. "I guess I'm just surprised you don't have a boyfriend."

Another blush. Vivi was starting to hate her skin. "Well, I did. We just broke up last week."

Jonathan slipped the sunglasses on and looked at her. "Oh? Why?"

Because he was a wuss bag who couldn't handle one small criticism. Well, one small criticism every hour or so. Like she was really going to tell Jonathan that.

"He was unworthy," she said with a sly smile.

Jonathan laughed. Damn that sexy laugh and the Hollywood eyewear.

She pulled up in front of his house and slid to a smooth stop. She was very impressed with her self-control. Slamming on the brakes would have been a much more satisfying move.

Jonathan removed the sunglasses and looked her right in the eye. "Yeah," he said. "I think most guys are probably unworthy of a girl like you."

Oh, God, kiss me, Vivi thought. *Kiss me, kiss me, kiss me.*

She found herself looking at his mouth, and noticed that tiny white scar on his chin again. "What's that from?" she asked.

"What? Do I have food on my face," he asked, quickly flipping down the visor mirror.

"No. The scar," Vivi said with a laugh.

"Oh, that?" Jonathan said. "I could tell you, but then I'd have to kill you."

"Ha ha. Seriously. How'd you get it?" Vivi asked.

"Doing something badass," Jonathan joked, his eyes teasing. He popped the car door open.

"Why won't you tell me?" Vivi demanded, not used to being shot down.

"Because it's more fun to make your face do that blotchy red thing it does when you're frustrated," he said, getting out and closing the door. "See ya!"

"Jonathan—"

"I've got a lot of work to do," he said, lifting his bags and waving. "Bye!"

"Fine!" Vivi shouted, half-laughing, half-annoyed.

"Fine!" he replied jovially.

Vivi shook her hand and peeled out, lifting her hand out the top of her car in a wave. She bit down hard on her bottom lip to stop herself from smiling.

"He's Izzy's guy. *Izzy's* guy," she said as she zoomed toward the highway. "Jonathan is all for *Izzy*."

★ ★ thirteen ★ ★

Lane glanced up from her English notes, yawned, and looked out the plate glass window at Lonnie's, where school buses and carpools were rolling by. It was so different here in the morning. Instead of the lively chatter of gossip, the place was relatively quiet, the peace disturbed only by the sound of the cash register pinging open or the occasional cell phone ring. Five men and one woman were in line, all wearing brown or black trench coats to ward off the slight drizzle outside. Lane glanced at her watch and wondered what train these people were catching. Her mother was out of the house by six every morning to get to breakfast meetings in the city by eight. Apparently the Lonnie-goers had less demanding jobs.

Outside on Washington, Vivi trudged by, the hood of her sweatshirt up over her head. At the same time, Isabelle approached from the other direction, walking jauntily, her pink plaid umbrella protecting her hair. They met at the door, and then Isabelle dragged Vivi inside and practically flung her into the booth across from Lane. Isabelle was all smiles. Vivi was giving off seriously irritated this-is-way-too-early vibes.

"Hey, guys!" Lane said brightly.

Vivi shoved her hood back and, with a grunt, accepted the coffee Lane pushed across the table to her.

"I am *so* sorry for the emergency meeting, but I have *the* biggest news!" Isabelle said, standing at the end of the table.

Lane looked at her quizzically. "What's up?"

"Shawn broke up with Tricia last night!" Isabelle announced, bouncing up and down on her toes.

Lane had never been punched in the stomach, but she had a feeling it would feel a lot like this. She actually lifted her two braids (a necessity for her frizzy hair in humid weather) and covered her eyes with them, not wanting to see Vivi's head actually explode.

"What!?" Vivi shouted, fully awake for the first time.

"He called me last night," Isabelle said. "Now, don't freak out. I did not get back together with him. And we didn't even talk about the prom."

"Thank *God*," Vivi said, slumping.

"But I do think he wants to go with me," Isabelle added.

"Iz! Come on!" Vivi blurted.

"But I was so good, you guys!" Isabelle said, ignoring Vivi's protestations. "I told him that he'd hurt me, and that if he wanted me back, he was going to have to earn it this time," Isabelle said, grinning like she'd just announced her biggest triumph ever.

"Wait, so you *are* getting back together with him?" Lane asked.

"What about Brandon?" Vivi added.

"Brandon will understand," Isabelle said, waving a hand. "You guys, this is Shawn. And it's our senior prom. And I'm sorry, but I think going with someone I know and love is a much better idea than going with someone I've never met."

Lane's heart beat an insane pitter-pat rhythm in her chest. This could not be happening. Isabelle could not really be considering getting back together with Shawn after everything he'd done to her—and after everything she, Vivi, and Curtis had done to try to protect her.

"But you're going to meet him! This weekend!" Vivi blurted, standing up.

"I can always cancel that," Isabelle explained. "Brandon won't mind not having to drive all the way down here."

"But . . . but . . . Isabelle! You like Brandon!" Lane said. "You can't just blow him off."

"She's right!" Vivi added. "Don't make any snap decisions."

Isabelle's face dropped slightly, and she looked at the freshly waxed floor, where her umbrella was making a small puddle. "You guys, I know you don't like Shawn—"

"This has nothing to do with Shawn," Lane lied. "We just . . ."

She looked at Vivi for help, widening her eyes.

"We just want you to keep your options open!" Vivi put her hands on the sides of Isabelle's arms and squeezed. "Iz, at least meet Brandon before you decide."

"Yeah. Just wait until after Saturday," Lane added, turning on the bench so that her legs were dangling over the edge. "Then you'll be able to make an informed decision."

"We saw how Brandon made you feel," Vivi implored. "And that was just on IM. Imagine what it would be like to hang out with him in person! Iz, he might be, like, your soul mate!"

Lane almost laughed, but bit her tongue. She knew how much effort it must have taken Vivi to utter the phrase "soul mate" without rolling her eyes.

"You think?" Isabelle said, raising her eyebrows.

"Totally!" Lane put in, feeling like a complete heel. But there was nothing else she could do. Jonathan was their only hope. "But, if you blow him off now, you'll never know."

Isabelle sighed, her shoulders slumping. She stared down at her manicured fingers and fiddled with the cord on her umbrella. "Maybe . . ."

"Come on. It's just one date. One meeting," Vivi said.

"And if you still want to go with Shawn after that, we'll shut up about it," Lane added. Vivi glared at her, but Lane shrugged. Honestly, if Isabelle picked Shawn after meeting Jonathan, there really *was* nothing else they could do for her.

"Okay. Fine," Isabelle said with a resolute nod. "I will not get back together with Shawn without giving Brandon a shot first."

"Yes!" Vivi cheered loudly.

"Good decision," Lane said.

"Thanks, you guys." Isabelle gave Vivi a quick hug, then leaned down to cheek-kiss Lane. "Sometimes you two are good to have around," she joked. "Want anything? I'm gonna grab a bagel and juice."

"I'm good," Lane said.

"Me too," Vivi added, finally sitting down again. She waited until Isabelle until was on line with the trench coat patrol and out of earshot before speaking again. "Whew. That was close."

"Tell me about it," Lane said, pulling her notebook closer to her. "But now we have to make sure that Jonathan is seriously irresistible. Shawn is going down!" Lane whispered, her eyes sparkling.

"Wow. You're really into this all of a sudden," Vivi said, amused.

"Well, that was scary!" Lane hissed, glancing across the shop at Izzy, who was inching forward on the line. "I do not want her getting back together with Shawn. And obviously Brandon is our best chance."

"Hm. Haven't I been telling you that from the beginning?" Vivi said nonchalantly.

"Yeah, yeah," Lane said. "So you were right. Don't let it go to your head."

They looked at each other and smirked. "Too late!" they said in unison.

Then Lane laughed and settled back to study. First she was going to ace her English quiz and then, this afternoon when she and Vivi met up with Jonathan, she was going to throw herself into this project for real. After this close call, *nothing* was more important than keeping Isabelle away from Shawn.

✵ ✵ ✵

Lane was hanging out in front of the school after the final bell, waiting for Vivi as the younger kids ran for the busses and the older kids headed for their cars. She tipped her head back slightly as the sun attempted to peek its way through the clouds, and she smiled. Her English quiz had been a snap. In face, she had finished twenty minutes before the end of the period and spent the rest of the time coming up with quizzes to test Jonathan's knowledge of the various books she'd given him. He had to have read at least a couple of them by now, and if not, Lane was going to sniff him out.

It was Taskmaster Morris from here on out.

"Getting a tan?"

Lane's head snapped forward, and she opened her eyes to find Curtis standing before her, one foot on his skateboard. Her face turned crimson. "Oh . . . I was just . . . uh . . ."

"What are you doing now?" Curtis asked, popping his skateboard up and into his hands.

Lane swallowed hard. "Vivi and I are going to Jonathan's."

"Oh." He looked off toward the parking lot, put the board back down, and pushed it back and forth with his toe. "I was gonna see if you wanted to do the Calc homework together."

The sun pushed its way farther through the clouds, and Lane's skin prickled with heat. "I'm sorry. I can't," she said, wishing more than anything that she could. "This morning

Isabelle told us she's getting back together with Shawn unless Brandon is, like, her soul mate. So we kind of have to—"

"Make him into her soul mate?" Curtis supplied.

"Yeah." It sounded stupid now that someone else had said it out loud.

"Okay. I guess I'll go, then," Curtis said, hopping on his board. He hadn't looked her in the eye in two minutes.

"Wait!" Lane blurted. "Are you mad?"

"No. Operation Skewer Sluttig is important," Curtis said flatly, shrugging and looking pointedly toward the parking lot. "You gotta do what you gotta do. Catch you later."

And then, he zoomed off down the hill, lifting a hand in a wave, but not looking back. Lane's stomach was all tied in knots. Curtis had never been that cool to her before. Not in all the years that she'd known him. Did he have a problem with Jonathan? With the plan? What had she done to offend him?

"Hey, Lane!" Vivi shouted, jogging up behind her.

Lane shook off her negative vibe and turned to her friend. Time to put her game face on. She could obsess about Curtis later.

"Hey! You ready to go?" Lane asked, trying to reclaim the determination and excitement she'd been feeling moments ago.

Vivi yanked her backpack straps onto her shoulders. "That's what I came over to tell you. You can have the after-noon off," she said.

Lane blinked. "What?"

"You can have the afternoon off," Vivi repeated, slapping

her shoulder. "Kick back. Relax. Or, you know, study. Since that's what you always want to do anyway," she joked.

She started past Lane, who stood there dumbly for a good five seconds before finding her voice.

"What are you, my boss?" she asked.

Vivi stopped and turned to her, looking surprised. "No. It's just that Jonathan's gonna watch some of the movies we gave him, so our services aren't needed," she said. "Well, yours aren't, anyway. I said I'd go over there and watch them with him."

Lane studied her friend. Vivi checked her watch and suddenly became very interested with the long line of cars jockeying for position at the parking lot exit. The longer Lane stared at her cheek, the pinker that cheek grew.

"What?" Vivi snapped finally.

"Oh my God. You like him!" Lane blurted. "That's why you don't want me to go! You want him all to yourself."

Vivi huffed, but still looked out at the traffic. "You're cracked."

"I so am not!" Lane blurted.

Vivi stood up straight and stared Lane right in the eye. "I do not like him. I only offered to go over there because I'm not entirely sure he's going to get the appeal of *Dead Poets Society*."

"But you don't get the appeal of *Dead Poets Society*," Lane reminded her.

"Well, no, but Isabelle explained it to me once, so I can just regurgitate that to him," Vivi replied. "It's just business," she added, looking away again. She could barely stifle a giddy smile.

"Oh, God! It is so not! You like him! I don't care what you say. You like our best friend's fake boyfriend!" Lane had to will herself to keep from screeching.

"Lane, please—"

"Vivi, you can't do this. If you go over there alone, you could screw up the whole plan," Lane begged, throwing her arms out at her sides. "You . . . Jonathan . . . alone in the dark. Watching semi-romantic movies . . . I know you. You'll jump him. You won't be able to stop yourself!"

"Do you really think I have no self-control?" Vivi snapped.

"No! But—"

But when you want something, you usually go for it without thinking about other people's feelings. Lane couldn't say that to her. Vivi would flip out.

"Okay. I know you like to think that you know me and Isabelle *so* well, but this is one time that you have no idea what you're talking about," Vivi said. "I am not about to jeopardize the whole plan and send Izzy running back to Shawn, just because I may be *slightly* attracted to Jonathan. Every girl he knows is probably attracted to him."

Lane glared at Vivi. "I'm coming with you." She pushed past Vivi toward the parking lot, but Vivi put out her arm, stopping her.

"No. You're not," she said, holding Lane back.

"Vivi!" Lane cried.

"Lane!" Vivi replied, crossing her arms over her chest.

For a long moment, Lane engaged in a staring contest with Vivi, feeling like she was back in kindergarten fighting over the last cupcake. She was not going to back down. Not after blowing off Curtis—who was now apparently mad at her—so that she could go to Jonathan's. She was as much a part of this plan as Vivi was. There was no way she was going to be shut out now. But the longer they stood there, the more Lane felt herself cave. There was no winning with Vivi. There never had been. There never would be.

"Fine. If you want to obliterate this whole thing, be my guest," Lane said finally. "I don't care anymore."

She turned on her heel and stormed off the other way, headed for home. For the first time in Lane's life, a pack of freshmen jumped out of *her* way. Apparently she looked intimidating when she was about to burst into tears.

"I'm not going to obliterate anything!" Vivi called after her.

"We'll see!" Lane shouted back, sure that Vivi couldn't hear her over the roar of an approaching bus.

We'll just see.

★ ★ *fourteen* ★ ★

Vivi couldn't move. If she did, her shoulder would brush Jonathan's. Or their hands would touch. Or their thighs. What the heck was up with this tiny love seat thing? Jonathan's parents obviously had money. They couldn't afford bigger furniture?

"Can't we watch this in the living room? There's no air in here," Vivi said, looking around the actually quite airy family room.

"DVD player in there is broken," Jonathan said without tearing his eyes off the screen.

Perfect. Whoever had put together that faulty piece-of-crap technology was going to ruin her entire plan. Because if she moved just one inch, if she took an extra deep breath, some part of her body was going to touch some part of Jonathan's, and then it would all be over. She would attack him. She wouldn't be able to stop herself.

"This is actually pretty good," Jonathan said.

Vivi turned her head to look at his profile. It was perfect. He was perfect. And they were sitting on this loveseat all alone while his brother was at a friend's. No parents, no nosy brothers . . .

Wait. You do not like him. He's just a hot guy, Vivi told herself. *There are hot guys everywhere. You wouldn't even be* thinking *about kissing him if Lane hadn't put the idea in your head.*

Yes. This was Lane's fault. All Lane's fault. And she could prove the girl wrong. She *would* prove her wrong. All she had to do was keep her hands and lips to herself.

"What?" he asked, turning to face her.

She ripped her eyes away, refocusing on the TV. Her heart pounded so hard, it was making her nauseated. "Nothing."

He was still watching her. Staring at her cheek. Vivi rubbed her hands together and shoved them like a wedge between her tightly crossed thighs, trying to make herself as small as humanly possible.

Suddenly, Jonathan's thigh grazed hers. Her heart completely stopped. She looked at him, and he was somehow much closer than he'd been a moment before. His eyes were heavy as he took her in, the question in them perfectly clear. The plea for permission. Every inch of Vivi's body throbbed.

Yes. Do it. Just kiss me.

Jonathan's lips swooped toward hers, and much to her own surprise, Vivi leaned away.

"Stop!"

"What? What's the matter?" Jonathan sprang back as if burned. Vivi was already on her feet.

"Nothing. It's just ..." Behind her, Robin Williams was going on and on. "It's just this is Isabelle's favorite part of *Dead Poet's Society*. You should watch it. You have to . . . to know it if you're going to go out with her on Saturday."

Jonathan glanced at the TV screen as if it were an alien ship that had just landed in his family room. He sat up straight on the velvety love seat and pressed his hands into the cushion.

"Right. I actually wanted to talk to you about that," he said.

"About what?" Vivi asked.

"About me dating your friend." Jonathan stood up, not taking his eyes off Vivi's face. He stood so close to her, she could feel his warm breath on her face. God, he was perfect. Why did he have to be so perfect? "Vivi, do you . . . really want me to date your friend?"

Vivi thought of Isabelle's tears when Shawn cheated on her. Her confidence after she met Brandon online. Her excitement after Brandon had asked her to the prom. The deal they had made that Isabelle would give Brandon a chance.

Vivi was standing in front of the only person who could prevent Isabelle from going back to Shawn. Izzy had been her friend since they were both in pigtails and pink overalls. Jonathan had been in her life for three days.

"Yes. I do," she said firmly. "Why wouldn't I?"

"No reason," he said, his face turning to stone. "I guess we should go back a couple of scenes."

He grabbed the remote and sat down at the far end of

the love seat, pressing his side against the arm, giving her as much room as possible. Vivi felt tears prickling behind her eyes.

"Actually, I have to go," she said loudly, grabbing her bag.

"What? We're not even done with the first movie yet," Jonathan said.

"I know. I just remembered I have to do something."

She was not going to cry in front of him. No way. No how.

"But, Vivi—"

"I'll see you later!" Vivi was already halfway through the kitchen. "Just watch as many of those as you can!" she shouted back.

She slammed the front door behind her and sprinted for her car. It was for her own good, for Isabelle's. For everyone's sake.

★ ★ ★ *fifteen* ★ ★ ★

Friday was gorgeous and sunny, and the courtyard in front of the school was jam-packed with students chatting and popping their skateboards, soaking up every last minute until they had to go inside for homeroom. Lane leaned back against the outer wall of the gym, waiting for Vivi to arrive so they could update one another on their progress. She kept one eye on the parking lot and one on Curtis and his skater friends, who were among the boarders, trying to impress a group of freshmen girls with their skills. Curtis hadn't spoken to her all morning, which meant her stomach was already clenched beyond repair, but it got worse every time one of the girls laughed or giggled. Was one of them Curtis's date? When Vivi's convertible finally pulled in, Lane jogged over to meet her friend at her designated parking space, happy for the reprieve from the low-rent X Games.

"Okay. What happened between you and Jonathan last

night?" Lane demanded before Vivi even had a chance to get out of her car.

"God! Give a girl a heart attack, why don't you?" Vivi demanded.

Vivi was wearing low-slung sweats and her track T-shirt, her hair in a ponytail with no makeup. Standard Vivi don't-mess-with-me gear. Lane knew it. She *knew* something had gone wrong with Jonathan.

"Did you guys hook up? Is that why he was acting so freaky on the phone last night?" Lane stepped back so Vivi could open her car door.

"You talked to him?" Vivi demanded. "What did he say?"

"Oh my God, I'm right! You kissed him, didn't you?" Lane demanded.

"No, all right? We did not hook up!" Vivi slammed her car door. "Why were you guys talking on the phone?"

"He called me to go over the IM conversations between Marshall and Isabelle," Lane told her. She watched her friend closely, gauging her reaction to every word. "He wanted to make sure he was ready."

"Okay. So why the big panic?" Vivi asked.

"Because, he was acting weird. Very businesslike. No jokes, no nothing. And he asked me if I'd talked to you since you left there," Lane continued as they turned and headed back toward the school. "Why did he ask me that?"

"Lane, I have no idea. I'm not a mind-reader, all right?" Vivi said with a shrug. "All we did was watch a movie. No big deal."

"If you say so," Lane replied.

"I say so. How did it go with the IMs?" Vivi asked, pulling her sunglasses out of her bag and sliding them on. "Are we all set?"

"Not exactly," Lane told her. "I mean, there were a *lot*. Have Marshall's grades been suffering lately? Because I honestly don't think he's been doing anything other than chatting with Izzy."

Vivi snorted. "Figures. It's the first time in his life a girl's spoken to him past the 'hey' stage," she joked.

"That's not true! I talk to him," Lane protested. They had arrived at the circle of benches in the courtyard and sat down on the only one that was still free.

"Yeah. Because you have to," Vivi replied.

"I don't understand what your problem is with your brother," Lane said, dropping her bag down at her feet.

Vivi rolled her eyes and tipped her head back with a yawn. "Whatever. Is Jonathan ready or not?"

"There's no way he's going to remember everything," Lane replied. "It's too much. I mean, he's a smart guy, but this is like cramming for finals in two days. Anyone would have a hard time. And if Izzy asks him one weird question on something he doesn't remember, we're dead. What're we gonna do?"

Vivi pulled her head up and stared out across the parking lot in a forlorn way that gave Lane an even deeper twist in her stomach. She looked almost resigned.

And then Vivi's entire face lit up. "I've got it!"

"What?" Lane asked, both hopeful and nervous at the same time.

"There you are! I've been looking all over for you guys!" Isabelle trilled suddenly, coming up behind them.

Vivi's face went ashen and Lane jumped in to distract Izzy before she could notice.

"Hey, Iz!" she said, grabbing her friend into a hug. "So! Tomorrow's the big date! Are you excited?"

"So excited," Isabelle said. "I can't wait to find out what he looks li—"

"Actually," Vivi interrupted suddenly, standing up. "Lane and I were just talking about tomorrow, and we think we should come with you."

"What?" Isabelle asked.

"Yeah, what?" Lane echoed.

"You know, what we were just talking about?" Vivi said pointedly, knocking Lane with her arm. "It's just, you met this guy online and he doesn't even have a picture up. He could be some, like, fifty-year-old perv or something. Or a kidnapper. He could be anyone."

Lane stared at Vivi. This was her solution to the problem? To go on a three-way date with Jonathan? What were they going to do, pass him notes under the table to tell him what to say?

"Well, we're meeting in a public place," Isabelle countered, shading her eyes from the morning sun.

"Yeah, but that's not enough." Vivi crossed her arms over her chest. "You've seen *Without a Trace*. Trust me. You want someone with you."

Isabelle bit her lip and looked at her friends. "You really think he's a fifty-year-old perv?"

"No! Of course not," Lane said, grasping Isabelle's hand quickly. "I'm sure he's a total gentleman. But Viv's right. It's better to be safe."

"You're right," Isabelle said finally. "And you guys should meet him anyway. We're all going to be hanging out together at prom!"

"Yes, we are," Vivi said through a forced smile.

Lane glanced at Vivi. Could it be any more obvious that *she* wanted to go to the prom with Jonathan?

"You guys are the best, have I told you that?" Isabelle reached out to hug them both. "What would I do without you?"

You'd be going to the prom with a jerk, Lane thought, her heart clenching painfully. Lane shielded her eyes and looked out over the school courtyard, bustling with kids reluctant to go inside on such a beautiful day. To her left, Curtis flew by on his board, jumping from an entire set of stairs on the pathway. *But at least you'd be going with the person you wanted to go with in the first place. Unlike the rest of us.*

There were couples everywhere. Lane wasn't sure if it was spring fever or the impending prom or just a random twist of evil fate, but everyone seemed to be holding hands, smooching in the halls, and flirting shamelessly everywhere she went. Standing in the cafeteria line behind Cara Johnson and Sanjay Medha was like watching a Skinamax production live and in full color. In front of the pair was a huge open space. Behind them was a long, long line. But all they could see was the extreme close-up of each other's noses as they nearly swallowed each other whole.

"Say something," the sophomore girl behind Lane urged under her breath.

Lane turned purple. She was no good at speaking up, but as the next person in line and the only senior in sight, she supposed it *was* her responsibility.

"Uh, excuse me?" she said meekly. "We kind of, um, need to get moving."

She was greeted with a loud, slobbery, sucking noise as they readjusted their faces. The kids behind Lane groaned. And then, like an angel descending from heaven, Curtis appeared, cutting the line to get in front of Lane. Her heart felt like it was going to explode at the very nearness of him.

"Yo! Gupta! If we wanted to see that, we'd rent the professional version!"

Sanjay and Cara pulled apart and looked over the line in a bored way, but they did move. They slid their one tray along, each holding one end, their legs practically entwined as they tripped forward. The kids in line cheered.

"Thanks," Lane said tentatively.

Curtis grabbed a chocolate milk and an apple. "Yeah, well, it was the least I could do."

"What do you mean?" Lane asked. She slid her tray behind his, taking nothing. Somehow food was the last thing on her mind.

"Just that I owed you one," Curtis said, glancing at her

from the corner of his eye. "I'm sorry about yesterday. I think I was a BFJ."

Lane laughed. She was so relieved, she could have kept on laughing for an hour. "You weren't a big fat jerk."

"Okay. Maybe a little fat jerk." Curtis joked. He took out his wallet and glanced at Lane's tray. She realized nothing was on it and quickly grabbed a bagel and juice. "I got both," he said to the lunch lady.

Lane was beaming as she emerged from the line. She and Curtis walked slowly side by side down the center aisle.

"I'm just irritated by this whole grounding thing. And you guys are so busy with Brandon. . . . I just feel like I'm never gonna get to see you unless we're studying together." He stepped sideways so he could look at her.

Lane's heart went kinetic on her. He was worried about never seeing her. This was the best conversation she'd ever had.

"Want me to call your dad and tell him he's evil?" Lane asked, trying to stay calm.

"Like you'd ever really do that," Curtis joked back, pausing in the center of the aisle. "Besides, he's not totally evil. We made a deal that if I get a B-plus or higher on that history test, I can go to this one party this weekend. So I have to wait till we get it back in seventh to find out if I can actually go, but I was thinking . . . if I can go . . . maybe you'd want to go too," Curtis said. "I'll pick you up, I'll drive you home. You don't have to do a thing."

"Really?" Lane squeaked. Was this a date? Were she and Curtis going on a date? "I mean, yeah, sure. That sounds good."

"Good!" Curtis said with a grin. "I'll pick you up around seven. Cool?"

I'll pick you up around seven. It sounded like a date. But no. She and Curtis were just friends. The guy quite possibly had a date for the prom. She had to calm down. Maybe his prom date was going to be there, too. Maybe he'd invite Vivi and Isabelle as well. *Do not let yourself get carried away,* Lane told herself.

"Okay. Cool," Lane agreed with a nod.

"Hey, are you guys gonna sit down, or are we eating lunch here?" Vivi said, coming up behind them.

Lane flinched, but managed not to drop anything. Together, the three of them headed off to join Isabelle at their table. Lane sat down, trying to invest herself in the talk about graduation and the post-graduation party, but she just kept waiting for Curtis to bring up this weekend's bash—to invite Vivi and Isabelle—but he didn't. He didn't so much as mention it.

Looked like it was just her and Curtis. Oh, and maybe his prom date. But Lane would deal with that if and when it happened. For now, she was just going to be happy. Happy and, for once, hopeful.

★ ★ ★ *sixteen* ★ ★ ★

Vivi's leg bounced up and down under the table in the back corner of Lonnie's. She pressed her hands down on her thigh to try to get it to stop, but it was no good. She was nervous. Like she was going out on a first date. Which, she supposed, she was. Only it wasn't her first date, it was Isabelle's. Isabelle's first date with Jonathan.

And of course, Isabelle looked like a goddess. Smooth hair, perfectly understated makeup, and a lovely, girly outfit that would have looked like a Halloween costume on Vivi. Isabelle had even refused to order anything to eat, not wanting to mess up her lip gloss. Vivi, meanwhile, had already polished off half a bagel with peanut butter and a bag of Doritos.

"Are you sure this dress isn't too much?" Isabelle asked, smoothing the front of her cotton Ralph Lauren strapless.

"Well," Vivi started to say. "Maybe—"

"No, Iz," Lane said, shooting Vivi a silencing look. "You look beautiful."

Isabelle smiled. "Thanks for coming, guys. What would I do without you?"

Vivi grinned, but Lane looked so uncertain it gave Vivi a sour feeling in her gut. But no. No. They were doing the right thing. They were keeping Isabelle away from the toxic substance that was Shawn Littig and handing her the most amazing guy on the planet. They were, quite possibly, the best friends ever.

Isabelle checked her delicate silver watch. "Where is he? You don't think he's ditching, do you?"

If he does, I will personally hunt him down and burn all his preppy little sweaters. "No," Vivi said, glancing at the neon clock on the wall. "He's still only fashionably late."

Just then, the glass door swung open. Vivi turned around, her heart in her throat. But it wasn't Jonathan who walked through the door of the restaurant. It was Marshall and his frizzy-haired, *Lord of the Rings*–obsessed friend, Theo. Vivi rolled her eyes and clucked her tongue as she slumped down again.

"Hey, Marshall!" Lane called out, waving.

Marshall looked up and smiled. "Hey, Lane." He said a few words to Theo, then came over as Theo got on line behind a pack of junior girls from the cheerleading squad. Marshall was wearing that new green jacket of his over a black T-shirt and yet another pair of trendy jeans. He even wore a studded black belt. His blond hair was uncharacteristically mussed.

"What are you doing here?" Vivi demanded, annoyed.

"Can't a guy get lunch?" he asked smoothly. "Hey, Isabelle."

"Hey," Izzy said. She glanced at him quickly, but then did a double take. "You look different."

"Thanks," Marshall asked, smiling shyly. "I think."

"Can I talk to you for a second?" Vivi asked through clenched teeth. Without waiting for an answer, she grabbed his arm and dragged him toward the counter. "What are you doing here? She's gonna know something's up!"

"Uh, Vivi? This place is always filled with people from school. Theo and I are just getting lunch. People do it all the time," Marshall said. "And besides, I wanna see this guy. I'm as much a part of this plan as you are."

Vivi glared at him. She actually couldn't argue with that. "Fine. But get your food to go. As soon as he gets here, you're out."

"Whatever," Marshall said, rolling his eyes.

Vivi balked as he turned around and strolled over to the counter. Apparently the new, tough wardrobe was going to his head. He said something to Theo, and they both chuckled, glancing over at Isabelle and Lane. Vivi could have killed him. What better way to ruin the vibe of a date than to have creepy genius boy spying on them? She stormed back to the table and dropped onto the bench. All she wanted was to get this song and dance over with already.

"Omigod. That's him. Is that him?" Isabelle said suddenly. She positively glowed.

Lane's face went totally slack. "That's him. I mean . . . it's gotta be," she added quickly.

Vivi whipped around, and the world stopped spinning. Jonathan stood at the door, slowly surveying the room. He slipped his sunglasses off, and his eyes finally fell on her. Vivi felt as if the heat emanating from her body could have warmed the rest of the shop. He looked incredible. His blond hair was perfectly disheveled, and he'd grown out a bit of blond stubble all along his cheekbones and chin—but not over his scar, she noticed. It was a hot day, so he had deviated from the agreed-upon wardrobe, but he'd done well. He wore a red T-shirt with black block writing over one shoulder and a pair of baggy, torn jeans. His black boots were scuffed, and he was wearing—unfortunately—the exact same belt as Marshall. Not that anyone other than Vivi would ever notice.

"Brandon?" Isabelle asked.

Slowly, Jonathan smiled. An intensely sexy, closed-mouthed smile. He strolled over to the table, his eyes never leaving Vivi's face.

"Hey," he said, looking deep into Vivi's eyes.

Vivi replied in a near whisper. "Hey."

"Hi," Isabelle added.

Vivi's shin exploded with pain—thanks to a kick from Lane—and she snapped out of it. She kicked Jonathan's foot, and he finally focused on Isabelle. Vivi watched with a mixture of dismay and triumph as his smile widened.

"Isabelle?" he asked, pleasantly surprised.

"Brandon," she replied, grinning wildly.

"Your photo did you no justice," Jonathan said, his voice low and husky.

Isabelle blushed with pleasure. "Thanks."

He reached into the back pocket of his jeans and produced a perfect pink rose. Isabelle gasped. "Pink's your favorite, right?" Jonathan said.

"You remembered," Isabelle said breathlessly.

Jonathan shrugged. "My grandfather always told me, never show up for a date empty-handed."

Vivi had to concentrate to keep from shaking her head at his brilliance. He'd been told how much Isabelle loved and respected her grandparents. This guy was good.

"That's so sweet," Isabelle trilled, sniffing her flower.

Jonathan sat down next to Vivi, across from Isabelle, and Vivi scooted away a touch, just to be safe. After Izzy introduced "Brandon" to her two friends, Vivi and Lane were finally able to exchange a look without being obvious. Lane beamed with pleasure, and Vivi smiled back. Her heart squeezed painfully, but she ignored it. It didn't matter what stupid reactions her body chose to have. Because Isabelle was obviously happy. And that was all that mattered.

"I have trouble sleeping sometimes. Too many thoughts, you know?" Jonathan said, narrowing his eyes in a smoldering way. "Like last night was really bad. I didn't get to sleep until about four in the morning."

He was slouched back in his chair, legs spread, toying with the straw in his soda. The complete antithesis of his usual, straight-backed, polite self. Vivi was amazed. He was doing it. He was really doing it. Isabelle was riveted. Vivi, meanwhile, was wondering how much of what Jonathan was saying was true, and how much was stuff he made up for his Brandon character. Because the more he talked, the more she and Jonathan seemed to have in common. If this stuff was, in fact, true.

"I have the same problem," Vivi couldn't help mentioning. "Like I just can't turn off my brain."

"Do you?" Jonathan asked, for a split second falling back into his real voice. That was how Vivi knew that this part, at least, was true. Then he seemed to recall himself and slipped back into character. "Anyway, so when that happens I usually play my guitar for a little while to relax."

Vivi's heart thumped, and she glanced at Lane, who went white as a sheet.

"Guitar? I thought you played drums," Isabelle said, confused.

There was the briefest, almost indiscernible twitch in Jonathan's expression, but Vivi was pretty sure she was the only one who caught it.

"Yeah, but it's kinda hard to play drums in the middle of the night," he said, sitting up and leaning in toward Izzy. "I do still live with my parents. Unfortunately."

Isabelle grinned. *Good save,* Vivi thought.

"But when the guitar doesn't work, I have all these lists I recite in my head," he continued. "That usually does the trick."

"Lists? What kind of lists?" Vivi asked.

"Oh, you know. The states and capitals. The presidents,"

Jonathan said, then glanced at Isabelle. "Boring crap like that," he added. "Usually puts me right out."

"Omigod! I totally do the same thing! Except I try to recite the names of all the people in our class," Vivi said.

"Really? That seems like a lot," Jonathan replied.

"It's a small class," Lane said flatly. She kicked Vivi's shin under the table again.

Jonathan glanced at Lane, cleared his throat, and then returned to Isabelle. "What do you do when you can't sleep?"

"Me?" Isabelle blushed. "Oh, well, I don't usually have that problem. Ever. I usually pass out as soon as my head hits the pillow."

"Oh." Jonathan looked disappointed for a moment, but then smiled a completely sexy smile. "Well, I envy you. And your pillow."

Isabelle giggled and blushed even deeper. Vivi rolled her eyes. She almost couldn't believe how easily her superintelligent friend was falling for this ruse. Not that she minded. She was feeling quite proud of herself, actually. When her heart wasn't panging in that annoying way.

"So . . . are you sure you don't mind coming all the way down here again next weekend?" Isabelle asked.

Vivi held her breath. Was this it? Had Isabelle made up her mind to go to the prom with Jonathan? And if so, why did Vivi suddenly feel like screaming instead of jumping up and down for joy?

"For you? Are you kidding? I'd drive to California," Jonathan said without missing a beat. He leaned his elbows on the table, hooked his finger around Isabelle's pinkie, and held it there. Vivi couldn't have ripped her eyes off those entwined fingers if the Starbucks across the street had spontaneously combusted.

Isabelle smiled and held his gaze. "Good answer."

Jonathan smiled back. Vivi could practically feel the attraction between them. She was actually growing hotter from her proximity to it.

"Does that mean I passed the test, then?" Jonathan asked, cocking his head to the side and smiling that sexy, intimate smile again.

Isabelle blushed. "This wasn't a test."

"Sure it was," Jonathan said. "But I was more than happy to take it."

Isabelle turned her hand, lifted Jonathan's, and laced their fingers together. There was no moisture left in Vivi's throat.

"Then yes. You passed the test," Isabelle said, never taking her eyes off his.

Jonathan squeezed Izzy's fingers, and he may as well have been squeezing Vivi's heart. *Please let this be over soon,* she thought.

"Good. Then I'll be here next week," Jonathan said. "Just name the time and place."

"We're meeting at my house," Vivi blurted.

Jonathan looked at her like he'd forgotten she was there—or that she existed at all—and dropped Isabelle's hand.

"Cool. Well, you'll e-mail me the details, right, Isabelle?" he asked, drawing himself up in his seat. "I should probably hit the road. I've got a . . . thing. Back home."

Isabelle jumped to her feet. "Okay. I'll walk out with you."

"Cool." Jonathan looked at Lane, and then held Vivi's gaze for a long moment. "Ladies."

"Nice to meet you," Lane said loudly.

"Bye," Vivi added.

As they walked out the door together, Isabelle turned around with a gleeful grin and mouthed the words *"Oh my God!"* like she just could not take how lucky she was. Vivi forced herself to smile back.

"Wow." Vivi swallowed hard and kept the smile on. "How perfect was he?" she said to Lane.

"Yeah. Perfect," Lane said in a strained voice. She pushed herself up and out of the booth. "For you."

"What do you mean?" Vivi asked, scooting to the edge of the vinyl booth. "Isabelle's freaking."

"Yeah, because she's blinded by his gorgeousness," Lane said, throwing up a hand. "But I swear, Viv, it was more like he was on a date with you than her. You guys talked practically the entire time!"

"Give me a break, Lane. They were drooling all over each other at the end there," Vivi stood as well, her adrenaline shoving away her melancholy. "I'm happy for her!"

I am. I really, really am.

"Yeah. Sure. You just keep telling yourself that," Lane replied.

I am! I really, really am!

At that moment, Isabelle burst back through the door and skipped over to Vivi. "Omigod. I cannot believe how perfect he is! I'm so glad you guys didn't let me get back together with Shawn. I had *no* idea there were even guys like him out there. And he was so nice to you guys! Could you even imagine Shawn chatting with you like Brandon did? That would never have happened."

"Nope. Never," Vivi said, smiling triumphantly at Lane.

"This is going to be the best prom ever!" Isabelle said, showing every one of her perfect teeth. "Okay. Now I have to pee. I've had to for, like, twenty minutes, but I didn't want to get up from the table."

She laughed as she ran past her friends for the bathroom at the back of the shop. Ever so slowly, Vivi turned to Lane, eyebrows raised. But Lane simply scowled, refusing to board the happy train.

"Great. Now she's totally in love with him," Lane said, putting her hands on her hips. "What's she going to do when she finds out that Brandon is not really Brandon?"

"Okay, do you even know what a bright side is?" Vivi snapped as Lane headed past her for the door.

"Not in this scenario!" Lane turned around again, her arms crossed over her chest. "She's going to get her heart broken all over again!"

Vivi looked around the now semi-deserted, post-lunch-rush shop, grasping for an answer that would actually appease Letdown Lane. "Well, then . . . we just won't let her find out."

"Uh-huh. And how's that going to work?" Lane asked, leaning one hand on the back of an empty booth.

Vivi drew a blank and raised her palms. "I guess I'll just have to figure something out."

"Yeah, well, good luck with that," Lane told her. "Because either they date forever with Jonathan calling himself Brandon, or he's going to have to break up with her without breaking her heart. Try pulling that off."

Lane turned and stalked toward the door again, all in a huff. Vivi jogged over to get in front of her, blocking the exit.

"What's the matter with you?" Vivi demanded. "You don't get to take the high road all of a sudden and act like this is my fault. You're just as much a part of this as I am."

Lane sighed, staring at the floor. "Yeah. Maybe you're right. But I really wish that I wasn't," she said, looking sad. "I'll talk to you tomorrow."

"Wait! Where're you going?" Vivi stepped in front of her again. "We're supposed to meet up with Jonathan."

"You go. You don't need me there, anyway," Lane replied morosely.

This time, Vivi just let her go, and Lane shoved the door open with the heel of her hand, so hard it seemed like the thing would snap off its hinges. Then she was gone. And the second she was gone, everything she'd said sank right in.

Vivi felt the sourness of guilt seeping in around her heart. All she had wanted to do was show Izzy that there were cool guys out there who were not Shawn Littig, but instead, Isabelle was clearly crushing hard on *one* guy— on "Brandon." Vivi was going to have to figure out a way out of this that wouldn't involve Isabelle's heart breaking.

After dropping Isabelle off at her house, Vivi drove straight to the Suburban Diner, where she, Lane, and Jonathan had had their first meeting. Her heart was pounding as she turned into the parking lot, but she told herself she was just excited to go over the next phase of the plan. It had nothing to do with seeing Jonathan alone. Her palms were not, in fact, sweating.

She expected to meet him inside at a booth, but as she tooled through the lot looking for a space, she saw him leaning back against the rear of his beat-up SUV. He'd smoothed his hair down again, but was still wearing the Brandon gear. Vivi grinned and waved, then pulled in alongside him and got out of the car.

"You were amazing!" she shouted, rushing around the car. Jonathan stood up straight as she approached. "Really. Unbelievable. I had no idea what a good actor you were. Isabelle bought it like you were giving it away on sale."

"Yeah. She seems like a cool girl," Jonathan said.

"I am so excited you are going to the prom with her," Vivi rambled. "Shawn Littig is finally, *finally* history!"

"Vivi . . . about the prom," Jonathan said, pushing his hands into the pockets of his jeans. "I don't think I can go."

Vivi felt like she'd just stepped in a tremendous pothole. "What?" she blurted. "You have to go. She's so excited! And you just told her you'd be there! You can't back out now!"

"Vivi." Jonathan took a step toward her, his blue eyes searching hers. "I don't want to go unless it's with you."

Vivi's heart spasmed. "What?"

"There's something here. Between you and me," he said. "Not between me and Isabelle. You're the one I want, Vivi."

Then he placed his hand on the small of her back and pulled her to him. Before she could suck in a breath, his lips touched hers. Vivi felt an explosion of attraction unlike anything she'd ever felt before. She sank into Jonathan, and his tongue parted her lips, sending shivers all down her back. Then her arms were around his neck. His thighs were pressed against hers. His hands were in her hair. There were no thoughts in Vivi's mind. Nothing at all other than how incredibly perfect this felt.

And then, a horn honked.

Startled, Vivi pulled away. "What the hell are you doing?" she shouted, half out of it.

A car full of teenage boys rolled by them, laughing and taunting them. Vivi wiped the back of her hand across her mouth as if she was disgusted, even though she was anything but. He had to believe that she was, though. He had to. Because she could not go there. Jonathan was Isabelle's date. He was meant for Isabelle.

"You're supposed to be dating my best friend!" Vivi said firmly, taking another step back to put more space in between them.

"No, *Brandon* is supposed to be dating your best friend!" he shot back, his face red. "*I* want to date *you*!"

Vivi's breath was short and shallow. This was not happening. It simply was not happening.

"Vivi. Come on," Jonathan said quietly, stepping toward her again. "Go out with me. We both know we want this," he said with an adorable smirk.

One look at Jonathan's hopeful face, and she knew. She'd screwed up. Big-time. It wasn't just Isabelle who was going to get her heart broken around here. All thanks to her and her stupid plan.

"No. I don't," she said flatly.

Jonathan took a step back and laughed in an awkward way. "What?"

"I don't want to date you, Jonathan. You are so not my type, you may as well be another species," Vivi said, the words coming as if of their own accord.

"You don't mean that," Jonathan said, his face turning bright red.

"Yes. I do. Look at you. You're like a nineteen-fifties movie. The uptight, preppy, fresh-faced jock with the little brother he just loves and the dorky clothes and the . . . the whole 'I'm so polite' thing. That's not me. None of that is me," Vivi said. "I'm messy. I'm loud. I don't do polite. You and me? We don't mesh."

"What about opposites attract?" Jonathan asked beseechingly as he reached for her hand.

Vivi groaned and snatched her arm away. Jonathan flinched. "God! Can you not take a hint!?" she shouted, exasperated. "We are not going to be together! I don't like you that way!"

Jonathan's jaw clenched and he stared at her, betrayed. He looked like Vivi had just run over his dog.

"I'm sorry," Vivi said automatically, her heart twisting. "That was . . . blunt."

"Yeah, but you don't do polite, right?" Jonathan snapped, backing away from her.

"No, it's just. I wanted to be clear," Vivi said, grasping at straws. "If you're going to the prom with Isabelle—"

"No. I'm not. I'm not going to the prom with Isabelle. This ends right here," Jonathan said, turning toward his truck.

"Jonathan, no," Vivi said desperately. "Stop."

Jonathan got in behind the wheel and slammed the door so hard that Vivi lost her breath. She couldn't let him go. She couldn't let him drive away and risk never seeing him again.

"I'm sorry, all right!" she shouted over the revving engine. "Come on! Let me explain!"

But he ignored her. He simply pulled out of the space and drove away, not even giving her one last glance.

★★ seventeen ★★

"Come on, come on, pick up!" Vivi said through her teeth. She was clutching the steering wheel with one hand and her phone with the other. Normally she was all about cell phone safety, but this was an emergency situation, and her headset had gone MIA. Probably crushed under one of the empty fast food bags or piles of gym clothes that polluted her car. "Pick up!"

"Hi. You've reached Jonathan. Leave a message."

"Dammit!"

Vivi threw her phone on the passenger seat, where it bounced and came dangerously close to flying out the window. She ran a yellow light, made a sharp left, and careened down Washington Street.

This was a nightmare. How could Jonathan do this to her? If he liked her so much, shouldn't he be trying to help? Shouldn't he not be backing out on her at such a crucial moment? Didn't he get it by now? This was not about her. It was not about the two of them. It was about Isabelle.

Her cell phone rang and her heart leapt. She nearly drove into a fire hydrant groping for it. When she finally grasped it in her sweaty fingers, it was almost on the fourth ring and she didn't even have time to check the caller ID. This call could not go to voice mail.

"Hello?" she said shrilly.

"Vivi? Are you okay?" Isabelle asked.

"Oh. Hey, Iz. I'm fine," Vivi said, stopping at a red light and cursing to herself for not making it.

"You sure? You sound a little weird," Isabelle said.

"No. I'm good. What's up?"

"I just can't stop thinking about Brandon," Isabelle gushed. "Did you notice that little scar on his chin? Where his stubble wasn't growing in? How insanely sexy was that?"

"Insanely," Vivi agreed morosely.

"What do you think it's from? Do you think he got it recently, like, skiing or something? Or do you think it's one of those old scars, like from a block battle in kindergarten or something?" Isabelle theorized.

Vivi took a deep breath. She was not going to lose it. She was not. But why did Isabelle have to be so darn romantic and dramatic and mushy? It was going to kill her when she found out Jonathan—Brandon—whoever—had backed out.

Maybe I should just tell her now. Get it over with, like ripping off a Band-Aid.

"I wonder if he'll tell me," Isabelle continued rapturously.

"Or maybe it's, like, some deep, dark secret thing from his past and I'll have to wheedle it out of him."

Vivi hit the gas when the light turned green and zoomed toward Lane's house. *Okay, we have to fix this. We cannot give up now,* she told herself. *Jonathan will go to the prom with Isabelle if it kills me.*

"Vivi? Are you there?" Isabelle asked.

"Iz, I'm sorry, but I kind of have to go. I'm driving," Vivi said, appealing to Isabelle's goody-goody nature.

"Oh! Sorry! Call me later, okay?" Isabelle asked.

"I definitely will. Bye!" Vivi dropped the phone again, slammed on the brakes in front of Lane's house, and ran up the front walk. She pounded on the door to let out some of her psychotic adrenaline. After what seemed like forever, Lane yanked open the door, her face creased with concern.

"Vivi! What's the matter with you?" she asked.

"Jonathan bailed," Vivi said, sweeping past her friend into her large foyer.

"What?" Lane gasped. Her face went white and she let the front door slam shut.

"He bailed!" Vivi grabbed the banister on the wide stairs and squeezed. She was so pent up, she felt like she could break the solid oak in half. "He said he's not going to the prom."

"What? Why?" Lane asked.

All right. This one was going to hurt. "Because he . . ." Vivi took a deep breath. "He likes me. He wants to go with me."

Lane looked suddenly faint. She leaned back against the wall next to the door and stared. "I knew it."

"Yeah, yeah, you were right. Congratu-freakin-lations,"

Vivi said, pacing in front of her friend. "He likes me and I like him. But that should not change the fact that we had a deal!"

"Forget the deal!" Lane blurted, covering her face with her hands. "We have to call it off. It is beyond time to call it off."

"No! We can't! Not now!" Vivi said, her fingers splayed before her like a condemned man begging for his life. "Not now that she's met him! Not a week before the damn prom! It's too late. If she doesn't go with Brandon, she doesn't go with anyone. And this is Isabelle! She's Suzy High School! If she doesn't go to her prom and win prom queen and all that she'll . . . she'll kill herself!"

Dramatic, Vivi knew, but even Lane couldn't deny it. Isabelle had been looking forward to their senior prom ever since ninth grade. She had made a collage for a health class assignment—a work that was supposed to represent the person she wanted to be—and every picture had been cut out of a prom magazine. She still had the damn thing stuck inside the inside flap of that stupid Prom Planner of hers.

"So call him," Lane said tiredly. "Call him and make him change his mind."

"You don't think I tried that? He won't pick up the phone," Vivi said. She collapsed onto the bottom step of the staircase. "You know, sometimes I think caller ID was the worst invention ever."

"Yeah, only when you're on the calling end," Lane replied.

Vivi sighed. It was go time. Time to tug on the last straw. "Lane, you're gonna have to go over there and talk to him."

"Me?" Lane looked like a cornered street dog.

"Yes, you! I know I screwed up, and I'd fix it if I could, but I can't. You're the only one that can fix it," Vivi begged. "Please. He won't listen to me, but maybe he'll listen to you." She glanced at her watch. "It's still early. You can catch him before dinner."

"You want me to do this *now*?" Lane asked.

"Yes, now," Vivi said. "We're already losing precious time. Besides, if we don't fix this, I'm going to be up all night worrying about it."

"Well, I'm sorry to hear that, but I can't," Lane said resolutely, shaking her head. "I can't go over there. I have plans."

For the first time, Vivi noticed that Lane's hair was pulled prettily back from her face and her eyes were all made up. And not only that, she was wearing a cute cotton dress Vivi had never seen before. She looked nice. But what could she possibly be doing that would be more important than saving Isabelle from a dateless prom?

"Please, Lane? We can't let this fall apart now. We've come too far," Vivi said. "You're the one who was all worried about Isabelle's broken heart. What do you think's gonna happen if we have to write her an e-mail from Brandon saying he can't come after all? She'll think he met her and didn't like her. She'll think he thought she was hideous or something. Talk about a broken heart—she'll be shattered."

Lane stared at Vivi, venom in her eyes. "You did this, Vivi. I warned you this was going to happen, but you didn't listen. It's not my responsibility to clean up your mess."

Vivi felt a brand-new thump of guilt in her chest. Technically, Lane was right. This was all Vivi's fault. But that didn't change the fact that it needed to be fixed. For Isabelle's sake.

"Please?" Vivi whispered. "Come on, Lane. For Isabelle. Please?"

Lane took a deep breath and stared off down the hallway to the kitchen. For a split second, Vivi was sure that she'd failed—that all hope was lost. But then, Lane looked at her again, her expression resigned and her shoulders slumped.

"Fine," she said, lifting a weak hand and letting it drop. "I just have to make a call."

* * *

Lane pulled her mother's Jaguar to a stop in front of Jonathan's house and killed the engine. She speed-dialed Curtis for the third time and held her breath. As the phone rang, she checked out Jonathan's house, half-hoping to find the driveway empty and the house all closed up. Unfortunately several windows were open to let in the warm spring air, and she could hear music coming from an upstairs window. Finally the phone clicked over.

"Curtis here. Today's song is 'Graduate' by Third Eye Blind."

Lane groaned through the few bars of the song she'd already heard two times in the past half hour. Finally, mercifully, the beep.

"Curtis, it's Lane again. Did you get my other messages?" she asked as she climbed out of the car and slammed the door. "I'm so sorry I had to run out, but if you call me and give me directions to the party, I'll meet you there. So, just . . . call me. Okay. Thanks. Bye."

She hung up and shoved the phone into her jacket pocket. Why hadn't Curtis called her back yet? Had he not gotten her messages? Was he at her empty house right now ringing the doorbell over and over again? Or had he gotten the messages and was just so mad, he didn't even want to call her back?

I hate Vivi. I hate, hate, hate, hate, hate her! Lane thought as she speed-walked to the front door and rang the bell.

Feeling murderous by this point, Lane rang the bell again, pushing it so hard, she was pretty sure she sprained her finger. She was still shaking out her hand when Jonathan opened the door. His face registered obvious surprise.

"Hey," Lane said, suddenly realizing she'd been so busy trying to call Curtis that she hadn't remotely planned out what to say.

"Hey," he replied. "Come in."

He ducked his head and shoved his hand in the pocket of his madras shorts. Maybe it was a good thing Vivi hadn't come herself, because in his baby blue polo, with his tan legs exposed, looking all sheepish, he was totally adorable.

Jonathan led Lane into the kitchen, where his mother—a tall preppy woman with short blond hair—was chopping vegetables.

"Mom, this is my friend Lane," Jonathan said. "Lane, my mom."

"Hi," Lane said, feeling awkward.

Jonathan's mother wiped her hands on her apron and

smiled. "Hi, Lane. Nice to meet you." Then she looked at Jonathan quizzically.

"We're just gonna go in the family room for a sec, okay?" Jonathan asked.

"Sure. Do you want anything to drink or eat, Lane?" she asked.

"No thanks," Lane said.

"Well, call me if you need anything," she said, before returning to her chopping.

Jonathan turned and walked down a couple of steps into the family room. Playing on the TV was an episode of *Junk Brothers,* one of "Brandon's" favorite shows. Lane raised her eyebrows at Jonathan.

"Yeah. You guys got me into this," he said, lifting the remote to mute it. He walked around the coffee table and stood, facing her. "So. What's up?"

"Nothing. Sorry if I'm bothering you," she said.

"You're not. But my friends are gonna be here in a minute," he said. "So . . ."

"So why am I here?" Lane asked.

"I think I know why you're here," Jonathan replied, scratching the back of his neck and looking away, like he was embarrassed. "Vivi told you what happened."

"She told me you quit," Lane said. "So I was just hoping to talk you back into it."

"Wow. And you sound very enthusiastic about it," Jonathan joked.

Lane managed a weak smile. She walked around and perched on the arm of the velvet love seat. "Look, I know you think we're both insane, but Isabelle's not. She's actually incredibly cool and sweet and awesome. And she's the one that's gonna be hurt if you don't come. Maybe we shouldn't have started this whole thing, but we did. So I guess I'm just asking you to consider her feelings."

Jonathan looked at her, almost amused, and Lane realized what she was saying. She chuckled and looked at the floor, feeling like a complete idiot.

"Consider the feelings of a total stranger who you are in no way responsible for," she said, nodding her head.

"I'm sorry," Jonathan said. "I really am. But I knew from the beginning I shouldn't have gotten involved in this. I know you think what you're doing for your friend is a good thing, but it's not. You took away her chance to make a decision for herself."

Lane's heart felt hollow. Jonathan had no idea how ironic his words sounded to her. She felt as if she'd never made her own decision for herself ever in her life, and now he was accusing her of making Izzy's decisions for her. Was that what she had done? Was it possible that, by participating in Vivi's insane scheme, she was taking more charge of Isabelle's life than she'd ever taken of her own?

She realized at that moment that she had known this was never going to work—that she had no chance of talking Jonathan in to coming back. After all, she wasn't the type-A personality of her particular group. But she'd come anyway. She'd come because it was somehow easier than looking at Vivi and saying no.

Jonathan picked up his backpack from the floor and yanked a thick envelope out of the outside pocket.

"Here," he said, handing it to her. "It's the money Vivi paid me. I appreciate your situation, Lane, I really do. But it's your problem. Not mine."

"Okay," Lane said, her voice thick with tears. She couldn't believe this was happening. Isabelle was going to be crushed, and it was all her fault. Hers and Vivi's. Not only was Izzy going to be dumped by the person she had called her "dream guy," she was also going to have no date for the prom. Unless Shawn hadn't asked someone yet, and then she'd be going with the devil himself. How had it all gone so wrong?

"You all right?" Jonathan asked. "You look like you just lost your best friend."

"Or all three of them," Lane said morosely. Vivi was going to be pissed. Curtis was going to be hurt. And once Isabelle got dumped, she was going to sink into the biggest depression of her life. All because of one stupid little scheme.

"What do you mean?" Jonathan sat on the opposite arm of the love seat and put his feet up on the cushions.

"You don't want to hear about it," Lane said, blushing.

"Wouldn't have asked if I didn't," Jonathan said with a kind smile.

Lane glanced at him. Could she really tell him what was wrong? She'd gone so long without really telling anyone what she was really feeling. But why not Jonathan? He was a nice guy, and it wasn't like he was going to tell anyone what she said. He'd basically just cut all ties with her and her friends. Lane shoved his money into her purse and turned to him.

"Do you remember Curtis?" she asked.

"The guy from the diner the first night. Sure," Jonathan said. "He's been IMing with my brother about video games."

Lane smiled. "He has?"

"Danny thinks he's way cooler than I am," Jonathan said with a laugh. "Why?"

"The thing is, I've liked him basically forever," Lane said, shoving herself up and pacing toward the bookcase on the wall. "And he . . ."

"He has no idea," Jonathan finished for her.

"Kind of," Lane said.

"Why haven't you said anything?" Jonathan asked.

"Because I can't!" Lane said, feeling pathetic. "I've planned it out, like, a million different ways, but every time I try I chicken out. And every time I chicken out I feel like an even bigger loser. Plus, he's been my friend, like, forever. And if things go wrong, I don't want to lose that."

"Ah."

"But then the other day he asked me to go to this party tonight and, I don't know, maybe I'm just reading into it or whatever, but I think he was asking *me*, you know? Like as his date?" Lane said hopefully.

"This party is tonight?" Jonathan asked, pointing at the floor.

"Yeah."

"Then why the heck are you here?" Jonathan asked.

Lane's face turned purple. She toyed with the spine of an old book on one of the shelves. "Because Vivi made me come."

"She *made* you?" Jonathan blurted.

"Well, yeah! I mean, we had to save the plan, right? And she couldn't come over here so—"

"Lane, don't take this the wrong way, but get out of my house," Jonathan said, not unkindly.

"What?" she gasped.

Jonathan walked around the coffee table and put his hands on her shoulders. "Do you realize what's going on here? You've wanted this guy your *entire* life and tonight might have been your best shot with him, but instead you're here, doing what you think will make Vivi happy. What you think will make Isabelle happy. What about you?"

Lane's heart started to pound. He was right. He was totally right.

"Vivi has totally messed with your mind," Jonathan continued, bringing his hands to his temples in frustration as he paced away. "She's somehow got you believing that her plan to help Isabelle is more important than anything. Even more important than you or me. Well, that's crap!"

"You're right!" Lane replied, her adrenaline pumping. "That *is* crap!"

"You're important! You're a beautiful, smart, funny girl! I think you should track this Curtis dude down and tell him he'd be an idiot not to go out with you," Jonathan ranted, throwing his arm out.

"Yeah! He would!" Lane grabbed her purse.

"Good! Now go!" Jonathan said with a smile, pointing at the door.

"Okay! I will!" Lane replied, all riled up. She turned and stormed up the stairs, but stopped at the door and turned her head. "You really think I'm beautiful, smart, and funny?" she asked quietly.

"Go!" Jonathan said with a laugh.

And she did, as quickly as possible, grinning the whole way.

"Everything okay, Lane?" Mrs. Hess called after her.

"Everything's fine! Nice to meet you!" Lane shouted back.

Then she slammed the front door of Jonathan's house and ran for her car, her heart pounding with excitement.

It has to work. It has *to,* Vivi thought, clutching her cell phone as she walked upstairs to her room after a big bowl of ice cream. *Please, Lane. Pull off a miracle.*

She was just shoving through the door to her room, where Marshall was sitting—as always these days—in front of the computer, when her phone rang. Vivi's heart slammed into her rib cage. Lane.

"Lane! What happened?" Vivi blurted into the phone.

Marshall turned around in the desk chair and leaned forward, elbows on his knees. Vivi had already apprised him of the situation, so he was all ears.

"He didn't go for it," Lane said, sounding strangely giddy. "He's out."

"What?" Vivi blurted. The room started to spin. Marshall hung his head in his hands.

"He's out," Lane repeated. "Sorry. I gotta go."

"Sorry? *Sorry!?*" Vivi blurted, gripping the phone so hard, her fingertips hurt. "Lane, where are you? You can't just give up! We've got to—"

But the line went dead. Vivi groaned and speed-dialed Lane right back, but it went directly to voice mail.

"Dammit!" Vivi blurted, tossing her phone on her bed.

"He didn't change his mind?" Marshall asked.

"No, Marshall, he didn't change his mind," Vivi replied sarcastically, crossing her arms over her chest. "Oh my God. What are we going to do? There has to be something we can do," she said, starting to pace.

Marshall stood up and walked to the window, staring out on their quiet street. "I hate to say this, Vivi, but I don't think there is," he said quietly, chewing on his thumbnail.

"Marshall," Vivi blurted, frustrated. "If you say 'I told you so,' I will hurl you right out that window."

"I'm not!" Marshall replied. "But what are you going to do? Hire a stand-in? It's too late! She's met the guy now. If he's not coming to the prom, then no one is."

Vivi's heart had never felt so sick. She moaned and sat down on the edge of her bed, putting her elbows on her thighs and her head in her hands. "This is not happening. It is not happening. . . ."

Isabelle was going to be devastated. Crushed. And why? All because Vivi had concocted this stupid plan. "I thought I was doing the right thing," Vivi said, looking up at Marshall, her feet bouncing up and down. "I didn't want her to let Shawn hurt her again. No one did."

"I know," Marshall said simply. "And there was a point there when I really thought it was going to work."

"Really?" Vivi said, tears springing to her eyes.

"Really. But unfortunately . . ." Marshall looked over at the computer screen. Vivi stared at its whitish-blue glow.

"It didn't," she said, her voice flat. Her heart was so heavy, it was making her shoulders curl forward. This was it. This was the end. She felt as if she'd just resigned herself to a life of friendlessness and solitude. "You need to write to Isabelle and tell her Brandon can't come to the prom."

"You're sure?" Marshall said.

"What else can we do?" Vivi stood up and letting her arms drop at her sides. "The sooner we do it, the better. We can't leave her waiting until prom night thinking she still has a date."

Marshall took a deep breath and laced his fingers together on top of his head, his elbows jutting out like wings. Then he blew out the breath and turned toward the desk, determined. "Okay. Let's do this."

He brought up Isabelle's MySpace page with her smiling face up in the lefthand corner. Just looking at it made Vivi want to smack her head against the wall. She couldn't be here for this. She had to go.

"I'll be downstairs," she told Marshall, grabbing a pillow off her bed.

"Wait a minute. You don't want to tell me what to write?" Marshall asked.

Vivi paused at the door. She felt the tears threatening. Like she had any idea how to let a person down easy. Like she could even remotely bring herself to do this to her friend. She looked at her brother, so wide-eyed and innocent, and her heart panged. "You're way nicer than I am, Marsh," she said. "I'm sure whatever you come up with will be fine."

Vivi jogged down the stairs to the first floor, suddenly needing to put as much distance as possible between herself and the mess she'd created. Her eyes stung from unshed tears and her throat felt tight. She'd failed. She'd failed her friend in the worst possible way. Just thinking about how Isabelle's face would look when she read Marshall's e-mail made her want to hurl something. And it was all her fault. She raced for the basement and its comforting, cool darkness. It wasn't until the door closed behind her that she finally let the tears flow.

eighteen

After driving around the entire town of Westmont twice, searching for Curtis's mystery party and finding nothing but a policeman's retirement bash at the VFW Hall, Lane sat on her front step and waited. Her parents were out at some big gala in the city and wouldn't be home until the wee hours of the morning. Which was good. Because at least she knew Curtis would get home before them and they wouldn't find her passed out in front of the door. At least she hoped he would get home first. If he stayed out all night, she was pretty sure her adrenaline rush would be gone by the next time she saw him.

Finally, a pair of headlights flashed around the corner. Jeff's Mustang. Lane stood up, her heart leaping into her throat. She wiped her sweaty palms against the back of her jeans and waited for Jeff to pull into Curtis's driveway. Waited for Curtis to get out and knock fists with the two guys in the backseat. Waited until he turned around and finally saw her.

"Lane?" he said.

Somewhere off in the distance, thunder rumbled. Wind tossed Lane's hair across her face. She shivered and pulled her jacket closer to her as she walked across her lawn to meet him in his driveway. He was wearing a blue sweater with frayed cuffs and a pair of cargo shorts, and his hair was all styled into a perfect mess. He was adorable.

"Hi," she said. "Did you get my messages?"

He lifted his hand to show her that he was holding his phone. "Just now," he said, his tone apologetic. "I didn't even realize I had my phone off."

"You just got them?" Lane asked, relieved.

"Yeah. When I came by to pick you up and no one was home, I tried calling your cell, but it kept going right to voice mail. I just figured you'd forgotten about me." Curtis laughed and scratched at the back of his head. "I was mad at you all night. But if I'd just checked my freaking phone . . ."

Like I could ever forget about you, Lane thought.

Okay. It was time. Time to do this thing. Time to throw herself out there. *He'd be an idiot not to go out with you,* Jonathan's voice said in her mind. "Curtis—"

"I'm really sorry," he said. "Tonight was supposed to be fun, but instead it got all screwed up. But you should have been there. It was totally insane. This guy came wi—"

"Curtis," Lane attempted. But he was rambling.

"And then he set up a turntable and it was like something out of a bad movie. He was jus—"

"Curtis!"

He flinched. "What?"

Lane's heart stopped beating. She held her breath. "Will you go to the prom with me?"

Curtis's face went slack. The whole world slowed to a crawl. Lane's hopes and dreams washed away with the first few drops of rain. *Petrified* was the only word she could think of to describe his expression. Big, fat drops of rain smacked down on the crown of Lane's head, as if taunting her.

"Never mind," she said, backing up. "I don't know why I just said that. I—"

"Lane. Wait," Curtis said. He covered his face with both hands for a second, then dragged them down. "Dammit. It's not that I wouldn't want to go with you—"

"But you don't. That's fine. I get it," Lane was navigating backwards across her lawn as the raindrops came faster.

"No, it's just . . . I already have a date," Curtis said.

Lane felt as if a spotlight had just snapped on, searing her with its hot, white light. She imagined the entire AV squad from school—along with everyone else she knew—standing on Curtis's roof, training the light on her and laughing at her humiliation. She wanted to throw up. Right there on the driveway walk. This was supposed to be her night. The first day of the new Lane—the Lane who spoke up for herself and got what she wanted. Instead it was a nightmare.

"Of course. Of course you do," Lane said, still backing away. "I mean, the prom is next week already. And you have a tux. How could you not have a date?"

"Well, I didn't until tonight," Curtis said, looking physically ill. "I asked Kim Wolfe. At the party."

Lane lost all ability to breathe. Tonight? He'd asked Kim Wolfe *tonight*? When she was supposed to be with him. Tonight when she was out doing Vivi's dirty work Curtis had still been dateless. The realization of her missed opportunity hit her like a lightning bolt to the head. If only she had known where the party was, if only she had gotten there first . . .

"Kim Wolfe?" Lane said, her brain not quite functioning. "I didn't even know you two were—"

"We're not. I mean, we're not, like, dating or anything. I just—" Curtis made a frustrated noise in the back of his throat and shoved his hands under his arms. "Kim is—"

"A total gossip with a completely ridiculous love of the word *woot*?" Lane blurted. "Which, by the way, isn't even a word!"

Curtis pulled his head back, stunned. "Lane—"

"I have to go," Lane said, whipping around. Her soaked hair swung around and smacked her in the eye. She tripped over one of the sprinklers hidden in the lawn. Pain exploded in her toe, but she kept right on walking. Insult to major injury.

"Lane!"

"I'll talk to you later!" she said, attempting to sound normal through her tears. Hand shaking and wet, she managed to grasp the doorknob and shove her way into her house. Inside she leaned back against the door and dropped to the floor, clutching her injured toe and trying very, very hard not to cry.

"Thanks a lot, Jonathan," she muttered under her breath. It was his pep talk that had convinced her to do this. His confidence in her that had finally made her believe it would all go her way. Well, she'd finally done it. She'd finally spoken up for herself and put herself on the line.

And now she was sitting on a cold tile floor, dripping wet, with her bare toe throbbing in her hand, her heart breaking, and tears streaming down her face. So much for that.

✳ ✳ ✳

Lane pulled up right behind Vivi's car in Isabelle's driveway the following morning. Vivi was just getting out of her convertible. Lane's body temperature skyrocketed at the very sight of her friend.

It's all your fault, she thought, narrowing her eyes. *If you hadn't forced me to go over to Jonathan's on a pointless mission, I would have been with Curtis last night and he wouldn't have been anywhere near Kim "Woot-Woot" Wolfe.*

Vivi looked over at Lane impatiently, shoving her sunglasses up on her head. "Are you coming or are you just going to sit there keeping the seat warm?" she snapped.

Lane narrowed her eyes. Was *Vivi* mad at *her*? For what? For being a good little errand girl and driving all the way over to Cranston for her? Lane got out of the car, slammed the door, and stormed right past Vivi on the front walk. "She called you, too, huh?" she asked curtly.

"Of course she did. Why wouldn't she?" Vivi asked, scurrying up behind Lane.

"Oh, I don't know. Maybe she somehow sensed you were the cause of all her misery," Lane said over her shoulder, her heart pounding like crazy.

"Me! You're the one who went over there to convince him not to bail and failed miserably," Vivi replied, shoving her hand into the front pocket of her large hoodie. "Did you even try, Lane? I mean, really try?"

"Of course I did!" Lane shot back. She reached out and rang the bell. "But *someone* had already offended him so badly, he wants nothing to do with us!"

"Uh!" Vivi exclaimed indignantly, her mouth hanging open. "You have got a lot of—"

At that moment, the door swung open, and there stood Isabelle, makeupless and wearing her pink Victoria's Secret pj's, tears streaming from her swollen eyes. She had about five tissues crushed in each hand.

"H-h-hi guys!" she wailed.

Lane forgot all about Vivi and Curtis and Jonathan. She forgot everything. Never in her life had she seen Isabelle look so horrible. Guilt seeped in like cold lead around her heart.

"Iz?" Vivi said uncertainly.

Isabelle stepped forward and wrapped them both into her arms, snotting all over Lane's shoulder. "I'm s-s-so glad you're h-h-h-here!" she cried.

Lane looked at Vivi over Isabelle's bent head. *We did this to her,* she thought, narrowing her eyes.

Vivi rolled her eyes right back, telling her to back off.

Then Vivi extricated herself and closed the door. "Come on, Iz. Let's go sit down."

"Okay," Isabelle said with a sniffle.

She held one of the tissue wads to her nose as she shuffled between her friends toward the living room. On the couch in the normally pristine, opulent room, was a bowl of half-eaten cereal, three Pop-Tart wrappers, ten romantic tragedy DVDs, and Isabelle's laptop. Izzy shoved the Pop-Tart wrappers aside with her foot as she sat, and placed the bowl on the floor to make room for them, weeping the whole way.

"It's gonna be okay, Iz," Lane said, sitting down on the couch.

"No, it's not!" Isabelle wailed. "He dumped me! Everything was totally fine and then we went on a date and then he dumped me! Do you realize what this means?"

There was a lump in Lane's throat the size of a soccer ball.

"It means he thinks I'm repulsive!" Isabelle cried, throwing her hands up. A few of the tissues tumbled to the floor. "I'm hideous!"

"Isabelle, you're not hideous," Vivi said, reaching out to stroke Izzy's hair. "Come on, you know you're not hideous."

"Well, why else would he have dumped me?" Isabelle asked, wiping her face. "You guys were there! What did I do? Did I say something wrong? Did I offend him?"

Lane was growing so frustrated, she wanted to scream. She would kill to be able to tell her friend the truth. Of course she hadn't said anything wrong. The whole thing was a freaking lie! But she couldn't. Because then Isabelle would hate them both and she would throw them out and then she wouldn't even have any friends to cry to.

"You didn't say anything wrong," Lane told her, stacking the DVDs up neatly on the coffee table and swiping some crumbs off the couch. "I'm sure there's a good explanation."

"Well, I'd *love* to know what it is, but he won't write me back," Isabelle said as she pulled the computer onto her lap. She struck the keys haphazardly like she wanted to break the thing. "Why! Won't! He! Write! Me! Back!?" She said each word with another slam of a key.

Lane and Vivi's wide eyes met, disturbed. As angry as Lane was at Vivi, they were in this thing together. And this thing was getting serious.

"Okay, Iz, let's just leave the nice computer alone," Vivi said, pulling the laptop away from her and setting it on the side table. She closed it with a snap, and Isabelle looked at it longingly. "Listen, you don't need him," Vivi said. "He's just a guy."

"But what about the prom?" Isabelle asked, looking at Vivi, then Lane, wild eyed. "I have no date!"

"So we'll all go together. Alone, together," Vivi suggested, putting her hand over Isabelle's.

"Really?" Isabelle said hopefully.

"Yes! It's a perfect idea," Lane said, taking Isabelle's other hand. Her heart panged as she thought of Curtis. Of her failed attempt at happiness. But she managed an encouraging smile. "Who needs dates? We have each other."

"We have each other," Isabelle repeated, looking at each of them with such deep thanks in her eyes, Lane wanted to tear her own hair out. "You guys are the best friends in the world, you know that?"

Then she reached out and pulled them both to her so fast, she almost knocked Lane and Vivi's heads together.

"I could never get through this without you guys," Isabelle said dramatically.

Lane's heart squeezed in her chest. Little did Isabelle know she wouldn't even be going through this if it *weren't* for them. She reached up and around Isabelle's shoulder and patted her awkwardly on the back.

"We know," she said, feeling like a total jerk. "We know."

★ ★ nineteen ★ ★

Vivi paced back and forth in front of the picture window in her living room, holding up the skirt of her floor-length black dress with both hands. Every few steps, her ankle turned in her high heels. She finally dropped onto the couch to yank them off. Why everyone seemed to feel the need to wear those torture devices was beyond her. She thought longingly of her black Converse lying on the floor of her room and wondered if anyone would notice if she wore them instead.

"She's late. Why is she so late?" Vivi asked Lane. "Did I not say pictures at six? You were here at six. Curtis *told* me he was going to be late because Kim had a dance recital thing this afternoon, but Isabelle said nothing. Where the heck *is* she?"

In the kitchen, her mother and Lane's parents chatted over drinks, waiting for the rest of the group to arrive. Their laughter was mocking Vivi's anxiety.

"Will you calm down already?" Lane said through her teeth. "You're making me tense."

"I'm just worried, all right?" Vivi said, looking out the window as a car rolled by. "What if she cracked? What if she decided she couldn't handle going without a date and she's curled up in a ball on her floor right now?"

"I'm sure she's not," Lane said, looking rather piqued anyway.

"Text her," Vivi said, crossing her arms over her chest.

"Why do I have to text her?" Lane asked.

"Because your bag and phone are right there and mine are upstairs," Vivi shot back. Why was Lane being so difficult lately?

Lane rolled her eyes and snatched her purse off the couch. "Fine."

Vivi stood there, tapping her foot as Lane texted Isabelle. While they waited for a reply, her mother came up behind her.

"Anyone else get here yet?" her mom asked.

"Not yet," Vivi trilled, sarcastically matching her mother's happy tone.

"Oh, honey. You look so beautiful," Vivi's mother said, snatching her up into a tight hug. "Have I said how fabulous I think it is that you have the confidence to go to your prom without a date?"

Vivi's heart panged. "You've mentioned it."

"Well, I do. I think if there's no one in your life who you think is worthy of sharing such a night with, it's a wise decision to go on your own terms," her mother told her, touching her face. "I'm so proud of you."

203

Vivi attempted a smile as her mother moved away. She wouldn't be so proud if she knew that she'd given up her chance at a dream date so that Isabelle could have one instead. Which wouldn't even be so bad if that whole thing hadn't backfired as well. What a waste.

Suddenly, Lane's phone beeped. Vivi stood next to her so they could both read it.

> **Isabelle:** Sorry so late. Mom wanted 2 tk some pix in R yard. Just me & my date!!!

Vivi's heart hit the floor. "Her *date*?"

"What date?" Lane blurted.

"Ask her!" Vivi demanded.

Lane texted back.

> **Lane:** What date?

It took Isabelle about two seconds to reply.

> **Isabelle:** It's a surprise!!! On r way now!!!

"Omigod. She's going with Sluttig! I know it! This is a nightmare!" Vivi exclaimed, shoving her hands into her hair. She paced to the window and back, feeling like a caged dog.

"We don't know that," Lane said.

"Who else could it be? Why would she have kept it a secret from us unless it was Shawn?" Vivi demanded, crossing her arms over her stomach. "I can't believe this. I can't believe that after everything we've done she ended up with Sluttig anyway."

How could this be happening? How had everything gotten so very far out of her control?

Just then, Vivi heard footsteps on the stairs and looked up to find her brother descending in a full tuxedo. His blond hair was gelled, but casually—not into a helmet like he used to wear it—and he looked very handsome. There was just one problem.

"What the hell do you think you're doing?" Vivi demanded.

"Going to the prom," Marshall replied, adjusting his lapels with a smile.

"Uh, Marshall, I hate to break it to you, but you're not a senior," Vivi said.

"I told him he could be my plus-one," Lane said, stepping forward.

"What?" Vivi blurted.

"Wow, Marshall. Very James Bond," Lane said appreciatively, dusting some lint off his shoulder.

"Thanks," Marshall said, turning around and striking a pose. "Swayne. Marshall Swayne."

"Dork. Major dork," Vivi amended.

"Vivi. What is your problem?" Lane asked.

"My problem?" Vivi said, pacing. "My problem is we're supposed to be going without dates, remember? We made a pact! We promised Isabelle."

"I'm not really her date," Marshall explained.

"Yeah, I just thought he should get to go. You know, after all the work we forced him to do," Lane replied. "And besides, Isabelle has a date now, so—"

"She does?" Marshall asked.

"Yeah, which means I'm the only one without one!" Vivi blurted.

Out of the corner of her eye, Vivi saw the stretch Mercedes limo pull up in front of her house. This was it. Everything had officially spiraled out of her control.

"They're here!" she shouted to her mother, just because she felt an extreme need to shout.

She and Lane and Marshall all fell to their knees on the couch to see out. The parents, meanwhile, headed right for the front door to greet the newcomers.

"I cannot wait to see Isabelle's dress," Lane's mother said as she click-clacked by in her heels. "That girl has always had the most impeccable taste."

"Except when it comes to guys," Vivi said quietly, feeling nauseated. "I swear on my life, if Shawn Sluttig gets out of that car . . ."

Isabelle's father's silver Infiniti pulled up behind the limo and her parents got out. Then, the back door of the limo opened and out stepped . . .

Jonathan Hess.

"Jonathan?" Vivi gasped without even thinking. She couldn't have formed another coherent thought if she'd tried. Jonathan was here. And if a Hollywood scout had driven by at that moment, he would have been snatched up and dropped on a red carpet within twenty-four hours. He looked gorgeous. Sleek black tux. Long gray tie. Sexily tousled hair. Perfection. He walked around the back of the car and opened the door for Izzy. Vivi suddenly couldn't watch anymore. She turned around and flopped down on the couch. "But how . . . ?"

"I guess something I said convinced him," Lane said giddily.

Vivi felt as if nothing would ever make sense again. "I guess it did," she said dubiously. "But why didn't she tell us he changed his mind? The girl was devastated all week. You'd think she would have told us he was coming. Why didn't she—?"

"Who cares?" Lane trilled, her eyes bright. "He's here! *Brandon* came through! Oh my God, Vivi! It worked! Isabelle has her dream date!"

Just like that, it was like all the tension between Lane and Vivi faded away. It hadn't all been for nothing. All the debating, all the plotting, all the angst. It had actually worked.

Out in the foyer, Vivi's mother and Lane's parents greeted Isabelle and her family and Jonathan.

"Oh, Isabelle! How lovely you look!" Lane's mother gushed.

"Just like a princess right out of a Shakespeare play," Vivi's mother agreed.

"And who is this handsome young man?" Lane's mom asked.

"Brandon. Nice to meet you."

Vivi's brain went foggy at the sound of his voice. She felt weak. Jonathan was not supposed to be here. He was not supposed to be standing in her house looking runway-worthy with her best friend at his side.

"Wrap your brain around it, Vivi. You should be psyched!" Lane said. "Your plan worked. She's not with Shawn. You did it!"

"We did it," Marshall corrected.

Vivi took a deep breath. Lane was right. This was a moment for celebration. They had actually pulled it off. Isabelle was happy. She was going to the prom with the guy of her dreams. Vivi just wished that the guy wasn't also the guy of her own dreams. But beggars could not be choosers.

"You're right," she said finally, smoothing her dress down. She cleared her throat, shook her hair back, and resolved to put her feelings aside for the rest of the night. This was for Isabelle. It was all about Isabelle. And maybe, just maybe, everything would be all right. "Come on," she told her coconspirators. "Let's get this soap opera on the road."

How the heck did I end up here? Vivi thought as the unrelenting sun beat down on her face. She stood in the center of the yard, flanked on one side by Isabelle the Pink Princess and Jonathan the Movie God, and by Happy Little Lane and Always-in-Vivi's-Face Marshall on the other. If someone had told her three years ago that she'd be going to the prom dateless while one of her best friends went with her brother and the other went with the guy Vivi was seriously crushing on, she would have decked that person. But here she was. And the more Jonathan made Isabelle giggle and preen, the more Vivi seriously considered changing into a T-shirt and hitting the basement with a pint of ice cream and an X-Men movie marathon.

No. Even they were too romantic. Maybe zombie movies.

"Hey, everyone! Happy prom!" Curtis announced, bursting through the back door and out onto the lawn.

"Woot! Woot!" Kim Wolfe cheered, pumping her palms in the air in her garish green dress.

Vivi's stomach turned and she looked at Lane, who had completely lost her smile. Okay. So maybe Happy Little Lane hadn't been the worst thing. Depressed Lane was going to suck. Curtis and Kim's parents appeared at the back door behind them, and Vivi's mom and the other parents rushed to greet them.

"How's it going, man?" Curtis asked, slapping hands with Marshall. Curtis was wearing a black tux and a red tie with colorful swirling designs all over it. It would have looked silly on anyone else, but on Curtis it was just cute. "Hey, Vivi," he said, putting his hands in his pockets. "Lane," he added somewhat awkwardly.

"Hi," Lane said. Just then Kim sidled up to him and slipped her arm around his.

"Hi, all!" she trilled.

Lane turned around and headed for the patio. "I need some lemonade."

Curtis looked at Vivi uncertainly, but before she could even think of something to say, Isabelle came over to introduce Jonathan.

"Curtis, Kim, this is Brandon," Izzy said.

"Nice to meet you," Jonathan said, shaking hands with them.

"You too," Curtis said.

And then, awkward silence ensued.

"Well, I'm thirsty too!" Curtis said finally. "Who wants a drink?"

"I'm in!" Isabelle said.

Then they turned and lead the group up to the patio, where Lane was sitting in a chair, sipping sweetened lemonade with a look on her face that was all sour. With Isabelle's back turned, Vivi saw her chance. She grabbed Jonathan's arm and pulled him behind the huge rhododendron by the back fence.

"Vivi! What are you doing? Isabelle's gonna be suspicious," Jonathan protested.

"I don't care. We have to talk," Vivi said.

Jonathan looked like a caged rabbit. All darting eyes and shifty feet. "About what?"

"Well, first of all, thanks for coming," Vivi said. "After the way we left things—"

"Yeah, well, *Lane* was very convincing," Jonathan said.

Vivi felt a pang. It wasn't like she expected him to say he needed to see *her* again, but it still, somehow, hurt.

"Okay. Well, good," Vivi said, her hands on her hips.

"Can I go now?" Jonathan looked extremely uncomfortable.

"No! Wait! We never had a chance to go over what happens next," Vivi said, her heart pounding in her ears.

Jonathan's brow creased. Even that was gorgeous. "What happens next?"

"Yeah. What you're going to say . . . you know . . . to let her down easy," Vivi said, feeling disgusted with herself. She knew he hated this stuff, the lying and scheming, but she had to do it.

"No one expects you to play Brandon forever. The deal was you take her to the prom. So we had an idea of what you could say to let her know you won't be seeing her again after tonight."

Jonathan looked incredulous for a moment, but he stood up straight and focused on her. "I'm all ears."

"We were thinking you could tell her you're going away for the summer to a conservatory or something. To study music. Someplace far away," Vivi explained quickly. "Tell her it's a serious immersion program and you're not supposed to have any distractions like e-mail or anything."

"Seriously? That's your plan?" Jonathan's tone was mocking.

"What? She'll love that you're so dedicated to your music. You can just tell her that you've loved knowing her, but you need to focus on your future. It's just like every crappy romance novel she's ever read. She devours them at a rate of two a day down the shore every summer," Vivi told him. "They're her guilty pleasure."

"Okay. So I'm going to a conservatory in a foreign country where I can't have access to e-mail," Jonathan said. "Fine. But if she buys that, she's not as smart as you guys have always made her out to be."

Wow. He really wasn't giving her an inch here.

"It'll work," Vivi said defensively. "I know her a little bit better than you do."

"Fine," Jonathan said. "We should go before they realize we're both missing. When's your date getting here?"

Vivi's stomach hollowed out. "I don't have a date, remember?"

She hated the almost hopeful tone of her voice, but it was too late to take it back now. And she was hopeful. Hopeful he'd do something. Take her in his arms. Kiss her. Tell her he wished he were here with her instead of Izzy. Anything.

But his beautiful face was blank. "Oh yeah. Right. Well." And that was it. He turned around and slipped back out into the yard, leaving Vivi there alone to hold back her tears.

Dancing in the center of the country club dance floor, surrounded by her classmates, Lane felt as if she had to be dreaming. It couldn't be her senior prom. How had it come so quickly? One second she was a freshman looking up at the tall, confident seniors in awe, and now she was a senior and she didn't feel confident or awe-inspiring, let alone tall. She had thought that by the time she was a senior things would be different. She'd be cool and secure, totally certain of who she was and where she was going—just like all those older girls had seemed to her when she first started high school. But now here she was, a month away from graduation, dancing at the prom with her friend's little brother because she couldn't get a date with the guy she wanted to go with. The guy who was currently grinding with Kim Wolfe on the other side of the dance floor.

Lane danced around Marshall until her back was facing

Curtis. That was something she did not need to see. At least she was certain of that much.

"Having fun?" she asked Marshall.

He managed to nod as he continued to step back and forth to the music—one of those sucky dance versions of a formerly poignant love song that Lane just hated. Unfortunately, if the last two sets were any indication, the DJ seemed to love them. "Sorry. I'm not the greatest dancer," Marshall said.

"You're way better than most of the guys here," Lane told him. "At least you can find a beat."

Marshall grinned. "Yeah. I guess that's good."

"Omigod, Lane, *who* is that guy with Isabelle?" Jenny Lang asked, grabbing Lane's arm.

"His name's Brandon. He's from Connecticut," Lane lied.

"Damn. I wish I'd applied to UConn. I mean if they grow 'em like that up there," Jenny said, blushing. "He is totally the hottest guy here." Her eyes flicked at Marshall. "No offense."

"None taken," Marshall shouted to be heard over the music.

"*Look* at them!" Jenny said, her eyes wide. "He's all over her! How long have they been going out?"

All over her? Lane thought, confused. She glanced over at Isabelle and Jonathan, and, sure enough, they were standing in the middle of the dance floor, locked together. Instead of dancing to the semi-insane beat like the rest of the crowd, they were moving slowly back and forth, staring deeply into each other's eyes. Jonathan's hand moved up and down Isabelle's back. She sighed, closed her eyes, and leaned her cheek against her chest.

"Uh . . . not that long," Lane answered finally.

"Well, they are clearly in love," Jenny said. "Everyone's talking about it."

"Really?" Lane asked.

"Are you kidding? No one ever understood what she was doing with Shawn Littig. Good for her. Ciao!" Jenny said before disappearing into the crowd again.

"Are you okay?" Marshall asked Lane.

"*What* is going on over there?" Lane asked him under his breath. "They look like long-lost lovers or something."

Marshall glanced over, then cleared his throat and quickly looked away. "Well, maybe he's just playing it up."

"No one told him to do *that*," Lane gasped as Jonathan's hand grazed Izzy's butt.

Isabelle looked up at Jonathan, startled, but then they both laughed. Isabelle was completely glowing. Her face was flushed; her eyes were bright. She was a total goner.

"Omigod, you guys!" Vivi trilled, weaving through the crowded dance floor to join them. "Have you *seen* Sluttig? He's totally green!"

Vivi lifted her hand to point Shawn out, but it took a moment for Lane to find him. That was because he wasn't on the dance floor, but sitting at a table on the edge of it, slumped down, staring at Isabelle and Jonathan with murderous eyes.

"Probably doesn't help that Tricia Blank has had her tongue down Dell Landry's throat all night," Marshall pointed out, nodding toward the corner, where Tricia was curled up in the quarterback's lap.

"Definitely not." Vivi laughed, swiping her long blond hair over her shoulder.

"I just hope Shawn doesn't start something with Jonathan," Lane said. "I don't think he signed up for an ER trip."

"Eh. He'll be fine," Vivi said. "I'm sure he can hold his own." For the first time, she looked over at the couple she'd engineered, and her face completely fell. Lane's heart went with it. She knew that Vivi was seeing what *she* was seeing. Two people who were totally falling for each other.

"Vivi," Lane started to say.

"You know what?" Vivi interrupted, recovering herself. She lifted her arm, her sleek silver camera dangling from a strap on her wrist. "I think I'm going to go take a picture of Shawn to record this for posterity."

Lane sighed as Vivi rushed off. She wished the girl could just admit how she felt about Jonathan already. But really, from the way things looked now, there might be little to no point. Jonathan touched Isabelle's face with his fingertips as they danced, still gazing into her eyes.

"This is unbelievable," Lane said, looking up at Marshall—who was staring longingly at Isabelle and Jonathan.

Suddenly Lane recalled all the times she and Izzy had been over at his house and he had attempted to join in on the conversation, only to be thwarted by Vivi. She remembered how great he'd been the night Izzy had found out about Shawn's cheating, bringing Izzy her favorite root beer. She realized how nervous he'd been at the idea of IMing with Isabelle at first, but how obsessed he'd become with it once he'd gotten started. And then there were the new clothes, the new haircut, the fact that he'd shown up at Isabelle's first date with "Brandon." He'd been there to check Jonathan out. To size up the person who was taking his place with Isabelle. And then it hit her.

"Oh my God. Marshall! You like Isabelle!" Lane gasped.

"What? No, I don't," Marshall said quickly. He blushed and looked away.

The dance song ended and a slow one began. Half the people vacated the dance floor, but Lane clung to Marshall.

"Yes, you do!" she whispered. "You were just totally staring at her! I know that look! You like Izzy!"

"I do not!" Marshall said through his teeth.

"I can*not* believe I didn't see this before," Lane said, grinning. "Marshall, why don't you—?"

"Lane, I don't like Isabelle, okay?" He sighed in frustration and looked around to see if anyone was in earshot, then ducked his head closer to hers. "Can you keep a secret?"

"Of course," Lane replied.

Marshall took a deep breath. For a brief second, he dug his teeth into his bottom lip, and then he blurted it out. "I wasn't staring at Isabelle. I was staring at Jonathan."

Lane stopped dancing.

"I'm gay, Lane," Marshall whispered, averting his eyes. "But you can't tell anyone. Especially not Vivi. You have to swear."

"I swear," Lane said, breathless. She wasn't completely shocked. Just shocked that she was the first person he told. And that he liked Jonathan. One more tangle for their big old web.

Marshall dropped his arms and blew out a sigh. "Maybe we should take a break."

"Sounds like a plan," Lane said, eager to sit for a second and collect her thoughts.

She turned around to head off the dance floor and nearly bumped right into Curtis. Curtis standing there in his perfect tux and his funky red tie, all alone. Lane's heart pounded painfully, and she looked around for an escape. But then Curtis opened his arms and raised his eyebrows. "Shall we?"

"Sure," Lane managed to say.

She could hardly even look at him as he wrapped his arms around her waist and started to move. She was too embarrassed, too tense, too everything. She glanced at him, found him staring right at her, then flinched and quickly looked away.

Say something! Say anything! Lane chided herself.

"I like your dress," Curtis said finally.

"Thanks. You picked out a good tux," Lane replied.

"I thought it was me."

"Well, it is."

"Good."

"Good."

There was a long moment of silence as they continued to dance. Lane was just starting to wonder if this damn song was ever going to end so that she could breathe again, when Curtis spoke.

"Lane, there's something I want to tell you," he said. He stopped dancing.

The entire world went quiet. For a split second, everything

was still. Lane knew whatever he said next was going to change her life. Somehow knew it with complete certainty. He was either going to break her heart or make her year. She looked into his warm brown eyes and braced herself.

"Yeah?"

"I just want you to know that—"

"Curtis! Come on!" Kim appeared out of nowhere and grabbed Curtis's arm. "They're taking our table picture! We can't not be in it! Woot woot!"

She yanked Curtis away and he tripped, staring back at Lane with an apology in his eyes. Just like that, the whole world came rushing back—loud music, laughing voices, bad perfume—and Lane had missed her moment once again.

twenty

Vivi slid all the way to the end of the seat in the limousine and stared out the window. If she had to watch Izzy and Jonathan make lovey-dovey eyes at each other for one more minute, she seriously might die of misery.

God, I wish I could skip the post-prom party, she thought to herself as her friends took their dear, sweet time getting in the car. But she couldn't. She had to be there when Jonathan broke up with Isabelle. *If* he broke up with her. From the looks of things, those two could very well be headed toward promise rings and two-point-five kids.

"Hey!" Curtis whispered, tapping her arm as he followed her in. "Operation Skewer Sluttig is in full effect, huh? Isabelle's loving that guy!"

Vivi's stomach turned. "Yeah. Great."

Curtis shot her a confused look and took the seat across the way. He was quickly joined by Kim, who was scrolling through the pictures on her digital camera. Marshall sat next to her and Lane squeezed in next to him, which left the space next to Vivi open for the couple of the century. Jonathan sat down right next to Vivi, his thigh grazing hers, and she pressed herself even closer to the window.

Kill me. Just kill me now.

"What are you doing all the way over there?" Jonathan said to Isabelle as soon as the door was closed. Vivi watched in horror as he pulled Isabelle up onto his lap and she giggled happily, her prom queen crown slightly askew.

"Brandon!" she teased, slapping his shoulder. She did not, however, move off him. Instead she kicked her silver shoes off and they promptly slammed into Vivi's feet.

"Yeah! Woot! Woot!" Kim Wolfe cheered, climbing into Curtis's lap as well.

Vivi stared at Lane across the wide expanse of the car. The plan was working, but somehow, this night could not get any worse.

"Driver! To Dell Landry's!" Isabelle called out cheerily.

"Yes, ma'am!" the driver replied.

Luckily, it was a short ride, and Kim filled the time by passing around her camera and making everyone look at her "awesome" pictures, most of which were of her random friends striking slutty modeling poses on the dance floor. Jonathan and Izzy, however, ignored her pleas to take the camera, whispering and giggling with one another, Jonathan's arms locked around Isabelle's tiny waist. When the limo finally pulled up the wide driveway to their classmate's sprawling home, Vivi had to press her fingernails into her palms to keep from clawing her way out.

"Are you okay?" Lane asked Vivi, falling into step with her as she beelined it for the front door and the mayhem inside.

"I'm fine. Totally, totally fine," Vivi said, her fists clenched.

"You guys! Wait up!" Isabelle called after them, jogging in her long skirt and high heels. Vivi didn't slow, but Izzy caught up with them anyway. "Omigod, you guys. How amazing is Brandon?"

Lane shot Vivi a pained look. Vivi appreciated the sympathy, even as it irritated her. All she wanted was to get the heck out of there.

"So amazing," Lane said, touching Izzy's arm.

"The way he looks into my eyes? You guys, it's so incredible!" Isabelle gushed as they crowded through the door. "I know this sounds insane, but I think he's going to tell me he loves me."

"What!?" Vivi blurted, stopping in the middle of the marble foyer. A bunch of kids who were already milling around with champagne and beer stopped to stare at them, but quickly saw nothing interesting was going on and got back to their cavorting. "You barely know each other," Vivi said.

"I know, but he's been hinting around about it all night," Isabelle gushed, hand to her heart. "Like he keeps saying there's something he really wants to tell me. And that he's never met anyone like me. And his voice gets all husky and I swear it just makes me gooey inside. It's so intense."

Vivi glanced back through the open door and saw that Marshall, Curtis, and Jonathan were all posing for a picture for Kim, Jonathan wearing his "I'm too cool as Brandon" smirk. What she wouldn't give to smack it right off his fickle face. Hadn't he just told Vivi that he liked *her*, like, a week ago?

"And you know what the really weird thing is?" Isabelle said. She looked around, grabbed each of their arms, and pulled them toward the wall, behind a huge potted plant. Vivi stared at her breathless friend, petrified to know what was coming next. "The weird thing is," Isabelle repeated, her brown eyes all dreamy, "that I think I love him, too."

"Isabelle," Lane said, her tone anguished.

Vivi's throat completely closed.

"Thank you guys *so* much for convincing me to come with him!" Isabelle gave them a quick hug and rushed over to throw herself into Jonathan's waiting arms.

"I'm the devil," Vivi said under her breath. "I'm so the devil."

"It's okay," Lane said. "It's gonna be okay."

But Vivi suddenly felt her chicken marsala was not quite sitting right in her stomach. She turned around, shoved Kim Wolfe aside, and sprinted for the bathroom.

"Go, Curtis! Go, Curtis! Go! Go! Go, Curtis!"

Vivi, Lane, and Isabelle all sat on one of the leather couches in Dell's living room, laughing their way to tears as Curtis solo-danced atop the slate coffee table. He'd lost his jacket, his tie was tied around his head, and his shirt was completely untucked. All around him, their tipsy classmates raised their arms and cheered him on. With Jonathan and Marshall nowhere to be seen, Vivi was more relaxed than she'd been all night. She wished her friends had stuck to the no-date rule. If they'd been alone like this all night, she might have actually had fun.

"Okay, what is happening right now?" Isabelle asked, laughing.

Lane giggled. "I think we're seeing drunk Curtis in *full effect*," she said, putting on a skater boy voice.

"Why do I not have a video camera?" Vivi wailed through her laughter. "This is prime blackmail material."

Suddenly Curtis jumped off the table and attempted a flying split. Which only split his pants. Everyone cracked up and cheered even louder as Curtis's face turned purple.

"It's not funny!" Curtis shouted, even as he laughed. "This is a rental!"

Lane doubled over laughing. Isabelle wiped tears from her eyes. Vivi watched them and tried to solidify this memory in her mind. Her one fun memory from her senior prom.

"You guys, this has been the best night ever," Isabelle said with a content sigh, sitting back as she got her laughter under control.

Instantly, Vivi's shoulders tensed. She knew from Isabelle's dreamy tone that she was thinking about Jonathan. The last thing Vivi wanted to be thinking about.

Isabelle looked up and her smile widened. "And it's only going to get better." Vivi's heart thumped. Jonathan had just walked into the room and was weaving his way toward them.

Isabelle struggled to push herself up off the sunken couch as he approached and he rushed the last few steps to take her arms and help her. Izzy tripped into him and giggled and Jonathan hugged her tenderly. Vivi suddenly felt like taking her shoe off and throwing it at him. It would be the first useful thing the damn heels had done for her all night.

"Where have you been?" Isabelle asked, blinking up at Jonathan. "I missed you!"

"I missed you, too," he said in a low, sexy voice, running his fingers across her cheek. "Can we . . . maybe . . . go outside?" he asked, glancing at Vivi and Lane like he wanted privacy.

"Absolutely," Isabelle said with a smile.

Jonathan started for the door, but Isabelle quickly turned around and grinned, giddy as could be.

Vivi's heart and stomach switched places in her body, which was not a pleasant feeling. "Do you think he's going to break up with her or tell her he loves her?"

"Vivi, there's no way he loves her. He hardly knows her," Lane said.

"Yeah, but I hardly know him and—"

Vivi stopped, a few words short of saying way too much. Lane, however, read her face like a book.

"Omigod. Vivi!" Lane moaned, realizing what Vivi had been about to confess. "This is like a Greek tragedy!"

Vivi's heart felt as if it might shrivel up and die. She couldn't just sit here and feel this.

"Come on." Vivi got up from the couch and grabbed Lane's hand.

"Come on where?" Lane asked in trepidation.

"I have to see what's happening," Vivi said, feeling panicked. She squeezed Lane's hand so hard, it was like their skin fused.

"Okay. Okay. Let's go," Lane replied.

Holding hands, they rushed across the living room and out the front door. Dozens of kids were hanging out under the stars, sipping their drinks or making out under and up against the huge oak trees that lined the drive.

"Where are they?" Vivi said through her teeth.

"There," Lane whispered, pointing.

Isabelle and Jonathan were huddled close together near the bubbling fountain a few yards away. Vivi would have given anything to be able to hear what they were saying, but between the party noise and the running water, she never would have been able to eavesdrop without being right on top of them.

"Over here." Vivi pulled Lane toward one of the columns outside the front door. She positioned her friend across from her and tried to keep an eye on the proceedings. "Try to make it look like we're just chatting."

"Ooookay . . . So, can you believe that awful mermaid-from-hell dress Kim Wolfe is wearing?" Lane said, clearly trying to lighten the mood. She glanced over at Izzy and Jonathan.

"Omigod. I know. You are about a hundred times hotter than her," Vivi said quickly. She had to keep reminding herself to breathe.

"Really? Thanks," Lane said. "I wish Curtis would—"

"Hang on," Vivi said, touching Lane's arm to stop her.

Across the way, Isabelle's eyes widened. Vivi wasn't a lip-reader, but she knew what the word *what* looked like, and that's what Isabelle kept saying. Jonathan reached out to touch her arm and Isabelle let him, but then she lifted her hands to her face. Vivi's heart turned to stone.

"Oh, God. Is she—," Lane began.

"She's crying," Vivi said. "Oh my God! She's *sobbing!*"

Jonathan said a few pleading words and Isabelle nodded quickly, but the tears kept coming. And even as Vivi's heart went out to her friend, she couldn't help feeling just the slightest bit relieved. He wasn't telling Isabelle he loved her. There was still a chance—

Oh my God. I am *the devil,* Vivi thought, sick to her stomach.

"This is awful," Lane said, turning away. "She thought he was going to tell her he loved her and instead he's breaking up with her."

Vivi attempted to swallow but couldn't. Her vision blurred with tears. This was wrong. It was all so, so wrong.

Then, Jonathan and Isabelle hugged. They hugged for a long, long time, Izzy's face turned to the side, her eyes squeezed closed.

Finally Jonathan pulled back and wiped his thumb across Isabelle's cheek, drying her tears. Vivi felt like her own heart was tearing open. His touch was so tender. So reverent. She cold practically feel his fingertips on her own skin.

"I can't watch this," Vivi said, turning away.

"It's okay," Lane said. "They're hugging again."

"Again?" The pain was excruciating.

"Yeah, and now he's going. They're saying good-bye. This is good, right? I mean, sort of," Lane said hopefully.

Vivi's breath caught and she looked up again. Sure enough, Jonathan was backing down the driveway toward a cab that was waiting at the far end, past all the haphazardly parked cars. He watched Isabelle the whole way as Izzy stood there, her shoulders shaking with her sobs.

He's going. This is it. Vivi felt as if her heart were being pulled right out of her chest. *I'm never going to see him again. And I don't even get to say good-bye.*

At the very last second, Jonathan looked up. Looked right at Vivi. Her heart stopped beating. She just needed him to nod at her. Or wave. Anything to show her that he still cared about her. But he just looked up at the house, and Vivi was suddenly uncertain whether he'd seen her there at all. Then he turned and was gone.

And just like that, tears were streaming down her face.

"She's alone. Come on," Lane said to Vivi, grabbing her wrist.

"I can't," Vivi cried.

Lane looked at her and her jaw dropped. "You're crying!"

"No, I'm not!" Vivi said, using her palms to quickly dry her face. "I'm fine."

"Vivi—"

Vivi's heart cracked at Lane's sympathetic tone. And she just started to babble. "It's just . . . you guys were right. I do push guys I really like away. That's what I do! Because they're not good enough or I'm scared of . . . of not having control or whatever. But this time, he *was* good enough. He *so* was, Lane. And what did I do? I not only pushed him away, I pushed him right at my best friend!"

"Oh, Vivi," Lane said. "I'm sorry. I didn't want to be right." She reached over and hugged Vivi, and Vivi clung to her, trying to get control of her breathing.

"He's gone," Vivi said. "And he hates me."

"Vivi, I'm really sorry. I *know* this sucks. But we have to talk to Isabelle," Lane said firmly, pulling away. "We did this to her. We need to be there for her right now."

"I can't," Vivi repeated, shaking her head as the tears continued to come.

"You *have* to!" Lane said. "Now come on."

Vivi took a deep breath and nodded. Lane grabbed her hand and squeezed as they headed down the driveway.

"Isabelle!" Lane called out. "Isabelle. What happened?"

"You guys!" Isabelle threw herself into Lane's arms. "He's gone! Brandon's gone!"

Vivi turned away and dried her face again, sucking in a big gulp of air to steady herself. She had to be strong right now. For Isabelle.

"Gone?" Lane improvised. "Oh, you mean he went home?"

"No. I mean he's gone. He's leaving for a conservatory in Paris tomorrow morning. He's gonna be there all summer," Isabelle cried. "I can't believe this! I thought we were going to be together and he just . . . he just . . . broke up with me!"

"Iz, I'm so sorry," Vivi said, feeling lower than she ever had in her life.

"But it's not like he didn't like you," Lane pointed out.

"He probably just thinks long-distance relationships don't work."

Isabelle's eyes widened. "That's exactly what he said! And I believe him. I do," she said, pacing away and toying with her clutch purse. "It's just I wish it didn't hurt so much. I'm never going to see him again!" she wailed, fresh tears streaming down her face.

Tell me about it, Vivi thought.

"C'mere," Vivi said to Isabelle. She hugged her friend as she cried, her own tears hidden behind Isabelle's back. "It's okay, Iz. It's gonna be okay. Sooner or later, this whole thing is just going to be a distant memory."

Lane stepped over and made it a group hug, her head bent to Vivi's shoulder, like she was comforting Vivi as much as she was comforting Isabelle.

"I'm just gonna miss him," Isabelle sniffled, putting her chin on Vivi's shoulder. "I'm gonna miss him so much."

Join the club, Vivi thought, reaching up to wipe a tear from under her own eye. She knew exactly how Izzy felt.

★★ twenty-one ★★

"I still can't believe Curtis split his pants." Vivi doubled over laughing as she and Lane sat at a table in Lonnie's the following morning. All around them their classmates sipped their coffees, everyone in comfy sweats or jeans, chatting about the night before. "I wonder if the rental place will take them back."

Lane tried to laugh, but couldn't. Her heart was way too heavy. "Do you think they hooked up?" she asked.

Vivi raised her eyebrows. "Who?"

"Curtis and Kim? Do you think they, like, made out?" Lane asked, pushing her coffee back and forth between her hands.

"I thought we agreed not to talk about anything depressing." Vivi glowered.

"Oh my God! You *do* think they hooked up!" Lane exclaimed.

"Uh, no," Vivi said. "No way. Curtis has better taste than that."

"He asked her to the prom, didn't he?" Lane pointed out.

"Only because you didn't ask him first," Vivi said. "I told you to—"

"Please do not go there right now," Lane interrupted, her shoulders tensing. She could not get into that particular conversation with Vivi. She wanted to try to keep today light.

"Fine," Vivi said, rolling her eyes. "Where is Isabelle?" she looked at the door. "That girl is never late."

"You don't think she's sitting around in sweats with Pop-Tarts again, do you?" Lane asked warily.

Vivi snorted. "Maybe she's with Shawn. You know, rebounding."

Lane laughed at the suggestion, but then her eyes locked with Vivi's and her stomach dropped. "She couldn't."

Vivi paled. "If all we did was drive her right back into Sluttig's arms . . ."

"We never should have done this," Lane said, holding her head in her hands. "I mean, could it have backfired any worse?"

"Hey! It did not backfire," Vivi said under her breath, leaning across the table. "The whole point was to keep her from going to the prom with Shawn, and she did not go to the prom with Shawn."

"I thought the whole point was to keep her from getting her heart broken again," Lane countered. "And instead, we just broke it for her. And yours, by the way."

Vivi sat back. "My heart is not broken," she said evasively. She picked up her bagel and ripped off a huge chunk with her teeth. "This was never about me. It was about Isabelle," she said through a mouthful of food.

"That's it. I'm calling her," Lane said, diving into her phone for her bag.

Just then, Vivi's phone beeped. "That must be her," Vivi said, producing her own phone from the pocket on her zipped hoodie. She read the text aloud.

"She says, 'You're never going to guess where I am,'" Vivi said, her brow wrinkling.

Lane got up and dropped down next to Vivi on the bench so she could see. Vivi typed back.

> **Vivi:** U'r supposed 2 B @ Lonnie's!!!
> **Isabelle:** cant make it. Im going to paris to surprise Brandon. Have noon flight. Am at Newark airport right now! Bought tix w/graduation $$!

"What?" Vivi shouted, silencing half of Lonnie's.

Lane's vision clouded over and she gripped the sides of the table. "Text her back! Text her back!"

Vivi typed furiously.

> **Vivi:** NO! You cant go to paris!
> **Isabelle:** Nvr felt this way B4! Have to go. Looked up his school on web and will be there 2nite!

"Do something!" Lane squealed. "Do anything!"

"I'm trying!" Vivi shouted.

> **Vivi:** DO NOT GET ON THAT PLANE!!!
> **Isabelle:** this is true love Viv. Crazy but true. Gotta go!
> **Vivi:** NO! Stop! Need 2 talk first.

overwhelming sense that at any moment she was going to be tackled by airport security, but she hardly cared. "We made him up. The guy that took you to the prom was named Jonathan. I'm really sorry. We just wanted you to get over Shawn. But you can't get on that plane. He's not even gonna be there when you get there because he's not real! Please, Iz, just . . . just call me back!"

She skidded to a stop next to Vivi, heaving for breath. Vivi, for her part, was a bit pink in the cheeks but otherwise fine. The perks of being on the track team, Lane supposed. Maybe she should have stuck with soccer past freshman year, because she really felt like she was about to have a coronary.

"What?" she asked Vivi, who looked flat-out helpless as she stared at a television screen full of flight numbers and departure times.

"We don't even know what airline she's on," Vivi said flatly. "We don't know what gate, what flight number. And you can't even get past security without a ticket. What was I thinking?"

"No," Lane said, desperate. "You can't give up now. We got here, didn't we? And it's . . ." She lifted her phone to look at the time. It read 12:02. "No!" Lane wailed.

"What? What's the matter?" Vivi asked.

"It's after twelve!" Lane shouted, lifting the phone to show her. "She's gone! She's gone, Vivi!"

"No. She can't be. Maybe she missed her flight!" Vivi said hopefully. "Or maybe it's delayed!" Her eyes scanned the screen again.

"What? In this weather!?" Lane flung her arm toward the

window, which was full of nothing but blue sky. "Face it, Vivi. She's gone. Oh my God. Oh my God! How could I have let you talk me into this!?"

"What!?"

"Don't give me that innocent face!" Lane shouted. "This is all your fault!"

"My fault?" Vivi demanded. "We were both in on this one, Lane."

"Oh, please! You knew I didn't want to do this! I tried to beg you to drop it a thousand times. But no-o-o! You've gotta be right. You're such a freaking control . . . freak that you have to make all the decisions in everyone else's lives! Well, look where it's gotten us, Vivi!" Lane shouted, throwing her arms out. "We're in an airport and Isabelle's on a plane to a freaking foreign country!"

"Oh, you are so innocent aren't you?" Vivi countered. "Do I have to remind you that just last night you were all proud of yourself for helping to convince Jonathan to come to the prom after he bailed on me?"

Lane's face stung. She *had* been rather giddy about that at the time—feeling as though she'd maybe done something right where Vivi had screwed up. But that was then—when Isabelle was happily posing for prom pictures. This was now—when Isabelle was watching a stewardess point out emergency exits.

"That is so not the point," Lane said.

"Well, I think it is!" Vivi shouted. "If you and Marshall hadn't talked Jonathan into showing up, we wouldn't be in this mess right now."

"If *I* hadn't talked him into showing up!?" Lane exclaimed, incredulous. "You made me do that! I could have been at a party with Curtis that night asking him to the prom, but instead you begged me to fix your problem and I did! It's always about you!"

Vivi's jaw dropped slightly, and Lane felt an instant pang of guilt as her words hung in the air around them. They had started to draw a bit of a crowd, and a few college guys standing nearby ooohed at her dig.

"Oh, really?" Vivi said, stepping closer to Lane. "Well, you didn't *have* to go. It's not like I held a gun to your head. Is the word *no* even in your vocabulary, you pushover?"

"*Oooooh,*" the guys chorused again.

Lane's eyes misted over. Vivi had just hit her where it hurt the most. In front of all these people. At that moment she hated the girl. Hated her more than anything. This *was* her fault. It *was*. And no one was going to convince her otherwise.

"That's it. I'm outta here," Lane said, grabbing the keys from Vivi's hands. She turned and started to storm away.

"Where are you going?" Vivi yelled after her. "You can't leave me here."

"Yes, I can! It's my car!" Lane turned to shout back.

"Lane, you can't be serious," Vivi said.

Lane paused and crossed her arms over her chest. "Fine, Vivi. You want a ride home, you're gonna have to ask me nicely."

Vivi looked around at their audience, the color rising in her cheeks. Clearly she was hating every minute of this.

But there was also no other way out. For once, Lane had the power. "Fine, Lane. Can I please have a ride home?"

"Um, let me think about that," Lane said, bringing a thoughtful finger to her chin. *"No!"*

Then, to the applauding crowd's delight, Lane turned around and stormed toward the automatic sliding doors.

★★ twenty-two ★★

Lane was so pumped up and petrified at the same time, she felt as if she were losing her mind. Before long she found herself driving down her sun-drenched street, having no idea how she'd gotten there. She had taken her mother's car on the highway—to Newark Airport, no less—and she didn't even remember which roads she'd taken or what exits she'd used.

Probably not a good sign. She hoped she hadn't cut anybody off or caused any accidents. That would be really bad.

The thought of unknowingly leaving a string of wrecks behind her somehow struck her as funny as she approached the corner where Curtis's house sat like a beacon in the sun next to her own.

"I made up a guy. I made up a guy for my best friend and hired someone to pretend he was him and now she's on her way to France to be with him, but he's not there. No, he's not! He's not there because he doesn't exist!"

Lane pulled into her driveway and gasped a few times, trying to get control of herself.

"And I told off my best friend! The only friend I have left! I told her off just for being herself! What kind of person does that? A crazy person, that's who," she said, tears squeezing out the corner of her eyes. "I am a crazy person who is shouting at herself and crying in her mother's car!"

She choked in a few breaths and yanked a tissue out of the box in the center console. She blew her nose loudly and wiped at her eyes.

"And I asked you to the prom!" she shouted at Curtis's house. "Do you have any idea how hard that was?" she cried. "Do you have any freaking clue?"

Just then, Curtis's garage door slid open and out Curtis came, straddling his dirt bike. He looked happy and carefree and adorable in his black cargo shorts and an old, faded concert tee. So happy and carefree and adorable, it sent Lane's pulse racing. Without thinking, she got out of the car and slammed the door. Curtis almost fell off his bike, he was so startled.

"Wow. Give a guy a little warning," he said, righting himself.

Full of sudden fire, Lane stormed across her yard. "I have to tell you something!" she shouted. Almost screeched.

"Okay." Curtis put his bike down in the driveway. He looked freaked, but Lane didn't care. The words were coming and she was not going to stop them.

"When I asked you to the prom that night, I wanted to go with you," she said, standing right in front of him. "I mean,

I *really* wanted to go with you. Not as friends. Not as some last-minute pity date. I wanted to go with you. In fact, I've wanted to go with you forever. And I know that might freak you out, but it's how I feel. And I'm tired of not saying how I feel!"

She stopped and shoved her hands under her arms, clinging to her sweater as her chest heaved up and down. Curtis stared at her.

"So. How do you feel about that?" Lane said, petrified.

"I feel like an idiot," Curtis said, shrugging slightly.

Lane blinked. "Okay."

"No. Not okay," Curtis said. "Lane, I really wanted to go to the prom with you, too. I almost asked you, like, a hundred times, but I kept chickening out. I thought you would laugh in my face."

"No," Lane said.

"Yes!"

"I thought you were gonna laugh in *my* face!" Lane said. "And then you told me there was that girl you were interested in . . ."

"There was a girl I was interested in. You!" Curtis said, throwing his hand out at her. "I only said that to see how you would react and you had no reaction, so I figured . . . you know . . . that you weren't interested. But even then I kept trying to set up, like, situations where I could ask you. Like asking you to pick out a tux with me. I figured that would be the perfect opener, but you said no."

Lane's jaw dropped. "No."

"And then the party. I was going to ask you there. . . ."

"No!"

"You keep saying that," Curtis said with a smirk.

"Well, I don't know what else to say!" Lane blurted. "I thought you were in love with Kim Wolfe or something."

"I only asked her because you bailed on me for the party," Curtis told Lane. "I was going to ask you that night, but when you weren't even home, I just kind of figured you couldn't care less. So I asked the first girl I saw."

"No."

"Yes!"

"So you're not in love with her?" Lane asked, her voice squeaking.

"Not even close," Curtis said with a laugh.

He stepped closer to her. So close, she could count the gold flecks in his eyes. Lane looked at the ground, suddenly shy, but Curtis ducked his head to get back in her line of vision. He was smiling. And before she knew it, his lips touched hers. His hand was on her lower back. His other hand pulled her closer to him. Her heart swooped as she gave in completely. She was kissing Curtis. Curtis was kissing her.

Before she could stop herself, she started to laugh.

"What happened?" Curtis said, his eyes half-closed. "Are you laughing at me?"

"What? No! No. Not at you." Lane was warm and happy and disbelieving. "It's this day. I'm laughing at this day."

"So it wasn't the kiss." Curtis wanted to be sure.

"It wasn't the kiss. I promise. The kiss was good. The kiss was great, actually."

Curtis stood up straight, all proud of himself.

"But I have to go," Lane said, backing away. "Can we do this later?"

The self-satisfaction disappeared from Curtis's face. "Are you serious? We wait this long and now you want to wait longer?"

"I don't want to, but I have to." Lane bit her lip. "I have to go find Vivi and apologize and then I have to go over to Isabelle's house and tell her parents that I shipped their daughter off to a foreign country."

"Pardon?" Curtis said.

"I'll explain later," Lane said. "Bye!"

Curtis lifted a hand in a confused wave and Lane giggled all the way to Vivi's house.

Vivi jogged out of her house with the cash to pay her cab-driver, just as Lane was pulling up along the curb. She was surprised by how relieved she was to see her friend. After Lane's unprecedented freakout in the airport, Vivi had thought there was a good chance she would never see the girl again.

"Thanks for waiting," Vivi told the cabdriver, handing over a good chunk of the money she'd gotten back from Jonathan. Which, she supposed, she actually owed him now. As the cab drove off, Vivi turned to face Lane, who was approaching with a sheepish look on her face.

"You had to take a cab home, huh?" Lane asked, biting her lip.

"Girl's gotta do what a girl's gotta do," Vivi said, pushing her hands into the back pockets of her jeans. "Lane, I'm *so* sorry! I didn't mean to call you a pushover."

Lane smiled. "I didn't mean to say you were a control freak—"

"But I am," Vivi said, lifting her shoulders. "We all know I am."

"Yeah, but it was still a mean way to say it," Lane replied.

Suddenly exhausted, Vivi turned around and dropped down on her front lawn, letting out a groan. "This has already been a really long day."

"No kidding," Lane said, sitting next to her.

Vivi took a deep breath and stared down at the patch of grass between her knees. Her face felt hot and her heart was sick with dread. "I really screwed up this time, didn't I?" she said.

"Well, this *is* the first time one of your schemes has gone intercontinental," Lane joked, squinting one eye against the sun as she looked at Vivi.

Vivi managed to laugh. "I'm really sorry, Lane. For everything. I don't know what I was thinking with this one. I must have been out of my mind."

"Well, don't be too hard on yourself. Somehow in all the insanity I did manage to finally kiss Curtis," Lane said.

Vivi felt like she'd just been spun around like a Tilt-A-Whirl. "You *what*!?"

Lane beamed. "I just went over there. I told him I liked him. He told me he liked me. And we kissed."

"Shut *up!*" Vivi said, shoving Lane over with both hands. Lane braced herself with her elbow to the ground and laughed. "I knew it! I knew he liked you back!"

"Appears that way." Lane blushed like crazy.

"How was it?" Vivi demanded, turning to face her.

"Amazing. Perfect. Everything I always wanted," Lane confirmed, her blue eyes shining.

For the first time in days, Vivi's heart felt full. It didn't feel jealous or guilty or nervous—just full of happiness for her friend.

"Lane, I am *so* happy for you," she said, reaching over to hug her.

"Me too," Lane said.

When they pulled back again, Lane picked at a blade of grass near her hip. "I just wish it could have turned out the same way for you and Jonathan."

Vivi sighed as her chest constricted once again. "Well, that was never meant to be."

"Are you sure?" Lane asked. "Maybe if you called him?"

Just like that, Vivi's tension was back full force. "Maybe, but we have bigger problems to deal with right now."

"Right," Lane said, looking across the street. "Guess I was trying not to think about that."

"Come on." Vivi shoved herself up and then yanked Lane to her feet by her wrist. "Let's go inside and figure out what to do next."

Lane took a deep breath and blew it out. "Sounds like a plan."

As they walked into the house, Vivi tried to look at the

bright side. At least she still had Lane. At least she wasn't in this entirely alone. No matter how forlorn her heart felt.

✳ ✳ ✳

Several hours and much procrastination later, Vivi and Lane stood before the red front door at Isabelle's house, unable to move. Every time Vivi even thought about raising her finger to ring the doorbell, her resolve left her.

"Maybe we don't really need to do this," she said. "They have to know, right? Isabelle's not an idiot. She'd tell her parents if she was getting on a plane."

"We can't assume that," Lane said firmly, sounding as if she was trying to convince herself as much as Vivi. "We have to find out."

"Why hasn't she called yet?" Vivi looked at her phone. She and Lane had calculated it out. If Isabelle's flight really left at noon, she'd be in Paris by now. This whole thing would be so much easier if Vivi could tell Izzy's mom that she'd heard from her and she was okay. "Maybe we should just wait until she calls."

"Enough stalling," Lane said.

With that, Lane lifted her hand and rang the bell. Vivi's stomach dropped out of her body.

"What are you doing?" Vivi blurted.

"Biting the bullet," Lane said.

Vivi closed her eyes, feeling as if she were cresting the top of the highest hill on a roller coaster. Her heart was in her throat. Her stomach was where her heart should have been. And suddenly she had to pee like she'd never had to pee before. She heard footsteps. Heard the doorknob turning. This was it. There was no turning back.

"Well, hello, girls!" Isabelle's mother was a vision of calm, unperturbed ignorance—all pearls and pressed cotton and perfect teeth. So she didn't know. She didn't know a thing. Vivi looked at Lane. Lane looked like she was about to bolt. Vivi grabbed her hand.

"Hi, Mrs. Hunter," she choked out.

"Come in! Come in!" Mrs. Hunter trilled, opening the door wide.

Vivi could feel Lane shaking as they stepped inside. She felt like a prisoner being walked out in front of the firing squad. What was Mrs. Hunter going to do when she found out? Was she going to scream? Throw things? Faint? Were they going to have to call 911?

"Isabelle's not home right now, but you're welcome to wait for her in her room," Isabelle's mother said.

That could be a long wait, Vivi thought.

"Actually, Mrs. Hunter, there's something we have to tell you," Vivi began, hoping against hope that this wouldn't be as bad as she was imagining.

"What's that, hon?" Isabelle's mother asked with a smile.

Vivi looked at Lane. Lane stared at Vivi. There was no air in the room. No turning back. And suddenly, Vivi heard the words spilling from her lips.

"We didn't mean to do it, Mrs. Hunter! Honestly! We were just trying to help!" Vivi blurted.

"Didn't mean to do what, Vivi?" Mrs. Hunter asked, nonplussed. "What's the matter?"

"It's Isabelle," Lane said. "And Brandon. You remember Brandon, right? From last night?"

Mrs. Hunter crossed her arms over her chest. Her expression grew concerned. "Yes . . ."

"He's not real!" Vivi blurted. "We made him up!"

"On MySpace. We made him up on MySpace to help Izzy get over Shawn," Lane said.

"We gave him a dog and drums and books and movies," Vivi rambled.

"And then we had Marshall IM her, pretending to be him—"

"All we wanted was to get Izzy over Shawn! That was it! But then she wanted to go to the prom with Shawn, so—"

"So we had Marshall ask her. Well, Brandon. Well, Marshall as Brandon," Lane rambled. "But then we had to actually *have* a Brandon—"

"So we hired one," Vivi said, swallowing hard. "We hired a guy from Cranston Prep and he was totally hot, right? Wasn't he hot?"

Mrs. Hunter gaped at her.

"So not the point, Vivi," Lane said through her teeth.

"Right, sorry," Vivi said, chagrined.

"Girls, as appalled as I am right now, I'm getting the idea that you haven't gotten to the point." Mrs. Hunter nervously fiddled with her pearls.

"Well, we had Jonathan—that's the guy who pretended to be Brandon—we had him break up with her last night and say he was going to Paris," Lane said. "We figured it was foolproof, you know? No one wants a long-distance relationship at eighteen, right? But the problem is . . . the problem is . . ."

Vivi took a deep breath and closed her eyes. The words all came out in one quick rush. "The problem is that Izzy is on a flight to Paris right now to find him!"

"What!?" Mrs. Hunter screeched.

"Except he's not there! He doesn't even exist!" Vivi couldn't stop herself. "Izzy used all her graduation money to chase after a guy who we made up!"

"Mrs. Hunter we are so, so, *so* sorry," Lane said tremulously.

"How could you *do* this?" Mrs. Hunter raved. "She's on a plane? Right now? To *Paris*!?"

"Mrs. Hunter—"

"Don't even speak to me, Vivi Swayne," Mrs. Hunter snapped, slicing a finger through the air.

Vivi pulled back, feeling as if she'd been slapped. The lump in her throat grew. "I'm sorry."

"Oh my gosh! My baby!" Mrs. Hunter covered her mouth with her hands, her eyes wide. "She's going to be all alone in a foreign country!" She turned around and rushed into the kitchen. After the briefest hesitation, Vivi and Lane followed. Mrs. Hunter grabbed her purse and keys and looked around in a panic. "My passport! I need my passport!"

"Mrs. Hunter, what are you doing?" Lane asked.

"I have to go after her! She's going to be all alone!" Mrs. Hunter rambled. "I have to find my passport." She turned again and swept past them, running up the stairs in her sensible heels.

Vivi stood in the foyer, gripping the banister, feeling hollow. She could hardly breathe. "Omigod, she hates us," she said, holding her hand over her chest. "Could this possibly get any worse?"

Suddenly, Vivi's cell phone rang. She pulled it out, shaking like a leaf, and saw Isabelle's name on the caller ID. "It's her!"

Lane gasped and huddled in to hear.

"Izzy!" Vivi shouted into the phone, barely able to grip it in her quaking hands. "Are you okay? What were you thinking? Your mother is freaking out right now. She's on her way to Paris to get you!"

Total silence.

"Iz? Are you there?" Vivi wailed in desperation. "Where *are* you?"

And then, a hand came down on her shoulder. Vivi whirled around, and Isabelle was standing right in front of her.

★ ★ twenty-three ★ ★

"What . . . what . . . what?" Vivi could not get past that one word.

"Izzy! You're here!" Lane threw her arms around Isabelle's neck.

"I can't believe you losers actually thought I'd follow some guy I barely know to France," Isabelle said, smiling at Vivi over Lane's shoulder. She was wearing a bathing suit and terry cloth shorts, glistening like she'd been out in the sun all day.

"But . . . but . . . I—"

Isabelle pulled away from Lane, lifted her phone, and snapped a picture of Vivi's face. "Nice. I really had to get that one for posterity."

"Isabelle," Vivi said finally. "What is going on?"

"Why don't you come out back and see?" Isabelle said, tilting her head toward the back of the house.

Vivi looked at Lane as they followed Isabelle through the kitchen to the back patio. Lane looked as baffled as Vivi felt. Baffled and relieved. Isabelle stepped outside.

"They're here!" she sang.

Confused, Vivi walked out into the glare of the sun. For a second she was blinded, but she could make out two figures sitting in lounge chairs alongside the shimmering pool. Two shadowy figures that ever-so-slowly came into focus.

Marshall kicked back, sipping an iced tea in distressed khaki shorts and a cool T-shirt, and Jonathan looking as Abercrombie-perfect as ever in a polo and linen pants. He was all clean-shaven now, his hair back to its preppy flatness instead of the tousled Brandon effect.

"Ladies!" Jonathan said with a grin. "How was Newark Airport?"

Vivi couldn't move. Could hardly process what she was seeing. Even in all her confusion, Vivi was ecstatic just to see him again.

"You remember Jonathan, right? He never really looked like a Brandon to me," Isabelle said with a shrug. "But then I guess he never was a Brandon!"

"How long have you known?" Vivi asked finally.

"Since last weekend. The night of our first 'date,'" Isabelle gloated, throwing in some air quotes.

"So this whole week . . . this whole week with you crying and moping and everything. It was all a sham," Lane said.

"Yep. Who knew I was such a good actress?" Isabelle preened. "And my mom did a great job just now, didn't she? Maybe she should audition for your mom's next show, Viv!"

"I think I need to sit down," Vivi said, dropping into a chair at the table. She couldn't believe it. She'd been outplayed. By Isabelle, of all people—the least deceitful person she knew.

"It was hard, believe me," Isabelle replied, sitting as well. "I *so* wanted to tell you that I knew. But it was way more fun to mess with your heads."

"But . . . but how?" Vivi asked.

"Brandon and I . . . well, *Marshall* and I were chatting online that night after our date and I asked him if he wanted to go so he could go to bed early," Isabelle replied, smiling. "And he told me that he'd slept like a rock the night before so he could stay up all night talking to me if I wanted. Which was sweet, but clearly a lie. Since on our date, *Jonathan* had told me that he had been up until four in the morning playing his guitar."

Vivi shot eye-daggers at Marshall, who sank down in his chair a bit and covered his eyes with his sunglasses.

"So after some IM grilling, I finally got his true identity out of him and he spilled about—what did you call it?— Operation Skewer Sluttig?"

Vivi winced. "Yeah."

"Spilled the whole can o' beans," Isabelle continued. "That was when I decided to come up with my own plot."

"So she called you," Lane said to Jonathan.

"Yep. There was a message from Izzy when I got home from my friend's house that night. Marshall got her my number and she called me and told me she knew everything and that she had a plan to get back at you," Jonathan said. "And

I don't know, but for some reason at that very moment, getting back at you seemed like an attractive idea," he added, smirking at Vivi.

Vivi's heart was spasming like crazy. *What does this mean?* She wanted to scream. *Was all that mushy stuff between you and Izzy last night just to get back at me? Or did you actually fall in love with each other while plotting your revenge?*

"Omigod! The look on your faces when I told you I thought he was going to say he loved me?" Isabelle said, cracking up. "That was so classic! I *wish* I'd gotten a picture of *that*."

"So you're not mad?" Lane asked.

"Not anymore. I was at first. I mean, I was like Count of Monte Cristo mad," Isabelle said. "But after I talked to Jonathan and Marshall about it, it sounded like your hearts were in the right places. I mean, who else has friends that would go so overboard just to make their friend happy?"

"I cannot believe you made us think you were going to Paris," Vivi said, laughing as she rolled her eyes. "That was so not cool."

"Yeah, and making me believe I had a brand-new dream guy just to keep me away from Shawn? Not cool either," Isabelle said sternly. She stood up and walked over to Vivi and Lane. "You guys, you don't have to protect me, okay? I can take care of myself."

Vivi sat up straight. "But I—"

"You have got to learn to keep your mouth shut," Isabelle said firmly.

Vivi snapped her mouth closed.

"And you!" Isabelle turned abruptly to Lane with her arms crossed over her chest. "You cannot tell me you thought this was a good idea."

Lane looked at Vivi. "I . . . well . . . no."

"Well, God, girl! Speak up! If you would just learn to stand up for yourself already, we could have avoided this whole thing!" Isabelle teased.

"Oh, she learned to stand up for herself, believe me," Vivi said proudly.

"Yeah?" Isabelle raised her eyebrows.

"I kind of left her at the airport," Lane said with a shrug.

"No way," Isabelle said, her jaw dropping.

"Yep." Lane preened.

"Wow. Nice," Isabelle said, slapping hands with Lane. "You'll have to tell me all about that later."

"I guess I deserved that one." Vivi shook her head, smiling. "I'm really sorry, Izzy. It all went very wrong."

Isabelle smiled slowly. "Well, not *totally* wrong," she said. "Thanks to you guys, I finally found someone who cares about me." She slowly walked around the table toward the lounge chairs. "Someone who really listens to me and treats me the way I deserve to be treated."

Vivi's heart pounded in her throat. Oh, God. So it was true. Isabelle and Jonathan really *had* fallen for each other. She could only imagine all the late-night phone calls they must have had, putting together their plans. All the whispering and scheming. So all that stuff at the prom—the touching and gooey eyes and lap sitting—it was all real. Vivi was going to die. Right here, right now.

"My perfect guy," Isabelle said, pausing between the two chairs.

And then, Marshall stood up, took Isabelle in his arms, and kissed her like there was no tomorrow.

"Marshall!" Vivi blurted.

"No! Isabelle! You can't date Marshall! He's gay!" Lane shouted.

"What!?" Vivi cried. She brought her hands to her head. "Okay. Is this what an aneurysm feels like?"

Marshall pulled away from Isabelle and laughed. "Lane, I'm not gay. I was just messing with you. You caught me staring at her and I had to throw you off, so I said I liked Jonathan."

"I'm so going to hurl," Vivi said.

Isabelle laughed and hugged Marshall and they kissed again.

"Ew. Okay. I cannot watch this," Vivi rambled. "What is wrong with you people? I did *not* sign off on this!"

"Vivi," Jonathan said, pushing himself out of his chair.

"I mean, Isabelle and Marshall? This cannot happen," Vivi continued.

Jonathan walked over and stood in front of her. "Vivi!"

"What?" she blurted.

"Would you shut up already?" he said.

Vivi's mouth snapped shut. Jonathan's blue eyes sparkled as he looked at her. "What did you just say to me?" she asked.

"I said, 'shut up,'" he told her. Then he reached out, grabbed her by the waist, and pulled her to him. Vivi gasped in surprise, and then he kissed her. He kissed until she was floating somewhere outside herself—letting everything go.

When he finally pulled away, all she wanted was to pull him back again.

"Okay! Feeling very fifth wheel out here!" Lane said with a laugh. She turned and headed inside. "I'll just be getting a drink!"

"So I didn't scare you away?" Vivi asked Jonathan.

Jonathan took a step back, but held on to her hand. "Takes a lot more than one freak-out in a parking lot to scare me off," he said with a manly shrug. "Just took me a couple of days to realize it."

"A couple of days? Try a week!"

"Well, a guy has to play hard to get . . . ," he teased.

"You suck, you know that?"

"No, you suck."

"No, it's definitely you. You definitely, definitely—"

"Okay, this could go on for days. I have a better idea," Jonathan said.

Then he pulled her to him once more, and this time neither one of them was about to let go.

★ ★ twenty-four ★ ★

A few weeks later, Vivi sat in the sun with the rest of her class in her white cap and gown, smiling at Jonathan in the first row of the bleachers. Next to her, Lane and Curtis clutched hands. Up on the makeshift stage in the middle of the Westmont High football field, Isabelle was just finishing up her valedictorian speech. Vivi felt nothing but excited and accomplished and proud. She was having a perfect moment.

"Congratulations to the graduating class of Westmont High!" Isabelle shouted.

Vivi jumped to her feet and cheered with the rest of the class, throwing her cap into the air. Hundreds of white and black disks sailed up into the cloudless blue sky. And then came back down again.

"Duck!" Curtis shouted. And they all did.

"Ow!" Vivi said with a laugh as a hard corner slammed right into her back.

"That tradition has got to go," Lane replied, shaking her head.

"You guys! We graduated!" Vivi shouted. She grabbed them into a group hug as everyone around them high-fived and snapped pictures.

"We are officially OOS!" Curtis cheered.

"Huh?" Vivi asked.

"Out of school!" Curtis explained with a grin.

"Yeah, and now that we're OOS, maybe it's really time for you to quit that crap already," Vivi said.

"Bite me, Vivi," Curtis replied.

"Not BM?" Vivi shot back.

Curtis chuckled. "You said BM!"

"You guys?" Lane said.

"You are such a . . . a . . . guy!" Vivi countered.

"Hey! You finally noticed!" Curtis replied. "Congrats."

"You guys!" Lane shouted.

"What?" Vivi asked.

"Where's Isabelle?" Lane peered around through the mayhem. Parents and friends had started to crowd the field to take pictures with the graduates. "We need to get a picture. She was supposed to come right down here."

"I don't know," Vivi said, looking around. "She probably just got snagged by some people wanting a picture of the valedictorian."

Jonathan arrived and planted a big kiss on Vivi's cheek. "Congratulations!" he said, handing her a big bouquet of roses.

"Thanks," Vivi said, beaming. "But where's my real present?"

"What's that?" Jonathan teased.

"You promised! You promised you were going to tell me the story of the scar!" Vivi cried. "So come on. Give it. Spill!"

"Okay, fine, fine." Jonathan turned her toward him, wrapping one arm around her waist. "I got this scar," he said, leaning in close as if he was going to tell her a dark, tragic secret. "Trying to jump a ramp on my tricycle when I was four."

"No way!" Vivi said with a laugh.

"I told you I could be badass," he said with a blithe shrug.

Vivi laughed and stood on her toes to kiss him. "That's the cutest, most pathetic thing I've ever heard."

"Tell me about it," he said with a grin.

"Okay, where is Isabelle?" Lane asked, growing frustrated.

Suddenly, Vivi's cell phone beeped. She lifted her gown and fished under the folds of fabric until she could get to the pocket of her shorts. When she pulled it out, the text message icon was flashing on the screen.

"It's from her. What the heck?" Vivi said.

Lane, Curtis, and Jonathan all huddled around her as she read.

Isabelle: Guess where I am. And no. Not with Shawn.
Vivi: Ha ha. Better not B! U break M's heart.
Isabelle: Im @ Newark Airport

"She's hilarious. Really," Curtis deadpanned.

Vivi: V. FUNNY!

> **Isabelle:** OK. Not there yet. But our flight leaves in 4 hrs. U, me, Lane going 2 paris. Go home and pack!!! HAPPY GRADUATION!

"What?" Vivi blurted.

"Yeah, what? What about me?" Curtis put in.

"She can't be serious." Lane grabbed the phone from Vivi.

"Hey! That's my phone!" Vivi protested.

"Back off, Vivi!" Lane replied.

"Wow. She's getting good at this," Jonathan gave Vivi a squeeze as Lane texted back. Vivi smiled. She was actually fairly proud of Lane's newfound guts.

> **Vivi:** its lane. r u serious?
> **Isabelle:** TOTALLY SERIOUS! Remember grad $$$? Now GO! Meet at my house 1 hr.! Don't 4get yr passports!!

Lane closed the phone and looked at Vivi, dumbfounded. "We're going to Paris."

Vivi's heart skipped with excitement. "We're going to Paris!"

She grabbed Lane's hand and they jumped up and down, squealing happily. "Come on! Let's go pack!" Lane exclaimed, squeezing Vivi's fingers as they started navigating through the crowd.

"Uh, ladies!?" Jonathan called after them, clearing his throat.

Vivi and Lane turned around. Jonathan and Curtis were staring after them forlornly. "Yes?"

"What about us?" Curtis asked, lifting his palms.

Vivi looked at Lane and grinned. "Well, you'll just have to pine for us until we get back," Lane shouted.

"Unless, of course, you want to hop a plane and follow us, but that's your prerogative!" Vivi added. "I'm done telling people what to do."

And with that, she and Lane jogged off, hand in hand, to go get Izzy.

acknowledgments

Special thanks to Katie McConnaughey, Emily Meehan, Josh Bank, Lynn Weingarten, and Courtney Bongiolatti for their patience and help in guiding this novel. You all know I couldn't have done it without you!

Check out the latest book in

Kate Brian's PRIVATE series:

PARADISE LOST

Not happening. This was not happening.

I walked down the hall of the ICU at Edward Billings Memorial Hospital, trying to look as if I belonged there. Holding my coat closed tightly over my now ridiculous-seeming gold minidress and trying to make the nurses and doctors believe I knew where I was going. But I didn't. I didn't know where I was going, or where I was, or how I'd gotten there. I had never navigated these sterile halls, never had to visit this cold, ominous place with its grim-faced orderlies and somber lighting. The one thing I knew was that this could not be happening.

In my mind's eye, all I could see was the blood. I had woken up on the floor of the solarium in Mitchell Hall, the back of my head throbbing with pain. Noelle had been hosting a preparty there for Kiran Hayes's birthday fête in Boston, and I had gone to confront Sabine DuLac about her relationship with Ariana Osgood. She had pulled a gun on me, I had blacked out, and when I'd come to,

I had seen Josh's prone body, his face pressed into the hardwood floor. And blood. Blood everywhere. The scream that had escaped my throat had sounded otherworldly, like something out of a science fiction film. Like nothing that could have come from my own throat. That was when Sabine had realized the bullet had missed me. Even though the gun was gone, even though Trey Prescott and Gage Coolidge were holding her back, she had made one final lunge, intent on strangling me or clawing my hair out—hurting me in whatever way possible. I had thrown myself backward in fear and had bumped into something hard. A second body. Dark hair had been splayed everywhere, arms bent at unnatural angles. Another scream, and after that, everything had become a blur.

The shouting as the police had hauled off Sabine. The Pemberly girl who, splattered with blood, had fainted dead away. The flashing lights of the ambulance. The EMTs shouting for us to stay back as they'd sorted out who was hit and who was unconscious and who might be . . . dead.

Now an orderly shoved a meal cart out of a room and right into my path. I was so startled that my hand flew to my heart. My knees felt like they could collapse at any second. I pressed my other palm against the wall to steady myself, my fingers landing just above a gold plate with a room number printed on it: 4005. Which meant that the next room was 4007. The room I was looking for. The room I dreaded.

Deep breath, Reed. You can do this. You have to do this.

I closed my eyes for a moment. This wasn't about me. Yes, Sabine had tried to kill me. Yes, the person who, all semester long, I had thought was my best friend had turned out to be a raving homicidal lunatic stalker. Yes, I had spent months living in the same room with a girl who had then tortured me and drugged me and sent out a lewd video of me to the entire Easton Academy community. *That* was all about me. And I could deal with all of that later.

But right now. This. This was not about me.

I took that deep breath and stepped tentatively into room 4007.

Josh's eyes instantly met mine, whisking the breath right out of me. I was aware of the machines—the beeping of the heart monitor, the strange twitching lines on the screen, the dripping IV. But for a moment, just one moment, all I could see were those eyes. The relief, the anguish, the longing, the fear. Everything I felt was right there in his eyes. He knew. He understood. But then he broke eye contact, and I dropped back to reality.

Reality, where Ivy Slade lay on a hospital bed, unconscious and pale, her eyelids appearing purple under the fluorescent lights. Tubes and wires and sensors were stuck to her temples and wrists, and her black hair was shoved back from her face in a haphazard, unparted way that she would have loathed if she could have seen it. The white hospital sheets were tightly tucked in all around her, giving her the look of a half-wrapped mummy. Only her arms were free, and Josh was holding her hand. Her delicate, seemingly lifeless hand. My throat went completely dry.

Why hadn't she stayed outside like the police had told her to do? Why had she run back into the solarium? In all the panic, I hadn't even realized that she had come up behind me. She didn't have to be there. Didn't have to come with me to confront Sabine. I had even told her not to come along, but she obviously was worried about me in my one-track state of mind. That track being the express train to confrontation with a homicidal maniac.

It was my fault that she was here. All my fault.

"Is she going to be okay?" I whispered.

Please say yes. Please, please say yes. I wasn't sure I could handle another death. Another funeral. Another good-bye. I wasn't sure if any of us could handle it.

"They think so," Josh replied. He looked hopefully over at her. "The bullet went through her upper shoulder and just missed her lung. If it had been half an inch lower . . . She lost a lot of blood, though, which is why she's unconscious right now. But yeah, they expect her to make a full recovery."

My eyes misted over as a crushing weight was lifted from my shoulders. She was going to be okay. *Thank you, thank you, thank you!* Ivy and I had just started to become friends. If it weren't for her, I may have never figured out that it was Sabine who was after me. That Sabine was the person who had killed Cheyenne Martin and had tried to make me believe it was my fault.

If it weren't for Ivy, I might have gone to Kiran's party with Sabine and ended up shot dead in an alley in Boston somewhere. Who knew what the details of the girl's plan had been? It seemed that, as long as it had ended with me dead, Sabine would have deemed it a success.

Josh placed Ivy's hand on the bed next to her hip and slowly got up to usher me out the door. As we left the room, I turned to him, prepared to be a good friend—a supportive friend and nothing more. To ask the right questions. The questions that

Noelle Lange and Rose Sakowitz and all the other people down in the waiting room wanted me to ask. But before I could even open my mouth, I was in his arms.

"I thought she was going to kill you," he said breathlessly.

Surprised tears jumped to my eyes. I savored the familiar strength of his arms, the crisp scent of his shampoo. I clung to him, gripping the smooth fabric of his oxford shirt like it was a life vest and I was about to go under.

"I can't believe what you did," I said as a tear spilled down my cheek. "Lunging for the gun like that . . ." I forced myself to pull back so I could look into his eyes. "When you hit the floor, I thought you were dead."

Josh placed his hands on either side of my face and looked at me as if he was trying to reassure himself that I was actually there. "I didn't even think. You were frozen, and there was a gun pointing at you, and I . . . I didn't even think. It was either throw you down or go for the gun, and I guess I was closer to the gun, so . . . I just did it."

"You saved my life," I said, a sob choking my throat.

He moved his hands to cup my shoulders and touched his forehead to mine, blowing out a sigh. "You're okay. You're okay," he said. "Thank God you're okay."

Just like that, my heart filled with bubbles of joy. Josh still loved me. He loved me so much that he couldn't stop touching me. He loved me so much he had put himself in harm's way to save me. Josh loved me. I felt so high, I could have floated right out the hospital window.

But then, reality. Like a lasso around my ankle, reality once again slammed me back down to the ground. Because Josh's attempt to save my life had resulted in Ivy's current state. He had knocked the gun just as it had gone off. Knocked it so that the bullet had passed me by . . . and had hit Ivy right in the chest.

In trying to save me, his ex-girlfriend, Josh had put his current girlfriend in the hospital.

We both looked over at Ivy's room. I knew that Josh was thinking exactly what I was thinking, that Ivy didn't deserve this. He let his hands slip from my shoulders, and he stepped away. Suddenly, I was freezing. For the first time, I noticed the bloodstains on the front of his shirt. On his hands. Under his fingernails. Ivy's blood. It was everywhere.

"What happened to Sabine?" he asked flatly, as we started walking back to the waiting room.

"They arrested her," I told him. "Pretty much everyone heard her confess, so . . . ."

"I can't believe this. I can't believe this is happening."

Josh pressed the heels of his hands into his eyes. I knew the feeling. It was all so overwhelming that it was hard to decide which part to try to sort out first. Cheyenne's pointless murder, Ivy's pointless injury, or the fact that Sabine was Ariana's sister and, apparently, had come to Easton for the sole purpose of torturing me. How were we supposed to deal with that?

And then, of course, there was the issue of us. The "us" that now included three: me, Josh, and Ivy.

"So . . . now we just . . . ," I trailed off. I knew Josh well enough to know that he always did the right thing. And the right thing at this moment did not include me.

We turned the corner and stopped down the hall from the waiting room. Josh leaned against the cinderblock wall. He looked miserable. Tired and gaunt and haunted. He raised his hands to his face again, making a little tent around his nose and mouth. For a moment, neither of us breathed. Then he dropped his hands, as if resolved, and looked at me. The emotion was gone. In its place was an expressionless wall.

"I have to stay with Ivy," he said firmly. "I have to know she's okay. She's going to need . . . someone."

My heart contracted painfully, and I allowed myself one moment of selfishness. One. *But what about me?* I thought. And then I let it go. Because he was right. Ivy needed him more than I did. Yes, I had been through a lot this semester. We both had. Cheyenne's murder, our breakup, my falling-out with Noelle, and the constant feeling that someone was stalking me. All the heartache and paranoia had been because of Sabine. It had all been part of her little "torture Reed for hurting Ariana" plan.

I wished that Josh and I could have talked through all of this right then. That we could have sat together and figured out what it all meant. But at that moment, it all meant nothing. Because he cared for Ivy and, as much pain as I was in, Ivy needed him more.

I glanced over my shoulder toward the waiting room. I saw Noelle hovering, watching me expectantly. We hadn't even had a conversation yet. Hadn't cleared the air after our massive breakup and her kicking me out of Billings. But she had made a peace offering—she'd invited me to the party tonight—and after everything we'd been through in the past few hours, I knew that things were going to go back to normal between us. At least I hoped they were. She was all I had now.

"I guess I should go tell them what's going on," I said slowly.

The last thing I wanted to do was leave him, but I had to. Standing in front of Josh and not being able to touch him was going to kill me.

"Okay," he replied, his eyes wet.

"Okay," I repeated, somehow getting the word past the lump in my throat.

I turned and started down the hall, my footsteps heavy. A few doors down, I paused and looked over my shoulder. He was still standing there, watching me. Watching me walk away from him. "Keep me posted, okay? On how she's doing."

"I promise."

So there it was. Good-bye. I was going to be strong. I was not going to pine and whine and wish. I was going to be good. For me, for Josh, and for Ivy. That was my promise to myself.

about the author

Kate Brian is the bestselling author of the wildly popular Private series, the Privilege series, *Sweet 16*, *Lucky T*, and *Megan Meade's Guide to the McGowan Boys*. She lives in New Jersey.

From bestselling author
KATE BRIAN

❤ ❤ ❤ ❤ ❤

Juicy reads for the sweet and the sassy!

Sweet 16
As seen in *CosmoGIRL!*

Lucky T
"Fans of Meg Cabot's *The Princess Diaries* will enjoy it." —*SLJ*

Megan Meade's Guide to the McGowan Boys
Featured in *Teen* magazine!

The Virginity Club
"*Sex and the City: High School Edition.*" —*KLIATT*

The Princess & the Pauper
"Truly exceptional chick-lit." —*Kirkus Reviews*

❤ Published by Simon & Schuster ❤

Some girls would die for a life of Privilege . . . Some would even kill for it.

Don't miss a minute of this delectably naughty series by bestselling author Kate Brian.

Available
Now

Available
June 2009

Get ready
for the newest
Private novel:

PARADISE LOST

And don't miss the first eight books in the Private series:

Check Your Pulse

Simon & Schuster's **Check Your Pulse**
e-newsletter offers current updates on the
hottest titles, exciting sweepstakes, and
exclusive content from your favorite authors.

Visit **SimonSaysTEEN.com** to sign up,
post your thoughts, and find out what
every avid reader is talking about!

About the Author

Robert Sachs moved to England from America during his late teenage years where he received his BA in comparative religion and sociology at the University of Lancaster. He began to study with Tibetan Buddhist masters, and embarked on a study of Asian healing systems, including Macrobiotics, with Michio Kushi and Rex Lassalle at the Kushi Institute in London, and hatha yoga. Before returning to America in 1976, Robert completed training as a mental health counselor with the Richmond Fellowship and became certified as a hatha yoga instructor. He returned to London to complete shiatsu training with Rex Lassalle and was instrumental in starting the Community Health Foundation's "Growing Family Centre." He later went on to receive a massage license from Central Ohio School of Massage and a Masters in Social Work at the University of Kentucky.

Following the death of one of his daughters, Robert was led into the study of the conscious dying practices as found in the Tibetan Buddhist tradition and is a member of Sogyal Rinpoche's Spiritual Dying Network and the National Hospice Organization. Along with his wife, Melanie, Robert has also pursued studies in Indian and Tibetan Ayurveda and their published works in this field are considered by such teachers as Dr Deepak Chopra to be the clearest and most usable texts available.

Robert now works with the medical profession to integrate contemporary scientific approaches with the ancient wisdom traditions in the areas of stress management and preventive health care. He is a guest instructor for the Chopra Center for Well Being in San Diego and lecturer in Tibetan Medicine for the Sino-American Rehabilitation Association College in Los Angeles. He lectures at holistic health care conferences nationally, has been featured in a number of magazines, and has hosted his own talk radio shows in New Mexico and California focusing on a unique system of astrology called 9-Star Ki and alternative health care.

Robert lives in San Luis Obispo, California where he and his wife Melanie co-own and direct Diamond Way Ayurveda. They have three children, Kai Ling, Harriet Christina, and Jabeth David-Francis.

By the same author

Nine Star Ki: Your Astrological Companion to Feng Shui

Tibetan Ayurveda: Health Secrets From the Roof of the World

Rebirth Into Pure Land

Perfect Endings: A Conscious Approach to Dying and Death

The Passionate Buddha: Wisdom on Intimacy and Enduring Love

THE BUDDHA AT WAR

Peaceful Heart, Courageous Action in Troubled Times

ROBERT SACHS

WATKINS PUBLISHING

LONDON

This edition published in the UK 2006 by
Watkins Publishing, Sixth Floor, Castle House, 75-76 Wells Street,
London W1T 3QH

1 3 5 7 9 10 8 6 4 2

Designed and typeset by Jerry Goldie Graphic Design

Printed and bound in Great Britain

British Library Cataloguing in Publication Data available

ISBN 1 84293 174 1

www.watkinspublishing.com

Contents

Dedication

On September 11th, 2001, while fanatics with limited and narrow fundamentalist beliefs were cutting the throats of airline crews and taking aim at the Twin Towers of New York, His Holiness the 14th Shamarpa (Kunzig Shamar Rinpoche), a high Tibetan lama and my teacher, was on a plane landing at New York's JFK airport. From the point of view of an outside, unenlightened observer, he had no particular reason to fly to New York that day. But that is how he is. He does what he does when he sees the need to do it.

As the Rinpoche's plane touched down on the airport tarmac, the first hijacked plane smashed into the first tower. As he cleared customs, the second plane smashed into the second tower. Having been picked up by his host and driving toward the city, they saw plumes of smoke rising above the towers, which were soon not to be. His car was one of the last cars allowed over the bridge into the city before police shut it down.

For three days, Shamar Rinpoche worked with the shocked and the grieving. He offered prayers for the fallen and grief-stricken and gave teachings about life, death, and the truth of impermanence. He provided comfort and showed a path that leads away from fear, hatred, and revenge toward peace, understanding, and profound compassion. Months later, he made a speech which, in fact, inspired me to write this book. This speech you will find in the appendices to this volume (see page 230).

In the spirit of what this great and dedicated teacher demonstrates through his Buddha-activity, I dedicate this book to the families of the September 11th bombing victims and to each and every being who has had to grieve for loved ones lost to the senseless slaughter perpetrated by humanity against itself. In the words of a Buddhist prayer:

"May sickness, poverty, and warfare subside wherever we may be.

May good omens and Dharma* increase!"

Robert Sachs,
San Luis Obispo, CA,
August 2005

*understanding of the way things are

Preface

by His Holiness the 14th Kunzig Shamar Rinpoche

In modern countries where materialism is strong, the concepts and practices of Buddhism can be effective in neutralizing the problems that naturally arise and create much suffering, including conflict and war. My student, Robert Sachs, has written this book to show what role Buddhism can play in creating lasting political and social change.

It is my sincere wish that *The Buddha at War* is helpful to all who read it and that it fulfills the need to bring strength and confidence to those wanting to see a world free from sickness, poverty, and warfare.

Shamarpa,
Los Osos, CA,
July 18th, 2004

Foreword

by Stephen Levine

Robert Sachs' concern for the well-being of others extends to the horizons in which we wish our children to be born, a world where mercy and awareness are its most treasured values and its rewards are from the hard-earned activation of compassion and care for other sentient beings.

Reading *The Buddha at War*, I hear a bell ringing. It is like the bell that begins and concludes a period of meditation, and it is also the "All Clear" bell that signals it is safe to venture out, the bell that rings the end of war. The Buddha said it was less difficult to overcome ten thousand enemies on the battle-field than it was to release attachment to the hindrances to the heart. It was easier to go to war than to find peace in ourselves.

Robert Sachs recommends that we look for the flowering of peace in a close examination of the seeds of war: separation, partisanship, all the way into the seemingly inconsequential "liking and disliking" which arise from moment to moment to nonetheless form the foundation of all such confrontations and aggravated allegiances. Our identification with a particular perception singled out from a hundred possibilities, which then becomes *our* truth, is the most potent cause in our insistence that there is something to fight for, something to make others suffer for not sharing. From a reinforcement of the natural but unfortunate tendency to become lost in an identification with "I" and "other", we find reasons to hoard resources, to starve the hungry, to burn fields and ravage villages, to leave the homeless to fend for themselves in the refuse piles of a society which furthers the violence to themselves and to others in the insistent misuse of what is only partially consumed or recycled.

It is our fear of our unknown interior, our uninvestigated suffering, which fattens the generals and reinforces the leap of faithlessness that flattens our world and breaks it off at the edges, a piece at a time, leaving us little refuge, perhaps a momentarily uncluttered square on the game board on which to stand, one-legged and confused at having to choose between safety and the sacred.

Until we begin to roll back the battlefield one insight at a time, with each moment of self-discovery, each uncovering of the mercy and peace of our inherent nature, the continual encroachment of wars and slavery continues – of more types of wars and slavery than we notice or acknowledge. Ultimately, this book is devoted to gaining access to the battlefield – the one inside us that spawns the one we see before us – and emerging victorious.

Stephen Levine,
author of *One Year to Live* and
Turning Toward the Mystery

A Ray of Hope

If you have picked up this book, more than likely you feel that the world is in a dire way. With more than forty wars brewing or under way around the globe; the growth of terrorism, both state-sanctioned and from radical groups; a growing chasm between the rich and the poor; the dramatic climatic and environmental shifts that are bringing us more powerful and frequent tornadoes and hurricanes; and the devastating, cataclysmic tsunami of 2004 – it all looks pretty bleak for the survival of the human race.

That all of these things are happening at once is considered by many people of a fundamentalist religious outlook to be a portent of the impending apocalypse. For others, in the East, these "signs" point to us being in a "Dark Age." While that in itself sounds bad, it is not without hope. The simple truth is that little of what we are witnessing is new. Global warming may or may not be a new "man-made" phenomenon. But regardless of whether you view this as a causal factor or "junk science," our Earth has gone through repeated climatic and seismic tumbles and flip flops. And, certainly, conflict has been a characteristic of the human race since the dawn of civilization.

While the frequency of most of these happenings does seem to be on the increase, we have also developed the media and information technology that allow us to be more aware of such phenomena, and indeed to witness them both in our midst and in distant lands. This frequent exposure to painful and traumatic events has any number of effects on our hearts and minds. Some of us may worry and find ourselves getting more and more anxious and depressed. Others may get frustrated and angry. Still others may try to get on with their lives without noticing too much.

What is heartening, however, is that at the same time, in response to the pain and suffering of those among us, we are also seeing more and more acts of individual and collective kindness, compassion, and heroism that remind us that there is nobility, decency, and love at the core of our being. Increasing numbers of people see the need to make their own personal contribution toward social, political, economic, and environmental peace and harmony. Often against seemingly overwhelming odds and circumstances, people are reaching deep within themselves, striving to connect with "something" in order to better their lives and the lives of their neighbors.

Disaster and dire circumstances are often the teachers that wake us up to the fact that something has to change. It would be nice if this wasn't true, but it is. Most of us would like to live our lives and go about our business without too much hassle or distraction. But, as John Lennon put it, "Life is what is happening when you are making other plans." Life intervenes, things get in our way and we are forced to awaken from the hypnotic trance and slumber of our own routines. We then try our best to meet the tests and challenges that face us. But do we have the focus and fortitude to know what to do? How do we overcome our own negative emotions, which can sabotage our efforts and lead us back into the same old mess, or worse? How do we center ourselves and learn to become skillful in making changes for ourselves? And, looking around us and seeing that our happiness is intimately connected to the happiness of others, how do we develop the wisdom and skillfulness to create positive and lasting change in the world about us?

Answering these questions is what this book is about. It is a book devoted to helping you find the inner resources that will make it possible for you to not be overwhelmed with sadness, despair, frustration, anger, or inertia. It is about changing your life from within and then reaching out to change the world around you. For, as you tap into the inner resources that you already have, new possibility begins to show through the apparent solidity of the oppressive and depressing illusion of a troubled world. And in the realm of possibility, change – no matter how small – has its effects. No good thought, gesture, or act is ever wasted and will slowly but assuredly bring about the changes that we all, as humans, want to experience and share with those we love.

What We Want...

There probably isn't a human being on this planet who doesn't wish to have a happy life. Although happiness can mean different things to different people, some of the more commonly shared aspirations are to feel safe, to have shelter and enough to eat and drink, to be with people you love and who love you, and to enjoy all of these in an atmosphere that is peaceful. And yet there are so many on this planet who do not feel safe, live in makeshift or inadequate shelter, have little to eat and unfit water to drink, and are always looking over their shoulder.

The ideal situation that we all wish for, the dire conditions many on this planet find themselves in, and all points between these two extremes, come about for reasons that are largely of our own making, whether we intend them or not. Some of the causes for the world's ills are glaringly obvious, and it would be comforting to think that with a few free elections, a few corporate shake-ups, and a call to higher ideals, the wrongs of the world could be righted. But such simple solutions are rarely sufficient, because the causes of human suffering are many and intricate, and form interlinked chains of events that lead back to the dawn of human existence. Some, needing a linear rational explanation as to why things are the way they are today, have scanned the annals of history and looked at the lives and legacies of political, religious, and military leaders, who used their charisma or force to claim or take what some would say was more than their fair share. Such leaders often passed what they had on to their children, lineage, or clan until, over time, the original reason for them being rich and powerful was lost under a mantle of legitimacy born of privilege.

One of the many problems with such analyses is that they usually end up simply making us either depressed or angry – neither state of mind being particularly useful in mustering what is needed to take things in a different direction. In the end, what is going to make the greatest difference – what is going to be the spark or catalyst for creating a world where we can achieve the ideals to which we all aspire – begins with our minds. For it is either the clarity or the confusion of our minds that leads us to pick up a pen, march in the street, or shoulder a gun.

Where to Start: Heart and Mind

"Mind" is the connection between the head and the heart, with the master of the two being the heart. When the full power of the mind is awakened – as we gradually awaken from the slumber of our habits, and from our confining superstitions and beliefs about the world and how it is or how it should be – anything is possible. We become wiser and our compassion deepens. Inevitably, we become conscious and engaged.

Positive change, even revolution, in any field of human endeavor, be it in the political, social, scientific, or spiritual domain, has come about through the efforts of those with minds informed and fueled by wisdom and compassion, who have transformed their worlds and inspired new ways of seeing and being. Such people have shaken, and sometimes even brought down, the fortresses of the powerful.

If we want to live in a land of freedom, if we want to see conditions in which the needs of all our brothers and sisters are met, we need to develop free minds. Neither external freedom (freedom from entrenched power structures and from such conditions as sickness, poverty, and warfare) nor internal freedom (freedom from the habitual mind that narrows our vision and in turn breeds the host of problems we face both within and without) is easily won. Both require commitment, diligence, and vigilance. Both require time to change. To want change, to create the causes and conditions for change to happen and to become lasting, is no small task, and we must surely celebrate the victories that are made along the way. When we see a tyrannical regime fall; a corporation restructured in accordance with wiser and more compassionate ideals; or social services provided to the disfranchised: all of these are testimony to the hard work – both external and internal – done by individuals pursuing our basic human desire to see good in the world.

However, creating a society where a sufficient number of people are attuned to the needs of the many, and who undertake to safeguard whatever changes for the collective good are attained, requires there to be a widespread awareness and appreciation of the unlimited potential of the awakened mind. In the final analysis, it is the awakening of this potential and the freedom that we experience from within that matter to us most. And, in times like these, which seem so dark and uncertain, it will be our inner strength that points us in a new direction, that will provide the inspiration, ideas, and resource-fulness to create a more positive future for us all. Toward this end, and as a part of the awakening of this potential within us, we need to create a valued tradition of wisdom that in turn produces holistically-minded citizens who are both spiritually attuned to their higher, ultimately good natures and able to function positively, powerfully, and with purpose amid the ambiguity and messiness of everyday life.

Cultivating consciousness

No book could possibly examine every detail of the complex and interconnected issues in our world that need attending to. However, it is possible to focus on the inner resources that we, as individuals, can cultivate in order to meet the challenges of addressing these issues. This is the sole purpose of this book. In a time that many Buddhist leaders have called a "Dark Age," the tradition of Buddhism provides time-tested methods that anyone may easily use to become what I shall call throughout a conscious, engaged activist.

The most important word in this phrase is "conscious," for in truth, no matter how oblivious we may be to our world, we *are* engaged and we *do* act. If we have a body, where we put it in space matters. Once we are born and inhabit a body, we stand on the ground and we are identified as partisan, on one side or the other of this or that. We cannot escape this. If we silently stand behind those who wave guns and perpetrate crimes against others, even if we never pick up a gun ourselves, but try to ignore, even disassociate ourselves from "them," there will be those who will identify us as part of the crowd that supports the gun-toters.

Our only option, therefore, if we are no longer to feel that we are the victims of circumstance or of the capriciousness of our times, is to become conscious – to make conscious choices, no matter how imperfect, and accept and live with the consequences of those choices. At least then we will have tasted freedom and will be able to stand taller in the face of the challenges that life will inevitably put before us. This foundation of becoming more conscious in our engagement with the world will only grow and mature with time. It is the bedrock of our freedom.

The above reflections, and what I am to present throughout these pages, are expressed in a language that comes from my training in the teachings of the Buddha. However, their essence is to be found in the words and deeds of the Founding Fathers of the country in which I live: the United States. In the Age of Enlightenment, a group of people came together not only to secure their independence from what they perceived as a tyrannical authority, but also to create a form of government and governance that would avoid the pitfalls of emerging states throughout the course of history. Much of what they said and wrote reflects a profound appreciation of education and of the awakening of our inner resources as the most important safeguards for an emerging democracy. As such, the United States has always stood as a country founded on higher, enlightened ideals.

However, it is not my intention in this book to represent the United States either as an embodiment of an ideal or, conversely, as a country that has *not* lived up to an ideal. As an American, I shall simply, from time to time, draw on examples of American history, recent and more distant, in addressing issues that individuals and groups need to be aware of in seeking to create positive social and political transformation. For it is my belief that the teachings of any philosophy or spiritual tradition can remain alive only if they can be made relevant in the context of our day-to-day lives and realities.

All this said, it is my wish that the reader find through these pages the strength and resourcefulness to awaken and deepen their own innate potential, not only for their own personal benefit but also for the benefit of each and every being that they meet. For true contentment and peace will only be attained when what brings us contentment and peace is shared.

There are many people in my life whom I wish to thank for inspiring this project. Inspiration comes from both negative and positive sources, both of which have the potential to draw us out and meet our world. Thus it is that I would first like to thank President George W. Bush. Without the illegitimacy of the 2000 and 2004 presidential elections, and the blatant corruption that ensured his assumption of the office of President, I would not have been roused from, and pushed past, my normal "comfort zone" of being only semi-informed, and partially engaged, when it came to the election of my public officials. Through watching the hubris of Bush's administration and the resulting debacle in Iraq I became inspired to look at the history of power and its abuse in my own country and at the wisdom of the Founding Fathers; and I was inspired also to appreciate the work of such modern presidents as John F. Kennedy, Lyndon B. Johnson, Jimmy Carter, and Bill Clinton. I was also compelled to look more deeply into the teachings of such dear friends and beloved masters as His Holiness the XIVth Kunzig Shamar Rinpoche, the Venerable Chögyam Trungpa Rinpoche, the Venerable Khenpo Karthar Rinpoche, and Lama Ole Nydahl, in order to see how their words and living examples could be applied to meet the current social and political climate in the U.S. and the world in general. Without such great masters, I would not have had a compass with which to navigate the ambiguities and conundrums that are part and parcel of the social and political realities affecting us all. Add to this mix the polar opposites of media pundits Rush Limbaugh and Michael Moore. May all the living teachers, leaders, talk show hosts, and satirists who have inspired me in this endeavor live long, healthy lives.

My appreciation also goes to Bob Silverstein of Quicksilver Books, who continues to inspire me to think bigger and act bolder in my writing projects. Also to Michael Mann of Watkins Publishing, who had the vision to see the long-term benefit of this effort.

Most importantly, I wish to thank my Beloved, Melanie. At Christmas, 2003, she gave me a pewter embossed dragon pen with a card that said she wanted to support my writing of this book. Melanie, you are my true muse, my inspiration, and the source of all wisdom that graces me.

May all of the effort and inspiration that has gone into this book bear fruit in the creation of conscious, engaged activists who feel greater freedom, joy, and possibility in their hearts and minds to seek and work for the changes that all of us have the potential to enjoy.

Robert Sachs
San Luis Obispo, California

CHAPTER 1

A Call to Action in a Dark Age

"We have nothing to fear, but fear itself."

Franklin D. Roosevelt, former US President

Buddhist masters say that we are in a "Dark Age." In my twenty-five years of studying with many Tibetan lamas and Rinpoches ("Rinpoche" is a Tibetan title meaning 'Precious One' given to especially wise and revered lamas), mention has been made time and again of this fact, and what it means. When I and many other Western students born in affluent nations first heard this, it was hard to imagine what such teachers meant by "Dark Age." We had our own ideas and images spawned by history classes on medieval Europe: a land infested with disease-ridden rodents scurrying about infecting millions of our ancestors with the Black Death. In the latter part of the twentieth century, as this sort of thing wasn't happening (at least not to *our* friends and neighbors), most of us thought existentially – that the "Dark Age" must refer to being caught up in the morass of our own confusion. That seemed bad enough.

However, the world is a much bigger place than your own back yard. To remind us of that, a good friend and Buddhist teacher, Lama Ole Nydahl, in his yearly travels around the globe, would suggest to students who came to him for personal interviews with the hope of being liberated from their personal miseries, that they should spend a week reading the *International Herald Tribune*. A week later, having acquired a new perspective on the world, fueled by the reality of the ongoing atrocities that we humans seem inclined to inflict upon each other and our environment, the students would then be told to look more closely at what they saw as "suffering" in their lives.

A Climate of Fear

Having traveled a bit myself, I have seen Lama Ole's approach as both clever and useful. However, since 9/11 and the falling of the Twin Towers in New York, a bubble protecting the Western psyche in the more privileged states of Europe and America has been forever and irreparably shattered. The illusion of safety, the illusion that the suffering in the world was not so bad or at least – if one were to be more selfish about it – not happening to "us," came crashing down. With this veil ripped from our eyes, the realities of terrorism, nuclear proliferation, political and economic injustices, AIDS, and the ongoing and escalating numbers of wars worldwide seem more vivid. No matter what spin is placed on these realities that our planet is going through at this period of history, they have become part of our daily diet of news.

According to some of the more apocalyptic traditions of the West, we are living in the end of days. Armageddon is near. We somehow slipped through the noose of the year 2000, when it was predicted that all computers would crash, and some even anticipated that a global cataclysm would ensue, and that a blessed few would ascend to the "kingdom on high." Nevertheless, a mentality encouraged by the real possibility of tragedy – a horrible end to it all – looms over us. This mentality is rooted in fear. In its least insidious expression, it makes us overly cautious, makes us shrink away from possibility and joy. As it eats away at our confidence and narrows our vision, we may experience paralysis, and some of us may become anxious or depressed.

For others, a feeling of despair may set in that in turn encourages myopic, black-and-white solutions to complex problems in our immediate lives and in the wider world. If such desperation leads us to espouse some form of fundamentalist religious persuasion – a trend that is sweeping the globe – or to take up arms, in order to wipe out the perceived sources of our discomfort, the engine driving such views and actions is always the same: fear.

Yet as dire as this all sounds, Tibetan Buddhist masters encourage us not to lose heart. Why? Because, according to them, such Dark Ages have happened before and, over the millions of years to come, will no doubt happen again. More to the point, these masters encourage us to look at what causes a Dark Age in the first place. They direct us to look at both external (in the world and cosmic) and internal (personal and psychological) causes. I shall address such matters in due course, especially as they apply to the phenomenon of war. For now, though, I wish to convey what lessons and information I have received from Tibetan masters that allow me to be cautiously optimistic even in the midst of this Dark Age. I say "cautiously" not because I have my doubts about what these masters have said but because a cautious mindfulness is very useful in helping us to move forward. Even in the current atmosphere, with biological terror and nuclear devastation as real possibilities, I have confidence in their message that we have gotten through such times before and can do so again. The risks are high, but they are not insurmountable.

The Time We Live In: Our Dark Age

Buddhist cosmology is vast in scope, embracing cycles of time that span hundreds, thousands, even millions of years. There are eras, ages, and epochs. In the 5th century BCE the Buddha Shakyamuni is said to have gazed into the future and, according to some Buddhist teachers, seen our own period as an age of decay in which mental, degenerative, and auto-immune illnesses would plague humanity. He saw it as a time of difficulty and strife.

However, many of us who were in our late teens and early twenties in the late 1960s were told that we were entering into the "Age of Aquarius," a time of love and light. Assuming we set any store by the predictive astrology of our own heritage, how can these two prognosticated realities – the "Dark Age" and the "Age of Aquarius" – exist side by side? Whatever happened to "flower power?" The answer for me came in a lecture given in 1978 by a Canadian Tibetan Buddhist teacher named Namgyal Rinpoche. In a presentation given to his students and the general public in London, Namgyal Rinpoche spoke at length about the Age of Aquarius. For many of us, being starry-eyed budding Buddhists, what he said was shocking as well as depressing. What I present in this chapter is an elaboration of what the Rinpoche said that day. My intention is to flesh it out to present a fuller vision of what, I can now see, he wanted us to look at and prepare for – and which, it seems to me, is in fact coming to pass.

An alternative Age of Aquarius

Namgyal Rinpoche said that we are, indeed, in the Age of Aquarius. That is to say, we are in an age that has the potential to see a total transformation of society toward more enlightened values and actions. Love and light can reign in such an age. It can be everything that every utopian, peacenik, beatnik, hippy, and spiritual aspirant would like it to be. However, the Rinpoche also described an alternative Age of Aquarius that looks more like the apocalyptic vision I presented earlier. This version of the Aquarian Age is what Chinese philosophers would call "interesting times," in which a high level of uncertainty and chaos is prevalent. Traditional social structures and cultural mores are shown to be obsolete or out of step with the demands of current times. One example is overpopulation, how it impacts and overwhelms current social infrastructures and support networks and challenges religious beliefs that procreation is God's will. This may seem exciting to some – a time of opportunity when the shackles of the past and parochialism can be cast off and we can then grow and express ourselves in new and unprecedented ways. But, for those with fewer material or emotional resources, such times can be tremendously challenging, if not downright frightening.

Those frightened by what they saw around them in such a period – and a good many people would be – could exhibit an extreme range of habitual, reactionary responses as they sought to survive materially and emotionally. At one extreme, with the social and cultural doors barely hanging by their hinges, some might find within themselves a rebellious, even anarchistic side that seeks to throw all caution to the wind and to live as if there were no past or future, only the present – a Generation X and a culture with a more lax view on drugs, alcohol, promiscuity, and so on. Such a reaction is not to be mistaken for a more "Zen" approach to life. In fact, in a more

bohemian, hedonistic "me-first" lifestyle, consciousness, con-
scientiousness, and conscience are bypassed in favor of
intoxication, where self-indulgence and entertainment-seeking
are paramount. This starts with the mind-dulling pabulum
we feed our young in the form of *Teletubbies* and other visual
valium, and the behavioral morphine we ingest to buy into a
more-is-always-better lifestyle, which numbs the senses and
blocks out visions of poverty, starvation, war...

On the other hand, and almost at the exact opposite
extreme, others might respond to the uncertainty of the times
by shrinking back and seeking security, stability, and predictability, expressed in a fear of stepping outside one's front
door, the need to rely on dogmatic, circumscribing faiths, or
believe unswervingly in well-crafted and spun political
rhetoric.

As if to answer the demands and challenges of these polar
responses, social structures and institutions become super-
bureaucratized and over-regulated, with more permits, laws,
and restrictions in completing even the simplest of tasks to
rein in the radicals and provide a sense of stability for the
fearful. In this alternative vision of the Age of Aquarius,
individual needs and personal expression take second place to
a tendency for government bodies and mega-corporation
interests to suppress and to dominate, in order to create the
illusion of stability.

As fear dominates the psyche and security becomes the
imperative of the majority of public and private power brokers
and of the citizens they govern, there must also be belief
systems that are simple and promise stability. Some may seek
out the well-marketed New Age-type ideologies that make
utopian promises and offer a "mother ship" to return to.
Others may turn to living out their own wants and dreams
vicariously through the lives of a plethora of TV and movie

stars and other marketed heroes and heroines. The truth is, however, that in uncertain times the majority want beliefs that are based in a black-and-white reality so that, again, they can know where they stand. For many, such beliefs may take the form of religious fundamentalism as the religious equivalent of a secular order obsessed with bureaucracy, regulation, damage containment, and control.

Sadly as history has borne out time and again, all of these conditions can come together to create the perfect atmosphere for the emergence of despots and tyrants. Capitalizing on fear is an old human tradition. It is, in fact, the main ingredient in leading people into armed conflict against one another. As the late Nazi commander Hermann Goering aptly put it:

> "Why of course the people don't want war. Why should some poor slob on a farm want to risk his life in a war when the best he can get out of it is to come back to his farm in one piece? Naturally, the common people don't want war...That is understood. But, after all, it is the leaders of the country who determine the policy and it is always a simple matter to drag the people along, whether it is a democracy, or a fascist dictatorship, or a parliament, or a communist dictatorship. Voice or no voice, the people can always be brought to the bidding of the leaders. That is easy. All you have to do is to tell them they are being attacked, and denounce the peacemakers for lack of patriotism and exposing the country to danger. It works the same in any country."[1]

1 Gustav Gilbert, *Nuremberg Diary*, Farrar, Strauss and Co., 1947. Recorded on April 18th, 1946.

As dire as all of this may sound, even if this is truly to be our planet's future, Namgyal Rinpoche was not wholly pessimistic. Of the two alternatives for the Age of Aquarius, the Rinpoche did not have much confidence that the utopia of love and light promised by the pop culture would be what emerged. Rather, he saw the coming of the darker version – but with pockets of light. Even in such circumstances, all joy and possibility would not be absent. The opportunity for growth and transformation would still be there, though not on the scale that our early Aquarian "pioneers" envisioned. The wisdom traditions and the possibilities for enlightened ways of being would continue to exist, but would manifest as pockets or beacons of light. Such places or groups of individuals committed to enlightened possibility would be small, and would attract those who had enough space in their hearts and minds to see through or beyond the marketed and media-based visions of reality. In such communities, the growth and awakening of consciousness would be intense and rapid.

Following the ancient oriental principle of a balance of forces, what has a front also has a back. The bigger the front, the bigger the back. In the midst of darkness – in the midst of mediocrity, sickness, poverty, and warfare – there *is* possibility. And as dark as the future might look, the pockets of brightness would be of equal intensity, albeit at first sight somewhat veiled.

Looking at the evidence of what is happening in the world around us, it appears that Namgyal Rinpoche's vision is coming to pass. We have seen the consolidation and bureaucratization of a united Europe; the Patriot Act and the evident erosion of constitutional rights in the United States; the machinations of affluent nations and the IMF toward the establishment of a homogenous, well controlled global economy fine-tuned under the watchful eye of multinational corporations; the familiarity, yet confusion, we now all have for the term *jihad*; the proliferation of religious TV and radio stations juxtaposed to such grotesque and banal reality-TV offerings as *Survivor*, *Temptation Island*, and *Fear Factor*; and the media obsession with telling us all the down-and-dirty details about our superheroes. And at the same time, we have seen the gradual, organic emergence of holistic and environmentally-conscious living, against a background of growing interest in Eastern and more esoteric spiritual and healing traditions.

Around the time that Namgyal Rinpoche was conveying his vision of the Age of Aquarius, from the mid-1970s to early 1980s, other Tibetan teachers began to address global and political issues that many students wished they could forget. The rather messy end to the war in Vietnam; the escalation of the "War on Drugs" and battles with drug cartels; a succession of oil crises over the last thirty years that can not be separated from Western policy and growing unrest in the Middle East; the increase in airplane hijackings and terrorist attacks worldwide; and the climaxing of Cold War tensions that would eventually lead to the collapse of the Berlin Wall and the ensuing chaos of a Europe in transition – these were just some of the political and historical factors that Tibetan teachers saw as challenging the seeming promise of Western democracy and freedom.

Shambhala: The enlightened realm

In the early and mid-1980s, perhaps because in their great wisdom they perceived the need, His Holiness the Dalai Lama and other great Tibetan spiritual masters began to offer for the first time in the West public teachings and empowerment ceremonies of Kalachakra, the tantric Buddha. At the same time, the late Ven. Chögyam Trungpa Rinpoche introduced teachings and training on the way of Shambhala. The Kalachakra teachings are considered the pinnacle of Buddhist thought and practice. Their goal is to create powerful beings free of illusion and focused on the benefit of all. They are the basis of all Buddhist tantra and the core teachings that inspire the enlightened citizenry of Shambhala.

Tibetan Buddhist tradition teaches that Shambhala is – for lack of a better word – a "supernatural" realm, or a more spiritual/etheric plane of existence that is around us on this planet, although we cannot see it. It is a realm of nobility and honor; a society governed by enlightened principles. It is believed that emissaries from Shambhala visited the Buddha and requested that he come to their realm to teach. He consented, and seeing the advanced and gentle ways of the Shambhalians, manifested himself and taught in the tantric form of Kalachakra, the Deity of Time.

Chögyam Trungpa Rinpoche, who was also known as Lord Ösel Mukpo, an emissary of Shambhala, teaches that there have been times when the realm of Shambhala has had a direct impact on humanity. The Samurai tradition of Japan; the Magyar warrior class of Hungary; and the legacy of King Arthur and the Knights of the Round Table were considered by Lord Mukpo to be direct links to Shambhala. Chögyam Trungpa/Lord Mukpo gave direct teachings toward the establishment of what is now a non-denominational meditation organization worldwide called Shambhala Training.

Other teachers who gave teachings on the Kalachakra ceremonies also made claims about Shambhala's role in relation to planet Earth. What they said is that the Earth is a unique planet, where humanity has a suitable environment to work with its innate potential to transform itself and awaken the love, wisdom, and compassion, which are hallmarks of what Buddhism defines as enlightenment. As such, the

Shambhalians consider Earth to be too precious to allow it to annihilate itself. According to this tradition, the Shambhalians are in a sense our local, invisible guardians, watching what we do, periodically interceding in earthly events when the stakes are too high. Although no teacher I have met has ever been specific about these interventions in modern times, I often have wondered about the abrupt end to the first Gulf War in the early nineties and whether there was some Shambhalian influence in the matter. Furthermore, although we may view our current world situation as dire, it is predicted that the trend toward fundamentalism in both its Eastern and Western forms will continue for another two centuries. The Ven. Khenpo Karthar Rinpoche, a contemporary Tibetan Buddhist master of incomparable insight, once commented that the times we are currently in will seem peaceful compared to the times we shall face over the next two hundred and fifty years as societies deteriorate, fundamentalist factions vie for superiority, and unrest grows. Then, at some time in the twenty-third century, it is predicted that the Shambhalians will once again intervene in earthly affairs to avert an all-out war between the fundamentalist factions.

We in the West have our own tradition of guardian angels and are used to hearing promises made from pulpits that all will be well. Some may think that such words are spoken primarily to keep attendance high and church coffers full. But perhaps there is more to these promises than we know. Similarly, it may just be that the words of Tibetan masters on the realm of Shambhala are there to let us know that we are not alone in the struggles that we go through, both within and among ourselves, and will not be abandoned to our baser and more negative impulses. Both visions, Christian and Buddhist, tell us that we are being watched and looked after. Hatred and war will not win, will not end us. Hatred is not at the heart of humanity. Buddhists take this even further by saying that the planet upon which we assume dominion is, by virtue of that dominion, centered around the force of love and our basic loving nature – what in Buddhism is termed *bodhichitta*, or "awakened heart."

The teachings of the Buddha do not agree with those Christian sects that foresee Armageddon or an "end of days" scenario. No matter how dire, desperate, or dangerous the times might appear, the Buddha foresaw that we will not annihilate ourselves. But in order for the full potential of our loving nature to emerge victorious over our confusion and despair, we need to be willing and committed to do the work that needs to be done. The degree to which we ignore or put off that work is the degree to which sickness, poverty, and warfare will continue to manifest in the course of human history. In other words, even though at the most basic level all is well and the survival of humanity is assured by those who stand witness to our struggle, our future is up to us.

The inner struggle

This book has a lot to say about war. For those concerned about the current political climate, I will go on to discuss how to live with, work against, and, better still, transform the self-interested and government, corporate, or otherwise partisan-sanctioned aggression that seems so apparent in these times. But, more importantly, these pages will look at the deeper causes of conflict and war. In fact, this book is about the greatest of all wars, the war against the cause of all the worldly conflicts that we have had to endure since the dawn of humanity. It is the war that the Buddha himself fought: the war with the forces of darkness that are in each and every one of us. These forces – what in Buddhism are known as the "Three Poisons" of ignorance, attachment, and aggression –

are reflected in our individual and collective thoughts, attitudes, emotions, and reactions, and are the root cause of our current Dark Age. They are the source of all our misery and mischief, whether it be in the form of personal suffering or excessive bureaucracy, the homogenization of culture to the point of global marketed mediocrity, religious fundamentalism, and the host of ways in which we torment our brothers, sisters, and fellow species on this planet we call home.

The Ven. Khenpo Karthar Rinpoche taught many years ago that the cosmic and external forces that appear as a Dark Age, and manifest as sickness, poverty, and warfare, are the result of the Three Poisons gathering as a cloud in each of our minds, and then gathering as one great stormcloud that covers us all in darkness. Whether the seemingly insurmountable external causes and conditions that we face are the result of a cosmic, divine, or human hand, it is the inner causes that need to be addressed. Once we are truly on a path of resolving and transforming these internal causes, the environmental and geopolitical chaos that we witness today will, in turn, begin to be resolved and transformed for the benefit of all. What is important to understand, however, is that working on the inner causes is always linked to working with the outer manifestations. They cannot be separated. We need to address the Three Poisons within ourselves and also simultaneously address them as they manifest in the world around us.

Conscious, Engaged Activism

Knowing that the Three Poisons are not who we really are and that at our core is a loving nature and "enlightenment-potential," the Buddha offers his teachings – the Dharma – as the medicine to transform the "poisons" and our self-created attitudes and circumstances that stifle and nearly destroy the possibility of our awakening. The goal is to encourage and support us to wake up – to become conscious of our true nature and our intimate relationship with, and role in, the world around us – and to focus our thoughts and actions on behavior that contributes to a peaceful future and the wellbeing of others as well as ourselves. This is what I mean by *conscious, engaged activism*. It is altruism with teeth. The Buddha wants us truly to "be all that we can be" – spiritual warriors in whatever form or capacity we can fulfill. Until we have won the inner war against darkness and the Three Poisons within us, until each and every one of us has actualized our potential for enlightened living and our lives are wholly conscious and engaged, the Buddha's gaze will not swerve: he and all those who serve as our guides and friends in this world, supporting our awakening, will remain at war.

For those who want to break free from the duality, inner turmoil, and partisanship that will only continue to polarize us and separate us from the common good that we seek, what follows are insights and tools from the Buddha's teachings, which can help the reader to become a conscious, engaged activist – a spiritual warrior. For in times of strife and warfare, if we are to awaken, we have no choice but to become warriors. To strive for a lasting peace, to put an end to war and all else that haunts us, requires the courage to embark on the sublime and arduous spiritual path in order to end the warfare of confusion and conflicting emotions within us. If we can base our actions on a mind and heart transformed, the global transformation we seek will be set upon a lasting foundation. That is the purpose of this book.

We cannot escape the times that we live in. We cannot escape the truth that to be alive and acting in whatever way we do has consequences, whether we like it or not. If the saying is true that a butterfly flapping its wings in one place can cause a hurricane thousands of miles away, there are global consequences whenever we step outside our front door. This is not meant as a flippant ploy to swell the reader's head with delusions of grandeur, or a means to goad us to do something against our will. It is just a simple, sobering reminder of our connection with each and every being. We are responsible to one another. It is not that we *can* make a difference, but that we *do* make a difference. The difference we make manifests in accordance with the choices we make.

In these dark times, we are being called to action. Our loving nature – the enlightened potential that the Buddha recognized as lying at our core of being – is calling us. For those willing to answer this call, there will be trying times. There will be tests along the way. These tests will often be very difficult. We may not pass some of them and have to try again and again. But in the end we shall not fail. For failure is not at the core of who we are.

CHAPTER 2

War and Buddhism

"In traditional societies such as the Tibetan society I came from, you ride your horse, you pitch your tent, you make a fire. Whatever you do, it is done simply and directly. If you have to kill your enemy, you do so in the same spirit of simplicity and directness. Your enemy should die in your lap rather than being slaughtered from a distance. And having killed your enemy, you're supposed to kiss the enemy. I don't know if you can understand this. In America, the white man just wiped out the Indians.

There was no sense of sacred warfare. What I'm talking about is quite the opposite of that approach."

Chögyam Trungpa Rinpoche[2]

For many Westerners, Buddhism is synonymous with pacifism. The Buddha himself is pictured as still, demure, and detached; and the most common image of a Buddhist is either a monk with a shaved head, wearing orange robes and sandals, or one of the peaceful and benign media shots of His Holiness the Dalai Lama.

If we were to look for examples of Buddhist leaders running imperialist, aggressive Buddhist nations, we would not find any. Nor has Buddhist doctrine ever been the sole justification for dominating one group or another economically, politically, or militarily. I say "sole" because in the case of Tibet, for example, aristocratic families with allegiance to particular Buddhist lineages have vied for power. No doubt, as in other nations of the world, one may find examples where leaders and politicians in Buddhist countries in Asia have used religion as the rationale for political, economic, or military action. But because Buddhism tends to cultivate independent thinking, its followers are generally less susceptible to being drawn into mass movements or mass hysteria, or to taking propaganda seriously.

When countries which have a large Buddhist population or are governed by Buddhist leaders have experienced political, economic, or military struggles, the actions of Buddhists at such times have not always been peaceful or passive. Contrary to the images of demure, passive monks, consider those Vietnamese monks and nuns who burned themselves to death in protest against American involvement in their country's civil strife. In my own life, I have had the privilege to meet one of the former kings of the Tibetan region of Kham, who told me how some of his people responded to the Chinese invasion

[2] Chögyam Trungpa Rinpoche, *Great Eastern Sun: The Wisdom of Shambhala.* Shambhala Books, Boston and New York, 1999, p.196.

of the late 1950s. Under his guidance, the locals sold drugs to Chinese soldiers by day so that they could more easily scare them off or – if there was no other option – kill them at night. More recently, there is the example given by one Western lama of his Russian Dharma students who run raids into Chechen strongholds to rescue those who have been taken hostage. Knowing the bad karma it is to kill, the lama advises them to shoot at the captors' kneecaps rather than kill them, to leave them crippled and unable to fight in the future.

Even more dramatically, I am reminded of stories passed on by His Holiness the 16th Gyalwa Karmapa. In his book *Dzalendara and Sakarchupa* he tells of his previous incarnation as an assassin whose purpose it was to murder a tyrant, who would otherwise have caused the death of countless others.[3] The tyrant's assassination not only prevented the suffering of others, but also prevented the tyrant himself from accumulating more and more negative karma in the future. The action of this "enlightened" assassin was an example of what in Buddhism is called "wrathful compassion" – a term which we shall address later in the book. The point is that from an enlightened perspective, pre-emption and pre-emptive strikes are permissible.

Is War Truly Evil?

Buddhism, therefore, does not shy away from conflict or war. In 2001, in his speech accepting the Nobel Peace Prize, former US President Jimmy Carter said: "War may be a necessary evil. But it is always evil." But while there is probably no person on this planet who truly prefers conflict and war over peace and

---

[3]   H.H. the 16th Gyalwa Karmapa, *Dzalendara and Sakarchupa*.
     Karma Drubgyud Darjay Ling, Eskdalemuir, Scotland, 1981.

harmony, does it stand to reason that war must always be defined as evil? The most profound of the Buddha's teachings speaks of what is called "emptiness," the notion that everything is "empty" of intrinsic, independent existence. All things are interconnected. Hence, nothing can be judged as wholly and ultimately "good" or "bad." The degree to which they are either is determined by the mind of the perceiver. Thus, whether conflict, even war, is – in the long or short term – good or bad depends on what side of the fence you are standing on. Another holder of the Nobel Peace Prize, His Holiness the Dalai Lama, expressed this in his own acceptance speech for the award in 1989:

> "War or peace; the destruction or the protection of nature; the violation or promotion of human rights and democratic freedoms; poverty or material well-being; the lack of moral and spiritual values or their existence and development; and the breakdown or development of human understanding, are not isolated phenomena that can be analyzed and tackled independently of one another. In fact, they are very much interrelated at all levels and need to be approached with that understanding. Peace, in the sense of the absence of war, is of little value to someone who is dying of hunger or cold. It will not remove the pain of torture inflicted on a prisoner of conscience. It does not comfort those who have lost their loved ones in floods caused by senseless deforestation in a neighboring country. Peace can only last where human rights are respected, where people are fed, and where individuals and nations are free." [4]

[4] H.H. the 14th Dalai Lama, *A Policy of Kindness*. Snow Lion Publications, Ithaca, NY, 1990, pp17–18.

If peace is merely the absence of war – if injustice, poverty, and strife are brewing underneath a seeming calm – then of what value is it? The forces that seek to maintain such a peace may succeed in preventing the chaos that could exacerbate conditions, but they may also suppress the free expression of frustration at the status quo which at times may also necessitate conflict beyond a level of verbal disapproval. The introduction of something new, the awareness of other options or possibilities, always brings with it discomfort, conflict, breakthrough, and reintegration. This is as true for our own hearts and minds as it is for the macro-structures of society around us. That is why civil protest is an essential ingredient in democracy and probably why Thomas Jefferson spoke of the importance of suspicion of government control as an important feature of an active, dynamic democracy truly focused on personal freedom.

There is an old Buddhist saying that it is far more difficult to cover the world in leather than it is to put on shoes. What this means is that it is very difficult when our own minds are not transformed to work on transforming the world around us. Hence, if we want to see qualitative change in the world around us, we must begin with ourselves. In his Nobel Prize acceptance speech in Oslo, the Dalai Lama went on to speak about the importance of developing inner peace as the prerequisite for external peace. This is a critical point and one that is central to what this book offers. At the same time, it would be overly idealistic to suggest that anyone with a conscience should suspend their actions against poverty, destruction of the environment, or violations of human rights because they have not reached a totally enlightened state – the state of inner peace. I do not believe that the Dalai Lama was suggesting this. However, his words are a warning of the risks of acting to resolve what we see as the world's difficulties without equally being committed to looking within ourselves. Until we do so, it will remain difficult for us to know whether our actions are skillful or wise; and our unskilled, unfocused actions will give rise, at best, to unskilled, unfocused consequences.

At the same time, despite the fact that most of us are gripped by the "Three Poisons" of ignorance, attachment, and aggression, because I hold to the fundamental Buddhist tenet of basic goodness or a loving nature being the core of who we are, I truly believe that unenlightened as most of us are, we always go into life's situations with the intention of doing our best based on what we currently know. Our knowledge may be flawed and incomplete and our actions imperfect, but in our desire to make and see a difference, we act nevertheless; and because our minds are not cleared of confusion, inner conflict, and unresolved feelings, we shall see these mirrored in the consequences of our actions in the world around us.

Thus the confusion within ourselves, and the uncertainty of knowing what is the most skillful path to take in order to change the world around us, can lead us to make hasty judgments that lead us down the road to what may seem to us to be justifiable conflict. And if a sufficient number of people around us also have less than adequate information and harbor a host of similarly unresolved inner conflicts, it is more than likely that, like clouds gathering to cause a storm, tensions may accumulate that may lead to actual physical conflict or war.

It is said that "The road to hell is paved with good intentions." In any given situation, we may sincerely believe that what we are doing is the right thing, and the only thing we can do. War that results from mental confusion may not necessarily be "evil." But the Tibetan Bön master Tenzin Wangyal Rinpoche describes such an outcome as "failure" – a failure to resolve matters in ways that most of us would prefer.

However, this is not necessarily to deny that there are times when conflict or war, however undesirable, may be the only way to shake up what may appear to be, as we are currently able to see it, an intractable situation. There may seem to be no alternative way of allowing otherwise suppressed feelings, needs, and forces to free themselves and be expressed. Is this messy? Absolutely. But reality is by nature relative, ambiguous, and messy. Until we are enlightened and have acquired the capacity to see the past, present, and future clearly, and our actions are pure and have only the consequences we intend, there will always be unintentional effects, or "collateral damage."

Hopefully, we learn and grow from our mistakes. Hiroshima and Nagasaki made us realize that the unchecked proliferation and use of nuclear weapons was a short cut to the total annihilation of the human race and most other forms of life on the planet. Thus we closely monitor the development of nuclear technology throughout the world. Having witnessed the effects of nuclear weapons only twice, we are more enlightened about the truth of a nuclear disaster. Hindsight, looking back upon what we have done in the light of the consequences of our actions, is definitely one way to learn what to do and not to do in the future. Unfortunately, it seems to be the teacher we end up relying on most.

The Four Aspects: Intention, thought, action, and reaction

His Holiness the Ven. Shamar Rinpoche made some poignant comments about conflict and war in the wake of 9/11. In an attempt to take the dialogue beyond the sentimental to a place where people could truly reflect and learn, he spoke of the Buddhist teaching of the Four Aspects that characterize each of our actions. To explain this briefly for now, every action consists of the following four stages: intention; contemplation and thought; action; then our reaction to the action we have committed. In other words, we want some action to happen and set our determination to perform it; we consider *how* we are going to perform the action; we perform the action; and then we look back and assess what we have accomplished. All actions proceed in this way.

If our actions are directed by positive intention and clear thinking, and we have the skill to perform what we intend to do, then more than likely the outcome will also be positive and clear. This is one end of the spectrum. At the other end is where we have negative, harmful intentions, focus all of our thoughts on accomplishing that intention, successfully commit an act that brings great harm, and take delight in our success. Such actions are the most "evil." While even these actions are, in Buddhist terms, intrinsically "empty" in themselves, we can call them "evil" from a relative point of view, in the sense that they are almost entirely negative, harmful, or destructive in effect.

Most of our actions fall into the wide range of possibilities that lie somewhere between these two extremes. Perhaps we have a positive intention, but don't think things out all that well, commit actions that do some harm, and then feel confused or ambivalent about the result. Equally, if we have negative intentions but lack the clarity of mind and the skill to pull them off, we may end up angered at our lack of success. Again, there is a mixed result and how we react afterward will more than likely reflect that. The action and what follows will generally provide us feedback on our lack of skill. In an appendix at the end of this book, Shamar Rinpoche reflects and gives advice on how to view the events of 9/11 based on this perspective (see pages 230–1).

If we look back on the long history of warfare, we shall

always find the motives of the participants occupying a similar gray territory. A side that goes to war usually does so for mixed reasons – to end a tyranny and free the people, say, but also to increase business opportunities and open new trade markets. If those who decide on war are not entirely focused or have a number of altruistic and self serving aims in mind, similarly – and more than likely – they may think even less clearly about the means they will use to achieve their ends. Consequently there are generally mixed results: a campaign may be well planned and the military well trained, but perhaps some of the necessary information about strategic and civilian sites is incomplete, resulting in "collateral damage" affecting noncombatants. In all wars, after the dead are buried and the wounded tended to and sent home, a legacy is spawned on both sides. The "victors" may think that the end justified the means. Those on the other side, the so-called "losers," however, may be embittered and disfranchised. The legacy of resentment often, down the line, leads to further conflict and war.

Of course, each side in a conflict will generally view the outcome differently. We should also remember that history tends to get rewritten by those who have control of the pens, so that a war seen as negative in outcome at the time, may be seen by later generations to have had a more positive impact, and vice versa. Probably the only reliable indicator that any given conflict has had a more positive than negative impact is whether or not it has been the spawning ground for further mayhem and pain. A Buddhist perspective and the tools which it offers may be helpful in guiding our assessments and seeking more skillful alternatives if and when conflicts arise in the future.

In the end, we learn from war, as from many other areas of human experience, that we are victims of our own frailties and need to view the past as no more than a foundation upon which we can build better ways to be, and act, in the future. And so, if we want a more positive, loving, and viable future, all we can really do is take ourselves in hand, commit ourselves to not reacting to our situation in a negative way, learn methods to transform our negative mental and emotional states, and perform all our actions with the best possible aims in mind.

Our Challenge And Our Potential

Is it possible to hone our emotional and perceptive skills, to develop deeper wisdom from the start? Can we learn right away to act appropriately and effectively in the predicaments we encounter – when to be peaceful, when to enter into conflict, when to let things mature in their own way, or prompt them along? The Buddha says in no uncertain terms, yes. The fact that we as humans prefer peace and happiness is a testament to what he saw as our inherent loving nature: the fact that we are basically "good." At the same time, because we are confused, in that we don't see the real correlation between our happiness and the happiness of others, our view of how to gain peace and happiness will more than likely disagree with someone else's view. When we do not see common ground, but only difference, conflict – perhaps, on a large scale, even war – is inevitable. In a 2004 campaign speech while running for the US presidency, retired General Wesley Clark spoke of entering into conflict only "reluctantly." If our basic nature is a loving one, it makes sense that to engage in conflict at all should only be a last resort, unless we are so wise as to be able to foresee the future accurately. But there are few of us who have that capacity.

Transforming the Three Poisons

To summarize this discussion so far, we have seen that all actions have consequences. If our actions are skillful and based on wisdom, we will more than likely achieve our objectives with few, if any, unintended side effects or "collateral damage." The degree to which there is "collateral damage" is the degree to which our actions were not as skillful as we thought or the knowledge we had was not as thorough as we supposed. Regardless, we do the best we can based on what we know. If we blow it, hopefully we shall be wiser and our actions more skillful in the future. Knowing that this is how it is for us as humans, and seeing the suffering caused by disasters that we are often so slow to learn from, the Buddha discovered methods that would skillfully guide us through the pride, jealousy, lustfulness, torpor, greed, and anger that distort our actions and lead to future calamities. Because he had first and foremost in his mind that we are all basically good and that at our core is a loving nature, he saw these negative mental states – what his teachings, the Dharma, call *kleshas* – not as permanent flaws, but rather the result of habit patterns.

Such habit patterns are formed as a result of the so-called Three Poisons that we are all inflicted with. These Three Poisons, which I already touched upon in Chapter 1 (see page 22) are **ignorance** (not understanding what the world is about or who we really are in relation to it), **attachment** (blind adherence, rooted in ignorance, to our own point of view), and **aggression** (toward anyone who disagrees with our point of view). The Buddha also came to know in his heart of hearts that if we transform our ignorance we can experience a wide array – "a rainbow" – of amazing capabilities, opening our minds to unlimited possibility and in turn transforming our attachment and our aggressive tendencies. In doing so we can release the heat and passion within us that create great joy and a spontaneous and effortless way of being and acting in the world. We can become who we are meant to be – ultimately, we can become just like him: an awakened or enlightened being.

The Buddha developed many methods to transform the Three Poisons. All of them encourage us to apply ourselves to developing what are classically called the "Six Paramitas" (Perfections) of patience, openness (or generosity), discipline, perseverance, meditation, and the deepening of wisdom, until these states of mind are the guiding forces in all our actions. **Wisdom** (the guiding light, which the Buddha saw as a female principle) conjoined with "**skillful means**" (the resourcefulness to bring that light to all our actions, which he saw as a male principle) result in actions that are inherently compassionate. Through training, our loving nature – our desire to be happy and to see happiness all around us – manifests as a compassion built on a foundation of wisdom and skill. Having fought the war within, and armed with the resourcefulness of an awakened being, the conscious, engaged activist is ready to meet the world.

The path one needs to tread to accomplish this noble task is what the reader will find systematically laid out in the following chapters. Each chapter will provide information, contemplations, and practical methods that will, in turn, become a foundation upon which the subsequent chapters are built. This organizational method was used by the Buddha himself to foster progressive understanding and growth for individuals wanting to connect with their loving nature and realize their inherent enlightened potential. The information, contemplations, and methods that are to follow, while Buddhist in origin, are universally applicable and will be of tremendous value in helping all those who wish to transform themselves and the world around them to remain focused, relaxed, and energized, when they work with the personal and global dimensions of the Dark Age as they inevitably arise in our lives. It is my fervent wish that what follows becomes an antidote to cynicism, apathy, and despair.

The Venerable Chögyam Trungpa Rinpoche used to say that it is always possible to cheer up. Ultimately, it is only from a mind that is transformed, free, and cheerful that actions to create lasting peace and happiness are possible. Let us enter on that path, starting now.

CHAPTER 3

Why Bother?
Revolutionizing the Mind

*"You can explore the universe looking for
somebody who is more deserving of your
love and affection than you are yourself,
and you will not find that person
anywhere."*

Anonymous

Human experience and the circumstances that humans find
themselves in vary dramatically. Some live in a Beverly Hills
reality with servants who lay out their clothes each morning
and make sure that their Mercedes is fueled, warmed up, and
ready to go for a light lunch in Malibu or a day of shopping.
Others wake up in the garbage dumps of Calcutta, scrounge
for restaurant morsels or spoiled fruit, then spend the
remainder of their day sorting mounds of rubbish to find
anything that might have a street value they can haggle for.
Most of us live our lives somewhere in between these extremes.

Yet, no matter how apparently idyllic or deprived our circumstances are, our experience of those circumstances can be surprisingly varied. Someone in the lap of luxury may be bored with life and take no delight whatsoever in their "good" fortune. At the same time, a poor person in Calcutta may cherish every moment of their "dire" life. And then there are the rest of us who at times feel good and motivated in our circumstances and at other times close to despair.

So, while the Buddha's teachings say that our circumstances are the direct result of our previous actions, which have led to the consequences we now encounter as a palace, a dump, or somewhere in between, it does not mean that our experience of these circumstances is cast in stone. The laws of karma, which I address in greater length later on (see page 133), teach that what you have done in the past – your actions and your attitudes when taking those actions – have led to your present. In the same way, your response to your current situation will lead you to act in a certain way, setting a course for you into the future. However, while where you are now is in a sense linked to your destiny, your future is neither predetermined nor inevitable. There is only possibility. The question, then, is how free and flexible is your mind when it comes to recognizing this possibility, when it comes to choosing options and attitudes that will create better rather than worse outcomes for you in the future?

Recognizing possibility is crucial in the life of a conscious, engaged activist. It is what allows someone in poverty not to give in to despair and hopelessness. It is also what prevents someone of wealth and privilege from hardening their hearts, becoming selfish and self-absorbed, or becoming too complacent to think that there may be something else, something better that can be done with their opportunities. In fact, it is important to learn to traverse a path that avoids the extremes of "I've got mine. I have worked so hard to get mine. Other people can do the same. Why should I bother with them?" and "My life is horrible. I can't change anything. I'm so worthless and small. What could I possibly do? Why should I bother?"

Between the numbing intoxication of self-absorption and self-aggrandizement and the depressing blackness of self-denigration is where most of us live our lives. And if we use enough gray matter we at least see how fickle life is and how the winds of fortune can blow this way or that. If we believe that all is capricious and that these changes are whimsically out of our control – if we don't understand the role of karma and our own authorship of the causes and conditions of our lives – then a "why bother?" attitude would make sense. But it doesn't. Our loving nature, the enlightened potential within us, is whispering to us. This is why somewhere inside us, to a greater or lesser degree, we know better. And that knowledge is what the Buddha appeals to.

The Four Thoughts that Revolutionize the Mind

To help us understand our situation better and to inspire us to seize possibility by learning methods to free our hearts and minds, the Buddha asks us to consider "Four Thoughts." These contemplations are seen as a preliminary to embarking on a more spirit-oriented life. For our purposes, they are the starting point for becoming a conscious, engaged activist. These four notions are called by different names: The Four Thoughts that Turn the Mind to Dharma; The Four Thoughts that Turn the Mind to Spirituality; and the one I like the most – The Four Thoughts that Revolutionize the Mind. These thoughts are presented in a set sequence. Yet, like interdependent building blocks, each thought reinforces and supports its predecessor and becomes the foundation upon which the logic of the next thought arises. Their goal is to cultivate a deep sense of appreciation for life and what it has to offer us. They are the perfect foundation upon which a revolution of the mind can occur.

Thought 1: Loving our lives

The first of the revolutionizing thoughts deals with what the Buddha called "precious human birth." He distinguishes between this and ordinary or regular human birth and life as being human. This distinction is significant and what is meant by a "precious human birth" exactly will be explained shortly. However, the Buddha saw that, in general *all* human birth is special. The reason for it being special is because of the "Six Realms of Existence" that the buddha identified. The human realm is, reatively speaking, the only one not governed by any particular overwhelming emotional experience. The "higher" realms of gods and demigods are governed by an intoxication with pride and competitive jealousy respectively. The "lower" realms of animals, hungry ghosts, and hell-bound beings are caught in the grasp of reflexive survival-based stupidity, insatiability, and hatred respectively. No doubt humans experience these emotions, and we may even argue with the Buddha's observations and conclusion that we do not experience such emotions as intensely as those in the non-human realms. Looking at all realms with an enlightened eye, what the Buddha saw was that human life is neither "too good" (like the life of a god) nor "too bad" (like the life of a lower being). What does dominate human consciousness with respect to emotional experience is desire and passion. Although this can be experienced intensely in such forms as ordinary lust or overwhelming longing, it also, when we desire something seemingly beyond our reach, gives us the impetus to change. Desire and passion, what the Buddha called "craving" will be discussed more fully in the next chapter. What is of importance here, however, is the Buddha's recognition of this craving as being central to our experience, hence central to our process of awakening and transformation. The highest expression of desire comes in the urge to awaken – to become enlightened, and ultimately free of all selfish desire – while passion can be transformed into compassion for all beings. It is these qualities that led the Buddha to assert that we are basically good and that there is in humans the unique quality of wanting, *and* actually having the capacity, to truly benefit others.

Returning to our distinction between precious and ordinary human birth, precious human birth is a life that has specific internal and external factors which the Buddha classifies with respect to what we possess as individuals and what the environment provides for us. From the point of view of achieving enlightenment, the most advantageous human birth is one where all of the sensory organs are intact and operating, the limbs and organs do what they are designed to do, and the mind is functioning within a "normal" range of intelligence. Ideal external factors include living in a peaceful and nurturing social and natural environment that provides access to education and training, which in turn lead us to becoming a resourceful and – ultimately – an enlightened being.

Classically, if all of these circumstances come together, the one who possesses them can take full advantage of the opportunity of human birth. This is both precious and rare. At the same time, this does not mean that enlightenment is not possible in other, less idyllic conditions, but that it is more difficult and consequently rarer. However, it is unfortunately also rare that individuals whose lives possess all the ideal factors do take advantage of them. Too often, like a pampered cat, we just lie there, basking in our fortune, falling asleep when we can. That is why Buddhist teachers say that to have the motivation to do something, to take full advantage of these circumstances, is as rare as when a tortoise comes up from the bottom of the ocean every thousand years and manages to slip its neck through a yoke that just happens to be floating along.

Motivating a person to take full advantage of the circumstance of precious human birth is what the three remaining revolutionizing thoughts are about. Many Buddhist teachers, seeing the opportunities that our Western, democratic culture provides us with, try to encourage us along this path.

Looking at the realities that so many face on this planet, the precious opportunity of a human birth may not bring these ideal internal or external advantages and may, in fact, come with an array of internal and external challenges. We are perhaps blind or deaf, or we may have a disease or some other physical limitation; we may live in a land and society where there is warfare or strife that allows little opportunity for much beyond basic survival; and our educators may focus on selfish or myopic goals reinforced by beliefs and superstitions that make us fearful to trust, love, or grow.

Yet the difficulties of such conditions may exist more in our perception of them than in how things really are. This point has been mentioned again and again by Buddhist teachers, who talk about the fortunate circumstances we are *all*, in fact, living in. For the most part, we live in a world that is a mixed bag, where as one Tibetan friend put it, "anything is possible." Thus, even though our internal or personal (physiological and psychological) causes are not optimal, a positive external environment can be supportive of tremendous growth and opportunity. Conversely, with a fully functioning mind and body we can find possibility even in the most hostile of environments. In the midst of warfare, someone can create something of exquisite beauty or demonstrate a heroic and inspiring compassion. Where such disabilities as blindness would once have been the cause of a limited quality of life, there are now technologies and schools, at least in some societies, that make education and the opportunity to live a full and fulfilling life possible. So it is that we see a heroic businessman like Oskar Schindler, a deaf and blind writer of inspiring words like Helen Keller, and a crippled world leader like Franklin D. Roosevelt. In the midst of conditions that seem less than ideal for growth, individuals *do* excel and societies *do* change.

Whether our own resources are plentiful or inadequate or our environment is supportive or challenging, what seems to be crucial to us as humans is that we recognize and appreciate what we have. **You cannot hate your life and despise what resources you have been gifted with.** If you can only feel poverty and lack in your life, your mind is caught in the extremes of either self-absorbed self-aggrandizement, where you think you deserve better, or self-denigration, where you convince yourself that nothing is possible anyway. With such a mindset, there is little room for, or consideration of, real change. In such cases the experience of love is based on someone or something distracting us from our basic sense of lack. Our sense of self-worth depends on our worth to others. The spiritual life or a life focused on spiritual revolution cannot begin with such a hollow, negative state of mind. It can only lead to change based on the whim of sentimentality and a co-dependency that robs life of its vitality.

Buddhist teachers coming from the East have noted that Westerners tend to be self-effacing and prone to self-denigration; that our bravado is often a cover for a weakness of ego structure. Although the ego is eventually to be dissolved in the process of aligning ourselves to our true spiritual potential, a certain degree of confidence in ourselves at a core level is something each of us needs. There is value in being familiar with our flaws in order for us to grow as individuals. But we also must cherish those existing strengths and qualities we have that make us more effective in certain areas of our lives. Spiritual teachers Stephen and Ondrea Levine speak of "treasuring" oneself. This means "warts and all." Many of us just get into accepting the warts; it seems that it is harder for us to cherish our qualities and strengths or accept compliments for them. Without a full embracing of both dimensions, our sense of lack will sooner or later spawn a desperation that will infect our minds, corrupt our intentions, and yield ineffective, even harmful actions.

Only if you appreciate and love your life, and can embrace what tools you have to help with transformation, will you be able to live and act in a manner that is open to possibility and free from constant second guessing. **To change the world, you first have to be friends with what you have. Only then are you able to use what resources you have effectively.** Consequently, it is important to take serious stock of your life and situation. Each of us is rich and resourceful in our own way. If we are materially rich in funds, then we have a capacity to reach out to many that others may not have. Or we may not have money, but we may have time to devote to others: to help the elderly, the dying, the homeless. Some may be rich in skills or the intellectual capacities to write, teach, and research. I shall discuss this further in Chapter 9, when I examine what a fully conscious, engaged activist looks like.

With this frame of mind there arises a wholehearted and genuine gratitude. When you love your life, you are not apologizing for being. Your resourcefulness, the richness that you discover you have, gives you an opportunity to do something useful with your life. However, this gratitude is not about being meek, groveling in thankfulness, or about being benignly content just with what you have. To help us to overcome such tendencies and to further inspire a gratitude that we feel, as Tibetans would say, "in the marrow of our bones," the Buddha offers the second revolutionizing thought, which focuses on impermanence.

Thought 2: Ashes to ashes

The Buddha said, "Life is as fragile as a bubble." Here today, gone tomorrow. All is impermanent. All that is created, all that I manifest, will eventually dissolve back into the elements from which they were created. When we are conceived, within the seed of our being that is to grow and live are also contained the processes and mechanisms by which we shall surely die. Life and death come as twins, never alone, each showing its face when it is its time. Wealth comes and goes, as does poverty. Wars come and go. Peace comes and goes. How slowly or quickly these all occur is generally beyond our reckoning.

If we look at our own life, there is no point in being smug about what we have, for all of us have seen others whose fortunes have come and gone. Can we be so certain that, at some point, it will not be our turn? Similarly, we may have seen friends in dire straits rise to fame and riches. Everything is possible and everything is transient. Nothing is set in stone and even stone will one day crumble and wear away. We change within ourselves, too. If we look at our own attitudes, we see that what once gave us pleasure may no longer do so. Our source of joy at one time can be our source of misery at another. Our joy, our love of life is not dependent upon what is "out there." Our attitudes, like the seemingly solid objects or situations to which they are tied, are also impermanent.

Impermanence teaches us not to take our life for granted, nor to expect that our current resources, either internal or external, will always be there for us. As we can lose our house, we can also lose our minds. However, as frightening as this may seem on the surface, the unrelenting truth of impermanence is actually quite liberating. It can transform the way we see the world in a variety of ways. For example, if we have not fully appreciated the First Thought and view our lives as a problem, impermanence teaches us that "this too shall pass." It can help us to "lighten up" or be the cause for us to develop courage. If we appreciate our lives in general, yet recognize difficulties we are facing at this particular moment, an understanding of impermanence can give us the strength to endure. On the other hand, even if we have everything we could ever want today, but know that there is no guarantee for tomorrow, we are prompted to action. We embrace the preciousness of our lives, what is available to us, and learn to maximize what they can yield. Impermanence teaches us to be focused and resourceful. If we were to put that in political terms, say, we would see that peace is both dynamic *and* fragile. Without constant appreciation and vigilance, it can soon easily degrade into discontent and conflict.

Impermanence, therefore, can give us a sense of urgency, but it need not be tainted with panic or desperation. However, if we should happen to lapse into thinking that we must desperately hold onto what we have, the third revolutionizing thought offers the antidote.

Thought 3: Responsibility

Once we appreciate our life and its impermanence, it is a logical step to consider what we need to do if we want to maintain or improve our conditions in the future. The third of the Four Thoughts asks us to look at time and causation. The

Dharma uses examples from nature to help us get a clearer picture.

Consider any plant that we wish to grow and harvest. We take the seed and put it in the ground. This sounds simple enough. But the process involves a number of steps. First, we have to be sure that we know what seed we are planting. Next, if we are to be successful with our planting, we need to know what season is best, what kind of soil is best, what depth to place the seed, when to water it, how to protect it while it germinates, sprouts, and grows. If we have inadequate information or are inattentive to any one of these details, our yield will be affected. If we cannot identify clearly what seed we are planting, why should we be so surprised if what we thought would be an apple tree turns out to be a fig? If we know we have planted an apple seed, but do not provide the right nurturing environment for the seed, why should we be surprised if the young sapling dies or the fruit is sour and infested with bugs?

The logic that applies to this example applies to everything. Everything in nature has a previous cause that is intimately and directly related to its outcome. From this we must come to understand that what we have in our life does not come to us by mere chance. The fruits of our lives, whether they are sweet or sour, are the direct result of the seeds we planted in the past, whether we see the link or not. Right from the start, we need to recognize and accept that where we are at, the resources we currently have, are the result of what we have done and how we react to what has been done to us in the past. So if we want to keep what we have, or change things for the better, it matters what we do next.

If it was positive previous actions that brought us to where we are now, then reinforcing and building on those positive actions, learning to be even more skillful, is the path we must pursue in order to improve things even further. The third of the revolutionizing thoughts is, therefore, about our own role in our own past, present, and future. In Buddhist terms this is expressed in terms of **karma** or the laws of cause and effect. In contemporary Western terms, the laws of karma are the laws of personal responsibility.

"Take personal responsibility" is almost a mantra in modern psychology. The Dharma takes this concept even further by helping us to appreciate the inevitable truth of responsibility. As we learn to love our lives and understand that rigidly holding on to what we have – or obsessively desiring what we view ourselves as not having – assures us of nothing, we learn to "let go." We release ourselves from the role of victim in our own lives, from judging ourselves in relation to others and what they have, and from seeing ourselves as being created in someone else's image. We lift our minds above a sea of self-absorption. We see "the bigger picture" – the world becomes larger and our place in it, and our hand in how things are, become more obvious. No matter how spectacular or disastrous our current lives may seem, consciously or unconsciously we have written the script in which we are acting. Knowledge of this helps us to keep our focus and to appreciate what potential our resources have. It teaches us to look down the road a bit, with a clearer sense of where we want to go next and how to get there. And, if we want positive results in the future, we must start off with a positive attitude, which is reinforced by loving our life and cherishing the possibilities we have in the moment.

Thought 4: No time to waste and nowhere to run

The fourth thought that the Buddha asks us to consider is both a summation and reinforcement of the previous three. If we love our life, know that it is impermanent, and understand that we need to accentuate what is positive in order to build something even more wonderful for the future, we have to feel a sense of commitment. We must develop the resolve to become conscious and engaged in whatever we do.

Ultimately, nothing we do is a "waste" of time, because even the time we use to distract ourselves, shirk responsibilities, or ignore what we don't want to pay attention to become building blocks in what is to come next. The author and Buddhist nun Pema Chödrön expresses this concept in the very title of her book, *The Wisdom of No Escape*: You cannot escape your own life; all that you do, all that you have done *will* haunt you, *will* be with you to the end of your days, and – if we accept the Buddhist notion of reincarnation – beyond.

Having awakened to the truth of the first three thoughts, we are set upon a course and it is up to us whether we want to embark upon it consciously and joyfully or fight it every step of the way. Our habitual tendencies will lead us at times to resist the course. This is normal, and we can always hope that we may learn from our mistakes. But can we be more proactive, more prevention-oriented? Can we inoculate ourselves against the Three Poisons of ignorance, attachment, and aggression and their resulting negative emotional patterns, so that we can avoid habitually diving into blind alleys? When we fully appreciate how precious our life is and that it can be lost more easily than it was gained, and understand also that we cannot escape the life that is our own handiwork, it dawns on us that there is nowhere else to escape to, and no time to waste. To think or act as if this were not true is merely an exercise in futility.

Moving Forward with Heart and Mind

Living in the truth of the Four Thoughts that Revolutionize the Mind brings us to a remarkable point where we cherish every asset we have and move forward more resolutely to do what life calls upon us to do. We embark on a life that is more conscious and engaged. And that usually means that our hearts and minds have expanded sufficiently to be able to see the absolute necessity of embracing others and working for their benefit in whatever capacity we can. **When we show up in our own lives, we find that we are actually showing up for everyone.**

Knowing that experience alone may not teach us this over the course of our lives, the Buddha set out these Four Thoughts right upfront for those who would be receptive to their message. Like a sun that burns away the fog, these thoughts bring with them warmth and possibility. They cut to the chase – bring us to our senses. There is no better way to embark on any action than by allowing the Four Thoughts to be a foundation. With the Four Thoughts in mind, let us now look at the steps we need to take next in order to develop the wisdom and skill to further awaken our potential and set ourselves upon a more conscious path.

CHAPTER 4

A Fine Mess:
Handling the Truth

*"First we make our habits. Then our
habits make us."*

John Dryden

The Four Thoughts that Revolutionize the Mind (see pages
41–51) go a long way toward awakening our potentiality. At
least, they build a sufficient foundation to allow us to
appreciate what life has to offer – they are the beginning of
embracing life in a positive way and an excellent antidote to
pessimism and cynicism. Life is rich. Life always holds
potential. But if this is so, if all people are equal in possessing
a loving nature and a "Buddha-potential," why do some see it
and others not? And why do we find ourselves slipping in and
out of the awareness of these possibilities?

The Four Noble Truths

These are all fair and very human questions. They are
questions that bespeak the truth that we are, indeed, endowed

with a loving nature at our core. These questions, set upon a foundation of appreciation inspired by the Four Thoughts, prepare us to handle what the Buddha wants us to contemplate and understand next. We are ready to deal with what he called the "Four Noble Truths."

Truth 1: Suffering is a part of human life

We suffer. For some, the first of the Buddha's "Four Noble Truths" may seem more obviously true than for others. Physical or mental sickness, poverty, warfare, and so on and on. We see all kinds of suffering around us. Yet, we also see that some people, in the midst of what we ourselves could not put up with, not only endure, but excel. Remember Helen Keller, Mother Teresa, and FDR?

On the other hand, what if we are oblivious to all of these problems? We're fit, we have our Mercedes, life is good. If there is suffering in the world, it must have to do with someone else. *We* don't suffer. *They* suffer. People can be so insulated as to think this way – and yet at the same time feel little or no motivation to care about other people's suffering. Sadly, this is one image that many in the world have of the very affluent, among whom the Americans usually feature highly.

However, this does not mean that such people do *not* suffer. The word the Buddha used for suffering was *duhkha*, which can mean anything from extreme physical pain and death to a general sense of unease or dissatisfaction with yourself and what you've got. This is the kind of underlying suffering we are talking about. This suffering is not inherent in any particular situation, but it is a part of our experience so long as we are not awakened to the strength and power of our loving nature and potential for enlightenment. **Because we are not enlightened, we are not free.** If we are not free, we suffer. Therefore, **suffering is about not being free.**

We are not free: each of us is trapped in some particular perception of how the world is and who we are in it. Of course, for the time being, everything may feel just grand. But the truth of impermanence teaches us that everything will change. Nothing is guaranteed. There can be no sanctuary, no refuge, in any knowledge that our world will stay this way. And if nothing else, even if things stay just the way we want them to, we are going to grow old and die. So we will continue to suffer until our minds are free and we can "embrace change," "go with the flow" or, as Werner Erhard, the founder of EST, used to say, "Ride the horse in the direction it is going."

As a person wanting to be an agent of social or political change, you need to understand suffering at this level. The extremes of physical and mental suffering – the suffering of personal or geopolitical adversity and disaster – is easy to see and understand. But the level of suffering we speak of here goes much deeper and is far more insidious. It can cause you to make grave errors of judgment. You have to understand that you suffer from your biases: your biases and preconceptions lock you into seeing only certain possibilities and not others. If you are not free to see the whole picture, the greater is the likelihood that your actions will be shortsighted and partisan, and have unexpected and unintended effects. If we want to be more accurately focused – if we want our hearts and minds to be free and thus have access to deeper wisdom and greater skill to accomplish what we set out to accomplish – we need to understand the underlying cause of this deeper suffering, this "unsatisfactoriness." The Buddha wants us to focus on what part we ourselves play in our not being free. To answer this question, he gives us the Second Noble Truth.

Truth 2: We suffer because we crave

According to Buddhist cosmology, there are Six Realms of

Existence (see page 42). Beings are born into various "realms," or types of existence, each of which is dominated by a particular strong negative emotional or psychological pattern. In the realm of the gods (*devas*), the dominant emotion is said to be pride. Beings in the realm of the "jealous gods" (*ashuras*) – the wannabe *devas* – are bound up in issues of envy and power. The inhabitants of the realm of "hungry ghosts," or restless spirits (*pretas*), are driven by insatiable greed that leaves these beings wandering and dissatisfied. Beings in the realm of *hells* – places of fire and ice – are caught so tightly in a mindset of anger and rage that they cannot but see the world as either too "hot" or too "cold" to endure. In the realm of animals, beings live instinctually, hard-wired to their senses, preying on others and in fear of being preyed upon. Then there is the human realm, in which the beings are governed by desire, or **craving**, which the Buddha called *trishna* (literally, "thirst").

The Six Realms are understood both literally, as a description of the beings that inhabit the universe, and also metaphorically, as a description of human emotional and psychological states. While we will all attest to having experienced most of these states at one time or another, craving – wanting, desiring – is the strongest force in the human psyche.

Each of these six negative emotional states are, in various forms, manifestations of the "Three Poisons" of ignorance, attachment, and aggression (see page 22). Simply put, and in human terms, we don't fully understand what is going on around us; we have our own beliefs about what we think is happening around us based on our desire to see things a certain way; and we actively resist anyone who tries to get us to see things differently. If we look at any aspect of our lives, we shall see these Three Poisons at work. For example, say we have a pain in our lower back but do not realize it is because our kidneys are not working all that well. Not understanding how various foods in our diet affect us, we carry on drinking ten cups of coffee a day. We may observe, even acknowledge, that our pain gets worse when we drink coffee. But, *we* just love coffee. What would life be without our Starbucks? But then our doctor diagnoses a kidney problem and suggests to us that we might want to cut back or eliminate coffee as it might be contributing to our kidney pain. Because we want to believe in a world where this is not true, we refuse to acknowledge the facts and carry on drinking coffee.

Or take another example, in relationships. We see a good friend talking to someone we despise. We have no idea what they are talking about. But, in the emotional turmoil of wanting not to believe what we are seeing, we draw erroneous conclusions about their interaction. "Maybe they were talking negatively about me? How can I ever trust my friend again?" And so the drama of a personal soap opera begins.

One final example from political reality. Most of us don't understand all of the ins and outs of the US government's Middle East policies. Nevertheless, in spite of our ignorance, some of us want to believe so badly that our officials know what they are doing that we become vehemently defensive in favor of the government. On the other side of the political fence, some of us – equally ignorant of the full picture – want not to believe what the government says and become equally emphatic about what we believe to be the administration's lack of credibility and even legitimacy.

Because everyday reality is so infinitely complex, relative, ambiguous, and multilayered, ignorance will remain a part of our consciousness until we are fully enlightened and can see all the interrelated factors and how they dynamically come together to create what they do. Ignorance causes us erroneously to see things in simple, seemingly solid terms, and informs our decisions and actions. What holds ignorance in place, what makes how we see things seem solid, is *not* their solidity, but our *wanting* to have things solid, so that we can feel more secure. But this is like trying to hold onto a handful of sand – it slips through our fingers. The solid and secure position that we crave in the universe is an illusion.

This wanting or craving arises from our illusory belief that we can know ourselves by fixing our relationship to what is outside of ourselves. But because that which is outside of ourselves is constantly changing, the belief is false and, in fact, our clinging to it only creates more insecurity. Thus, while the other two poisons of ignorance and aggression wreak their own havoc in our lives, the Buddha focuses on the linchpin of our humanity, which is our craving – our attachment to things, sensations, beliefs, and emotional patterns.

Truth 3: There can be an end to craving

To reassure us that not all is hopeless, and to motivate us to change our point of view, overcome the Three Poisons that drive our lives, and activate our potential, the third of the Noble Truths tells us that **there is a way out of this mess.** The way out is to free our minds of craving. For until we stop wanting the world to be a certain way, we shall have no option but to limit our possibilities and drive away – even, on a larger scale, wage war with – those who see the world differently from us. Our actions will become reinforced into reactive, habitual patterns that seem intractable and irreversible. And the cycle of suffering, unease, dissatisfaction, will continue.

Because we are beings of desire, to eliminate craving altogether seems a bit rash. It sounds inhuman. After all, what about the desire for something good, something better? Then again, how can we really know what is good or better if we are still wallowing in ignorance? Understanding this dilemma and knowing that our humanity and how we express it will always be marked by desire, the Buddha is not asking for some immediate or radical shift that renders us passionless automatons. Rather, he offers a well-developed plan to dismantle this craving and transform it into a wellspring from which to benefit others. This is what he presents to us as the Fourth Noble Truth.

Truth 4: To be free of craving, follow the Eightfold Path

The Fourth Noble Truth is to help us free the unlimited potentiality of our minds and bodies. It is about helping us "to be in the world, but not of it." We can learn to be detached, but engaged; passionate, but not obsessed. This is the purpose of what the Buddha spelled out as the **Noble Eightfold Path**, which he described as: "right view, right thought, right speech, right action, right livelihood, right effort, right mindfulness, right concentration." They are traditionally divided into three categories: morality (right speech, right action, right livelihood); meditation (right effort, right mindfulness, right concentration); and the development of wisdom and insight (right view, right thought).

The Eightfold Path or *Middle Way* is a blueprint for a life lived as a conscious, engaged activist. The eight aspects of this path are essentially an educational process that embraces all the ways in which we become a well-rounded, intelligent, civilized, and useful member of humanity. The Buddha's teaching, the Dharma, outlines ways of focusing and deepening our minds, and provides guidelines for how we behave in the world. Through meditation, the application of morality, and the cultivation of insight, our thoughts become clearer; our view of the world becomes more based in reality, our speech becomes more precise, our actions become more skillful and focused; our livelihood becomes more productive and beneficial to all those around us; our efforts focused and constant, our memory unlimited; and our meditation practice unending – and the constant source that underpins and fosters all the other seven aspects of the Path.

The word "right" as an adjective before each aspect suggests that what is offered supports an unfolding of the true Buddha-nature, our loving nature, that the Buddha knows is our birthright. As we build each of these dimensions in our lives we grow as individuals until, in the end, we manifest and contribute to a positive vision of the future for all those around us. It is a model for enlightened citizenship.

For someone "wanting" to tap into and grow through the wisdom that informs all aspects of this conscious, engaged lifestyle, meditation is a key ingredient. It is one thing merely to understand intellectually the workings of the Three Poisons and the incessant allure of craving in our lives. However, because as humans we have the in-built capacity to change, the main emphasis of the Dharma is on us actively taking greater responsibility for our lives by learning methods that allow us to see the strands of the web that holds together our habitual patterns. As we work with these meditative methods, freedom begins to emerge and inform our choices. We access our inner resources more easily and effortlessly and can discern how to use them and when.

This may seem a long, lonely road to walk. But with workable methods and the support of friends along the way, it will not be long before we begin to develop a lightness of being. When that happens, the fresh air of freedom will be exhilarating.

CHAPTER 5

Intention: Planting the Seed of Action

"If you always think what you've always thought,

You will always do what you've always done.

If you always do what you've always done,

You will always get what you've always got.

If you always get what you've always got,
You will always think what you've always thought."

Anonymous

As a therapist, I periodically work with relaxation techniques. Many years ago, I learned of a method that ended a period of deep rest with the thought of "intending to move." I would say to my blissfully resting client, "Now, I want you to think about moving. Just think about it. Focus all of your intention on moving, but don't yet move a muscle." The effect of this preparation for coming out of relaxation was dramatic. The client would come out of the exercise both deeply relaxed and totally charged and alert to get on with the day.

So powerful are our intentions that the Vajrayana, or Tantric, Buddhist tradition goes so far as to say that intention is the key: it is even more important than the act that follows from it. As the inspiration of what arises from emptiness to become manifest, one cannot speak of action without first speaking of intention. The power of intention is the beginning of a gathering of a force: a focusing that is possibly more dynamic in terms of what it mobilizes inside us than the resulting act itself. It is intention that informs our thoughts and emotions about the action we plan to carry out. It moves us to the threshold of action, and the degree to which we are certain or uncertain, committed or reluctant in our intention will determine the energy and force that go into making our action deliver the impact that we intend – regardless of its positive or negative virtues. But before we get too carried away, let's look at action in general first.

The Force of Karma

The biblical adage "As you sow, so shall you reap," is a Western way of expressing what in the East is called **karma**. The word karma itself means literally "action." Such "action" is a part of a continuum of events – which we conventionally distinguish from one another although in reality they are all interlinked –

which leads from the past, through the present, into the future. This can lead some to assume that there is a kind of "predestined" quality to things that happen, as when we hear people saying "It's your karma," or that such-and-such an incident was "karmic." The result can be a fatalistic view which certainly is neither Buddhist, nor, to my understanding, what the biblical adage was driving at. Rather, all events or actions are "precursors," which predispose what follows to have one outcome rather than another.

However, in a universe where anything is possible, the unexpected can occur. In the realm of human action – in the karma that we as humans create – it would seem that this possibility often arises because of our capacity to choose. The degree to which *we follow* the path along which the precursors seem to point determines the predictability of the outcome. This is neither good nor bad. It just is.

Karma, as we speak of it here, is a process. Circumstances that arise in our life in the present are the result of the past. How we interpreted situations in the past and acted on them, and our mental/emotional state following those past actions, determine how we act and feel now. How we act and feel now, how we interpret our current experience, is the basis of what we are to experience in the future. Thus in our lives, we have a habit of returning to "the scene of the crime." The "crimes" are ours, rooted in the Three Poisons (see page 22), reinforced into well-trodden, seemingly intractable habitual patterns. These patterns can create the illusion of predestination – the tangled web we weave, the vicious cycle – and cast us into a despair that seeks salvation at the hands of something or someone outside of ourselves.

The possibility of change
However, the Buddha taught that the reins for steering a new

course are always in our hands. We always get a chance to make something new from our past. If we reenact our old pattern, more than likely the pattern will go on into the future. As the quote at the beginning of the chapter says, "If you always do what you have always done, you will always get what you have always got." On the other hand, if we learn to step back, learn ways of being able to create space mentally and to see openness and opportunity – rather than another scene of a soap opera or tragic drama – then we can take a new course. History need not repeat itself if we sincerely make the effort to wake up from what would otherwise be habitual, reflexive reactions that have been reinforced time after time "since beginningless time."

To stop the repetition of history – what the Buddha called cyclic existence as depicted in traditional Tibetan paintings of "The Wheel of Life" – requires work. This work is, in fact, the purpose of the Dharma, the Buddha's teachings. These teachings are rooted in what he himself experienced in the process of his own enlightenment. As a fellow human going through the full array of thoughts, emotions, and experiences that we all go through, he saw that the work he had done in himself was a useful path for others to consider putting into practice in their own lives. Just some well thought out suggestions based on his experience. And for generations it seems that these suggestions have been useful.

The path that the Buddha suggests is not based on something so radically different from how we might try to resolve and work with matters in our own lives. However, he offers a systematic way of looking at and using our own resources wisely and with skill. If ever there was a "roadmap for peace," the Dharma – which literally means "the way things are" – is the Buddha's recommended route.

In Chapter Six, you will be presented with various meditative exercises and practices to help you to focus your mind more clearly. They can be done alone or in a group. Their purpose is to help the mind to disrupt the habitual patterns that send us blindly following courses of action that afterward leave us with varying degrees of regret. These universal mind tools can be applied to whatever course of action you will choose, providing you with greater discernment through each stage of every action.

In Chapter Two, I mentioned the idea that every action has four distinct aspects, or components (see page 32). Therefore, the action of stepping onto the path of the Buddha – or any other path for that matter – has the same four aspects. These elements and how they come together determine whether an action yields positive, negative, or mixed results for the future. To recapitulate and elaborate on what I said earlier, the four aspects of every action are **intention, contemplation, the act committed as a result of these**, and lastly, **one's attitude or demeanor both while doing the act and in response to its result.** As intention is the beginning of the process, it is now time to give it our attention.

Intention: The Road to Hell...

History offers us countless stories of individuals and nations whose intentions were good – at least from their own vantage point. Looking back, we can now say with some degree of certainty that these intentions and what followed from them were not particularly beneficial. The siege of Canaan in the name of God; the Babylonian conquests in the name of many gods; Hellenic and Roman imperialism; the Crusades; the Spanish Inquisition; the Mogul invasions; the American Civil War; the Russian Revolution; the rise of the Nazis; Hiroshima and Nagasaki; the Chinese Cultural Revolution; the Korean War; Vietnam; "ethnic cleansing" in former Yugoslavia and

Rwanda; and now the conflicts in the Persian Gulf: conquests, empires, and wars perpetrated by people convinced of the supremacy of their own spiritual or secular ideology, believing that the world would be a much better place if only everyone was like them, agreed with them or, if necessary, was controlled by them – for their own good.

But to focus only on extraordinary individuals and events, misses in many respects the ordinary workings of intention in the everyday lives of each and every one of us. Our own conquests, empires, and wars may be on a smaller scale but they happen for very much the same reasons. Achieving mastery over our delusions at the most personal level is the essential antidote for preventing disasters of greater magnitude.

Chain reactions

Buddhist philosophy speaks of what is called **dependent origination** (the term is also rendered as "dependent arising" or "interdependent origination"). The Buddha explained it as follows: "Because this is present, that will arise, and because that was born, this is being born." Simply put, it means that nothing arises independently – everything has causes and consequences. This is also described as a "chain of becoming" called the Twelve Links, or *Nidanas*. These twelve steps, each leading to the next, flesh out the process by which the Three Poisons of ignorance, attachment, and aggression are linked together. These links, which our minds naturally go through in forming our likes, dislikes, or sense of indifference, may be distilled as follows: Not knowing who we are (out of ignorance), we fall prey to a cascade of mental, emotional, and physical events that we classify according to one of three categories: attachment, aversion, indifference. In other words: what we like, what we don't like, and what we don't notice or care about one way or the other. We habitually set our intention to have more experiences that we like (things to which we are attached), and eliminate or minimize those experiences that we don't like (things to which we feel aversion). Perhaps we like chocolate ice cream, but gag at the taste of strawberry or butterscotch. Most likely we'll arrange our lives in order to have more chocolate and less strawberry or butterscotch. Or say we like cold weather and skiing; this may plant in our minds the intention of moving to Colorado in the future. And when people talk about vacationing in Florida, we scratch our heads and don't understand why anyone would want to hang out on a humid beach on the edge of a swamp.

And so it goes on. Maybe these choices aren't the best for us. Maybe we don't have the full picture and are missing out on something. But our intentions are driven – for better or worse – by craving, as the Second Noble Truth tells us (see page 55). The choices we make are subjective, for obviously others might choose the opposite with just as much zeal and intent. Let's look at a more interpersonal example. We may intensely dislike someone who is deeply loved by another. We may even see someone as a demon or a tyrant, while to another they are a saint and savior. And consider how even our own view of someone may change radically, depending on time and circumstances.

An extraordinary example of this is the case of Osama Bin Laden. For years he helped in the resistance against the Soviet Union in Afghanistan, for which the US government paid and praised him. Then, following his various attacks on American interests where Bin Laden demonstrated that he was no longer happy with his relationship with the US, he became a demon in the West. Yet he is viewed as a saint and savior by those who believe that what he is doing is upholding their traditions.

This process of dependent origination, which takes us

through our likes, dislikes, and indifferences, happens in an instant and over time. It is the commonplace path we have trodden since birth and (in the Buddhist view) before. Because it is commonplace, it seems "natural." But, because it is rooted in the Three Poisons, we can easily mistake what is *habitual* for what is natural. That is why, when it comes to breaking habits, everything seems so topsy-turvy and unnatural. We get caught up in the belief that what we think and the meanings we give to things, how we act and how the world appears to us, are all solid realities. We fail to look behind the scenes to see that it is our cravings and intentions based on those cravings that lead us along our habitual well-trodden way. Possibility is limited as we follow the path of predictable outcomes. This pattern is neither good nor bad, but if we want to change it and go in a new direction, we need to be a bit bolder.

The truth is, as the Dharma teaches, that all phenomena are characterized by "**emptiness.**" What this term means in a Buddhist context is that nothing has a permanent, constant, unambiguous identity, because everything is dependent on something else. Nothing exists purely in and of itself. So there can be no clear distinction between good-bad and like-dislike. The so-called reality that we perceive is merely an intellectual convenience, a way of ordering the world so that we can try to understand it. But we do not see this. How we measure and define the world and our reaction to it is based on misinformation and a craving for things to be a certain way. As long as this remains true, it is completely out of the question that our intention can lead to whatever perfect consequence we are pursuing. Our course of action will inevitably have pitfalls and unintended effects, no matter how "perfect" it seems for the moment.

The Ultimate Intention: The Four Limitless Meditations

His Holiness the Dalai Lama and other Buddhist teachers say that in the final analysis, all any of us ever wants is to be happy. And because, as the Buddha himself believed, we have an inherently loving nature, we also want the people around us to be happy too. As we focus on becoming conscious, engaged activists, happiness – for ourselves and others – is what we would like to see as the consequence of whatever we do, be it a small personal act or one that has geopolitical implications. The Buddha suggests that we hold this intention as the general, ultimate basis that informs and shapes every other intention we have to change the world for the better in some way. In Buddhist terminology, we are speaking about ultimate and relative bodhichitta. Bodhichitta means "awakened heart." Ultimate bodhichitta is the clear, unbridled, profound, altruistic intention of wanting all to be truly happy. Relative, or actively manifested, bodhichitta is how we set out to accomplish turning that intention into an everyday reality.

Bodhichitta underlies a wonderful meditative prayer of aspiration in the Buddhist tradition called the Four Limitless Meditations. In one translation, it reads as follows:

> "May all beings have happiness and the causes of happiness.
>
> May all beings be free from suffering and the causes of suffering.
>
> May they never be separated from the great happiness that is beyond suffering.
>
> May they dwell in great equanimity which is beyond passion, aggression, and prejudice."

Each line of this prayer has multiple layers of meanings, from the most mundane, everyday way of understanding the words to more profound levels of Buddhist philosophy. The prayer can in itself be a foundation for focused meditation practice and study. My comments will stick to the more general meanings, as they apply to setting one's intention for actions that create the most beneficial outcomes. To accomplish this, let us briefly examine each line of this prayer separately.

"May all beings have happiness and the causes of happiness."

We all want to be happy, and this line expresses the intention that happiness will come about in our lives. This happiness is not the feeling most of us have from time to time: a pleasant experience but an all too transient one. What the prayer is aspiring to is a *true and lasting* happiness, which is another matter. Rather than being tossed about on an ocean of highs and lows by the Three Poisons, we are seeking a happiness rooted in the enlightened freedom achieved by transforming these poisons. We wish to see ignorance transformed into an experience of our unlimited potential and capacities; attachment transformed into a mental and emotional state that is light, spacious, and capable of knowing anything and everything; and the heat of our aggressive tendencies transformed into the fire of joy and spontaneity.

But even before our happiness becomes rooted in such enlightenment, any experience of happiness, however fleeting, itself creates space and possibility. When we are happy, "in a good mood," we tend to act in ways that are more benevolent and beneficial. At such times we may be happy for reasons growing from the shaky ground of selfish desires, and the benevolence or kindness we show may be limited to those who in turn will bring about more happiness for us. Still, there is virtue in it and it demonstrates that at our core, there is a loving nature.

Of course, we may not agree with what another person does or find the reasons for their happiness acceptable. We may even challenge them directly about their actions, and this challenging may express itself in the form of conflict at every imaginable level. We may, in fact, be their active adversaries. But if we understand that the greatest good comes out of a happy mind, we shall retain at all times the ultimate compassionate wish that how they think and what they do now will become transformed into a better way of being – a way of being that guarantees a lasting happiness.

What often makes this difficult for us is when we see someone being happy at our or other people's misery or misfortune. Because a positive emotion is associated with what we find disagreeable, we want to lash out, to make them suffer like we have suffered. We want to "wipe the smile off their faces." To curb a mind inclined towards retaliation is no small thing. But it is the high road, the noble road that this particular line of the meditation encourages. I can recall seeing on television the jubilant Palestinians celebrating the fall of New York's Twin Towers. For certain, such jubilation more than likely arose from a general dislike for American policies or values. It may, therefore be understandable. But, happiness at someone else's expense is always problematic and sows seeds for further enmity. It is born out of attachments to mental and emotional patterns – rooted in the Three Poisons – that have given rise to a skewed view of the world. We don't want anyone to stop being happy. But we sincerely want them to be happy for the right reasons. That is compassion in action.

Along the same lines, in a conversation about the current US political situation, Lama Surya Das commented that he was dismayed to see Western Buddhists entering into the political fray for negative reasons: being depressed with the current situation, disliking the current administration, the president, the military, and so on. Although we may have perfectly valid reasons for not being pleased with what is happening around us, to succumb to negativism, name-calling, belittlement, and the deriding of character just poisons the situation further, making people defensive and weakening our own character in the long run. Former President Bill Clinton believed in trying to operate on higher moral ground by avoiding such negative tactics. While he may not always have succeeded, I believe that this generally positive approach may, in the long run, lead to more people and historians remembering his presidency in a favorable light.

More to the point, if we really want people to be happy, then does it matter who is creating the conditions for them to become happy? If it were possible for our political opponents to create better circumstances in the long run, should we be so partisan as not to be supportive and wish them good luck? If winning comes about only through attacking and destroying everything the other side wants and does and not valuing it for whatever it has contributed, then we do not move on. We are always in the position of starting over again – and more than likely having to fend off the enemies we have created with our negative attitude.

This doesn't mean that we let up on our vigilance. It does not mean we don't vote for change. What it does mean is that we value everyone and appreciate that they are doing their best based on what they know. And, if their actions are rooted in the Three Poisons, then we hope that the causes and conditions that will allow them to see things differently will arise for them.

Toward this end, we look at the last portion of the first line of the prayer: may all beings have "the causes of happiness."

The causes of happiness can be all of the conditions we looked at in the discussion of the "precious human birth" (see page 42). We would like people to be strong in body and mind, to have good mental and emotional capacities, and to find themselves in an environment that is conducive to supporting their experience of a lasting happiness. The Buddha's idea of the precious human birth reminds us of both the internal and external conditions needed to bring happiness about. It provides us with the general guidelines for what needs to happen. It is then for us to see where we are and set our minds and hearts on whatever aspect of these conditions we can improve.

At a deeper level, there is one single cause of happiness: the transformation of the Three Poisons. As we can see that all of our suffering and despair are the result of the Three Poisons, creating the conditions for us to learn how to uproot and transform the Poisons is, in the long run, the only guarantee that "happiness follows us to the end of our days." Depending on our capacities, we may have a greater or lesser ability to transform our living conditions and situations, or those of others. Having few material resources, we may nevertheless possess the ability to influence others by uplifting their experience and providing them with ways to transform. If nothing else, we can at least start with ourselves.

The attitude behind this meditation is **unconditional love**. Understanding that every single being looks for happiness, we realize the power that lies in first and always looking for the best in ourselves and others. For as we do this, and as the space this creates in our hearts and minds becomes a more ever-present reality, it encourages us to work in the world in even stronger, more dynamic, and more powerful ways. This leads us to the remaining three of the Four Limitless Meditations, each of which must be built upon a foundation of love.

"May all beings be free from suffering and the causes of suffering."

None of us wants to suffer. None of us wants to endure conditions that cause us to suffer. We try our best to eliminate those things in our lives that make us suffer. However, because we often fail to understand fully how we got into our predicament in the first place, we are usually at best only partially successful in our efforts. We may be able to get out of a particular abusive relationship or become free from some other oppressive force in our lives and our suffering, as we currently understand it, may be diminished dramatically. However, unless we understand that the reason this suffering *arose* is the result of the work of the Three Poisons in our lives, it is likely that we shall fall into a similar pattern in the future.

If we meditate on this we see how difficult it is to make real, lasting changes in our lives. Certainly our worldly, material conditions may change for the better. But how hard it is to overcome our own impatience, anger, frustration, pride, greed, or torpor. Real, lasting change – to be "away from suffering" – requires us to cultivate the Six *Paramitas*, or Perfections, of a compassionate, awakened being: diligence, patience, generosity, wisdom, exertion, and meditative insight. Developing these attributes within ourselves ultimately transforms us and they become the basis upon which we work with and transform the lives and conditions of others.

Understanding this meditation fully, we do not get discouraged when we work at changing something in someone else's life, only to watch as they re-enact the whole scenario over again. Nor do we disregard or disparage those whose lives it seems are devoted to creating suffering in the lives of others. Of course, it is much easier to show care and compassion for a victim than for a perpetrator. But here, we must understand that even the most heinous villain, torturer, or despot is living their lives in the midst of the Three Poisons. They may be hopelessly misguided, but we must always remember that they *are* misguided. Hopefully, in creating positive conditions around someone, we support them in accessing their own resources to make the necessary internal changes.

But, as we know from the chemistry lab of our own experience, making these internal transformations can be an incremental, painstakingly slow process. While the transformation of the Three Poisons within ourselves yields the greatest, lasting results in ensuring that our old habits do not prevail, we should not abandon trying to improve the external conditions that hold back the process of internal change. Changing the world takes time. Changing the mind can, in the Buddhist view, take lifetimes. We need to do both, and accept that the time frame for the transformation of each is radically different. Our world can look so different from one election to the next. But, until our minds are truly transformed, the change we so desperately wanted and celebrate upon its arrival will, once again, fade from view and the cycle of suffering will continue.

We may look around our world and see that we are not doing a very good job at eradicating or preventing suffering. But I think it is important to remember that we *are* capable of overcoming sickness, poverty, and warfare. Indeed, we have done it, time and again. There are parts of the world where most people live in peace, free from many dangerous illnesses and from extreme poverty. That we desire to see an end to these things *at all* is a testimony to the compassionate heart of humanity. This is what this line of the meditation appeals to. If we can reinforce this tendency through overcoming what is base in our habitual personal and collective lives, then we can create a society whose foundation for change, growth, and transformation is assured.

According to the Buddha, this is not just some Utopian dream. It is said that in all of the universes that can be seen with the eye of enlightened wisdom, suffering-free societies and worlds do exist. That we even imagine a world without such suffering lets us know that it is conceptually in the realm of the possible. At times we may seem closer, at times further away from this as a reality in our own lives. This is natural while we have not yet cleared our own lives of the effects of the Three Poisons. Nor can we ever really give up, for to give up would be to disregard fully our loving nature – our humanity. Ultimately, we cannot do that. Our loving nature will not stand for it.

In committing ourselves to developing the love and compassion expressed in these first two of the Four Limitless Meditations, we are undertaking to cease contributing to the perpetuation of suffering. And that is no small thing.

"May they never be separated from the great happiness that is beyond suffering."

The "great happiness" that is referred to in the third of the Four Limitless Meditations is the lasting happiness of enlightenment; that is, being free from the fetters of the Three Poisons. Our craving no longer exists so nor does the suffering that it generates. This releases all of our potentiality and makes it available to benefit everyone around us.

No effort, however small, that we make toward attaining this end is ever wasted or lost, if that effort is made with love and compassion. We understand that if we seek to become a conscious, engaged activist committed to seeing good happen in the world, love and compassion are not options. They are prerequisites. By developing a loving attitude and acting in the world compassionately, we create healthy positive conditions in which the true cause of suffering, the Three Poisons, can become transformed. Knowing that this is how true change for the good takes place, we embrace whatever we do whole-heartedly, with joy.

"Joy" in Tibetan is *tsultrim*, a word that also means "discipline." This does not mean pushing yourself or placing some kind of external constraint on yourself in order to force compliance. "Discipline" in this sense is what naturally arises when you know that what you are doing makes sense and guarantees a positive result. You can put all of your energy into what it is that you are doing and, if it is truly a worthwhile effort, a natural warmth or joy will arise.

Knowing that what we do is worth doing bolsters our commitment and resolve. This in turn can inspire the actual willingness to stand up for what we are doing and protect those who need to be protected. Hence this line of the Four Limitless Meditations not only contains the grandest of all wishes – that all may be uplifted and transformed – but it also inspires courage and a willingness to go the distance. It is a line of unshakeable conviction.

"May they dwell in great equanimity, which is beyond passion, aggression, and prejudice."

This last line of the Four Limitless Meditations is about our altruistic intention to benefit all *impartially*. With the gathering up of our love, compassion, and conviction, we are asked to meditate on the importance of using these assets for the benefit of all. Many Buddhist texts talk about altruistic intention and doing whatever you do "for the benefit of all sentient beings." If one fully understands that we are inextrica-bly interlinked with everyone and everything around us, then to be preoccupied only with one's own wishes and interests is a horrible miscalculation. Holding to an illusion of separation from those around us ensures that cooperation in our efforts will always be limited, partisan, and eventually attract attention from other parts of reality denied. For usually what is denied must, in effect, speak louder to get its fair share of attention. Thus it is that those who feel disfranchised or disregarded in society must often resort to tactics that draw attention, whether they be brash, outlandish, or antisocial. Protests, civil disobedience, even terrorist attacks basically aim to get their perpetrators acknowledged as part of the equation, worthy of consideration.

In essence, then, this line is about overcoming self-interest or partisan behavior. There may be some short-term benefits to such behavior, but in the long run a strategy of exclusion will eventually leave us out in the cold. The truth of this is evident and can be witnessed at almost every level of human interaction. Putting our earlier examples in more theoretical or philosophical terms in the public arena is the way partisan interests have spawned (and have always spawned) political polarization; where the gray, ambiguous realities of relative reality are forced into the starkness of simplistic black-and-white, good-versus-evil debate. In such an atmosphere, even if "your" side prevails, the tactics deployed to counter the "opposition" often simply serve to generate further partisan behavior that in turn reinforces and perpetuates the polarization – and so on and on.

If we embark on the process of transforming the Three Poisons – in this meditation referred to as "passion [craving/attachment], aggression, and prejudice [ignorance]" – we logically begin to enter the state of equanimity, treating all impartially. This state progresses as the Poisons weaken and our being and actions take on more enlightened qualities. At the same time we should not understand equanimity or impartiality as meaning that we treat everyone and everything equally, in exactly the same way. Impartiality has more to do with an attitude than an action. It involves greater discrimination.

For example, let us look at the saying, "One man's meat is another man's poison." Supposing we make a meal for two visitors, and for dessert we offer one visitor ice cream and the other just a plain apple. From an outsider's point of view, this seems unfair. And certainly, if we are basing this selection on liking one person more than the other, then we are acting from bias based on the poison of ignorance and the judgment against us is true. However, if our decision is based on the simple fact that we have taken the trouble to find out that one visitor prefers ice cream and the other prefers fruit, we are displaying a concern to be impartial based on discernment. In doing so we have taken a step away from ignorance toward true knowledge and compassion. And compassion, as we shall learn in a later chapter, is best applied with knowledge born of discernment.

Nor does impartiality necessarily mean that you have to *like* everyone equally. The great Tibetan teacher Gampopa once said "It is the sign of a superior person that he treats all with equanimity, yet still has a few good friends." We each have our preferences, and tend to befriend those with whom we feel an affinity. Buddhist teachers say that much of this is karmic, based on bonds created in previous lives. Regardless of whether or not you believe in reincarnation, we still feel a kinship toward some more than others. This is only a problem if your view of others is skewed by prejudices rooted in ignorance. In political terms, this is the basis of "good old boy" or "school-tie" politics and "cronyism." Preferential treatment and favoritism is always divisive.

What this line of the meditation helps guard against, therefore, is elitism. Meditating on the meaning of this line, and thus committing oneself to opening up to others and to making the effort to live and act in a more enlightened way, a natural charisma emerges. This charisma, together with all the other positive attributes we are now committed to developing, leads to a widening of our sphere of influence. The four meditations are considered "limitless," or immeasurable, because the more one lives in their truth, the greater the effect one has in the world – an effect that potentially knows no bounds.

Reflecting upon, and attempting to embrace, the Four Limitless Meditations is a tremendous antidote to corruption. Truly contemplating its meaning in relation to the acts one is intending to embark upon in the coming day, and then reflecting upon those acts in the evening, is a way of keeping us honest and disciplined. Until we are completely enlightened and can see beyond the illusions of time and space, the outcome of any of our actions will always remain a mystery unfolding. No doubt there will often be times when we blow it. If we have a small influence on what happens in the world around us, more than likely we shall see small mistakes. If we have more power and influence in the world, we shall more than likely see larger mistakes. At the end of each day, consider asking yourself the following questions:

> Am I happy tonight? Are the people around me happy tonight?

> Am I upset by what I have done today? Has anyone been harmed by what I have done today?

> Are there ways I can improve what I do to ensure that any harm caused is reversed, that those around me are protected from harm, and that those who are happy can continue to be happy?

> Did I act in a way today that is impartial? Did I treat all around me with the same degree of fairness

and loving concern?

If we ask ourselves these questions daily, then recommit ourselves to fulfilling the Four Limitless Meditations in the days to come, we anchor our lives and actions in a way that helps us to grow into the potentiality that we are now beginning to awaken.

The Power of Confession and Dedication

When we begin our day with the altruistic intention to be of use and service, and end it with a reflection on the fruits of our actions and attitudes, what we are creating is a spiritualized life. This way of being is reflected in the Vajrayana Buddhist practice of *sadhana*, a highly structured meditation form that follows the ways in which we psychologically prepare for action in the world, then carry it out. A sadhana starts with focusing on creating the inner resources to act in accordance with our altruistic intention, our "awakened heart," or bodhichitta (see above, page 69). We seek to access, then expand, the energy of particular positive qualities (wisdom, compassion, power, protection, and so on). Following such a template, we can focus our intention, assess what positive resources we have or need to have to carry out the action that is the manifest expression of that intention, and then act with clarity and good heart. What rounds out this process is our ability accurately and honestly to reflect upon what has happened as a result. In most of our activities the longer term results of our actions may barely be known, camouflaged in the clouds of the future. So, while we cannot necessarily judge the outcome of our action, we can certainly reflect on our efforts. We can assess our efforts honestly.

Throughout our day, did our mind stray? Were we always

thinking altruistically or did some self-centered wishes and thoughts invite themselves in? Did these wishes and thoughts make our efforts sloppy and less effective, and if so, how? We examine these shortcomings with an eye to making our actions even more precisely focused and effective in the day to come.

To clarify this process and to demarcate it more succinctly and powerfully in our minds, the formal practice of sadhana ends with confession and dedication. In the ordinary course of carrying on our business, these words may sound a bit too religious or sanctimonious. However, the psychological discipline and willingness to go through these processes as part of our actions makes their effects even more potent.

Confession embraces all of the daily questions we can ask ourselves in order to evaluate how well we have carried out our intentions through our actions. To make this process more dramatic and effective as a cause for change in the future, confession is about fully acknowledging where our actions were done with less than pure motive, where they were ineffective, and where they created unintended outcomes. We accept our responsibility for this and take it on board, not in order to punish ourselves, but rather to acknowledge *with compassion* our human frailties. We show compassion toward ourselves and do not lapse into negative self-denigration, and so create a positive springboard upon which to recommit our efforts to act with clear intent, more skillfully, and free of self-interest or partisanship.

Confession reintroduces us to our purity. It brings us back to our loving nature in a very simple and direct manner. And then we can go one step further. We can dedicate our efforts.

As I have said at other times, nothing is ever lost. No positive thought or action, however small or seemingly insignificant, is a wasted effort. Just as it is possible to compound misery, it is also possible to compound virtue and goodness. For this, we need to celebrate. We celebrate in order to connect with the joy and warmth that is an expression of our loving nature. We do this not because we want some warm, fuzzy, feel-good pleasure from what we've done. We do it for others.

Focusing again on the altruistic intention that we started our day with, we use our warmth and joy as a force to spread out the fruits of our actions to each and every being. Initially, we may think of seeing these good feelings spreading to those whose lives and hearts we wished to touch today. But, in improving the lives and conditions of these people, we create a ripple effect that touches those to whom these people are in turn connected. And so on and so on… Therefore, in dedicating the fruits of our efforts today, we don't hold back. We see them as limitless, touching more and more beings.

In the Vajrayana tradition of Buddhism, altruistic intention and dedication are the crown jewels. Altruistic intention immediately makes the application of our actions more effective. But dedication is even more powerful, as it takes the wish that you started your day with and sends it out into the world, riding on the energy of our tangible efforts. In a very powerful way, we turn our intention into a reality. It becomes a building block upon which tomorrow's renewed efforts can be constructed, inviting and generating more virtue and goodness.

Dedicating our efforts is more than simply *wishing* to make a difference. In dedicating, we celebrate that we *are making* a difference. And we invite everyone to join the celebration.

It would be interesting to speculate whether world leaders, present and past, have ever begun or ended their day with their intentions focused in the way outlined in this chapter. If so, particularly in the case of those known as tyrants or the perpetrators of great crimes and wars, would they have stopped before they went as far as they did? Was there any degree of self-awareness that would have allowed them to choose another course? Or were they, like most of us, so blinded by the Three Poisons that they could see no option, and just did the best they knew how based on the information they had at the time?

In the midst of difficult times, if we are to strike out on a more promising course, we need to learn and affirm ways that demonstrate love, compassion, conviction, and impartiality – even to the point of embracing those we deem as "evil" or "enemies" and acknowledging them compassionately as part of our human family. And if we do not yet possess in our hearts and minds the wisdom and skill to embrace others whom we view as dangerous or misguided, we can at least begin and end our days with the Four Limitless Meditations that set our intention for cultivating and affirming the possibility of doing so.

CHAPTER 6

Meditations and Mantras for the Conscious, Engaged Activist

*"May I be a guard for those who are
protectorless,
A guide for those who journey on the road.
For those who wish to go across the water,
May I be a boat, a raft, a bridge.*

*May I be an isle for those who yearn for landfall,
And a lamp for those who long for light;
For those who need a resting place, a bed;
For all who need a servant, may I be their slave.*

*May I be the wishing jewel, the vase of plenty,
A word of power, and the supreme healing;
May I be the tree of miracles,
And for every being, the abundant cow.*

Like the great earth and the pervading elements,
Enduring as the sky itself endures,
For boundless multitudes of living beings,
May I be their ground and sustenance.

Thus, for every single thing that lives,
In number like the boundless reaches of the sky,
May I be their sustenance and nourishment
Until they pass beyond the bounds of suffering"

Shantideva.[5]

Through his own personal examination of the human predicament, the Buddha saw meditation as an essential method of
uprooting and transforming the Three Poisons in a truly
lasting way. As the son of a king, he also saw the practicality of
meditation for slowing and averting the course of conflict in
the world.

For the Buddha was quite aware of partisanship, intrigue,
and the ways in which belief could be used to create harm.
Not unlike the medieval European crusaders, inquisitors, and
witch-hunters, the kings and empires of ancient India went to
war believing in, and motivated by, their own special relationship to God. Seeing this, the Buddha posed a simple question:

[5] Shantideva, *The Way of the Bodhisattva*
(Bodhisattvacharyavatara). Translated from the Tibetan by the
Padmakara Translation Group. Shambhala Books, Boston, 1997.
The passage is from Chapter 3.

If God is an objective truth, how can both sides in a war claim to be on God's side or to hold the right view, the right beliefs? It is not possible. Such claims and beliefs must, therefore, be subjective and based on preconceptions – in other words, based on the Three Poisons. The Buddha therefore concluded that if we are ever going to get to the objective truth about God, we need to begin by taking God out of the equation and examining our own minds. Peace does not come from believing in God. Peace comes from creating peacefulness in our own minds. Wisdom and skillfulness in action are not *bestowed* upon us. We need to work to obtain them. Again, we come back to our own minds.

If we sit quiet and relaxed, free from being too tight or too loose, our loving nature will become more and more evident. As we become accustomed to just *being* – here and now – our identification with the turmoil and confusion in our life is disrupted. We can then access whatever resources we need to face whatever life puts before us. We also come to understand how easy it is to get sidetracked, lured by one emotion or another. Thus, our compassion for others grows naturally as we come to understand how easy it is for others, too, to be trapped in realities that they may not want but don't know how to get out of. In the laboratory of our own experience, we come to an inner recognition of the value of altruism – being with and helping others.

Buddhist Meditation Practice

The Buddha taught a number of meditative methods. Some rely on nothing but an awareness of the breath. Others involve visualization or gazing upon an object. Most of the visualization practices also involve the use of archetypal sounds, such as mantras, to invoke specific qualities in our being. There are also meditations that have a particular philosophical or moral focus, such as to generate compassion, healing, or protection, or to dispel negativity between people or in the world in general.

The meditative practices offered in this chapter are either traditional Buddhist meditations or meditative exercises based on Buddhist tradition. All of them are suitable for everyone, regardless of your faith or orientation. At the same time, the format that they follow can be used as a framework upon which you can build other meditations or visualizations that you think will help you in your activist work.

The benefits of meditation

If I were to summarize what benefits you should get from meditation practice, it is that you should become more open, flexible, spontaneous, joyful. You won't "burn out" from the exertion that is demanded of you in the face of those habitual forces within and around us, which reinforce and make the scourges of sickness, poverty, and warfare almost seem permanent. The resistances that make your work difficult dissolve as the wisdom and skillful means inherent in your loving nature more easily manifest. No matter what task we face, the furrowed brow of zealousness, stress, and despera-tion is no hallmark that you are being any more effective in doing what you are called to do. And, more than likely, if such stress to your mind and body is not released – not transformed into naturalness – it will eventually undermine your efforts.

A good friend, Lama Ole Nydahl, speaks of meditation "teflon coating" your neurons. From the perspective of the Ayurvedic medical tradition, this metaphor is not far from what are claimed to be the physical benefits of meditation on our body and mind. With greater peace, joy, and equanimity you develop a natural immunity to getting too attached to irritations and challenges as they arise in your life and activities. You are able to let go of what is petty and inessential and get on with what matters.

Spiritual conviction born of the open-mindedness created by meditation – regardless of the tradition from which it comes – is an important asset for world leaders as they confront the turmoil of the twenty-first century. A number of leaders in the world are known to have a deep spiritual life and practice: His Holiness the Dalai Lama, Kofi Annan, Nelson Mandela, Aung San Su Kyi. Each demonstrates how their convictions need not create a close-minded exclusivism of the sort exhibited by those of fundamentalist persuasions, who see themselves as so unswervingly and exclusively right as to be prepared to line up against each other in preparation for Armageddon. Each of the above mentioned leaders has borne an immense burden of responsibility. And yet, in their measured continence, one has seen how peacefulness has informed their decisions.

How To Begin and Stick With a Meditation Practice

When we add something new to our schedule, such as the regular discipline of practicing meditation, other parts of our life get shoved around. For most of us, time is one of the things we perceive ourselves to be short of. Our schedules are, more than likely, too full to begin with. Therefore if we are thinking of scheduling a time to meditate, we might define it as one more thing to get done in the day and as such turn it into a burden. But this is no way to approach meditation. In his *Instructions on Meditation*, the great Tibetan master Dudjom Rinpoche wrote:

"Allow yourself to relax and feel some spaciousness, letting your mind settle naturally. Your body should be still, speech silent and breathing as it is, freely flowing. Here there is a sense of letting go, unfolding, letting be. What does this state of relaxation feel like? You should be like someone after a really hard day's work, exhausted and peacefully satisfied, mind content to rest. Something settles at the gut level, and feeling it resting in your gut, you begin to experience a lightness. It is as if you're melting." [6]

You settle down to meditation in this way. It is a time to feel nourished, to feel replenished. Enjoy it! This doesn't mean that you shouldn't take your meditation seriously, but if it becomes stiff, habitual, and an enforced discipline, meditation will provide you little benefit. More than likely, in the beginning, you will feel a certain amount of awkwardness. That is natural when you are rearranging your life a bit and also starting to practice something new. To get over these bumps, a little serious push is necessary. But, be cautious of getting too uptight, self-righteous, or judgmental with yourself.

Start with meditating for a short period and gradually build up your sessions in small increments of time. Work up to a time frame that feels comfortable and doesn't make you feel like you are being squeezed in other aspects of your life. At the same time, if there is a weekend or other period that you can devote to more meditation, go for it. Over time, as you allow the discipline of meditation to infiltrate your daily life, it will feel more and more natural and your sense of joy and commitment to the process will grow.

[6] H.H. Dudjom Rinpoche, *Instructions on Meditation*, a small pamphlet published by the Vajrayana Foundation, Hawaii.

Clarifying intentions

As we have said previously, Buddhist practice is based on altruism. This altruism comes from a profound understanding of our interconnectedness. Our happiness, our healing, our enlightenment itself is dependent upon this recognition and on placing everyone else in our thoughts as we meditate. To help develop and hold this perspective, in preparation for a meditation session or a meditative exercise, it is useful to contemplate the Four Thoughts that Revolutionize the Mind (see pages 41–51) and the Four Limitless Meditations (see pages 69–80). Many traditional Buddhist practices begin in this way. Spend a few moments reflecting on both.

A Preliminary Breathing Exercise to Transform the Three Poisons

The following exercise was taught to me by Dr. Lobsang Rapgay, a Tibetan doctor and former monk who is now a well established clinical psychologist in California. It can be done on its own or as a preliminary to other forms of meditation. Energetically, it can be like a more advanced version of counting to ten when emotions are running high. The exercise aims to help us loosen the grip of the Three Poisons on our consciousness by focusing on the movement of breath and also on working with the "subtle energy body." Before I describe the exercise itself, let me explain a few things about what this means.

The subtle energy body

Classical yoga as well as the most advanced Tantric Buddhist practices make reference to a subtle energy body, a system of *chakras* and spiritual energy channels in the body. Many in the West are familiar with the term chakras, or energy vortices.

These are envisioned as whirling centers of energy at various points in the body, from the base of the spine to the crown of the head. Hindu tradition relies on theories and practices based upon there being seven chakras. However, in Buddhist Tantra, the root chakra (*muladhara*) and crown chakra (*sahasrara*) are considered points of entry and exit respectively, with the five chakras in between being the ones that we need to work with. Thus, following the instructions given to me in the context of Buddhist Tantra, these chakras are linked to spiritual energy channels: two that run from about three finger-widths below the navel and finish at the edge of each nostril, and a central or main spiritual channel (*shushumna*) that begins in the same area below the navel, rises to the crown of the head, then drops down to around the middle of the forehead, finally turning inward toward the center of the brain. The two side channels twist and criss-cross around shushumna and it is at the constricted points where they cross one another and around the central channel that the chakras are said to be located.

Meditations are done to focus on the various chakras, loosen the constriction of the two side channels and allow for the movement of spiritual energy to ascend more freely through the central channel. According to Tibetan tradition, the chakras can only be "opened" either through the strong blessing of a master, or through the individual performing intense and effective meditation practice. No one else, like a massage therapist or a healer placing special stones or toning over your chakras, can open them for you. If they say they can, thank them and run in the opposite direction.

Some may ask, does this subtle energy body actually exist? It is true that if one were to try to find the exact anatomical location and physical presence of the chakras, you would be hard pressed. There is "something" there – for instance, the third (abdominal) chakra is regarded as the "survival" chakra, the seat of ego and personal power – and this area is indeed where we physically feel a "gut reaction" in the face of a physical or verbal threat to our person. And the chakras and channels may, like Chinese acupuncture meridians, be related to the modern understanding of the nervous system in some way (like Chinese meridians). But exactly *what* the subtle body is proves elusive because it is essentially an intangible, non-physical notion. Yet Tibetan masters and yogis of the East learn meditations where they focus on the chakras and the channels in very specific ways and venture to access and utilize the energy that arises. In their practices, the chakras will be visualized mentally as lotuses of different colors and numbers of petals that are sat, stood, or danced upon by small gods and goddesses. There are some of a more materialistic persuasion who get caught up in these details and try to make such descriptions into solid realities. His Holiness the Dalai Lama calls these "useful fictions," not necessarily to be taken literally. If we can relate to these chakras and channels as such, something of value does happen.

So in doing the following exercise, please relax. Try to imagine that these energies and their channels are as ephemeral as a rainbow. In the visualization for this particular exercise, the two side channels do not wrap around the main channel. The right channel should be viewed as a transparent RED tube, hollow and about as thick as your little finger. It is representative of the female energy (wisdom). It starts three finger-widths below the navel and moves deep within the body at a distance of one *tsun* (about half an inch) from the right side of the spine. It passes through the neck, over the brain but underneath the skull, drops down from the right side of the central fontanel, ending at the outside tip of the right nostril. The left channel is a transparent WHITE color, also hollow and of a similar thickness. It is representative of male energy (skillful means) and its path mirrors that of the RED channel but on the left side of the body.

Shushumna, the central (or spiritual) channel is visualized as a straight tube that is two little-finger-widths in diameter. It is often visualized as having a yellow tint, but in this exercise we see it as a transparent BLUE tube that starts four finger-widths below the navel and goes up through the body just in front of the spine. It goes through the neck and head to the central fontanel point, where it makes a tight downward turn to the area of the "Third Eye" (behind the center of the forehead) and hooks inward toward the pineal gland. It is understood as neither male nor female.

The exercise:

1. Begin the exercise by assuming a sitting position, either cross-legged on the floor or on a chair. You want to be comfortable, without your lungs or diaphragm feeling constricted in any way. If it feels comfortable and natural to sit cross-legged on the floor, sit so that you maintain the natural curve of your lower back. You may need to sit on a few cushions to achieve this. Generally, it is best for your behind to be somewhere between four to six inches off the ground, with your knees below the level of your navel. If you know other yogic or meditative sitting poses, feel free to choose one of those. If you need to sit on a chair, sit with your spine away from the back of the chair so that your chest can expand fully. Place your feet squarely and firmly on the ground, about shoulder width apart.

2. Visualize that the beginning of the WHITE channel or tube is slightly smaller and inserts into the beginning

of the RED channel, below the navel.

3. With your right thumb resting at the base of the right little finger, wrap all the fingers of your right hand around the thumb, with the exception of your index finger. Keep this finger extended. Block your right nostril with your right index finger and inhale through your left nostril. Imagine that the air you are breathing in through your left nostril is pure and fresh, and that this pure and fresh air is being drawn through the WHITE channel to where the WHITE channel is inserted into the RED channel, just below the navel.

4. At the point where you visualize the pure, fresh air reaching the opening of the RED channel, let go of the right nostril and, with your left hand in a similar arrangement as your right one, block the left nostril with your left index finger. As you exhale through the right nostril, visualize that the pure, fresh air that entered through the WHITE channel is pushing whatever is unclean, contaminated, and polluted out of the RED channel, like wind that blows away dust. As you breathe out, see especially that you are releasing the defilement, or poison, of **attachment** or clinging. Visualize these negativities as smoke leaving the right nostril.

5. Repeat this process two more times. After this, allow yourself to breathe through both nostrils and visualize the right, RED, channel as being luminous and purified of all negativities. Breathe in and out naturally three times, and as you do so visualize the right channel as radiant as a ruby.

6. Now repeat stages 1 through 4 for the cleansing of the WHITE channel. This time, visualize the end of the RED channel inserted into the end of the WHITE tube. Start by blocking the left nostril. As the fresh, pure air goes from the RED channel into the WHITE channel, you breathe out the impurities and the defilement of **aggression**. Do this three times and then breathe in and out normally three times, seeing the WHITE channel now as luminous and pure, like a diamond.

7. Now visualize shushumna, the central, spiritual channel. It is a BLUE tube the thickness of two little fingers. Visualize that the ends of both the WHITE and RED channels are inserted into the end of the BLUE channel. Once you have this in your mind's eye, place your hands in your lap. Allow the back of the right hand to rest in the palm of the upturned left hand. The thumbs then touch to form a triangle. With your hands in this configuration, raise them enough to place them around your navel so that it is in the center of the triangle.

8. Breathe in through both nostrils and visualize the pure, fresh air going up from the nostrils, through the RED and WHITE channels, and down to where they join the entrance to shushumna, the central BLUE channel.

9. As you exhale, feel this pure air moving up and cleansing the BLUE channel and with it the defilement of **ignorance**. You visualize that ignorance and all other impurities are pouring like smoke out of your forehead in the region of your Third Eye.

10. Repeat this two more times. Finally, lower your hands to

your lap and breathe normally three times, experiencing the central channel as luminously blue, supple, and purified. It is radiant like a deep blue sapphire.

Peacefulness Meditation

Peacefulness or "Calm Abiding" (Sanskrit *shamatha,* Tibetan *shinay)* Meditation is intended to encourage the development of a calm and clear mind. It is an excellent method for developing equanimity – toward others as well as ourselves. As agitation in our mind settles, a sense of wholesome aliveness arises naturally. And rather than feeling trapped in the predictable patterns of our ignorance, attachment, and aggression, there is a spaciousness that allows us to "think out of the box," as it were. New solutions and new possibilities emerge out of the "clear blue."

In Peacefulness Meditation, we focus on the breath. We do not do this as in the previous exercise, or as in the yogic *pranayama* practice, where we actively regulate the flow of our breath. Here, all we do is *observe* the natural rhythm of the breath, in and out. The exercise has six steps. As usual with any meditation or visualization practice, we begin with our sitting posture.

1. Sit in a comfortable manner, either cross-legged on the floor or in a chair, as described in the previous exercise (see page 94). Allow your hands to rest, palms down, on or just above your knees. Alternatively, you can place your thumbs at the base of your little fingers and wrap the other fingers over the thumbs. This is the sealing *mudra* (hand posture) of a Bodhisattva, or Buddha-to-be. It connects you more with your compassionate heart. If doing this mudra, rest your hands so that your knuckles

face up and your folded fingers are tucked and resting downward on your knees.

2. Allow your neck to relax with your chin slightly tucked in and your throat soft. The head should not be craned back or tilted forward. Wet your lips with your tongue and then rest your tongue on the palate, just behind your top teeth. If you are sitting on the floor, your eyes should have a slight downward gaze, resting approximately eighteen inches to two feet in front of you. If you are on a chair, aim your gaze between your knees, letting it go a bit further. In either case, it is generally considered best to have your eyes slightly open. This helps to keep you grounded, oriented in the space that you are in, and relaxed. If you find the room or space too distracting, then you may close your eyes. However, if what you get when you close your eyes is a great movie, it is best to keep your eyes partially open.

3. Take a deep breath in, draw up your pelvic muscles, tense your buttocks and abdomen, straighten your arms so that your palms or hands are pushing down on your knees, and lift your spine. Hold the tension for a moment; then slowly breathe out, and as you do so, let all the tension leave with the exhalation, giving you the sense of feeling more settled on your cushion or chair. Allow your diaphragm to become soft, your breath natural as it rises and sinks from deep within.

4. Now concentrate on the cycle of your breathing. Bring your attention to the natural breath as it passes in and out past the tip of your nostrils. Breathing in, feel the air passing in through the nostrils and moving down into

your abdomen to a point about three finger-widths (about one and a half inches) below your navel. As you breathe out, the abdomen contracts slightly as the air moves upward and passes out of the nostrils. Its invisible stream travels along the pathway of your gaze. As your eyes softly remain fixed on a given point, imagine that this stream dissolves about an inch above the ground.

5. To further this initial concentration, we count the cycle of the breath, especially focusing on the out-breath. As you inhale, be aware of the breath passing in through your nostrils, but pay particular attention as the out-breath leaves the nostrils. As the breath goes out, count to yourself "One." The next breath comes in, and as it passes out at the nostrils, you count "Two." Continue to count like this for twenty-one cycles of breath. There are two ways of counting: either count up to twenty-one, or count up to seven three times. In either case, if you find your mind drifting from the counting, start at one again until you complete the counting without distraction. This is easier than it sounds, so be patient with yourself. There are times when I have found myself spending a whole meditation session just getting through the counting!

6. Once you successfully complete the counting, allow your concentration to relax, focusing only on the passage of air as it leaves your nostrils and dissolves into space. If you get distracted by thoughts, just tell yourself, "Thinking," and then come back to the breath. It doesn't matter what you are thinking. What you are trying to do here is break your habit of being hooked on one thought after another. If the thought is truly important or some amazing inspiration, rest assured it will come back to you later on,

after your meditation session. For now, let it pass.

Begin your practice of this meditation slowly. Five or ten minutes to start with is a good beginning. Gradually increase the meditation to twenty minutes. When you have time, you can do it for longer. Some people will spend weekends or entire months meditating like this for hours a day. What matters most is consistency. A daily practice is best. If you can periodically get time to do it for longer, great.

Taking peacefulness one step further

The Peacefulness Meditation is a wonderful practice to do with a group of people. Like the principle of the "hundredth monkey," where the consciousness of a collective becomes synchronized, the turmoil within each person can be affected by the peacefulness generated by the group. At the same time, it can be an excellent meditation to create peacefulness between people who are in conflict or have communication difficulties. In this regard, it does not even matter whether the person you are having problems with is there or not. Just visualizing them in your presence, meditating with you, can yield a powerful, healing result. The person that you imagine sitting with you doesn't even need to be someone you know personally – it could be, let's say, a world leader toward whom you have difficulty feeling any compassion.

To make this visualization more powerful, Tantric tradition suggests imagining that if the person you want to be at peace with, or communicate with more effectively, is female, imagine that they are sitting beside you on your left. If they are male, imagine them on your right. The positioning of males and females has to do with the subtle energy theories and practices of Tantra. As we are each a blend of male and female energies, it is possible to utilize these energies for better results.

This can be a simple, unobtrusive way of breaking the ice or beginning the process or transforming our perceptions of others. See whether or not it helps when you actually do come face to face with them.

Tong Len Meditation: The Practice of Taking and Sending

Through observation, contemplation, and meditation, we come to the realization that nothing lives in isolation. We are inseparable from everyone and everything around us and this at-oneness is also quite intangible and ever changing. Furthermore, in our inter-connectedness, we see that we are always as much a part of the problem as we are part of the solution. So, even if we cannot solicit the participation of others in the resolving of tensions, conflicts, and problems, we can begin by working on ourselves and our relationship to others and to these difficulties. One practice that can be useful toward this end is *Tong Len*, or "Taking and Sending," Meditation.

In the context of our relationship to the world and our attempt to dissolve the imaginary boundaries created by the Three Poisons, which in turn lead to confusion-laden judgments and projections, Tong Len can be an effective meditation. It can be practiced on its own or with other meditations, and can even be done on the spot when we face a crisis. One of its foundational benefits is that it helps us to own and acknowledge our projections.

According to the great Indian Buddhist master, Atisha, the first person we need to do Taking and Sending for is ourselves. There are many levels of meaning in what he is saying. At the simplest level, we realize that all of our suffering arises from our own unmitigated Three Poisons; it is therefore useful for us to breathe in and *take back* from the world around us the thoughts, words, and actions that we have committed based on ignorance, attachment, and aggression. Breathing in with this thought in mind, we place in action an intention and commitment no longer to pollute our world and the people we love. As we breathe out, we send a breath of freshness, vibrancy, and good intentions out into the world.

As we come to own our projections and create more space for others, we become sensitive to their projections, the effects of the Three Poisons on them. We become more sensitive to why they are the way they are. As we breathe in, we then feel more compassion to take in and transform *their* pain and confusion and send waves of understanding and love out to *them*. If, in the context of a seemingly intractable situation, we breathe in whatever pain, confusion, or horror we see before us along with our own projections about the situation, we create a space within us that allows us to come to a problem afresh, less burdened by the weight of history.

What is offered below is a basic Tong Len meditation that can be done both formally, as when sitting in meditation, and informally, when dealing with difficult or painful circumstances on the spot.

1. If you are doing this as a formal meditation, begin by sitting and adjusting your posture and breathing in a similar fashion to how you worked with the Peacefulness Meditation. Come to the point where all you are doing is observing the passage of air at the tip of your nose.

2. Begin the Taking and Sending process with yourself. As you breathe in, put your intention and commitment into

absorbing all of your tendencies to project ignorance, attachment, and aggression out into the world. If you are stuck at this time with any particular negative emotion, breathe it in, knowing that this emotion colors and distorts your actions. The negativity that you breathe in goes to your heart, in which there rests a deep blue syllable, HUNG, pronounced hoong. You can visualize the letters H-U-N-G in the center of your heart, or just a deep BLUE light. This light is considered in Tantric tradition to be the nature of your mind. It is also a powerful healing color. Thus you are allowing the Three Poisons and their projections to be dissolved and healed in the deep blue light.

As you breathe out, imagine that pure, radiant love pours from your heart center, floods your entire being, then expands into and fills the space around you. Feel this radiant love as clear and WHITE, extending out as far as you can imagine.

3: Having done several breath cycles like this with yourself in mind, it is now time to bring your attention to others. Imagine that behind you are people in general, people you have no particular thought or emotion about one way or the other. Some teachers say that you should think of these people first, as you have few strong emotions or biases about them. For them, you start by focusing on their general pain and confusion. As you breathe in and out, repeat for them what you did for yourself. In your mind's eye, see their negativity come out of their bodies and minds and enter into that BLUE light in your heart where such negativity, the Three Poisons and their residues, are dissolved and healed. Imagine this negativity as being like black tar or smoke. As you breathe out, see the radiant clear WHITE light spread into their bodies and minds, filling them with clarity, joy, and love. You are forging a closer connection to them – to humanity and all beings in general – as a result.

4. Now, focus on those with whom you have a close or personal relationship. See these people on either side of you. As in the variation on the Peacefulness Meditation (see page 97), place the women on your left and the men on your right to make the meditation more energetically effective. Breathe in and out on behalf of these people in the same manner. Do this for several cycles of breath as well. Of course, you may even focus on a particular individual whom you are concerned about.

5. You are now ready to go to the next step of focusing your attention on people you have difficulty with. These can be those with whom you have a personal relationship, or a world leader, and so on. Imagine that they are sitting directly in front of you. Repeat the process for them as you did for all of the others in steps 3 and 4.

Take your time building up your strength and resolve to do this practice. Start with yourself. Gradually include others in a way that does not push you past a general sense of equanimity. There is not much value in finding yourself obsessing in the meditation about someone you love or someone you totally despise. Certainly, you want to work past these emotions to get to a place where you see a more workable relationship or situation. But it is more useful to acknowledge first where you are within yourself and build Tong Len slowly as an effective tool.

As mentioned earlier, besides being a formal meditation practice, Tong Len can be done on the spot in situations with others where there is pain or difficulty. In such circumstances, you can always breathe in and breathe out in accordance with this practice without others needing to know what you are doing. As you hold the intention of wanting to absorb rather than react to the pain, suffering, bad feelings, or confusion of the moment, this will have an effect on how you relate to the situation. In hostile situations, Tong Len can even dispel the tension or bring it to a resolution more quickly. In any event, you have stopped yourself, through your intention and breathing, from contributing to the problem. This can go a long way in moving relationships and situations forward.

Visualizing world peace

The bumper sticker with this slogan is found everywhere. Perhaps it is even translated into a variety of languages. The sentiment is obviously something many share. But is it possible to make this wish more potent? In this regard, Tong Len can be a useful practice. With respect to the visualization, you can imagine that you are out in space looking down on the planet. Alternatively, you can have the sense of sitting on the planet, feeling its presence underneath and all around you. Whatever way makes you feel most connected to the Earth is probably the best.

Imagine that as you breathe in, you are taking in all of the negativity, the harsh and negative forces that you feel contribute to the pain and suffering on the planet. Dissolve these in the HUNG syllable or BLUE light in your heart. As you breathe out, see WHITE light radiating out from you and enveloping the entire planet. See the power of goodness in this light changing people's attitudes, ending wars, ceasing pollution, or whatever you want to focus on. Expanding your vision to be so inclusive is very powerful and liberating in its own way. It can help to dispel hopelessness and give you a greater sense of connection, love, and compassion.

In this visualization, as with all the variants on Tong Len Meditation, remember that nothing is ever lost, and that the power of a well focused thought and intention is never wasted.

The cloak of light: A self-protection exercise

The deep blue light that is used in the Tong Len practice can also be used like a "cloaking" device; a way of not being noticed or detected when one does not wish to be. This was explained by Lama Ole Nydahl, who has found it useful while driving or in difficult or dangerous circumstances. It is not a Buddhist practice per se, but is in keeping with the energetic logic of these practices. All you need to do is to imagine that a layer of deep blue light surrounds your entire body in these situations. If you are traveling, you can even imagine that this light envelops your entire vehicle, plane, and so on. What this does is to make you seemingly less detectable by malevolent or other forces that may interfere with what you want to do. Like any energetic exercise, intent and concentration strengthen the affect. See how it works for you.

Helpful Mantras from the Tibetan Buddhist Tradition

The reciting of mantras is an important aspect of meditation in the advanced methods of the Tibetan Buddhist tradition. They are archetypal sounds, either single syllables or a combination of syllables, that help us to focus our energy and access our inner resources for specific purposes. For example, there are mantras that help us to access compassion, power, or protection, and others for developing deeper wisdom. They are connected with visualization meditations that are about seeing the world for what it is, based on a certain enlightened angle or viewpoint. Combined with a positive intention and the recitation of a mantra, these visualizations can dramatically enhance our personal transformation and our ability to access our inner resources to benefit others.

Intention, visualization, and mantra recitation are a powerful threesome when combined, but positive intention and the use of the sacred sounds of mantra on their own can be a potent means for mustering the compassion, power, wisdom or other quality you need to meet a given challenge. Lama Ole Nydahl cleverly describes mantras as syllables that "put a virus in our neuroses programs." While these syllables are often words or parts of words in Sanskrit or Tibetan, their actual meaning is of little consequence and it can even be an impediment to using them effectively as we might then focus on the meaning rather than the vibration. What is more important is their vibrational quality. Reciting mantras over and over again, we bypass our discursive mind, cutting through the mental obstacles to compassion, intelligence, power, protection, healing, or whatever quality the mantra aims to enhance. This allows that quality to shine forth more clearly in our being and action.

Before using the following mantras, which are all given in a simple phonetic transcription, begin by thinking about the quality you especially wish to access, then choose the mantra that helps you to access that quality and the energy within you directly. Include the altruistic wish that not only will *you* access and manifest that quality, but that each and every being will also access that quality. As you recite the mantra, feel as though the energy of the mantra is vibrating in all of your cells and imagine that its sound vibration reaches out and touches everyone around you in all directions in the same manner. This is an important step in becoming less self-centered and partisan, and more equanimous.

At a later stage you may wish to investigate the use of visualizations to enhance the power and energy of these mantras. If you do, I encourage you to seek out the advice of a qualified lama or meditation master. In the meantime, I have provided a bit of background regarding the mantras that you can use for visualization purposes. You can also find pictures of all these visualized aspects of enlightenment online and in many reference books on Tibetan Buddhism.

The Medicine Buddha mantra for dissolving the Three Poisons

TAY-YAH-TAH OM BEH-KAHN-DZEH BEH-KAHN-DZEH MA-HA BEH-KAHN-DZEH RAH-DZAH SAH-MOOD-GAH-TAY SO-HAH

Using the power of the Medicine Buddha mantra is excellent for uprooting and transforming the Three Poisons. It is for this reason specifically that it is included as the first of the mantras that is helpful to the conscious, engaged activist. Although the historical figure named Siddhartha Gautama is commonly know as *the* Buddha, the term Buddha ("Enlightened One") itself does not refer to any single individual. All the various Buddhist traditions claim that other Buddhas existed before Siddhartha, and that more will appear in the future. One of these earlier Buddhas is the Medicine Buddha, who according to Tibetan Buddhist tradition is the source of all healing. As a Buddha, he too awoke to the awareness of what caused us to suffer and what we need to overcome suffering. Specifically, he identified the Three Poisons and various means to cut through them. Although Medicine Buddha meditations are used by Tibetan healers and by those wishing to be healed of specific physical or mental illnesses, as we all suffer from the effects of the Three Poisons, it does not matter whether we are physically sick or not.

The mantra of Chenrezig for developing compassion

OM MAH-NEE PEH-MEH HOONG

The mantra of Chenrezig, *Om Mani Padme Hum* (given above in its usual Tibetan pronunciation) is probably the most famous of all Buddhist mantras. Carved on stone tablets found across Tibet, it is for generating and developing the qualities of compassion. Alongside the various Buddhas, the Buddhist traditions recognize many enlightened beings called *bodhisattvas*, "Buddhas-to-be" who work actively to help all beings to become enlightened. The bodhisattva of compassion is called Avalokiteshvara in Sanskrit and Chenrezig in Tibetan, and his name may be translated as "Loving Eyes." In the Chinese tradition, he became female, in the form of the goddess Guanyin. Loving Eyes is the functional aspect of the great Buddha Amitabha's discriminating wisdom in the world, manifesting as compassion in all of its forms.

The mantra of Green Tara for Accessing Fearlessness and Generosity

OM TAH-REH TOO-TAH-REH TOO-REH SO-HAH

According to legend, the female bodhisattva Tara was once an ordinary human being who was very devoted to spiritual practice. So impressive were her diligence and the results of her meditation that great masters told her that in the future, she would have good enough karma to be reborn as a man and thus have the best opportunity for reaching enlightenment. Hearing their words, she vowed that if she attained enlightenment, it would be in the form of a female, not a male. Tara's fearlessness to fly in the face of convention, and her dedication to giving to and helping others are the qualities one helps to access when reciting the mantra of Green Tara, a popular form of the bodhisattva. This is true whether one is a man or woman. Tara generously shares with all. Generosity is also, therefore, one of the qualities gained when accessing the energetic qualities of Green Tara.

The mantra of Guru Rinpoche: A mantra for our time

OM AH HOONG BEN-ZAH GURU PEH-MAH SID-DHEE HOONG

Padmasambhava was an Indian Buddhist Tantrika who came to Tibet in the eighth century and successfully introduced Vajrayana, or Tantric, Buddhism to Tibet. Others had tried before, but Padmasambhava had the wisdom and skill not only to speak clearly to the Tibetan people and their rulers, but also to subdue many of the adversarial forces that did not want him to succeed. So successful was he in his transmission of Buddhism to Tibet that he became known simply as *Guru Rinpoche* – Precious Teacher.

Guru Rinpoche was also renowned as an alchemist and wizard who had clairvoyant abilities and could see far into the future. It is said that he hid many teachings throughout Tibet that he knew would be useful to people of future times. Although many tried to find these hidden teachings, or *terma*, searching in caves, under rocks, and so on, only those who were destined to do so, and had the proper karmic connection to Guru Rinpoche, discovered them. One of these *terma* is the renowned *Tibetan Book of The Dead*.

It is said that Guru Rinpoche himself never died but simply disappeared, and his activity and power are still considered a potent force to this day. Sincere supplication to him, and using his mantra with the intention of benefiting others, are said to help clear away obstacles, eliminate disease, remove famine, and overcome unrest, to name a few. I have met Tibetan teachers who say that of all the mantras that are useful in a Dark Age, this is one of the most special.

"Be All That You Can Be..."

The purpose of sharing all of the meditations, meditative exercises, and mantras in this chapter is to give the conscious, engaged activist a daily focus or practice that will help to elicit the qualities he or she needs to meet the challenges of this Dark Age. These practices take the thoughtfulness and intention discussed in earlier chapters and give them greater focus, clarity, and power.

Depending on what you are called upon to do, you will, no doubt find that different qualities are demanded. The mindfulness of the Peacefulness Meditation and Tong Len are always indispensable. The mantra practices will help you to summon and access those qualities we all know that we possess, but have never had the tools to awaken. Regardless of whether you use the meditations as they are presented here or take them to deeper, more profound levels, in the end, the goal is the same – to awaken and make fully manifest that loving nature which we already embody in full measure.

Our resourcefulness is limitless. As we learn to access those resources in ourselves, we will also learn to evoke them in others. In this alone we shall begin the process of dissolving the causes for our Dark Age.

CHAPTER 7

The Power of Compassion

"If you plan revenge, dig two graves."

Old Welsh saying

Compassion is action informed by wisdom. When we understand what needs to be done, and choose the most appropriate means to carry it out, based on an altruistic intention to help others, our action *is*, in itself, compassion. It is a demonstration of *caring enough*. Compassion, therefore, is not neutral and *dis-passion*-ate, but rather *with-passion*-ate. It is intimate and involved. It is conscious and engaged. Compassion may seem an obvious quality to have in dealing with others and the world, but true compassion only comes about through all of the steps we have discussed so far. We need to understand the Four Thoughts that Revolutionize the Mind (see pages 41–51), the Four Noble Truths (see pages 53–60), and the altruism of the Four Limitless Meditations (see pages 69–80), and develop meditation and contemplation as a regular part of our lives. With these as a foundation, only then does compassion become truly integral – the basis on which we initiate any action.

Discriminating Wisdom

According to the Buddhist understanding, compassion is the active, functional aspect of what is called "Discriminating Wisdom." This means understanding situations for what they are. When we have trained our minds to understand the transitory, yet precious nature of every moment and cultivated the strong altruistic intention to step forward in our lives so that our world is made better along the way, compassionate action becomes both logical and inevitable. It is not an easy journey. For as we turn from the path of self-interest or prejudice, we walk into a minefield – or maybe we should say a *mind*-field – of progressive tests that arise from the resistance of our habitual minds, which are still ruled by the Three Poisons. We encounter deeper levels of avarice, covert intention, and tendencies of self-preservation. As these arise, the journey that started out so peacefully takes a wrathful turn as we face the tough psychological and emotional issues in our lives. The Tibetan doctor, monk, and clinical psychologist Dr. Lobsang Rapgay explained that this is why in the Tibetan Buddhist tradition new Dharma students are introduced to peaceful meditations and visualizations of such beatific deities as Chenrezig, or "Loving Eyes" (see page 108).

As progress is made and stability is developed, the teacher then begins to introduce the student to forms of compassion that have less appeal until – in the deepest, most profound dimensions of practice – the meditation student meets the "protectors": wrathful deities that represent the most difficult forms of compassion. These forms confront us to see if we really have the resolve to go farther, to really get the job done. In many respects, knowing how starry-eyed and idealistic we tend to be when embarking on something new, such as starting upon a quest or joining a group, be it a meditation or political action group, the Buddha was well aware that familiarity and time would eventually lead us to the "underbelly" of the situation. The more we get involved, the more we have to deal with the "dirt," so to speak. Rather than allowing us to lapse into cynicism, depression, and apathy, the Buddha engages us with teachings about the wrathful side of compassion. For if one cannot embrace and develop a compassionate attitude when facing the negative emotional states that every group or situation offers us over time, then bitterness and backbiting are inevitable.

This is an important lesson for the conscious, engaged activist: if you are really doing your job, if you are really creating something that is going to make a difference, you should expect confrontations and disagreements, both internal and external. Thus, while we may dismiss a saying such as "No guts, no glory" as bravado or macho nonsense, the Tibetan images of gore-spattered wrathful deities sporting garlands of human skulls while chomping on entrails with bloody fangs, are reminders of the truth that the path of compassionate engagement is not always a pleasant or comfortable one. A fellow Buddhist practitioner who was responsible for a military coup against a corrupt government and spent eighteen months of his life on death row, used to say that committing oneself to a route devoted to any significant change, be it at the personal or geopolitical level, is "not for tiny tots."

The four forms of compassion

In keeping with what arises as we develop along a spiritual path, there are four types of compassion that arise from discriminating wisdom. They are usually presented in the following naturally arising sequence: **pacifying** or peaceful compassion; **enriching** or empowering compassion; **magnetizing** or what could be described as seductive or charismatic compassion; and **wrathful** or destroying compassion.

This order is in keeping with a logical progression that is found in every action we initiate as humans. Initially, we hope that what we do will meet with no resistance, and can be accomplished peacefully. When this is all that a situation presents us, then our actions will be peaceful in nature. But more than likely, we will encounter some resistance and think of how we can win support for our cause. We attempt to convince those who are resisting us of our way of seeing. We attempt to overcome their hesitancy by trying to convince them that to join or support our efforts is in their interest as well. If such promises and guarantees do not *work,* we try to draw them to our side, through a charismatic display of some sort, something that is overwhelmingly impressive, or makes what we offer almost irresistible. If we still meet resistance, we may need to use stronger means to overcome it so we can get on with what we want to do. We render them powerless, irrelevant, brush them out of the way, or vanquish them in some way if necessary.

A similar progression occurs whether our intent is compassionate or malicious. How compassionate it is will reflect the degree to which we have transformed our actions with altruistic intent, skillful means, and wisdom. Such is the way of things between us in playgrounds, corporate boardrooms, halls of power, and on battlefields.

As I mentioned above, the four forms of compassion also reflect what happens to us internally on the spiritual path. Each stage of the sequence presents its own challenges as we move from a self-centered to an all-serving perspective. For an example of this sequence we can look to the Buddha's own progress to enlightenment. Each stage – as in most stories of great heroes in all world cultures – represented an initiation on his road to becoming, and manifesting for others, compassion in all of its dimensions

The Buddha's private war

The Buddha's spiritual development culminated in the final hours that he sat in meditation beneath a *bodhi* tree as his enlightenment fully manifested. At this point, the climax of a process which, according to Buddhist tradition, had taken many lifetimes, he faced his final tests. Siddhartha, the Buddha-to-be, was engaged in a private war; a final struggle against all of the inner and outer forces that keep us engaged, mesmerized, and locked into a matrix that thrives on predictable outcomes and shrinks in the face of true freedom. And, in his enlightenment story, what leads to war and how to be ultimately victorious is revealed.

Like each of us, Siddhartha started off confused and suffering. He was a wealthy prince, and did not suffer in a physical or material way, but he had no satisfaction in what he had, or in his experience of it. He sought for something else, and in his seeking he saw how distraction, and the craving that brought riches to some and disaster to others, needed to be dissolved. Being rich and privileged, he first thought that if he gave everything away and led a more simple life, this would bring him the peace of mind he was seeking. But, he soon learned that simplicity is a state of being that is determined by the mind, not by whether or not one lived in great material comfort or total austerity. So he sat quietly in simplicity, neither indulging nor starving his human senses; neither mentally engaging in the world around him nor retreating from it. Agitation and sloth were both overcome, and became a relaxed alertness. His attachments and fixations to things around him, even states of mind within him, began to loosen, and his mind became more and more aware of its vast potential. Siddhartha became wholly peaceful, and his peacefulness expressed itself in his ability to empower others to experience the same.

As his peacefulness deepened and his mind expanded into its natural, undistorted state, the illusions that he had been living under began to leave. But more subtle aspects of these illusions and other unseen illusions remained and came into Siddartha's awareness. Each of these illusions has a hook, a way of saying to us, "Do you really want to get rid of me? After all, haven't I served you well so far? I'll stay around if you really want me to." Images arose in Siddhartha's mind: images of wealth, power, and lustful delight. Why should he bother himself with overcoming what so many desire? Surely he, more than most, knew what was out there for him if he were only to give up on this silly quest. After all, he was a royal prince, a king-to-be, one who could possess many lands and riches, and plenty of opportunities to do whatever he wanted to with them.

But Siddhartha persisted against these disempowering thoughts and images. We can *never* know what really went through the Buddha's mind, but at this stage in the process of self-development, we can all fall prey to various ploys of disempowerment from voices within ourselves or from those around us. Such voices might tell us: "What you are doing is a waste of time and worthless. There is nothing virtuous in what you are doing. What's the point? You're missing out on so much!" Equally, pride and self-aggrandizement can arise: "Wow, I'm really great. I'm so serene. I'm the serenest of them all!" Such thoughts only keep you hooked to an egocentric, non-altruistic way of being. Alternatively, you can fall prey to the premature congratulations of others who want to identify with you. Whatever the Buddha thought or saw during his own process, he sat still. With peacefulness as a foundation and altruistic intention extended even to himself, he gave in neither to self-denigration nor to self-aggrandizement. He transformed both into the compassionate activity and state of being that could grace others with a sense of their own inner richness. And Siddhartha's enlightening deepened and his personal power grew.

As his power grew, what manifested in his mind was the discovery that anything he wanted he could have. He did not need to go out and seek what he wanted. Things would just come his way. It is said that on this part of the final spiritual journey, temptation arose, and Siddhartha saw before him beautiful, seductive women, offering him anything he could possibly want. He no longer needed to ask. He would just be given. All he needed to say was "yes" and allow himself to be indulged.

But with an eye steadfast on what he felt was his true destiny, Siddhartha continued to sit still. With his peacefulness and his enriching power growing, he cut through another web of self-deceit. His attraction to such physical desires withered, and with it the possibility of being seduced into reconsidering his choice. Transforming his in-built, animalistic desires and the power of seduction, Siddhartha was empowered with the charisma to divert others caught in the web of seduction with visions of freedom and the possibility of being able to relate to something far greater and of lasting beauty: their own awakening potential.

Yet Siddhartha's transformation was not complete. In the deepest recesses of his mind, the forces of attraction and seduction were replaced by one last challenge: fear. This test was not so much rooted in residual self-centeredness, as in self-preservation: the threat of not-being – of no longer being identified by all that is familiar. To shake us up, to "bring us to our senses," all that seemed beautiful becomes hideous and threatening, to entice us to recoil into the familiar, the predictable, the seemingly safe. In his mind, Siddhartha saw demon warriors hurling spears and shooting arrows, and vicious beasts set loose to attack and devour him – before it was too late.

But with his compassion toward himself and others growing indestructible, Siddhartha saw these fears, too, as just a phantasm of his own creation. Siddhartha still persisted in his commitment to awaken. With his inner foundation of peace and the powers to repel any forces – within or without – that distracted him from his task, he summoned his courage and mentally met his foe, disarmed him, and made him a powerful ally. As all vestiges of an ego rooted in selfish desire died away, Siddhartha absorbed these demons, harnessing them with a "wrathful compassion" that could protect others from harming themselves and, at the same time, scare them to action when he saw them to be braver than they saw themselves.

As the energy inherent in his enlightenment potential was no longer trapped and focused on preserving one fixed reality over another, what had been used for self-centered pleasures and self-preservation were now the limitless resources the Buddha had at his command. He had opened up to, and become, the conduit for endless possibilities in a universe focused on the wellbeing of all its inhabitants.

The four forms of compassion embody all the potential of what is powerful and good in what we do. The Buddha did not invent them or come up with them as some kind of doctrinal contrivance. What he accomplished was to develop the wisdom and skill to strip away the neurotic and habitual ways in which these positive qualities remain hidden in the progressive stages of our actions. In fact, our neurotic and habitual patterns that either covertly or overtly display our self-centered, unenlightened perspective, are veiled, confused manifestations of these four compassions, expressing themselves in our sloth or inaction, our agitation, our pride or self-denigration, our lust and manipulations, our destructiveness. If we awaken to the truth of this and work with methods to transform the Three Poisons, when we experience these tendencies within ourselves or witness them in others, we can call forth the power of the necessary compassionate action to change them into something more uplifting, more enlightening.

Compassion in Action: Taking Up the Challenge

If you are going to embark upon a path of change in the political or social sphere, you have to prepare yourself to fight the fight, no matter what comes your way. The resistance you face will be both internal and external. In the course of becoming an activist focused on any given issue, you will have to work through your own emotional labyrinth as well as contend with those forces outside you that will test your resolve. The Buddha said to love your enemies, not because they are loveable (at least from your perspective), but because they actually give you the opportunity, as mirrors of what is unresolved within you, to manifest higher, nobler qualities in your world. They may not be your friends, but they are your gift: they test your compassion. Just think of how the face of the social and political process would change if liberals showed compassionate consideration toward neo-cons, right-to-lifers did the same toward pro-choicers, and Muslims knelt down to pray beside Jews. What could open, honest, and caring dialogue do toward creating workable solutions, as opposed to intractable positions arising from brains and hearts unwilling to change?

Standing your ground

In the face of those who might want to distract you from your course, you will need to keep your focus and relax enough to be able to maintain a steady energy for the long haul. Expending too much energy in the beginning may lead to burn-out. By maintaining your equanimity, those around you will begin to see the shallowness of their own distractions and the agitation in their own hearts.

When those who represent the forces or causes you wish to see changed discover that you are not giving up, they may try at first to ignore you, playing down your significance. Can you stand being considered irrelevant? Try to see those who pit themselves against you not as adversaries, but as potential allies, and try to embrace them. If you retaliate defensively or otherwise go negative on them at this time in order to maintain your own sense of self-worth, they will note this weakness and exploit it later. Alternatively, they may want to inflate you so that you can trip yourself up. Here you need to remind yourself of what you are doing and for whose benefit you are working.

Seeing you are not swayed from your course, these forces may also try to co-opt your energy and efforts. In such cases, you may expect ploys of bribery and manipulation, and "offers you cannot refuse." If seductive offers cannot sway you and at the same time you show love for those who would see your downfall, expect to be further tested through the ploy of embarrassment and humiliation.

If building your pride and offers of power don't appeal, your opponents will seek to find weak points in your character. When they know what your weaknesses are, they may lay tempting morsels in your way. And any vague attention you give them will be turned into a scandal. Finding and exploiting "dirt" is an old political ploy as is fabricating dirt out of thin air. (I am reminded of a political campaign in Texas where a well known political figure in the White House planted bugging devices in his own office, claimed to have "discovered" them, and blamed his opponent. The ploy worked and destroyed his opponent's credibility.) In either case, whether one is snared by the lure, or the whole scenario you are confronted with is fabricated, you are tested to be honest about your own character. In a sense you have to be your own most loving friend *and* fiercest critic. In accepting these frailties in yourself, you build your own strength to resist. In admitting them or acknowledging them to others, much of their sting and potential for harm disappears, or at least becomes less relevant.

Embracing yourself entirely, warts and all, empowers those around you to examine their own shortcomings and points them in a direction within themselves where they, too, can let go of what sabotages their own growth. It also defuses their claims against you and, in turn, endears you to those who appreciate such honesty in the face of their own frailties. The spaciousness we create in embracing our own ambiguous natures invites others to embrace a vision of the world that is greater than they would have otherwise imagined.

If you are still standing after all of the attempts to seduce, disarm, or discredit you, your opponents may go to more extreme lengths to stop you bothering and challenging them. They may try to scare you, bring you to your knees, or even harm you. In the face of such action, you just stand your ground, because at this point you know that you are not turning back. You have the peacefulness, the power, and the charisma to withstand whatever is put in your way short of severe physical violence. You have become a formidable opponent that has turned the tables. You have no doubts, and are driven by truth to defend yourself and what you stand for.

Even if you must use force or destructive means to protect and advance a cause that benefits others, you do so not out of anger or hatred, but out of a profound love that understands that those who inflict harm on others also inflict it upon themselves as they entrench psychological and behavioral patterns arising from the Three Poisons. Because your actions are rooted in compassion, they are strategic and applied only to thwart what needs to be thwarted. With this intent and focus, "collateral damage" is kept to a minimum, sincerely regretted, addressed, and possibly willingly and publicly atoned for. As when a mother slaps away a child's hand as it reaches into a fire, the pain, fear, and upset caused is only temporary compared to the burns that could maim for life.

The inner challenge

I indicated earlier that problems and challenges arising from the outside are a reflection of our own lack of mental clarity, which in turn arises from our own fixations and aggressive attitudes and the full gamut of our own unresolved emotions. These aspects are what hinder us from using peace, empowerment, magnetizing, and wrathful compassion (see page 114) effectively. Therefore, if we want to become more effective against external challenges, we need to wake up to, and transform, the challenges within ourselves.

We may have some goal in mind, some change that we would like to see, but our mental confusion may lead us to be too attached to what we want. Consequently we may look for short cuts. Because we just want to cut to the happy ending, we may be lazy in our actions and oblivious to forces around us that really need to be addressed. Being fixated only on the goal, but not on doing what it takes to achieve the goal, we are easily prey to distractions, to being led on wild goose chases by others who perhaps actively do *not* want what we are seeking.

Before we know it we may have been led in some totally different direction and our goal may be as distant as ever, and perhaps even more difficult to reach.

If we go along this path without proper attention, because we feel that our cause is justified, we may get cocky. We may act, and believe ourselves to be, more powerful than we actually are. Afraid that self-criticism makes us appear weak, we may use bravado to win others over. We try to look bigger in the eyes of others. This merely invites others to discredit or ignore us. It also makes our opponents look more appealing if our own cause appears more power-seeking, self-righteous, and hollow.

Avoiding self-criticism and trying to prove to others that we are bigger than we actually are, we may take on more than we can handle. Drunk with our own sense of power – or in denial of our actual lack of power – we may overextend ourselves and drive ourselves toward bankruptcy of means and character. Our lust for survival arises and we make poor choices.

In the end, if our world fails to conform to our goal, we may abandon our ideals and lapse into self-denigration and depression, or in extreme cases resort to a violent and destructive attitude toward anything or anyone not supporting our illusion. In other words, we may well end up manifesting all of the traits and characteristics that we set out wanting to change. On the other hand, by training our minds to understand the logic and power behind altruism, we become less self-destructive and the same ego-building neurotic tendencies begin to be transformed more and more into a foundation of true compassion. When that happens:

You try to make the world around you more peaceful.

You try to encourage others in order to bring out
the best in them.

You try to offer those on the edge of disaster
something that can turn them in a better direction.

If all else fails, you try to take assertive action,
stopping them in their tracks or prompting them to
act differently, for their own good.

The degree to which these are well-informed and skillful
actions on your part will be revealed to you in time by what
occurs as a result. Once you have set out upon the path of
compassion, the world with all of its beauties and mishaps
becomes your ally in supporting and enlightening you as an
agent of change.

Wrathful Compassion – A Further Examination

The last form of compassion, wrath, is the trickiest. The reason
is that we often find it difficult to distinguish between a justifiable sense of outrage at unfairness or injustice, and confused
anger. There is usually so much heat and force behind both. In
the first case, we are being pushed to choose a course of action
that we would prefer not to engage in. All other options have
been exhausted or may seem to be ineffective in addressing
the severity of the situation. Maybe we have the luxury of time
to explain our case. Maybe we don't. In either case delay or
hesitancy may only make matters worse. In the second case,
confused anger, we have not paid enough attention and our
emotions brim over; we lash out, then with hindsight we try to
justify our words or actions to make ourselves feel better.

But even in the case of anger unskillfully unleashed, we
should not be too hard on ourselves. In fact, more than likely,

in such situations, we first try to keep calm and be reasonable (peaceful); try to find common ground or give the other party the benefit of the doubt (enriching); try to convince them to think or act differently, or appeal to something inside them to draw them toward our viewpoint (magnetizing). Note that here we are going through the logical process discussed earlier – a process which, at each step of the way, could have been more informed with skill and wisdom in order to create the compassion that would abate the fourth step, our wrathful response.

But regardless of our wisdom or skill, if none of these ploys works it is only after this process that we finally give up in frustration, snap, or lash out. This sequence can happen over a matter of moments, hours, months, or years. In the end, as Bön master Tenzin Wangyal Rinpoche says, our miscalculations and failure to find a less messy path lead us to conflict, and in extreme cases perhaps even to war.

However, such failures on our part should not necessarily be seen as a negative judgment on our actions and character up to this point. How we handle any difficult situation usually takes us to the limits of our wisdom and skill. We try our best, given our current level of skill and wisdom. And it just might be that it is better to do something, to act with the right intention, in the face of injustice, than to do nothing at all. **Feeling sorry for the suffering of others, but failing to intervene just because you do not think yourself skillful enough to act without anger, is just wimping out. It is not a sign of compassion.**

Rules of engagement

Until you are a long way down the road toward perfecting and applying the first three forms of compassion, the use of wrathful compassion will more than likely be problematic. To have the presence of mind to act with the purest intention, while deploying the fiercest forms of skillful action, demands that all vestiges of malice have been rooted out from within you. If this presence of mind is not firm within, the Dharma offers the following guidelines to those who see no choice but to use such means:

> First and foremost, you must understand that those toward whom you are deploying wrathful compassion are not *bad* but *misguided*. They are confused and intoxicated by their own Three Poisons.
>
> As such, they are deserving of compassion and you must try not to judge them or harbor feelings such as hatred toward them.
>
> In being minded to act wrathfully, you should feel a sense of reluctance to do so. This has nothing to do with hesitating, for you might not have this luxury.
>
> In your heart, there should be a remorseful quality that informs your action. This will prevent you from getting carried away in the energy of your destructive means and doing more damage than is necessary.
>
> In the end, you should not celebrate your victory, but rather show regret for actions that needed to be done.

Such an approach protects you from falling into the chasm of self-righteousness and rationalized justifications. For one thing, until you are enlightened, you really cannot tell if the person or cause you oppose *is* in error or more steeped in the Three Poisons than yourself. Thus, if you are truly trying to act with wrathful compassion, you hope for the best possible outcome, free from self-interest or partisanship. In that way, you can more easily accept and work with what befalls you as a result of your actions. For in the Dharma, there is no such thing as retaliation (see box). There is a desire to see justice, but not out of a sense of revenge or leveling the score. Aggression met with aggression just creates bad blood – and bad karma – on both sides. The Buddha would have agreed with the old Welsh saying at the beginning of this chapter.

Conclusion: Starting at Home

Before my son was a year old, many Tibetan teachers had gifted him small *phurbas*. A *phurba* is a Tibetan ritual dagger

---

In the face of external attacks, the Buddha did not recommend doing nothing, but warned against responding in kind, because this would keep us in a state of being rooted in the Three Poisons. These are a few things he said on the subject:

> *"Do not retaliate with anger when attacked with rage."*

> *"Do not retaliate with abuse when reviled."*

> *"Do not retaliate with criticism when blamed in public."*

> *"Do not retaliate with blows when threatened with physical violence."*[7]

[7] From Erik Pema Kunsang's *A Tibetan Buddhist Companion*. Shambhala Books, Boston, 2003, p.155.

---

used symbolically to "cut through" the Three Poisons. Fascinated by weapons as early as he could hold one, our son reveled in being able to hold one of his many daggers and as soon as he was old enough, he would run in the back yard, piercing the ground every so often. He told my wife that he was "taking care of demons."

Although I have never heard a story quite like ours, friends have told us similar tales of their own children, who have grown up either to be avid Nintendo game warriors or committed to martial arts. It seems that in an age of uncertainty, where war and terrorism are the daily bread of news that our children are fed with, some children are sensing a call to warriorhood in their lives. What seems paramount in these times, therefore, is that children are not only shown how warriors behave in conflict, they need also to understand how to be warriors of peace: warriors *in* peace, and *at* peace.

Toward this end, I feel that it is essential that children learn how to resolve conflict in a variety of ways. Within the home, parents often think that they should not allow their children to see them argue. They go behind closed doors, work things out and come out smiling. If a child does not see the process by which the conflict was resolved, but only sees two mad parents go into a room and two smiling parents come out, how can they possibly understand the process?

Pacifying, enriching, magnetizing, and wrathful compassion – each demonstrates a triumph over the Three Poisons. Each is inspiring. Each seems appropriate and just. What makes this so is that they come out of a conscious, engaged attitude toward the world. This is what parents, teachers, and leaders need to model more than anything else. For if children hear only hollow rhetoric from people from whom they feel disconnected, and see themselves as disfranchised, can we really expect them to show any conscience or impetus in wanting to shape their world for the better?

CHAPTER 8

"The Wheel of Sharp Weapons"

"It is an absurd assumption that religion and morality have no place in politics."

H.H. the 14th Dalai Lama [8]

Whether we have contemplated the Four Thoughts that Revolutionize the Mind; realized the implications of the Four Noble Truths; applied skillful methods at working with our minds; planted the seed of positive intention with the Four Limitless Meditations; and acted in the world skillfully applying one of the four forms of compassion; or are still caught in the turbulent sea of a confused habitual mind governed by the Three Poisons – or are somewhere in between – the world lets us know. Outer always reflects inner. If a bear stands in front of a mirror, it doesn't see a rabbit, even if it wants to. Whether we are prepared to see it or not, what is in the mirror is direct and accurate.

---

[8] From *The Little Book of Wisdom*. Rider, London and Sydney, 1998, p.153.

In the latter part of the tenth century, two notable books were written that address how to conduct our lives so that more and more positive qualities will naturally arise: one was Shantideva's *Bodhisattvacharyavatara*, or *The Bodhisattva's Way of Life*; the other Dharmarakshita's *The Wheel of Sharp Weapons*. A great work in the Mahayana Buddhist tradition by a great meditator and scholar, the latter is a verse text about behavior: what happens when we act in the world on the basis of our own misconceptions, greed, ambition, and other expressions of the Three Poisons; and how we can reset our way of thinking to commit to a path that is uplifting for all, including ourselves. Rather than taking the high, idealistic road of Shantideva, Dharmarakshita looks at where most of us find ourselves. Understanding with compassion that the suffering we are experiencing is something we would like to escape from, he offers antidotes to our dilemma. What I find most fascinating about its message is that the lessons it offers can be applied to individuals, groups, and even nations, depending on where we want to focus. As such, I consider it a vital text to ponder for anyone who wants to become a conscious, engaged activist.

Peacocks in the Poison Jungle

From the start, Dharmarakshita makes it clear that *not* to consider changing our motivation and action in the direction suggested is, to a greater or lesser degree, courting disaster. He explains this by using similes that distinguish the actions of bodhisattvas – those Buddhas-to-be among us who have committed themselves to a life and activity based on compassion and ending the suffering of others (see also page 112) – and the rest of us, who are more or less caught up in our own world of wants and desires. In the following extract, the world that most of us live in is considered like a jungle infested with poisonous plants that breed suffering and pain. Rather than blissfully living in the serene and healing places where there are medicinal plants that free one from suffering, the bodhisattvas chose to dwell in the jungle in order to help other beings. Here they work to transform whatever is poisonous into opportunities and situations for our awakening.

1.

"In the jungle of poisonous plants strut the peacocks,
Though medicine gardens of beauty lie near,
The masses of peacocks do not find gardens pleasant,
But thrive on the essence of poisonous plants.

2.

In similar fashion, the brave bodhisattvas
Remain in the jungle of worldly concern.
No matter how joyful this world's pleasure gardens,
These Brave Ones are never attracted to pleasures,
But thrive in the jungle of suffering and pain.

...

4.

Now, desire is the jungle of poisonous plants here.
Only Brave Ones, like peacocks, can thrive on such fare.
If cowardly beings, like crows, were to try it,
Because they are greedy they might lose their lives.

...

6.

And thus Bodhisattvas are likened to peacocks;
They live on delusions – those poisonous plants.
Transforming them into the essence of practice,
They thrive in the jungle of everyday life.
Whatever is presented they always accept,
While destroying the poison of clinging desire."[9]

One of the challenges we all face, as individuals, in collectives of societies, or as nations, is to look at our own behaviors and be able to identify clearly and admit to ourselves when we are acting for everyone's benefit or just for ourselves and our friends or allies. For along with our plans and actions often come rationalizations, which over time we may forget *are* just rationalizations, justifying what we have done. And the further we get from events, these rationalizations can become hardened or reified into doctrines with an internally consistent logic, or into religious beliefs perhaps supported by a divinity that we claim holds *us* dear and above all others.

But the true fruits of our actions are not that difficult to observe. In the Buddhist view, karma is infallible. The world we live in, and what befalls us individually and collectively, is the direct result of all our previous intentions, actions, and attitudes. If we live in a Dark Age, then as the Introduction spelled out, we have feathered our own nest to be that way (see page 1). If we do not transform our own Three Poisons, they

---

[9] Dharmarakshita, *The Wheel of Sharp Weapons*. Translated from the Tibetan by Geshe Ngawang Dhargyey, Sharpa Tulku, Khamlung Tulku, Alexander Berzin, and Jonathan Landaw. The Library of Tibetan Works and Archives, Dharamsala, India, 1981, pp.7–8.

will not only govern our emotions and actions from within, but they can also be used like weapons by others from without. In truth, the weapons that are used against us are made of our own hands, then given to those around us to deliver their blows. For example, if we habitually display aggression in order to get our way, why should we consider it odd or an affront to our sensibilities that resentment may one day, in turn, be expressed as aggression toward us?

Looking beyond our own personal conundrum, history is replete with leaders and nations who have thought of themselves as peacocks in the Western metaphorical sense, proud and superior to the fray, strutting through the world, seeing it as a garden whose treasures they have been manifestly destined to pluck, plunder, control, or destroy. But such would-be peacocks often pay a price in the frustration, anger, bitterness, and vengefulness felt by those who feel victimized by them. Sooner or later, the "treasures" they have gained from their behavior and treatment of others become like a poison. The victor either drowns in his own obsession or is swallowed up by the obsession of another who takes his place. Such was the fate of Romania's tyrannical leader, Ceausescu, who in 1989 was toppled and killed almost before anyone had time to think about it or reconsider. Such was the vehemence and overwhelming force of the pent-up resentment that he had provoked through his actions.

This cycle of events is, according to the teaching of the Dharma, inevitable in a world where ignorance, attachment, and aggression still inform the choices made by most people. As there are four variable aspects in any complete action – intention, thought, the manifestation of intention and thought in the action itself, and the resulting emotional response (see page 65) – what we do can have any number of possible outcomes. *The Wheel of Sharp Weapons* spells out more specifically what the logical outcomes are when the Three Poisons influence any of these variables.

The Wheel proves useful in enlightening us on many world issues and situations of our time, pointing directly to the logical, inevitable responses and consequences of how we are facing up to global problems, including one phenomenon that many Western governments are currently contending with: terrorism. The examples I will use relate to the current situation that the United States in particular finds itself in. I use these as examples because I am most familiar with them. I have no doubt that anyone looking at their own country and society will find similar examples. No country has a monopoly on the Three Poisons. To begin with, let us take another verse from *The Wheel*:

14.

"When we hear only language that is foul and
abusive,

This is the wheel of sharp weapons returning

Full circle upon us from wrongs we have done.

Till now we have said many things without thinking;

We have slandered and caused many friendships to
end.

Hereafter let's censure all thoughtless remarks."[10]

Consider the harsh words in foreign media and the street protests around the world in response to US foreign policy, especially with respect to the war in Iraq. We hear Americans expressing dismay and confusion when they hear and see such protests, and when foreign governments do not stand side by

[10] Ibid., p.9.

side with the American way of seeing the world. Less than a year after 9/11, with much of the goodwill toward the US which that atrocity had generated ebbing away as America pursued its new aggressive policy in Afghanistan and the Middle East, some Americans innocently asked: "Why do people hate us?" Newspapers ran articles and editorials examining this question. Children were shown on TV discussing this issue in their schools. But rather than engaging in considered debate, the Bush administration just tried to rationalize the issue away with the answer: "They are just jealous of our American way of life."

If we follow the wisdom of *The Wheel* and look at a broader picture that includes the perspective of those who are perceived to "hate us," we will come closer to a less simplistic, but more accurate, answer to the question of why the US has generated so much hostility around the world. To start with, there is a long-standing history of grassroots hostility in the Middle East, especially in the Muslim community, toward the US because of its foreign policy in the region. For years, the US government and the corporate interests that they support, and are supported by, have masterminded resource (especially oil) exploitation as well as actions to ensure the continuation and expansion of American influence in the region. US involvement has entailed years of covert interference in the affairs of sovereign Arab nations; the propping up of unde-mocratic or tyrannical regimes (including that of Saddam Hussein); and a refusal to do more than benignly pressure the Israelis for their policies toward the Palestinians, much to the dismay of the entire Muslim world.

Rationalizations, rhetoric, and the skewing of history have whitewashed and sanitized a bloody history – something that may blind those who benefit from cheap oil and petroleum-based products, but enrage those who have been suppressed and disadvantaged as a result. With such a history, it does not take a stretch of the imagination to foresee such hostility manifest as it did on September 11th, 2001. To make matters worse, there is the recent US invasion in Iraq and the lies, rhetoric, and denial that went into that decision. Consider the US administration's refusal to listen to UN weapons inspectors; its belittlement of those European leaders urging caution in the Middle East; its viewing as irrelevant the coop-eration of many of our most important allies of the last fifty years. The US has seriously strained relationships and alliances forged over generations.

At the same time, we should not ignore the fact that the war of words across the Atlantic has gone both ways. In recent years US administrations have sometimes been sharply critical of America's traditional friends, and the allegiances and alliances that have looked so seemingly stable in the decades after the end of World War II, particularly in Europe, have shifted over the years since America's inception. They have been rocked by scandal, and military and trade conflicts, and so on. Such incidences over time have also spawned – or reinforced – stereotypes that set people against each other at the most basic of levels; Yank, Limey, Mick, Spic, Frog, Kraut, Wop, Loud-Mouthed American – our bigotry, whose in, whose out… The Three Poisons make it impossible to think beyond self-interest and partisan alliances.

With such history to live with, and live down, the only remedy for developing international friendships that can be of lasting value into the future is to curb negative speech, to "censure all thoughtless remarks," be it at the personal or political level. *The Wheel* points to a truth that every diplomat probably knows: **It is important to be mindful of one's own tongue.** There is further discussion of what the Buddha called "right speech" in the following chapter (see page 152). For now, let us look at another verse of *The Wheel*.

13.

"When we lack any freedom, but must obey others,

This is the wheel of sharp weapons returning

Full circle upon us from wrongs we have done.

Till now we have looked down upon those who were lowly

And used them as servants for our own selfish needs;

Hereafter let's offer our services to others

With humble devotion of body and life."[11]

If we look at American history, we see the subjugation of individuals, races, or foreign groups as a part either of culture or official policy. Witch-hunts, slavery, the conscription of immigrants right off the boats, Chinese labor gangs, the internment of ethnic Japanese citizens. Of course, nations around the world have done similar things or worse. No doubt, if we were to examine what these cultures are going through today, we would see the laws of *The Wheel* applying in just the same way. But focusing on my own culture, when we in the US begin to see a growing bureaucratic stranglehold on our way of life with more repressive and restrictive laws and law enforcement agencies; ever more suspicion of citizens in general; growing invasion of privacy and loss of freedoms as so aptly demonstrated in the nebulously written Patriot Act – can we glibly point the finger and simply blame what Michael Moore calls an elite of "Stupid White Men?"

The domination of humans over other species, however undesirable, is a fact. Because of our craving to have what we

---

[11] Ibid., p.9.

want, whatever gets in our way has to be either used or removed. This Darwinian reality only speaks to the animal, instinctual side of our nature. Because of our ignorance, domination fueled by craving seems a better bet for getting what we want than cooperation. This view is shortsighted because if we place others below us on the food chain, the chances are that whenever our power weakens we, too, will become food for those of greater hunger.

Great philosophers have mused over "man's inhumanity to man." During the creation of the United States, no problem vexed the Founding Fathers more than the issue of slavery. Men of great vision, they saw that a democracy could not survive if the principle of equal rights was not treated as paramount and the importance of "life, liberty, and the pursuit of happiness" not acknowledged as the wish of all human beings, regardless of race, creed, or color. But they also saw the strength of habitual tendencies and feared that to try to break the culture of slavery in a newly formed, uncertain nation would meet such hostility that it would more than likely see the dissolution of the union before it had even begun to establish itself. Not only that, because the new country was in debt to Europe, it seemed only pragmatic to let the slave trade continue as a way of paying off the debt. So slavery was allowed to remain in those states where it already existed. It was a compromise.

Though it would seem that in not confronting the injustice of slavery the Founding Fathers left the US a mess that led to the Civil War and is still being worked out today politically and socially, the awareness of the injustice was there, together with the altruistic intention to overcome it, one day. This awareness was built into the US Constitution and is what keeps alive in people's mind the idea that America is "the land of the free." Embedded in the very fabric of the Constitution was the knowledge that such dilemmas were not just for lawmakers and leaders to decide upon, but for an informed and conscious electorate to participate in solving.

In reading about the lives of such men as Benjamin Franklin, Thomas Jefferson, George Washington, John Adams, and James Madison, what strikes me is that many of their qualities and ideals are in keeping with Dharmarakshita's antidote to the dilemma set up in the above verse. These men had a strong sense of serving others in the cause of freedom. Several of them exhibited a humility that allowed them to identify with the people they served. Each of them knew that they were seen by their people as special, but wanted to avoid seeing the establishment of an American aristocracy to replace the British one they had just gotten rid of.

Raising Consciousness

The world shows us what we are up to. Dharmarakshita is not inventing what isn't there anyway. The value of his verses is that they sober us up, make us aware what we have been doing. Drunk from intoxication by the Three Poisons, it's useful to be pulled over and given a breathalyzer. In "sobering up," learning to cut loose from our "evil ways," it only stands to reason that we would have to go through an emotional and behavioral "hangover" and the painful memory of what it was we did in our drunken stupor. It is important to remember, reflect upon, and understand what we have done and what resulted – and how to not go there again. Dharmarakshita demonstrates his compassion for us in *The Wheel*.

Although our modern civilization appears to be a good distance from being enlightened, it seems to me that as more people become literate and information is more widely available, the wisdom inherent in our enlightenment potential *is* being awakened. In the not-too-distant past, we may not have known what one Tibetan monk friend said to me was the "evil that men in suits do behind closed doors." This is true everywhere, be it Washington D.C., London, Paris, Delhi, Moscow, or Beijing. We are less automatically deferential to our leaders and we do know, or suspect, more of what goes on. And because we now have a multitude of instant-access media sources, word does get out, censorship or no censorship. "The truth will out" and nowadays the consequences of unbridled ignorance, attachment, and aggression are plainer to see.

Even if we do not know how to get ourselves out of the messes we find ourselves in, and although so much of what we witness becomes sensationalized and exaggerated through the tabloid media filter, a consciousness raising *is* taking place. This has two thrusts. One is where people try to turn away from the suffering. And so through such distractions as drugs and simplistic belief systems we seek to dull the impact of the fear, anxiety, depression, and despair that we feel at the constant bombardment of suffering witnessed night after night on the evening news. In this approach, the lengths we are prepared to go in active denial, betrays the awareness, somewhere inside us, of what is *really* going on.

For those who choose the alternative path, and can use the energy that is manifest in the fear, anxiety, depression, and despair to rise above them and challenge them, one of the first tasks is to have compassion for and work skillfully with those who are in denial. **Denial and defensiveness are defenseless in the face of love**

Monitoring ourselves

Lawlessness, corruption, terrorism, and warfare will not go away by making them illegal or seeking to destroy them by equally insidious means. Violence begets violence. *The Wheel of Sharp Weapons* would attest to this, and even schoolchildren know it as a playground truth. Thomas Jefferson once made the comment that governments become corrupt when people are corrupt. In one form or another, each of us is responsible for what we are witnessing around us. How could it be any other way? And, if we understand this, we must also accept the truth that we *are* our brothers' – and sisters' – keepers. We are intimately associated with *all* life. If we see corruption in those around us, we have a relationship to it for which we must take responsibility. That responsibility begins with an honest examination of ourselves. It is a futile and wasted effort if we solely busy ourselves with trying to monitor the attitudes and behaviors of others. We may effect some apparent change in this way, but may also create a lot of resentment in the process and it may be that when we are not looking, things will revert to what they were before. Using a political example, consider what happened after the ending of communism in Romania and Yugoslavia, when various clans or cultural groups resumed old hostilities and vendettas that had merely been ignored and suppressed for decades by the communist regime that had claimed all its citizens were equals.

In the end what other people do is their own responsibility, even if we may endeavor to assist them. Similarly, it is of primary importance for us to monitor our own attitudes and behaviors, employing with the highest standards of scrutiny to which we can hold ourselves. In this way, if we are successful, we will rid ourselves of corruption and create a backbone of integrity.

Because we all share the reality of this Dark Age, each of us has a connection to its cause, its continuation, and possibly its diminishing. What we are experiencing in these troubled times is a culmination of both positive and negative causes, and therefore most of us in affluent societies need to accept that we are the beneficiaries of blood money; that each of us has blood on our hands. Many of the appliances and conveniences we enjoy come to us as the result of the pillaging and depletion of the world's natural resources and the sweatshop labor of the less fortunate. Perhaps our good karma has allowed us to enjoy a comfortable life. But being born into a position of material privilege where what we enjoy comes to us through the blood, sweat, and tears of others, we have an obligation to understand, minimize, and possibly even transform whatever has come to us from corrupted intentions and actions.

This is hard work and goes a long way toward explaining why individuals, groups, even nations go through purification, a cleansing as it were, in the process of turning harmful or aggressive tendencies into positive benefits for all to share. Buddhist history is replete with stories of corrupt individuals whose fortunes were ill gotten, but were eventually put to good use. Still, the karmic "wheel of sharp weapons" came down hard upon them and they could not escape the karma of mishaps, crises, and problems in their lives as a result of their nefarious ways. But, in the end, they triumphed in helping others.

Such was the life of the great Tibetan saint Milarepa, who, misguided by his naïve love for and obedience to his embittered mother, committed mass murder, and had to work through the karma of that before becoming a great spiritual master. Then there was the powerful Indian emperor Ashoka, who took up Buddhism and became one of India's greatest and most benevolent rulers after he had begun to question what he was doing as a leader and had been further shocked into conscious awareness and compassion after witnessing the carnage that his own armies had inflicted.

Anyone looking at noted people of wealth and influence

anywhere in the world could find similar, more mundane stories. In that regard, I am reminded of an influential southern US family whose fortune was gained through prostitution and bootlegging. Today they are great contributors to many worthy humanitarian causes. And yet many in the family suffer health problems and difficulties arise in many of their undertakings. Sheer luck of the draw? Mere coincidence? Or "the wheel of sharp weapons returning full circle?"

For the most part this chapter has explored geopolitical examples of the presence of the Three Poisons and what they can be seen to have laid at our door. But before we act too cockily about what should be changed in the world, who should lead this or that nation, we need to see *ourselves* as both part of the problem and as a possible conduit for a solution. Before we step outside our door, we have to begin with ourselves and our own responsibility for those situations in the world where we are – in truth – *never* only a spectator. To become as bold as bodhisattvas in the jungle of poisonous plants, we are called upon to uproot and transform the poisons within, so that whatever we do in the world, our intentions, thoughts, acts, and emotions will successfully digest and transform the poisons of ignorance, attachment, and aggression that we see manifest as sickness, poverty, and warfare in the world around us and convey a brighter vision of what is possible.

CHAPTER 9

The Conscious, Engaged Activist

"The purpose of our life is not simply to be healthy, live a long life, become wealthy, get educated, or win many friends. None of these is the ultimate goal of life. Whether we are healthy or unhealthy, rich or poor, educated or uneducated, our ultimate goal is to benefit other living beings. The purpose of being alive, of continuing our present association of body and mind, is to benefit others, to use our body, speech, and mind to bring happiness to others. All our past, present, and future happiness is received through the kindness of other living beings, and our self-cherishing is the source of all our problems."

Lama Zopa[12]

So far we have discussed general considerations, as well as particular contemplations and meditations, which we need to be aware of and work with – to the best of our ability – in order to be a conscious, engaged activist. They apply at any time, but especially in the seeming morass of the Dark Age that we live in. That being said, it is now time to flesh out our image of a conscious, engaged activist. How would they look? What would they do? How would they act?

The face and activity of the conscious, engaged activist will be different for the circumstances that they find themselves in. It's easy for someone of my age to think of the term "activist" in the context of the 1960s and Vietnam. Young men and women with long, unkempt hair, radicalized and marching. Or more modern images of serious, concerned citizens focusing on issues, getting petitions signed, emailing members of Congress. But the image and notion of a conscious, engaged activist I wish to portray here goes beyond these images, beyond left and right, beyond any sense of partisanship whatsoever.

A conscious, engaged activist interjects wisdom and skillful means into whatever field of action or endeavor they are a part of. Briefly, Buddhist tradition teaches that there is a female and male aspect to enlightenment (a bit like *yin* and *yang*, but in Tibetan referred to as *yab* and *yum*). Wisdom (*yum*, literally translated as mother) is considered the female aspect of the enlightening process that tempers our awareness with heart and directness. "Skillful means" (*yab*, literally translated as father) is the male aspect that provides us with the precision and power to act. These two aspects are necessary for any venture to be successful. If one is lacking, then problems

---

[12] Lama Zopa, *Ultimate Healing: The Power of Compassion.* Wisdom Publications, 2001, p.27.

naturally arise. If there is no skillful means and only wisdom, then there is waffling and ineffectual action. If there is skillful means and no wisdom, situations become restrictive and tend towards fascism. But when they exist together in balanced measure they produce the intelligence, conscience, and compassion to do whatever it takes to make life better and meaningful for others, beyond partisanship.

Even though we may commit to embracing the various tools and considerations that I have spelled out in this volume, more than likely we shall find ourselves drawn to various fields of action based on our own karmic inclinations, or on preferences derived (in the Buddhist view) from many lifetimes of experiences. These strengths and weaknesses are reinforced in our current lifetime by the circumstances that we find ourselves in. So for some, being the consciously, engaged activist may mean working to bring the troops home from a war we deem unjust. On the other side of the equation may be a dedicated infantryman in a war-torn region of the world whose sole intent is to manifest patience and compassion for citizens caught in the crossfire. One person may work in a social action group and choose to be out in the streets to protest unfair trade practices. Another may be a policeman dedicated to maintaining peace and order in an economically deprived inner city neighborhood. The conscious, engaged activist could be a grandmother, emailing her friends with MoveOn updates or someone sitting quietly in a retreat somewhere, generating thoughts of love and compassion. The change that is sought by one activist may be a material change of circumstances. For another, it may be a change of conscience and consciousness.

Such activists can find themselves labeled as social misfits, anarchists, fascists, revolutionaries, terrorists, saints, freedom fighters, upholders of justice, even righteous avengers. What must be understood is that if we enter and act in any given situation on the basis of the principles we have set out thus far, it does not matter what the circumstance is. The conscious, engaged activist will make that situation better by bringing into it more wisdom, skill, and compassion, thus creating the context for the emergence of something more lasting and beneficial for all.

Because we breathe in and out, because we get up in the morning, go about our business in the day, and go to sleep at night, we are active and, to a greater or lesser extent, conscious and engaged. We bring to any and all situations we encounter whatever level of understanding we have, and then engage in that situation with varying degrees of enthusiasm or reluctance. Objectively speaking, we are never *not* acting in our world. There is no such thing as doing *nothing* about a situation. We are always doing *something* – and that something extends far beyond what we may think we are doing. In the matrix of our connection to each and every being, we continually affect our world in every dimension, whether consciously or unconsciously. The more we commit ourselves to becoming conscious and awake, the more we will understand this. In turn, our knowledge puts us in touch with our own role and responsibility in the grand scheme of things. This may seem a terrible burden and lead us the point of feeling paralyzed. So what should we do?

Equally, as we grow spiritually and become more conscious in our lives, the more we begin to notice those areas of our lives where we are *not* conscious. As a group of jazz musicians in Woodstock, New York, once sang, "The confusion is endless."[13] This predicament is depicted in the Buddhist story of the life of Loving Eyes (Avalokiteshvara or Chenrezig), the

[13] Lyrics from a song by Karl Berger and Friends.

bodhisattva of compassion (see page 108). His vow was to save all sentient beings from suffering, and at one point he actually thought he had accomplished this amazing feat. He soon learned that he was wrong, and in his sadness, he exploded into thousands of little pieces. Other enlightened beings, seeing how vast his compassion was, decided to put him back together again, this time with eleven heads and a thousand arms so that he could resume his work, but with greater capacities. Each head and set of arms was devoted to one of the Four Forms of Compassion (see page 114). Thus the bodhisattva's activity became limitless, to match the limitless number of sentient beings he was now prepared to save.

As the story of Chenrezig is intended to imply, we have the capacity always to expand what we do. It is just that as we awaken our loving nature and express compassion through our actions, we grow more keenly aware of how much more there is to do. One of the challenges in this situation is how to maintain balance. How do we respond to the tests of our strength? How do we learn not to overextend, yet at the same time to grow even stronger?

The shortcomings we face and the unintended disasters that befall us along the way are the result of us still being partisan: not having the wisdom or skill to work in a balanced and intelligent way with our energies. Not being able to comprehend, let alone access, the amazing potentiality we possess, our focus remains narrow and we become zealous or fixated in one direction and dimension of our life at the expense of others. Only knowing limited ways of using our energies, we pour them into a limited range of tasks. There have been great geniuses and eccentrics in the course of history who have done amazing feats that have helped advance civilization and culture. But it is also true that they often had areas of their lives that were not well attended to. And, as a result, their legacies may be mixed and the results of even their greatest efforts may be skewed or used in unintended, even undesirable ways. This may have to do with the actual thing one creates, as in the case of Alfred Nobel, who invented dynamite to make mining easier, but didn't consider that it would – almost at once – be used for bombs and shells. Or, it could be someone like President Bill Clinton, who could not foresee how his effectiveness, and the fruits of his efforts domestically and internationally, would be tarnished and diminished because of his wayward personal lifestyle and habits.

To my mind, there have always been countless "unsung heroes" whose lives may not have been so exciting, but gave something of lasting value to others. Rarely do we hear of ordinary citizens who act in a conscious, engaged way in all spheres of their lives. We seem to be more intrigued by the heroes and icons of creativity, power, and spiritual attainment who may suffer in certain parts of their lives but rise to fame and universal attention in another sphere. However, the Buddhist story of Vimilakirti gives us an example of a man who was at the same time a husband, father, businessman, statesman, and spiritual teacher. We shall look more closely at his activity and legacy towards the end of the book. Suffice to say at this point, in learning methods to cut through and transform the Three Poisons, Vimilakirti's mind was open and receptive to all that he encountered. No aspect of his worldly life – such as the care for his children, his wife, his business – was considered an obstacle to some noble cause. He embraced all and saw obstacles as opportunity, rising to each situation. His wisdom and skill to act with intelligent compassion endeared him to all around him.

What is important in Vimilakirti's example is that it was in his training to awaken his enlightened potential that he developed the capacity to handle every facet of his life more effectively. He personified the Buddha's Eightfold Path, which was introduced briefly in an earlier chapter (see page 59). It made him a better, more effective person in every dimension of his life.

Doing Our Best: The Eightfold Path

"The Noble Truth of the path leading to the cessation of suffering: it is simply the Noble Eightfold Path, namely right view, right thought, right speech, right action, right livelihood, right effort, right mindfulness, right concentration." As summarized by the Buddha in the last of the Four Noble Truths, the goal of the Eightfold Path is to create a well-rounded, awakened individual, free of the grips of the Three Poisons, and hence effective at every level of his or her being and action. The eight aspects of this path engage our spirit through cultivating the wisdom of right view and thought/intention; our bodies through the cultivation of ethical conduct in speech, action, and livelihood; and our mental/emotional development through the cultivation of focused effort, mindfulness, and concentration. When we take into consideration what the Buddha suggests in each of these aspects, we become dignified, upright, and certain about how we conduct our lives and where we need to place our energies.

Of course, at this point, it is logical to think to yourself, "OK, so what do I need to do? What is the best profession or calling for me to be an effective change-maker?" or "If I get into such and such a situation, what is the best thing to say or do?" In all the vast number of books available for self-help and improvement, wouldn't it be a relief to find one that gave you the simple answers to these questions?

But, the Eightfold Path is not about convenience. The Eightfold Path does not necessarily focus on what you *should* do. Much of that has to do with the particular situation you find yourself in. For certain, in the category of "Right Livelihood," there are some professions or career tracks that are more problematic and necessitate more skill than many can muster. Beyond these, however, the Eightfold Path is pretty wide open. The Buddhist teachings on each aspect of the Path have less to say about exactly how you *should* be and act than about how *not* to be and act. The reason for this is simple: If you begin to live your life with the considerations we have outlined thus far, your speech and actions will clear themselves up. You will awaken more and more wisdom and skillfulness in your actions and, increasingly, you will know what to do in each situation as it arises. At the same time, as imperfect beings, we shall periodically lapse into our old negative patterns of speech, thought, and action based on our unresolved, nontransformed emotions – residues of our Three Poisons. Thus, the Buddha spends a little more time providing us with a thorough understanding of these negative emotions and their resultant actions, so we can be more aware of the usefulness of avoiding or minimizing them.

Much of the discussion up to now has focused on the spiritual and mental/emotional components of the Eightfold Path. Let us now focus more closely on the ethical components: right speech, action, and livelihood. We shall begin with right speech – how to communicate with integrity and clarity.

Right Speech: Communication

The Bible says: "In the beginning was the Word." God first manifested in the unformed cosmos as an act of communication. The divine Word was the very agent of creation, the means by which everything in the universe came into being. It was also the means by which God related to Creation. Likewise, we shape our own personal universe, and ultimately the wider world beyond, through how we communicate.

It used to be said that a person was known by their word. Their word was a sacred bond and meant something, because it carried the intentions and the vibratory qualities of its speaker to the listener. In this light, effectiveness in speech, or any other form of communication, goes far beyond words and their specific meanings. That is why corporations, politicians, and organizations hire speechwriters, public relations professionals, or spin doctors who are paid to charge the words to create as positive, and memorable an impact as possible. A person's sincerity, intent, and "vibe" can make words powerful. As words, whether spoken or written, are commonly what set actions in motion, we need to be clear and speak from the heart if we stand any chance of getting the most out of what we say. If we want our words to be valued, the Buddha makes the Four Recommendations for Right Speech, as follows:

> **Do not lie or deliberately deceive others;**
> **Do not slander or speak maliciously of others;**
> **Do not use harsh or hurtful words;**
> **Do not gossip.**

In the next few pages we shall deal with each of these recommendations in turn.

Do not lie or deliberately deceive others
This is actually harder than it seems. With respect to lying, due to our Three Poisons, more than likely our ignorance will ensure that what we say is not entirely accurate. As beings in a

relative world filtering everything we look at through our subjectivity, we can skew just about anything; data is never objective, facts are never objective facts. Because of our subjectivity, what we communicate is immediately and always open to a vast array of interpretations. That is why the legal oath "to tell the truth, the whole truth, and nothing but the truth," is an impossibility in a reactive, litigious society such as currently exists in the US, and leads to the legal hairsplitting that gets criminals acquitted and innocents condemned. This is probably why Tibetan masters generally encourage people to stay away from the legal profession and litigation if at all possible. They believe that the law of karma will usually take care of people's misdemeanors better than we can.

Considering the number of frivolous or unnecessary lawsuits and the booming "compensation culture" that we are famous for in the West (especially in the US), and how we have all seen certain cases blown up into hysterical media circuses that preclude sober common sense reflection, the advice of the Tibetan masters seems warranted. The same masters will also tell you that two careers worth not pursuing are acting and politics. They consider both careers to be focused on creating illusions in the minds of others. And as for lawyers and actors becoming politicians...

Because we are social animals and communication is vital to our survival and the quality of our lives, the intention behind our words can be of far greater importance than the truth or accuracy of the words themselves. The Buddha was once asked about the matter of lying and told the following story as an example. A man is walking home from the marketplace and sees a fire in the distance. As he gets closer to the smoke, he sees that the fire is in his own home. He looks up at the second story window and sees his children playing, unaware of the danger that is engulfing them. Wanting to get them out of the house quickly, but without alarming them into a state of panic, he calls: "Children, come downstairs. I have brought each of you a beautiful present from the market!" Excitedly, the children run down the stairs to find what their father has brought them and as they reach his side, the house crashes to the ground in ruins.

At one level this father blatantly lies to his children. He has no gifts from the market and he is fully aware that he is deceiving his children, who are expecting toys or sweets or something similar. On another level, he *is* giving them a far greater gift – their lives – but understands that they are too young to grasp the magnitude of this. But in the few moments he has before the house's imminent collapse, an act of deceit is the only means by which the father can fulfill the more important task of preventing his children from suffering terror, pain, and certain death. In this case, the harm that comes from lying – his children's disappointment – is overwhelmingly outweighed.

The issue in lying and right speech, therefore, has more to do with the *intent* behind the deceit. We should try being honest about our intent, but there are times, as in the last story, when that might not be appropriate.

On this subject of honesty, we should remember that **it is easier to be honest than it is to be truthful.** We can be more frank about our thinking process, our biases, perhaps the emotions that are fueling our reasoning; the more honest we can be about what our assumptions are, about what lies behind our words, the more we show our openness and invite openness from others. And in that spirit of openness, we come closer and closer to what is true.

In the context of this thought, I will take a brief look at post-9/11 America and the use of speech by the current US administration. On the one hand, US citizens have been encouraged to relax and go about their business, travel, go to the malls, and so on. But alongside these reassurances there are periodic orange alerts, warnings about travel, bomb threats to malls, and so on. With such a schizophrenic message, what can the administration think is a reasonable response on the part of the people? And, more to the point, I look at the timing of such warnings and ponder what the intent really is.

The great British psychoanalyst R.D. Laing once said that if the average person knew what was really going on with respect to the forces operating behind the scenes in foreign relations, most of us would commit suicide. Similarly, governments have *always* lied to their citizens. At times, when war was wanted, fear was woven into the dialogue. When peace was wanted, platitudes and reassurances put the citizens back to sleep. As Goering well knew (see page 17), this has been one aspect of how leaders manipulate their nations since the beginning.

I think that a digression at this point to look at the events in the times that I am writing will highlight the Buddha's concerns and guidelines.

With regard to the War on Terror, it is interesting to learn that in the prosperous 1990s, President Bill Clinton was carrying on a covert war against the likes of Osama Bin Laden. Periodically, such news made its way to the forefront, but most of the time it was played down. And the country had a more positive, upbeat feel to it. Other than the "millennium bug" scare, the twenty-first century was generally anticipated with optimism.

But since 9/11/01, under the Bush administration, this covert war has gone public. Of course circumstances are different in that terrorism finally and officially made it to American shores. It would logically be more in the forefront of our minds and concerns. However, I cannot but feel that this fact is being used as a weapon against US citizens; a weapon to manipulate forces and funds to benefit some more than others, and to secure those benefits for years to come. The "Downing Street Memos," the "Plame Affair"(the outing of a covert CIA operative to get back at her ambassador husband, who had published the simple truth that there were not uranium deals happening between Niger and Iraq) – these and other controversies let most who wish to see such things know the transparent truth, that the war in Iraq was fabricated. And when no-bid business contracts with ties to the US administration were in place without there being an "exit strategy" following the "liberating" of Iraq, it is not a matter of rocket science to deduce that a small number of powerbrokers and their friends played the American public and the "coalition of the willing" like a well-tuned fiddle. I have gone to political meetings where people have wanted the US government to announce when they will leave Iraq. My answer to them is simple: The US will pull out when the contracts with these private companies come to an end. In the meantime, the soldiers that are there act as mercenaries for private moneyed interests.

In the pre-9/11 American press, an attention to politicians' words seemed to be matched by an observation of their body language. Body language communicates how clearly and honestly we are behind the words we utter. Post-9/11, the media seem to have suspended commentary on this and focused on words alone. Speeches by the administration have been "good" if the "right" words are being used and provide some choice, newsworthy "sound bites." Even though the furtive glances, grimacing lips, and defensive postures might be telling a different story, few in the media have been willing to comment on body language. As in the story of "The Emperor's New Clothes," those wanting to believe the bullish, upbeat words of the Bush administration, have continued to take their claims about the threat of terrorism and America's success in fighting it, at face value. Sharp observation or criticism from astute political analysts willing to separate fact from rhetoric has been sorely lacking. Of course, in a highly charged political atmosphere, one may think that the reason few people stand up and ask questions is that they fear being deemed "unpatriotic." This may make some people cower, but for the most part, the reason for the absence of serious critical analysis in the American media is simple: Along with building a monopoly over energy sources and large world commodity interests, the same small group has invested its money in the media. What Americans have come to hear more and more on the "news" is less news and more spin.

State-run or monitored media outlets are nothing new in most countries of the world. Friends from Eastern Europe told me that one thing that seemed to distinguish Americans from themselves was that Americans tended to believe what they heard or saw in the news. A free press was the hallmark of a young America. Over time, this has been eroded to the current sad state of affairs that many in the US lament. Still, this doesn't stop the administration's apologists defending what a small but growing group has become more and more suspicious and concerned about.

But with the passage of time, deceit always begins to wear thin and the strings holding the marionettes become plain for all to see. In the end, the results of this deceit may actually prove beneficial and bring us back to a Jeffersonian-like suspicion of government. In the end, it may mature the American citizenry and hone their discriminating awareness by making them more conscious, more observant, and less likely to be seduced. Like the citizens of our western European allies, who have witnessed the folly and devious machinations of their governments for centuries, Americans may become more conscious, critical, and engaged in the political process. As this happens, the issues that bind cultures and economies around the world will, more than likely, enter into our consideration and we shall, once again, cooperate with the international community as equals rather than try to bully the world into following what America wants. However, knowing that we are in a Dark Age, I believe this process may take longer than many of us would like.

For the conscious, engaged, activist the challenge becomes how to advance a cause or issue without undue exaggeration, and in a way that does not cause harm. There are certainly times when one needs to employ great skill to grab the attention of others and get your message across, but if we remember that "what goes around comes around," if we "spin" something one way we only ensure that in the future, things will get spun in the exact opposite direction, to our disadvantage. If we do lapse into spin and then get caught out, the only protection we have in such situations is to be honest about the intent behind our spin. For some reason, officials and those who get caught in the spotlight often forget how forgiving human nature can be in the face of honesty. How often have we seen people who, in their reluctance to demonstrate such transparency, have come to be haunted by their words down the line? It is better not to "spin" or misrepresent things in the first place.

Do not slander or speak maliciously of others

The Buddha's second recommendation for right speech warns of the damaging effects of slanderous speech: speaking maliciously or with ill will about others. These damaging effects are not only to others but to ourselves, because such behavior, in the end, destroys our own credibility. One aspect of this is rumor-mongering: deliberately infecting other people with negative, hurtful beliefs about someone. What is interesting about rumor-mongering is that, seen from the perspective of The Wheel of Sharp Weapons, it may be that the rumor itself is not wholly untrue. But the point is, again, what is your intention in spreading information about a person that is likely to make others think less highly of them? Or, if their reputation is already poor, what is your true intent in reinforcing it? Think on your reason for getting involved in spreading some negative piece of news or information. Is it really to draw attention to yourself? There is wisdom in the childhood expression, "Nobody likes a tattle tale." In the end, your own reputation can be on the line just as much, if not more, than the person you are tattling about.

To speak ill of another with the intent of helping a noble cause, protecting lives, and so on, may perhaps be justified in certain circumstances. But you must carefully monitor your intent to ensure that it is truly altruistic, in order to respond firmly to any accusation of acting maliciously and with ill will.

Do not use harsh or hurtful words

The Buddha next admonishes us to be careful of the words that we use in speaking directly to another person. He warns of the damage that can be caused by harsh, hurtful words. When we deride or belittle someone, or use angry and aggressive words toward them, that is often a defensive reaction that reflects our own unresolved issues. Unable to deal openly with what we see or hear, we may lash out in aggression and anger. According to the Buddha, though, anger destroys virtue. The positive rapport we may have established in our communication with someone can be destroyed in an instant. And the weakening effect of "lashing out" not only harms our relationship to the person we have attacked, but it can infect other relationships, too.

However, there may be times when we need to shake someone up, confront them about their own actions or behavior, for their own good or for the good of those around them, and our words can seem harsh in order to get through. Again, this boils down to the question of *intent*. There is of course a difference between defensive, ego-centered *anger* and the sort of compassion-centered *wrath* discussed earlier (see page 114). Shaking someone up with compassionate intent aims to provide an opportunity for self-reflection and honesty. Harsh words said not out of anger, but with concern and care, are likely to be less damaging to a relationship in the longer term, even if the immediate fall-out is a personal rift. Indeed, confronting someone with an honest appraisal of their conduct may well have a healing effect that makes a relationship closer than before. In this respect I reflect upon the falling out of friends, neighbors, nations who have, over time, come back together, even stronger. However, the choice of this form of communication always carries a risk, unless we are certain that the Three Poisons played no part in our motives.

With respect to the harshness of words, one additional point needs to be added. This has to do with a more sociological perspective, taking the Buddha's advice and looking at it from a more macro-perspective. I mention this because within circles attempting to be more conscious, there is, I believe, a movement toward taking the concept of *ahimsa*, or nonviolence, too literally and too far. In a nutshell, the admonitions and recommendations in the Buddha's teachings on Right Speech are the essence of nonviolent ways of communicating. This is the basis for such techniques as "Nonviolent Communication," or NVC, that are taught today. For certain, I have seen the benefits of such techniques in the lives of individuals and couples. But we must understand that, as mentioned earlier, everything is empty of intrinsic, independent existence. All words and actions may be positive, negative, or neutral depending on the perceiver. What may cause harm in one situation may be beneficial in another, and vice versa.

What that implies is that there *is* a place for harsh words, for painful frankness, for inciting those to act who would otherwise remain on the sidelines of life. These are hard judgment calls. But, they should not be wholly discarded as means that can be used when necessary by the conscious, engaged activist. As one Tibetan monk friend used to say to me, "Sometimes you need to call black black." Even the the proponents of NVC recognize this, but add – and rightly so – that with harsh words, with confrontations where there is a lack of mutuality and one side prevails over another, there is always a price to pay. And sometimes that price is unavoidable.

The discussion here focuses on power differentials and legitimacy. Such factors do influence what type of speech is most effective When a power is perceived as legitimate, for example the head of the class, the CEO of a company, the ruling party or class, the words and actions initiated by that power can often be rationalized away or sanctioned by what appears to be a higher authority of some sort, be it historical precedent, God, or whatever. If what they are doing or how they are acting is questioned by others, those in power can often respond in a benign, understanding manner that can descend into condescension toward those levying the challenge. More than likely, because those who have the legitimated power have more access to people's opinions, the news media, and so on, anyone justly challenging that power may need to become more provocative in their message to overcome their lack of legitimacy in the eyes of others.

This is why the words of radicals and revolutionaries often deliberately set out to appeal in a very direct, emotional way.

One of the future Founding Fathers of the United States, the young Thomas Jefferson, concurred with the French anarchist, Denis Diderot, who was quoted as saying that "The last king should be hung by the entrails of the last priest." We may never know how literally Jefferson was willing to consider Diderot's statement. Other equally provocative statements were made by the circle of men and women responsible for inciting the population of America to go to war to cast off what they defined as tyranny. John Adams, the second president, was quoted as saying, "I must study politics and war that my sons may have liberty to study mathematics and philosophy." Benjamin Franklin said at the signing of the American Declaration of Independence: "We must all hang together, or assuredly we shall all hang separately." And there are the famous words of Patrick Henry: "Is life so dear or peace so sweet as to be purchased at the price of chains and slavery? Forbid it, Almighty God. I know not what course others may take, but as for me, give me liberty or give me death!"

No doubt, if we gathered the words of other radicals, revolutionaries, and "insurgents" around the world over the course of history, we would hear similar sentiments. The point here is that in the absence of being under the mantle of what is deemed circumstantially legitimate in the eyes of God or man, a biting turn of phrase or well-crafted pronouncement from a charismatic leader can stop people in their tracks, incite comment, raise questions. In times when wrathful actions seem the only option to effect change, the speech that is necessary to set in motion those actions will also be wrathful.

All this having been said, confrontational or provocative speech need not be filled with vitriol and harmful intent. Of course, those whose legitimacy or authority is called into question may feel the sting of words against them and claim that they are being treated unfairly or worse by their challengers. This is just a political matter. But it is not infrequently the case that the rhetoric that is used by those wishing for change also includes comments that are demeaning or degrading to their opponents beyond what is necessary. I am reminded of various left-wing or liberal talk show hosts in America in recent years who seem to think nothing of going head to head with their right-wing or conservative counterparts when it comes to slanderous comments that really have nothing to do with the matters at hand. Such words uttered in a noble cause will degrade that cause, lower the bar, so to speak. They indicate that the consciousness of those using such tactics is not too dissimilar to that of those whom they rage against. In the end, there is cause for concern that if the tables were turned, those who sought change would become just as recalcitrant and problematic as those whom they sought to oust for the better – it would be the same soap opera with different players

Do not gossip

Lastly, the Buddha talks about the **damaging effect of gossip.** Gossip may seem benign, but in fact it is probably the most devious and destructive form of communication. There is a saying, "Loose lips sink ships," and there is truth in these words. Gossip has to do with poorly monitored communication. It is idle talk – unthought-out, ill-considered, lazy language. Behind the seemingly harmless banter of gossip is usually some poorly defined driving force. Are we speaking because we are nervous? Are we saying something so we get noticed, don't feel left out? Perhaps we are blabbering on just to make the other person feel at ease. What can follow is the passing on, with only partial consideration, of inaccurate information. A vague, unfounded, theoretical notion that you don't give much attention to can slip off your tongue, pen, or keyboard and become an idea "out there" that someone else takes seriously and acts upon.

Gossip creates collusion and conspiracy. Among friends, it creates a secret society of those who are "in the know" and those who are not. It can spread information in such a way as to make something insignificant into a big deal, a rallying cause. Or, as modern day spin doctors know, you can also make a big problem go away by just making something else seem more important. (I think of the days when Enron was falling and the CEOs close to the US administration were falling prey to scrutiny. Suddenly, everyone was chattering about two notorious criminals, Winona Ryder and Martha Stewart. And we all but forgot about Enron...)

Whereas rumor-mongering is direct and has more immediate consequences, gossip creates a nexus of confusion that can be the cause for the acceleration of rumors, harsh words, and other forms of ill-conceived communication.

It is probably because gossip is the greatest source of our communication problems that the Buddha recommended silent retreats and times when we sit silently so that we can quieten the banter of our minds. It is interesting to note that some of the most successful corporations in the world are run by Quakers, who are reputed to start their business meetings with several minutes of silence. What this does is to clear the space, and prevent anyone from coming into the meeting on a roll. And, if there are prior ideas or intentions, having them come out of silence exposes them to greater scrutiny, both from within and without.

As we become more conscious of the cacophony within our own mind and see how it steers our communication one way and the other, we have more compassion in understanding the willy-nilly nature of what most people go through in their own minds. We can then make the ecological decision not to pollute the world with our own confusion.

Some thoughts on the media

Knowing the Buddha's teaching on speech and actions that damage reputations, wreak havoc in people's lives, and lead to karmic repercussions, further down the road, it becomes painfully obvious that much of our media and news focus almost exclusively on just the sort of thing he warns against. The media are constantly churning out exposés and personal dramas that have as their central themes lies, deceit, murder, corruption, sexual misconduct, and so on. Some would like to argue that focusing on human depravity and immorality actually encourages it, by advertising its existence. Others feel that the entitlement to free expression, as enshrined for example in the US Constitution, guarantees the right of the media to put out such material, and that those who do not want to watch it or read it do not have to.

I look at such material in the context of gossip; the media rarely has a well-defined moral purpose for putting something out into the public domain, but rather observes what people currently seem to be fixated on and feeds those fixations in order to maximize profits. As the media and news services grow in importance in our lives, it is only logical that issues of morality, ethics, and intent become part of the dialogue in discussions about regulating them. This dialogue should not favor one ideology over another. An overly liberal media can be just as problematic as an overly conservative and restrictive one. In the ambiguity of relative reality, all we can ask of those who have the power over media services is that they occasionally think about providing just that – something that genuinely *serves* their audience.

Right Action

In the chapter on compassion, intent was considered as the driving force behind action and indeed synonymous with action when deployed for the benefit of others. What we now address, as with the discussion of speech and communication, are those actions which should generally be avoided.

In discussing "right action," the Buddha again broadly summarizes what he means in a series of admonitions:

> Do not cause deliberate harm to others or yourself;
> Do not commit theft;
> Do not engage in sexual misconduct.

Do not cause deliberate harm to others or yourself

The Buddha's first admonition under Right Action is against us causing deliberate harm or taking life, including our own. As I have said repeatedly, there is an endless cascade of events spawned by whatever we do. If we were enlightened, then not only would we know how our actions would be interpreted and responded to by others, but we would have the omniscience to see how they, in turn, would act upon others. Until cleared of the force of the Three Poisons, we have limited control over the possibly harmful effects of our actions. However, when it comes to our own actions, we can hone our intentions to ensure that what we do, even if it seems hurtful, is not done with a vengeful, spiteful, or retaliatory attitude. Thus, defending oneself or others from harm is acceptable. It may even be that in such a situation you need to use deadly force. From a Buddhist point of view such acts will have karmic repercussions, but they are mollified by the intent from which you were compelled to act and an attitude of regret to have done so. However, if you step beyond the minimum necessary action to prevent harm and act out of a desire to punish or exact revenge, then you will have crossed a line and the consequences, karmically speaking, are more severe.

The word "deliberately" in the Buddha's admonition is important. There are, of course, situations where one accidentally or unintentionally harms, maims, or kills another being. Someone may run out in front of our car; machinery fails on a job site; we accidentally tread on worms. The Buddhist understanding of karma sees a subtle link between those who find themselves behind the wheel, operating the machinery, and so on, and those who are harmed or killed. Our Western tradition seeks to exonerate of guilt those who end up as inadvertent killers in such situations, but does not go far enough in recognizing how infinite the repercussions of such events are in the wider cosmos. This probably has to with our general cultural denial of the truth of impermanence, and our limited understanding of the interconnectedness of all life.

My friend Lama Ole Nydahl works a great deal with European Buddhist students. World Wars I and II are still vividly in the consciousness of most Europeans, as war was a direct reality for many people who are still alive today. Lama Ole has looked closely at these wars and has found evidence that demonstrates that our basically loving nature was not suppressed even amid the brutality of those conflicts. One statistic he often brings up is that of the millions of rounds of ammunition that were fired by infantrymen during World War II, it is estimated that less than twenty per cent were ever aimed directly at another person. *We are not, by and large, natural born killers.* Most of us prefer peace and cherish life. And the disparity between this basic fact of human nature and what is demanded of soldiers in armed warfare is the foundation for the Post-Traumatic Stress Disorder suffered by many former combatants.

There are those among us who, in their darkness and confusion, somehow think that harming or annihilating others is justifiable. Even leaving aside clear cases of mental illness, there are people who see it as their duty, their destiny, their right, or whatever rationalization they use to themselves and others, to take life in certain circumstances.

Beyond possibly the examples of "enlightened assassins" and others who can see that their actions will protect the many (see the Tibetan story recounted on page 28), it is difficult to justify any intervention that deliberately ends life. A good intent may lack the component of sufficient remorse, turn vengeful, or go further than strictly necessary. History cites countless examples of battles that went too far, or happened after treaties had been signed, leaving behind a legacy that precipitated hatred in the future.

In our everyday lives, few of us have to consider whether or not we are going to enter a situation where we may have to decide whether to kill someone or put ourselves in harm's way. For those who do, such as agents of law enforcement or the armed forces, it would seem both prudent and necessary to encourage a mindfulness that addresses this dilemma, and sharpen the skill to be able to use deadly force sparingly and with genuine regret.

On the issue of taking ones own life, Buddhism naturally does not encourage suicide. It is considered, for the most part, a demonstration of a lack of compassion toward oneself, rooted in rigid beliefs. The Ven. Khenpo Karthar Rinpoche once said that if a person deliberately shortens their own life, then that person's consciousness will re-enact the suicide day after day until the time that their karma would otherwise have determined as the end of their life. In other words, we may want it all to be over, but that's not what we get. (I shall not discuss here euthanasia when a person is in extreme pain; my views on this are expressed in *Perfect Endings: A Conscious Approach to Dying and Death*).

But then there are examples of Vietnamese monks who willfully burned themselves in protest of a war in their country. In this case, using Buddhist logic, these monks no longer saw their bodies as personal. Their intent was to use their body as a vehicle of expression, to create images that would provoke reflection and dialogue. It is hard to know if the impact they desired made a difference one way or the other in the course of the war. But it certainly demonstrated a fierceness of spirit that left its mark on the minds of many an American GI.

Another example is the self-induced death of Tibetan monks when facing Chinese execution squads. These monks, adept in the yogic conscious dying practice known as *phowa*, elected to eject their consciousness out of their own bodies. The Chinese thought that these monks died from fright. But, in fact, they chose to cause their own deaths out of great compassion for their executioners. The Dharma teaches that it is a crime with serious karmic consequences if one takes the life of a person devoted to spirituality. Thus, their executioners were spared these consequences.

In recent times, we have become sadly familiar with those who commit suicide in the pursuit of a military, political or religious objective. In itself this is nothing new, as the world has long had its share of willing martyrs. However, whereas these acts have often been carried out against perceived aggressors ("enemy" troops or police, the predominant targets in the Iraq war, for example), many suicide bombers of today, such as those of 9/11 in New York and 7/7 in London, often choose to attack defenseless civilians in order to influence political outcomes.

Of course, such suicide bombers of today (notably in Iraq and Israel-Palestine) usually hold the religious or ideological belief that what they are doing is noble, an act of redressing injustice, for which they will be rewarded in heaven. However we may recoil in horror from the outlook of such people, it is naïve, foolish, and insensitive to dismiss them as beyond the pale, or to think that the only action we can take against such misguided souls is, in the words of President George W. Bush, to "hunt them down and bring them to justice."

Religious zealotry and the seductive words of dangerous and malicious charismatics is usually most effective in places where there is poverty, unemployment, and poor education. Where do the young and disfranchised in such places find ways of displaying their nobility, their higher purpose? Taking these common human desires and coupling them with anger, frustration, and a sense of futility is one recipe for creating people who are willing to strap on bombs to make a point, to further a cause, to proclaim the glory of their God. In addition the stark truth is that many of these same people have also been direct or indirect witnesses to the effects of the civilian "collateral damage" of bombs dropped on military targets; of covert operations; and of martial law, often imposed by Western "aggressors" or the regimes they support.

In some respects, acts of terrorism and suicide bombings are the weapons of those who, once again, do not have legitimate power, or feel cut off from it. Their presence is a leveling of the playing field. Consider dropping a daisy wheel bomb into an area from 5,000 feet above the ground. You never see the faces of those you kill with the countless bits of flying shrapnel. Then consider what it takes walking into a crowded market, seeing the faces of those around you as you detonate your bomb-laden vest. Perhaps those who do such acts are trained to be dispassionate or cut off in the moment so that they do not back down, do not hesitate. If so, this is actually a testimony to our loving nature and the fact that, in order for us to do such harm to others, we need to override our sensibilities through extreme belief, charged rhetoric, and brainwashing. Thus even if, in the act, suicide bombers are numb or out of touch other than with their mission, their choice comes out of a fierceness of purpose.

The resolve of these men and women, therefore, is very powerful. As such, we cannot simply "root them out," because the root causes that create them are perpetuated, both from within and without, by a mind confused with the Three Poisons and living in a world which, karmically speaking, is of their own making and is reinforced by others who, caught in their own Three Poison and, lacking the wisdom and compassion to know better, support or encourage them to act atrociously. And if they *do* know better, it is doubly worse for them.

(As a side note to this discussion, I cannot help but ponder how different the training of terrorists is compared to those who are trained as special forces and those involved with covert operations. To get people to do what would be, in "normal circumstances," heinous would seem to require a similar overriding of normal decency and sensibility. Thinking of such fierce and abnormal devotion reminds me of a conversation I had many years ago with an associate who knew the leaders of US Strategic Air Command. While at dinner and getting very drunk, senior commanders – who were directly under the order of the president of the United States – began to weep in an expression of their devotion to the office of the president and believed that the president was carrying out the will of God on Earth.)

To counter terrorism of this nature therefore, we need to look more closely at our own behaviors and actions. It is more than "hunting" the terrorists and bringing them to "justice." We need to think about bringing justice to the lands where terrorists are bred. What can we do to end poverty, create opportunity, and educate people? What can we do to challenge our own governments and leaders not to march to the tune of corporate greed and avarice that leaches the life blood from countries and peoples all over the world? What can we do to stand in the way of another daisy wheel bomb being dropped? These are the issues we must address if we want to see an end to terrorism.

The bottom line in this whole discussion about harming others is that we should generally try to avoid situations where harming or killing are the options laid before us. And even if we have no choice but to elect either action, there is no escaping the karmic repercussions that harming or taking of life has. Even if the reason seems justified or enlightened, there will be some hell to pay – and that is part of the equation we need to accept.

Do not commit theft

The Buddha then addresses the damage done by robbery, theft, and fraud. We want what we do not have and under the influence of the Three Poisons try to get it by deceptive and dishonest means, often because we cannot think of any other way. However, our motivation for doing so may not always be negative. Perhaps we pilfer to get money or food for our starving children. Perhaps our family is on the verge of being evicted. Not seeing any other option but to steal, the intent is to keep the family fed and safe.

But the truth is that such actions usually invoke someone's negative response. Few people thank you for stealing from them. Most people respond with disappointment, fear, or outrage; they recoil and hold on to what they have more tightly, or desire reprisal or getting even. Thus the poverty in one mind that leads to the unskillful act of stealing encourages negative responses in others. It is a self-perpetuating "lose-lose" scenario.

There is the old saying "Property is theft." We can all think of historical examples where robbing, stealing, fraud, looting, and so on have "seemingly" paid off. The seizure of land by one group or another, be it a clan, a landlord, a church, or a nation state. The bankrupting of natural resources of entire regions by fortune seekers, or governments in search of more resources. In recent years we have watched the greed of powerful executives misleading shareholders and employees, bilking their own corporation of billions and leaving thousands of people without pensions or retirement funds. And whereas a breaking and entering charge against an inner city person on welfare may see them in jail almost immediately, the crimes of such executives have yet to be looked at with the same level of scrutiny.

Witnessing such events, it is not hard to see that more often than not, those who have the power and the money lay down the rules (the golden rule of "he who has the gold makes the rules.") Empires, kingdoms of religious and secular nature are founded on the blood and backs of others.

Because those who feel left out or wish they had more are fixated on poverty and the feeling of not having their due or entitlement, most look at the rich and mighty with awe. It is they who seem immortalized most in art, song, literature: the rich, powerful, and famous. Especially in our Dark Age, where material wealth is the measure of success, magazines, TV entertainment exposés, and newspapers focus on the lives of such people. We are supposed to be entertained by how they dress, where they go, and who they are with, and we revel in their scandals. The simple fact is that when wealth is ill-gotten or disproportionate to what our being can embrace or handle skillfully, mishaps, disasters, and scandals are bound to occur.

If we look into the history of families who have ascended within society by such means, we often see that they, too, suffer. And if the laws of karma are to be believed, part of their suffering results from having taken what is not theirs to begin with.

The Buddhist mind training slogan says, "Don't reduce a god to a demon."[14] In our poverty, in our feeling somehow deprived, we should not wish to see the downfall of those who have more than us. We may think they deserve it, that they have got it coming, but, their falling or not will be determined by their karma. And our karma will just be made worse by harboring negative thoughts about others.

On the other hand, if we admire the wealth, success, power, or influence of others we should not mimic their misdemeanors, thinking that if they do it, why shouldn't we? I have heard such an argument by those who cheat on tax forms, or lie on legal forms. For one thing, this usually doesn't work well for those who do not have a wall of accountants, legal professionals, or armed protectors. But more importantly, such actions weaken us. Even if we steal or rob for seemingly altruistic reasons, the act of stealing brings us down, lowers our standards of behavior, leaves us open to reprisal. If nothing else, we subject ourselves to self-denigration – which does more to disconnect us from our loving nature than anything else.

In matters of property and finance, it behooves the conscious, engaged activist not to invoke the enmity of those who would like to scrutinize our actions in order to weaken our efforts or for other negative reasons. Within any society there are rules around property. Even if we are not in

[14] *The Great Awakening*, by Jamgon Kongtrul. Shambhala Books, Boston, 1987, p.34.

agreement with these laws or regulations and we consider them to be unfair or unjust, to challenge them overtly by not adhering to them will – in most situations – create two problems. For one thing, the collective mentality around us, the reified cultural reality of which we are a part, *does* have its impact on our mind. It can, therefore, be quite difficult to justify our lack of compliance – our bending of the laws to suit our needs – even to ourselves. The result can be nagging thoughts of doubt, and the energy we need to expend in order both not to think negatively of ourselves and to live in the rationalization of what we have done, can take its toll. As a mirror to these doubts, there will appear from the outside those who consider us a cheat, a scoundrel, someone not to be trusted, a criminal.

By not giving in to these tendencies and "rendering unto Caesar what is Caesar's," we stay under the radar. It also gives us a firm foundation upon which we can then address the injustices that we see around us. For disparities we see do more than just factually bespeak God's, or karmic, justice. It is a call for those with the resources to practice such virtues as generosity. And the power of doing so and the benefits yielded thereby do far more to ensure the constancy and growth of what one has, than the hiring of accounting book-cookers, attorneys, and private armies.

It is admittedly hard to stand by and watch people with power and wealth ignore, oppress, or seize the rights and property of others. When this happens, some may feel compelled to become active rebels against legitimated authority. But such efforts risk perpetuating the cycle of haves versus have-nots, if their goal is simply to even the score, to seize for ourselves what others possess. A Buddhist – the Dalai Lama is a famous example – would always advocate nonviolent action and dialogue, so that when change is achieved, those who are perceived as having disfranchised others do not in turn become disfranchised. This is the only way to guarantee a solution that is truly fair and does not leave a legacy of resentment and envy. Nonviolence and dialogue are also a way of ensuring that changes in wealth patterns are nurtured gradually. When generation upon generation has reaped the rewards of materially exploiting others, it can similarly take time to alter habitual patterns and set things on a new course. In our impatience or outrage we may want to see things happen tomorrow, if not today. But the risk in such haste is to alter the entire fabric of society so radically as to bring chaos, disorder, and suffering.

Do not engage in sexual misconduct

In the discussion of compassion, I spoke of acquiring an unshakeable charisma and an ability to influence others. This is based on overcoming the seductive power of craving and attachment and becoming equanimous. A possible problem is that as our power increases, we have to beware of becoming attached to an erroneous belief in our specialness – a belief that in our case, the ordinary rules of mortals no longer apply.

When one engages in sexual relations with another, especially intercourse, be it consensual or otherwise, Dharma teachers say that there is a bond that is created on the level of the etheric between the two people. Thus, while you may think nothing of a one-night stand or a well hidden tête-à-tête, the fact is that the person you have had sex with is stuck to you, energetically, like glue. So when your spouse or special friend thinks that you are being distant or that something has changed, they are right, even if you proclaim your love, protest vehemently, and so on. You are also stuck like glue to the other person. And, more than likely if your mate or theirs sees the two of you together or just saying hello to each other in passing, the bond or history that you share will get noticed. Beyond the duplicity in the most intimate of your relationships and the damage this will eventually have, suspicion will begin to have its effect in your other relationships. Illicit or harmful sexual relationships will always weaken, if not destroy, your credibility. That is why, beyond all of its various karmic implications, it can be used as an effective political weapon. For when the cover is blown and the illicit affair is in the open, it will usually create all-out scandal. Even if you are not actively setting out to destroy your own credibility by tempting fate, those who know the seductive side of power may place sexual temptation in your path.

Beyond such cases, which for some may seem confined to the antics of high-flying politicians and those in the espionage business, the simple truth is that sexual energies always form a part of the mix of any group that comes together. I have seen many organizations come unglued as a result of an affair between key players, sexual harassment, and so on. Thus, if you want to remain effective as an individual or you want to see a cause move forward more smoothly with less distraction and dramatics, the Buddha suggests gaining some control over your own sexual energy and its display. This is not about being prudish, but rather prudent. (Note: A detailed discussion of sex and what is meant by sexual misconduct is presented in my book *The Passionate Buddha: Wisdom on Intimacy and Enduring Love.*)

Some thoughts on mindfulness in action

Acquiring the ability to bring mindfulness to what we do and say comes about in a variety of ways. Our history can show us the skillfulness or lack of skillfulness in our actions. But, as we are habitual creatures and tend to repeat our actions rather than reform them according to the lessons of history, the

Buddha offers us advice about how to steer clear of certain major stumbling blocks that will always thwart our actions, and gives us meditative methods to dismantle the habitual mind that finds itself continually lured into the same traps.

In the Japanese meditative art of archery, or *kyudo*, the mind is observant, poised in the moment prior to the arrow being set free. Freed from the Three Poisons, the mind is intent upon the bullseye, and the arrow is the connection between the two. If the mind is not freed of the Poisons, and our intention is mixed, then the arrow will miss the mark. The arrow lets us know this in the moment of its release, and where the target is hit shows us how far we have gone astray. Of course, as in life when something demands to be done, in kyudo one cannot wait forever. You place your arrow, draw your bow, rest your mind on the target, and release. It is like breathing in and breathing out. The next arrow is like the next cycle of breathing. You boldly let go, accept the consequences, then take another arrow and make a commitment to be even more mindful – even freer of the Three Poisons.

The German writer and philosopher Goethe once wrote: "Whatever you can do or dream you can do – begin it. Boldness has genius, power, and magic." The magic and power that is transformation happens when, in the present moment, you trust your loving nature and let go. This usually requires conscious work on our part, even though it is in fact the most natural thing in the world. To find the "middle way" between "too loose" and "too tight," – to become natural in our actions – is the realization of this aspect of the Eightfold Path.

Timidity stifles creativity and possibility – and usually yields a mediocre result with an assortment of regrets. But the polar opposite of timidity, recklessness, is equally problematic. The problem we face is that regardless of how conscious or not we are, act we must. Perhaps our greatest challenge in effectively doing whatever we do is knowing how to move forward in mindful action between the looseness of recklessness and the tightness of timidity. We risk falling into a state of paralysis – not wanting to act at all – as if that were some kind of solution. But it is not, and we *shall* have to act, one way or the other, which is why to have the willingness to step forward in the first place takes boldness. **Having the boldness to put full heart and intention behind what you do ensures that you will learn the most from your actions. Properly observing the results of what it is that you have done, guarantees that your future actions will be even more effective.**

Many contemporary Buddhist teachers have written about mindfulness in action, especially when it comes to ordinary, everyday life. One such text that I have found immensely useful is Tarthang Tulku Rinpoche's *Skillful Means*. Tarthang Rinpoche looks at the pitfalls each of us can get into in the course of embarking on a project or cause. Probably the single most useful idea he puts forth is following through; following the course of action from beginning to end and trying to stay on task until you see it through.

This may seem obvious, but it is interesting to see how the mind strays in the process of doing any one particular task; group dynamics, sexual inklings, boredom and wanting to change track or approach prematurely. Distraction and wanting to be entertained often get in the way of doing effectively whatever we want to do, even if it is important to us. In effect, we are looking at how we can apply our meditative mind, come back to the breath, and translate that into coming back to the intention, to the task at hand. In the process of doing this we learn about endurance, patience, and generosity, and so on. **In mindfulness, we learn what it means to care.**

Right Livelihood: Being Practical, Pragmatic, and Useful

The Buddha saw that it is a natural part of growing as a human that we learn to take our place and make some kind of contribution to the world around us. This helps us to develop the independent state of mind that is a feature of enlightened being. There are no dead-beat Buddhas or Bodhisattvas. Each has their job, which is synonymous with their being. Until our mere presence is all that is needed to transform a situation in an enlightened direction, the rest of us will grow from having an ethical livelihood.

Livelihood takes action and translates it into how you will support yourself and take care of your responsibilities to others in an ethical way. When looking at a career, calling, job – however you want to define what you do on a day to day basis to secure the lifestyle you wish to lead – what choices can you make in what you do that will have a positive short- or long-term impact on those around you? This naturally includes activities related to social and political activism.

Please bear in mind that I am not saying that your livelihood needs be the focus of what you do as an activist. Those for whom it is, usually see their work as their calling: how they get their livelihood and their heart's interests to happily coincide. On the other hand, others make a living in order to have the time and resources to devote their thoughts, intentions, and actions to a different activity. The conscious, engaged activist is not someone who can be solely judged by looking at one dimension of his or her life, such as livelihood. Rather, it is the intelligent use of their resources and skills, focused on their intention to benefit others which matters most. At the same time, an ethical livelihood can support the energy to accomplish this, while a livelihood of more questionable deeds and aims can detract, if not negate, the good one is trying to accomplish elsewhere.

To accomplish the good that he or she seeks, the conscious, engaged activist requires self-knowledge. The Dharma teaches that this is primarily achieved through contemplation and meditation – the various methods I have presented earlier. As you familiarize yourself *with* yourself and discover what potential you have and the roadblocks that you habitually place in your own path that hinder that potential, you begin to lighten up, become more pliable, see ways of being that help you to access new skills within, and more resources without. Whatever your personal circumstances, attributes, and available resources may be, all can be turned into assets to help you along the way. If you are rich, you can learn to use your wealth wisely so that you create more opportunity and enrich the lives of others. If you are poor, knowing how to live without in a dignified manner can inspire those trapped in a mindset of poverty to give up the negative attitudes that create jealousy, greed, and other emotions that limit possibility and keep people in their place. If society deems you beautiful, you can often magnetize people to listen to you, and hence contribute to something that is worthy. If you are strong, you can engage in activities that physically protect others.

Of course, you may well have other internal attributes that you value in yourself more than these external ones – your honesty, your depth, your sincerity, and so on. You don't want to be recognized as the cute blond, the rich kid, the poor kid from the ghetto, the jock. But the truth is that, karmically speaking, you have been graced with whatever attributes are attached to these labels and to align your inner qualities with these outer attributes gives you added resourcefulness. It also helps us to break through stereotypic thinking that constrains us as much as it does others.

With respect to action and livelihood, how do you know where to put your efforts and energies? More than likely, based on your karmic inclinations, you will find yourself pulled in a particular direction. Your loving nature will bring out your affinity to this or that particular cause, plight, and so on. Trust this, "You cannot be all things to all people." Even the peacocks, the noble Bodhisattvas, have their specialties. These were not given to them as assignments. Rather, there was a calling they felt from within that they then perfected in opening up to their loving nature and their Buddha-potentiality. Thus your job in becoming a conscious, engaged activist is to develop the wisdom, skill, and compassion to use your inner and outer resources for maximum benefit.

And even if society becomes so repressive as to limit how and what we can do with the resources and capacities we have – for example nullifying or canceling elections, taking away personal freedoms in the name of patriotism or national security – unless each of us is lobotomized or restrained by mandatory psychotropic medicine, we always have our own mind. **And, we should not underestimate the transformational power of a thought well formed and directed.**

Rather than giving the student or reader a rundown of the *best* careers to choose, the classic Buddhist texts on right livelihood prefer to elaborate on those career choices that fundamentally help no one and, in the long run, cause harm that can last for generations. These careers are discussed here mainly because to be engaged in them while also claiming to focus on doing good in the world is either a blatant contradiction or a very uphill battle that few, if any, can win. On the contrary, it is an extremely worthy cause for an activist to work consciously and in an engaged way to curb or alter such practices, or halt them altogether, because of their global consequences. Again, the particular calling or work chosen in order to accomplish this may differ from person to person.

Wrong livelihood 1: The arms trade

The first of the wrong career choices is **being involved with the dealing or selling of arms.** Soon after the first Gulf War, His Holiness the Dalai Lama was visiting Albuquerque, New Mexico. In a full auditorium, he was asked what he thought about American involvement in Iraq and his opinion of Saddam Hussein. His Holiness said that while it may be true that Saddam was not a good person, it must be remembered that it was the US and other foreign governments and weapons corporations that had supplied him with the weaponry to invade Kuwait in the first place. We gave him the tools to act on his worst impulses. In this light, His Holiness felt that those who supplied the weapons were far more immoral than any action Saddam could commit, because his Western suppliers knew he would use the weapons he was sold. They just did not anticipate that he would use them against his own people, and against allies of the West.

It is problematic enough to possess one's own weapons with the intent, according to one's own ethical standards, only to use them in self-defense. We see this dilemma daily in the blurring of the line between self-defense and the idea of "pre-emption." What is the difference between a pre-emptive strike as a means of self-defense, and out-and-out militaristic aggression? Beyond the current debacle around the US' (and the "coalition of the willing") invasion of Afghanistan and Iraq, history is replete with despots and tyrants who whipped their populace into a frenzy based on fear of others, in order to justify invasions.

Bringing our discussion back from foreign policy to the act of making money from arms sales, I discussed earlier the fact that war is the failure to find other, more peaceful methods of settling our differences. To be engaged in the manufacturing and selling of weaponry, therefore, is cashing in on humanity's failures. Encouraging someone to buy your AK-47s, tanks, and missile launchers is basically pushing for a worst-case scenario to come about. Success in this endeavor usually breeds more worst-case scenarios – a win-win scenario for the arms industry.

On a personal note, I recall teaching at an international holistic health conference where great healers, speakers, and proponents of spirituality were invited to present. The conference was poorly attended and there were endless problems with staff, facilities, and funds. Only later did we learn that the company responsible for organizing the event mainly did conferences for weapons dealers.

Of course, nothing is ever entirely black or white. Applying the new nuclear technology to create the atomic bomb may or may not have shortened the Second World War. After the first two were dropped on Japan and the world recognized their horrific effects, some wanted to see a ban on such weapons. But for years they have continued to proliferate worldwide and the desire to acquire them is the aim of many governments convinced that to hold such destructive capability generates respect and acts as a deterrent. The problem is that when one has a nuclear arsenal, what temptations are there to go one step further? How often has time erased the memory of the sins of our fathers only for new generations disconnected from the nightmare of earlier history to go, once again, down the road of doom?

Rarely do we stop in our tracks or reverse course. The pride of the powerful and those seeking power is hard to tame and easy to capitalize on. And no matter how ethical a weapons dealer may want to be – claiming to balance the forces of opposing sides, or whatever rationale they may try to convince themselves and others with – their ethics and reasoning will be warped, as the demand for their goods and potential profitability inevitably lead them down a path that few, if any, can negotiate skillfully.

Seeing the heinous effects that the marketing of weaponry can have, the courageous step of being involved with, or supporting, groups that work to stop nuclear proliferation, ban land mines, and seek stronger laws regulating gun and weapon sales, is surely a worthy cause for a conscious, engaged activist.

Wrong livelihood 2: Trading in other living beings

The next of the worst career choices, from a Buddhist viewpoint, is **to be involved in the direct manipulation of the lives of others.** Here I am speaking of slavery, the sex trade, and raising animals for slaughter. All sentient beings want happiness and the causes of happiness. None want to suffer, to be used or manipulated against their will. Few if any of us need to be lectured on the nonvirtue of the sex and slave trades. If nothing else, we can look at history and see the negative social and cultural effects of these practices and institutions. Such negative fallout comes as no real surprise.

However, as far as the treatment of animals for slaughter is concerned, I believe this issue is a karmic powder keg that deserves far more attention than most of us have probably hitherto given it. In my discussion of this matter, I will include the actual slaughter of animals.

It could be argued that with a growing human population and the dwindling of open land for animals to range freely, raising animals for the sustenance of one's family or village makes sense. We can argue about the virtues of vegetarianism all we like. The Buddha saw the virtue of it, and orders of the Theravada tradition of Buddhism are exclusively vegetarian, as are many Mahayana orders. Even in those traditions where eating meat is accepted, there are practices and meditations that encourage becoming vegetarian for a time.

However, more human beings eat meat than not. Therefore, as this is an activity that most people participate in either directly or passively by consumption (directly through the slaughter or eating of meat and other animal products, and indirectly by consuming animal by-products such as leather for shoes, coats, and so on), it seems relevant to come up with moral and ethical standards for it. Most traditional and indigenous cultures have such an approach. But in our society, the commercialization and industrialization of the activity leads us away from such sensitivities by disconnecting consumers from the animals they consume. This in turn takes us down a very slippery slope where we more and more risk losing our connection to the sacredness of life itself.

The animal rights activist John Robbins has said that one of the legacies of our time will be that we were extremely cruel to animals. Although there are exceptions, commercially raised animals these days usually lead a tortured existence. They are often raised in close quarters, which increases their stress levels and creates the easy spreading of disease. Rather than change these living conditions (giving the animals more space would mean raising fewer animals), the owners just feed them antibiotics and other medicines that swell their bodies (good for pound per dollar ratios) and leave residues in their blood and muscles which we eventually consume (and probably accounts for more and more people being resistant to the benefits of certain antibiotics). Stressed, underexercised, and bloated, the beasts are then slaughtered with little thought that they, too, have consciousnesses and if degraded and killed with no regard for this fact, the pain, confusion, and fear that they experience in dying will be infused in their meat and byproducts. Animal stress hormones form part of the legacy we partake in at our dinner tables. So if we eat pounds and pounds of meat from distressed, frightened animals, why should we not expect our own state of mind to be affected, our own consciousness to go to similar places?

Our consumption of meat is disproportionate to our needs. Few of us live in climates, or do the physical labor, that would warrant the volume of meat we consume daily. As our healthcare systems corroborate this, perhaps this will have an impact on how much land is assigned to creating animals for slaughter and how much used to grow grains, fruits, and vegetables. But this is more than a healthcare issue. It is an issue with global economic, political, environmental, and moral consequences. It is one of many issues raised by those protesting agri-business, genetic modification, and proposals for cloning for consumption.

It is possible (and there are some groups already demonstrating this) to raise animals in healthy environments, to feed them well, and take them to slaughter in ways that minimize their suffering. Native American slaughter practices, Jewish Kosher practices, and the Tibetan tradition of butchers knowing *phowa* so they can eject the consciousness of the animals before slaughter, demonstrate that it is possible to bring consciousness into a meat-consuming nation.

To my mind, this is an area where activists can be extremely valuable, even more than against slavery or weapons sales. As we all eat daily, to bring consciousness into this area is to encourage consciousness and conscience across the board. As we value the life we take in order to sustain our own, this may lead to greater consideration in other dimensions of our lives, and hence curb the attitudes that encourage slavery and weapons dealing in the first place.

Wrong livelihood 3: The trade in intoxicants

The last of the careers that the Buddha would consider as anathema to a life that is conscious and engaged is to deal, market, or sell intoxicants, those substances that, in fact, are designed to make one *less* conscious and engaged – drugs and alcohol. Generally speaking, the Dharma frowns upon intoxication, a state where one loses mindfulness and consequently can find oneself wandering unchecked into the minefields of the Three Poisons. In the interest of health, consciousness, and desirable behavior, we are encouraged to "drink responsibly" as it were: to know our limits. In that regard, the Buddha was not necessarily against intoxicants per se, but it is a rare individual who can maintain their clarity while partaking in them, let alone resist overindulging. And, as someone who sells intoxicants is more interested in making a living and expects the buyer to beware and to monitor themselves, more than likely they will encourage us in directions few of us would really want to consciously take ourselves. **To sell intoxicants is, therefore, an assault on the mind itself.**

When it comes to other nonvirtuous professions, it is interesting to ponder their interrelationship – how alcohol and drugs fit into the arms trade, gambling, prostitution, and so on. To think that the money that is generated by such businesses is not tainted, again, flies in the face of karmic law. In my own experience, I can think of several examples, some personal. My great-grandfather was a rabbi whose sons chose nonreligious livelihoods. My grandfather became a dentist, but several of his brothers became bootleggers and went west during Prohibition. As they got involved with bootlegging whiskey and such, they soon found themselves embroiled with organized crime syndicates. Scandal or tragedy ruined many of their lives and the lives of their families. Again, this is much the same as the well-known American philanthropic family that I mentioned earlier (see page 143) whose money came from alcohol and prostitution. Despite all of their grand contributions to various causes in society, this did not prevent family members from suffering a disproportionate amount of mental illness and disease.

Of course, one can argue that at least *someone* wanted to take these dubiously gotten fortunes and put them to good use. Indeed, such actions can be virtuous and stop a habitual process that may have further negative consequences in the future. But this does not avert negative consequences incurred up to that point. Karmically speaking, someone still has to pay the piper. And I do wonder if even the most humanitarian projects funded by such philanthropy will not find themselves at some point in the future in crises that are somehow directly related to the means by which the donated money was earned.

In modern times, the issue of intoxication needs to be addressed beyond the traditional/historical/cultural intoxicants we all know or have addressed in our schools, churches, temples, mosques, and homes. We need to look at ways in which we have culturally sanctioned intoxication *as a normal state of being*. By this I am referring to the vast array of psychoactive drugs promoted by the pharmaceutical industry and the allopathic medical community that it serves.

In "The Spectrum of Life" program that I teach to teens, I talk to them about the failure of the DARE (Drug Abuse Resistance Education) program in American schools. This program has been in existence in American elementary and middle schools for over twenty years. Statistics seem to indicate that despite such education, the use of illicit drugs in a younger and younger population increase year after year. DARE fails not because the message is not a good one. It fails because it does not recognize that *we are a drug-taking culture*. I tell these kids that the theme should not be "Dare to get kids off drugs," but rather *"Dare to keep parents off Prozac."* The use of psychopharmaceuticals in the West is pandemic. We need not be so worried about keeping our kids away from dealers and peddlers of drugs and alcohol. For one thing, so many homes already have alcohol available as a matter of course – albeit supposedly for the adults. And then there are Prozac, Valium, Librium, Elevil, Xanax, Zoloft, Ativan, and a host of other mood-altering substances, that more people are addicted to than to any drugs that can be found on the street. These are legal and prescribed. Thus we model addiction to our children. They don't have to learn somewhere else.

We are living in a Dark Age where denial of the Three Poisons running amok in our lives leads us to be very intolerant of any mood that bespeaks our dissatisfaction, our alienation, our suffering. And rather than look at the causal factors, rather than begin the process of dismantling the Three Poisons, we are offered, and choose, substances that blur them, keep us synthetically in an "OK" gray zone. And this leads to our intolerance of slightly more active children in the classroom who "obviously need Ritalin" to agitated old people afraid of dying who "need" to be "snowed" with morphine. In between there are the intolerable ups and downs of conditioned, everyday life that show the cracks in the illusion of everything being OK, 24/7. We are looking at the fulfillment of Aldous Huxley's vision in *Brave New World*, where citizens are kept tame and in-line with *soma*.

To me, the culturally-sanctioned drugs sold to those who have not been given any mind training to learn how to relax and cope with what life throws at them, can be just as devastating in their effect and just as difficult to overcome or withdraw from as illegal street drugs and alcohol. The social consequences of the latter may be more dramatic, but in the end, a consciousness denied is a consciousness denied; and the profits made by the socially-sanctioned drugs corporations far exceed the money generated by alcohol producers and illegal drug cartels. To date, pharmaceutical companies rank as some of the top producers in terms of commodity profitability in the world, making some people who work for them wealthy almost beyond imagination.

Admittedly, many pharmaceutical drugs are produced for other purposes; and even those psychoactive drugs that I have mentioned do have their place and merits. But the degree to which money is generated by the sale of these drugs, without there first being much attempt to develop consciousness-enhancing methods for social unmanageability, is the degree to which these corporations reap the consequences that are not dissimilar to those facing the drug runners and bootleggers among us. Thus, as with other bad career choices, I believe that people should be wary of involvement with the pharmaceutical industry. And I also think that **the monitoring of such enterprises is another noble endeavor for the conscious, engaged activist**.

Another culturally sanctioned enterprise that encourages our intoxication is the marketing/advertising industry. **Because we are basically good, we also have the tendency to be basically gullible.** It may be true that everyone is doing the best based on what they know, but that does not mean that everyone comes to what they do with the best of intentions, wisdom, or skill. Part of enlightenment, and becoming a conscious, engaged activist, is losing our gullibility by developing discriminating awareness, the source of compassionate action. But, while we remain blind and unable to perceive things for what they are, there will be some who will capitalize on our frailty. Such people know the mechanisms of craving and seduction and will exploit them to lead us by the nose.

This is nothing new. Whoever sold the first donkey or chicken to another person had to have some marketing skills. The art and skill of influencing has always been a two-edged sword. Thus, the marketplace has always been rife with tantalizers, snake-oil salesmen, con artists, and confidence men and women. But as we learn more about psychology and the mind, we also learn the mechanisms by which we become influenced and make choices. This information can be used with integrity by teachers effectively to leave deep, positive impressions in our minds. But those with less noble, ethical and moral standards can use the same information to enslave us – to brainwash us. It really depends on intention. Neurolinguistic programming (NLP); visual and auditory subliminal messaging; spin-doctoring by repetition; and "operant conditioning" – all are part of the weaponry used by the media and advertisers to get their messages across – whether it is for us to buy soap or a car we can't afford, or vote for a particular candidate, *or go to war.*

To be involved in a livelihood and industry that promotes hyperbole and distortion for self-serving aims, or generally leads people away from their sensibilities, is exploitative, hence a questionable choice of life-direction. **To be actively involved in supporting organizations that are consumer watchdogs and promote truth in advertising seems a warranted endeavor for the conscious, engaged activist.**

Sickness, Poverty, and Warfare

In the Dedication of this book, I used a line from the vow of a Bodhisattva about being committed to seeing an end to sickness, poverty, and warfare. If I were in any way to narrow the definition of what I would consider to be the most appropriate livelihoods or causes for conscious, engaged, activists, I would say that these three issues are the most central.

Sickness, poverty, and warfare are closely interconnected. Each has influenced or contributed to the other two over the course of history. Depending on your inclinations and what

THE BUDDHA AT WAR

you see around you, therefore, addressing any of these problems in what you do will have merit and probably a positive effect on the other two problems.

At the same time, if I were to reduce the definition of right livelihood even further, I would focus on poverty. I say this not out of any great love for socialism, but rather, from a Buddhist sense of logic. The Buddhist laws of karma teach that if one is born into poverty, there has to be a personal cause. If we are to trust the examples and logic presented in *The Wheel of Sharp Weapons* (see Chapter Eight), if one has been cruel to others and deprived others of what they need, more than likely the wheel will come around and one will find oneself reborn into a situation where you too experience a lack of resources, similarly created by others, repaying the favor. Whether you accept this idea of karmic retribution or not, it is a concept that leaves out no player in terms of allocating responsibility for the circumstance of poverty. This is the key point. It is too simplistic and too sentimental to see people who live in dire poverty as solely victims or pawns of clearly identifiable "perpetrators" of poverty. We have to look not only at the role of the "perpetrator" but also at that of the "victim" to see how causes and conditions come together to reinforce poverty on both sides.

Craving, as we have discussed, is the greatest cause for our suffering. Not knowing the way things are, not understanding reality or how it works, as beings of desire, we crave. Rarely are we satisfied, regardless of how good we have things. And, as mentioned previously, there are those who in the most impoverished situations can demonstrate a spirit of generosity far greater than those living in wealthy iron-gated communities.

But, let us say that we are not so wise or enlightened. We live in situations which most would agree are impoverished in the relative sense. If we have little education, we may be receptive to forces within society, perhaps state-sanctioned religion and religious education, which praise the virtues of poverty and the evils of wealth. Perhaps they encourage us to be fatalistic about our place, as in the words of the old hymn: "The rich man in his castle, / The poor man at his gate, / God made them high and lowly / And ordered their estate." Or we may be susceptible to radical forces within society saying that we are poor because of other people, such as corrupt officials, corporate tycoons, foreign invaders. Add to this mix the growing access to media: along with useful information, it presents us with images of what others have that we do not. When we have little and see that others have a lot, it would seem to be a rare individual among us who is able to embrace a moderate approach to transforming their predicament – the moderate approach that teaches the middle way of personal responsibility and the need to change both the inner and outer causes of the difficulties you find yourself in. In craving an end to suffering, both in the ultimate and relative sense, it stands to reason that the habit patterns of greed, jealousy, and a host of other emotions associated with dissatisfaction arise strongly. When the habitual mental patterns that help to breed and reinforce poverty are coaxed to a higher state of agitation by those who see or can sense the energy and force of the frustration beneath the surface, then it is not hard to see how one might motivate those who are poor, starving, homeless, or feeling disfranchised to join *jihad*s, the ranks of suicide bombers, and so on.

Of course, this is a very sociological interpretation of a very complex phenomenon. But such an interpretation generally makes sense, and policy makers would be well advised to pay attention to sociologists, social psychologists, anthropologists, and others who spend their time examining the intricacies of societal interaction. However, we must also bear in mind that only a tiny number of people actually do join *jihad*s or become terrorists. Does this mean that they are brainwashed by those who wish to keep them subdued? Or is it because people are basically good and really do not wish to cause harm in their lives or in the lives of others?

Ultimately, helping all beings, through mind training, to overcome the strong craving that leads them to suffer is the greatest gift you can give them. It is especially helpful if it can turn the mind of someone who has considered violence and wants to try another way. Mother Teresa once said, "To a starving person, God comes in the form of a loaf of bread." Similarly, unless we help to lift vulnerable people out of their immediate material distress, it will be very difficult for such people to feel a motivation to make changes to more fundamental levels of consciousness.

Although, from a karmic point of view, such people may find themselves in such conditions by their own hand over the course of lifetimes, the fact that these conditions exist in the world is a call to us to grow spiritually, to use what resources we have to lessen the suffering we see. Some will benefit from food, some from education, some through programs like Habitat for Humanity, and so on. In some instances, forcibly ending civil war and strife may be necessary. Perhaps political and economic reforms will need to be put in place, and you will find yourself wanting to work with a lobbying group, seek political office, or join organizations that feel called to protest actively or directly challenge the powers-that-be in more wrathful ways.

So, there is plenty of work to do and each of us has the capacity to do *something*. What matters is that we make love and compassion manifest in a practical, useful way. For if we do not, then it's like the saying, "use it or lose it." Karmically speaking, the benefits that we currently have are because of positive deeds we have done in the past. To just hoard what we have and turn a blind eye to the suffering of others around us is to squander a precious opportunity that has the potential of in turn opening the doors of opportunity for others. In the end, actively using this opportunity will do more to bring us to a deeper level of peace and happiness than the pursuit of any real or imagined trinket.

To work truly on poverty, then, the conscious, engaged activist must not only put his or her efforts into whatever worldly organization or cause inspires them, but must also spend time meditating on the power of craving and attachment. For as we understand the power of what we crave and loosen our own attachments, a greater understanding for what needs to be done will arise in our work.

The Daily Life of an Activist

Most of us possess a blend of habits that are good, bad, and somewhere in between. Throughout our lives we then create well-trodden routines that will either consciously and willfully or unconsciously and seemingly capriciously reinforce our habits, for better or worse. In consequence, when we have established the thought and intent to reinforce what is good and eliminate what is harmful or of little value, putting that intent into action will require effort. If we want to become more conscious and engaged in what we do and in the lives of others, we need to go beyond just making that wish or holding that intention. We need to do something on a day-to-day basis that focuses our thoughts and actions on bringing us closer and closer to the awakening, enlightenment potentiality that we each know is our birthright. Therefore, setting some kind of daily activist schedule is useful.

What is presented here is not a template for what *must* be

done. Be flexible. At the same time, recognize the value of each of these components as part of making our daily lives more meaningful and productive. Hold each aspect in your mind. Do the things you can and acknowledge the significance of the others to maintain a thread.

1. Upon waking, tradition teaches that we should appreciate that we have woken up to a new day. Each day holds the promise of transformation. What makes our day look predictable and end predictably has more to do with our habitual mind than what is lying in wait behind each corner. To shake us from our complacency and the humdrum of our minds, there are the Four Thoughts That Revolutionize The Mind (see pages 41-51).

2. Orienting our day with the recognition of the preciousness of what time and space provide us, we come to the Four Limitless Meditations (see pages 69–80) that link our happiness and wellbeing with the happiness and wellbeing with all whom we encounter. Such an altruistic focus takes us beyond our obsession with ourselves, lightens our load, and makes us more open to our own loving nature and the potential it conceals.

3. With such thoughts and intentions in place, it is good to take some time to center the mind with some form of meditation or mantra that helps to dissolve the Three Poisons (for example, the meditations and mantras given in Chapter 6). Dissolving our fixations and residing in a more natural state of being, we are immediately put in touch with our resourcefulness.

4. We then go out and meet our day. We perform our livelihood or whatever activity we do in a day. Regardless of what that activity may be, we try to feel some direct or indirect connection with others and the world around us.

In a mindful, relaxed state fueled by positive intention, we strive to be compassionate in our actions: sometimes peacefully; sometimes needing to empower others; sometimes exerting more influence and charisma; sometimes confronting. We try our best to do what we feel is most beneficial with the greatest amount of wisdom and skill we can muster.

5. As the day is drawing to a close, we can spend some moments reviewing what has happened. We should look closely at our successes as well as our failures. When we feel we have fallen short, we should admit it clearly to ourselves and recommit our efforts for the days to come. When we feel we have been successful, imagine that the value and merit of that success spreads out to more and more people.

Structuring our days in this way makes life like a *sadhana*, a deepening ritual that enriches each moment, and nothing that is done is ever wasted. In emphasizing what is positive and committing ourselves to act accordingly, we begin to steer our lives in a direction that will naturally dissolve whatever barriers we have in our path. This does not mean that this process is easy. But it is more rewarding. And when we embark on anything with a reward at the end, we embark on a journey.

The Journey of the Conscious, Engaged Activist

The world that we see and experience around us is the sum total of all previous intentions, whether good, bad, or indifferent; their resulting actions, whether skillful or not; and the ensuing emotional reactions and responses, which prompted a cascading of other intentions and their actions – and so on throughout time to the present. Our interpretation of our world is filtered through our cognitive and perceptual filters. If we are awakening to our enlightened potentiality, we see a world in suffering that beckons us to action. If we are more steeped in the Three Poisons, we choose to ignore what we see, put on rose-colored spectacles, and try to pretend that it really isn't happening; or we fight to get our way or that piece of the pie we think we are being deprived of. Apathy, endless distraction in limited *material or mundane* pursuits, frustration translated into self-destruction, war-mongering, and terrorism are naturally spawned by our lack of intelligence, skill, and/or willingness to actively engage in new ways of being and acting in the world. It is the dominance of this mentality that determines a Dark Age.

Regardless of how enlightened we are – or not – we would all like to live in a world that is peaceful and safe, whether it be for personal or collective happiness. When we think of the world around us and wish to see changes in foreign policy, a change of cultural or social imperatives, or economic reform, we often do not see our part in the picture. Many place the lion's share of such jobs and responsibilities upon officials – those who have or presume dominion over our lives and nation. Regardless of whether such officials are elected or not, if we do not ourselves actively participate in the processes that determine the course of what our world is to become, is it reasonable to assume that the actions of others, even if supposedly on our behalf, will yield the consequences we want?

Certainly, as we have seen again and again throughout history, those leaders who detach themselves or feel themselves to be different from the people around them, create circumstances that often lead to something other than what many had hoped for – even the opposite. If we live in a society where we can elect our leaders, they are charged to do the will of those by whom they have been elected. We may also have the seemingly peaceful choice of influencing legislation and changing government policy through the election process. Those living under less democratic systems, where the powers-that-be derive less of their legitimacy from the will of the citizenry, may need to seek allies and other ways of influencing how change can be initiated. Situations where the powers-that-be control by manipulation or intimidation may require someone of great charisma, who can magnetize and galvanize people around them to deal with an issue that needs to be addressed, to emerge as the force behind change. In a situation where people live in terror of a dictator, if all other peaceful means to ease the suffering of those at the hands of such a ruler seem ineffective, it may be necessary to take up arms and rebel.

Regardless of our situation, change is always possible. We can always participate more fully in effecting change. And the wisdom and skill we need to apply will be different depending on the individual circumstances we are facing. More profoundly, the circumstances we are facing are a mirror reflection of who we are. And if they appear to us as circumstances that need to be changed, then the resources that we need to call up from within are the ones most necessary for our own development and enlightenment. **Our world tests us and perfects us.**

The Last Straw: Saint, Sinner, Martyr, Madman, Hero...

In a world caught up in the Three Poisons, we may get the illusory idea that being a conscious, engaged activist would invite praise, admiration, adulation. After all, if we all possess enlightenment-potential, wouldn't we all want to celebrate someone who demonstrates these potentials in their life and is doing great things to change social systems, policies, governments, nations, and so on?

The fact is, however, that the Three Poisons, true to their name, "poison" this perception for many. Hence while some may well honor your courage and effort, there will be many others who see what you do as an embarrassment, creating tension and awkwardness. Deep down, people know that *they* can do better, but the habitual patterns that dominate their thoughts and actions bind them to an illusion of impossibility. And your actions are an affront to this reality.

The conscious, engaged activist is someone who strives to live according to higher, spiritual principles. The joy that we discover from within through living and acting in accordance with these principles must not be dependent upon what is outside us. In this light, I am reminded of the words of two of my closest teachers from the mid-1970s and early 1980s. At one teaching, in 1978, the Venerable Bardor Tulku Rinpoche was speaking to a class on making the choice to follow the Dharma, the teachings of the Buddha. "When you enter the Dharma," he said, "you will be treated lower than a dog in the street."

What his words were driving at was the fact that even though the Buddha teaches that we all have enlightenment-potential, most beings live in a state of mind governed by self-centeredness and self-preservation. When an individual makes a commitment to opening up to this inner potential and living in a way that demonstrates universal love and compassion, such light creates embarrassment to those around, who feel the same potential inside themselves, but somehow do not know how to pull themselves away from their habit of trying to have the world just the way they want it. And so, the "dog in the street," the spiritual aspirant, may be viewed as different, delusional, crazy, heretical, and perhaps even worth crucifying. In secular terms they might be viewed as "unpatriotic," as they are not a patriot according to the preferred, culturally reinforced paradigm.

Thus, to commit oneself to a life and a path based on spiritual or higher principles and practices is noble, but fraught with emotional turmoil and the distinct possibility that unpleasantness, even danger, will be part of the process. At a minimum, don't expect gratitude. In the face of hostility or condemnation, it may prove difficult to maintain equanimity. Your defenses, the Three Poisons attempting to ensure your sense of importance – at least to yourself – may translate into an attitude of superiority. This will only lead you to feel more isolated and probably give you a condescending air. It can even translate into a sense of feeling like a martyr. History has very few examples of truly noble martyrs. Let's not make the list any longer than we have to.

Along these lines, but in a more pragmatic vein, remember what was said earlier about rendering unto Caesar what is Caesar's. All too often, those who seek change are struck down by their own inattentiveness to the social and cultural norms around them – paying taxes, curbing the dog, participating in their own children's education, and so on. Not that you have to kowtow to morals and mores that you sincerely do not approve of, but consider: what would the ideal citizen look like? By not (or not overtly) breaking the rules that most people around you see as reasonable, and by participating in your community in ways that make you seem less alien, you can set a remarkable example: someone committed to principles of change and growth who, at the same time, exemplifies that which is upright in the eyes of those around you. Presenting people with such a quandary will invoke less wrath and more inquisitiveness.

Several years after the teaching with Bardor Tulku

Rinpoche, I attended a group interview with the Venerable Khenpo Karthar Rinpoche. A rather distraught woman asked him why her life was so hard, even though she did her meditations faithfully and daily and tried to help others wherever she could. In answering her, he also turned to the audience and posed a rhetorical question. Why would we think that entering on a spiritual path would be easy? If we are truly committed to stopping the self-perpetuated nonsense of our lives, wouldn't it stand to reason that "the buck would stop here?" **Once we commit ourselves to stopping ways of being that are unhelpful to ourselves and others, isn't it logical that the momentum behind such habits would come crashing in on us all at once? That there will be a quickening, an acceleration of the resolution of the karma created, as it were, which demands our utmost attention if we are not to backslide into negativity and the old habitual knee-jerk responses from which we are trying to liberate ourselves?**

By committing ourselves to a life of becoming more and more conscious and engaged in our actions, we run into the protests from within of our own Three Poisons, and the protests from without of others whose Three Poisons wish not to be disturbed by us. If we are to stick to our convictions, we must be prepared to tread a path not dissimilar to that of the Buddha's. To make a difference in our lives and the lives of others, we need to accept internal and external resistance to our intent and actions. As we face down the habit patterns that lead to sickness, poverty, and warfare, we must be prepared to be tested at every possible turn and to view these challenges not as grounds for turning back, but as confirmations of the value of our struggle.

Of course, because we are human, we can only exhibit human behaviors, whether we are delusional (caught in the web of the Three Poisons) or on the path to awakening. Either way, our actions may lead some to cheer us on, while others point the finger at us, accusing us of various crimes and misdemeanors. If we are committed to a path of awakening, rather than reacting by isolating ourselves, creating more disconnection and the likelihood of more confusion, we openly step forward and embrace those who challenge us along the way. This doesn't mean we necessarily become friends, kiss, and make up. Perhaps they will remain adversaries. But, in being willing to listen, to remain open to communicating, there is a greater likelihood of a resolution that makes things better for all.

Treading the path of a conscious, engaged activist as laid out in this chapter can be lonely. But because we are all interconnected, change within ourselves or in the world around us will not happen in isolation. Along with those who challenge us, there will also be friends and helpers along the way. They are indispensable in the changes and transformations to which we are now committed. In the next chapter, I move on to address the issues of community and support – the "pockets of light" mentioned in the Introduction.

CHAPTER 10

Pockets of Light, Sources of Inspiration

Whatever work we set out to do as conscious, engaged activists, we can never succeed by our own efforts alone. The simple truth is that because we are all inextricably interconnected, there will have been those who go before us and pave the road; well-wishers providing support as we pursue our goals; skeptics and others who challenge us to live up to our dreams and visions by their negative input; and those in the future whom we hope the seeds of our actions will inspire, so that the good that is done carries on. Thus, the past, present, and future, and all of those who we come into contact with along the way, provide the context of our efforts and always contribute to them.

All that being said, we *do* make choices with regard to whom we associate with. Generally speaking, we prefer to be around those who agree with us, try to avoid those who annoy us, and care little one way or another about everyone else. Such is the nature of the Three Poisons. Even if we have the equanimity of a Buddha, as in the earlier quote of Gampopa (see page 79), it *is* nice to have a few good friends. This is who I am referring to when I speak of "pockets of light and sources of inspiration."

Unless our minds and hearts are stable like those of a Buddha or bodhisattva, more than likely we shall not have the veracity and courage to endure and prevail in situations where all we get are challenges and negative feedback for our actions and our desire to transform ourselves and the world around us. We can learn to love our enemies and those who challenge us for the gifts of molding our character, even become Bodhisattva-like peacocks who learn to thrive in the Three Poisons that they offer us. But, for the most part, and especially in a Dark Age, it behooves us to seek out those who inspire us and those of a like mind – friends and helpers along the way. This is not a cop-out or a sign of weakness, it is a sign and testimony to the human way in which we most effectively manifest our loving nature.

Refuge

In the Buddhist tradition, there is the notion of seeking refuge. Refuge is like seeking shelter, protection, succor, a place where one is nurtured. In a sense, we do this in relative ways all the time through associating with what we like and staying away from what we don't like. We seek refuge in our friends, our favorite foods, in acquiring what we think will make us feel more complete as a person. The Buddha saw this human tendency and translated it into a path with more ultimate goals in mind. Seeking refuge in the Buddhist sense is about identifying and associating with those persons and things in our life that encourage us to grow; that help us to cut through the Three Poisons that imprison us and develop our enlightened potential.

In the Buddhist tradition, there are three primary dimensions in refuge that contribute to accomplishing this goal. This is called the Triple Refuge, or seeking refuge in the "Three Jewels": the Buddha, the Dharma (his teaching), and the Sangha (community of practitioners). They are called "jewels," because the Buddha saw them as precious and invaluable to our growth and development. In a broader sense, we are speaking about what I have referred to as sources of inspiration – learning and practicing methods that help us to transform our Three Poisons so that we can be more effective in what we do – together with some form of community support. All three of these jewels come together in a tangible way when the third, a supportive community, is present; this coming together is what "pockets of light" specifically refers to, and explains why the Buddha saw and emphasized the importance of "*sangha*" or community. That being said, let us look at each of the dimensions contributing to these "pockets of light."

Seeking refuge in the Buddha

To seek refuge in the Buddha is the desire to make a strong connection with all of those who manifest their full enlightened potential. We do this not out of a sense of worshipping them like a god or gods, but rather because they represent, and can show us by example, what it is we can accomplish in our own lives. In the Tibetan tradition, living people may indeed be recognized as incarnations of Buddhas and bodhisattvas. Called *tulku*s, these special individuals are often lamas or monks, but not necessarily so. There are also laypeople who do work in the world in a variety of ways. They can be ordinary people or those of note in history.

With this in mind, who inspires us? If it is true that nothing is ever lost, then those who have gone before, our ancestors, our nation's forefathers, the mothers and fathers of various humanitarian causes, those who have been sainted – are more than just historical figures. What endures is more than the memory of their actions. We can feel their energetic signature: their intentions, thoughts, and actions well focused and released in time and space that carry on to this day. When we reflect upon them, visualize and meditate upon them, and try to emulate them, we forge a direct connection to their cause, their being.

Tantric Buddhist tradition formalizes this in various visualization meditations. The Buddhas or bodhisattvas meditated upon express qualities that we wish to identify with and manifest in our own lives, be it compassion, wisdom, the ability to protect others, heal, and so on. Because these meditations have been done for centuries with great success, they are, according to tradition, reliable and guarantee results. But whether one does these particular practices or not, **the act of invoking and seeking refuge in the example and energy of a source of inspiration, identifying with that being or person and seeing ourselves becoming just like them, can be done regardless of whether it is a saint, a national leader, or any very powerful figure. In this way we connect with and become a conduit for a worthy way of being, cause, or goal, and by taking it forward one more generation, we can deliver something of value to the future.**

Spending a little time each day showing appreciation for those who inspire us is valuable and creates connection. This may be done as formal meditation. We might make a special space where we have pictures, artifacts, books, or other reminders invoking our connection to what and/or who inspires us. Going on a pilgrimage to where such people lived or taught – be it Bodh Gaya in India (where the Buddha found Enlightenment), Rome, or Washington D.C. – and meeting, spending time, or studying with those who continue their work or example, can strengthen our qualities and appreciation and give us a deeper resolve to do the work we are inspired to do.

Seeking refuge in the Dharma

The second refuge in Buddhist tradition is the Dharma. Most appropriately translated, Dharma means "the way things are." As mentioned earlier, the Dharma is what the Buddha taught – an entire cosmology and explanation of how things are in this world and beyond. But this is not so unusual because all cosmologies and philosophies do the same, and proclaim themselves to be true.

The fundamental teachings of the Dharma do not in any way contradict any of the world's great wisdom traditions, of East or West. At the same time, as a pragmatist and one who respected science and experiential learning, the Buddha did not want anyone to take what he said about what was going on in blind faith. He wanted people to know things from the inside out. And so he gave methods of contemplation and meditation that worked with dismantling the Three Poisons, the root causes of our biases and prejudices. In that way, people came to knowledge of the world through experience and intimacy. Many other traditions in the world have similar methods and practices of enquiry, contemplation, and meditation. It is interesting and refreshing to note that once people get beyond their sectarian biases, there is often a sharing of methods and information that enriches all traditions and those who practice them. (I recall doing some work for a Trappist monastery in Kentucky where the brothers of the order did yoga and meditation as part of their spiritual practice. As far as they were concerned, any method that got them closer to God was fine by them.)

Seeking refuge in such wisdom traditions is the conscious, engaged activist's commitment to employing methods that always cut to the chase; that always aim to dismantle mechanisms that create partisanship, boundaries, suspicion, or barriers to peace and harmony among people and nations.

The methods outlined throughout this book, employed with skill and wisdom to accomplish the noble intention of the Four Limitless Meditations on love, compassion, joy, and equanimity, fit well with any of the great wisdom traditions or with any other positive, life-embracing philosophy to which one may feel aligned.

The term Dharma is usually classified as either "absolute," or "ultimate," and "relative." Absolute or ultimate Dharma has to do with the meditation and contemplative methods that aim directly to counter our intoxication in the Three Poisons. This will help us in whatever endeavor we apply skillful means and wisdom. Relative Dharma has to do with the information and practical day-to-day things we can do in the world in order to foster a positive and encouraging environment for us to engage in the practices of absolute Dharma. Among the fields of knowledge that were considered part of relative Dharma, the Buddha spoke of philosophy and dialectics – pondering the world from a broader perspective and understanding some of its underlying mechanisms. Thus there are great treatises on Buddhist philosophy, cosmology, earth sciences, and medicine which help us to see how the Three Poisons play themselves out in the world as the Five Great Elements. These elements are common to virtually all wisdom traditions as the matrix that comes together at all levels in manifest reality. There is no room to elaborate on such a vast topic here. But the point is that if we do *not* know how these elements come together and function in the normal run of things as they unfold, then we shall be less able to know what to do for ourselves or others.

In all the ages humans have existed on this planet, there have been seminal thinkers and visionaries who – steeped in the forms of prayer, meditation, and contemplation of their own spiritual and cultural context – have examined their world at the level of physical science, philosophy, linguistics, political and social sciences, and economics. They have presented models of understanding that at times have brought stability to uncertain times, and at other times challenged people with revolutionary ways of seeing. The works of such thinkers have stood the test of time for good reason.

So we should not be satisfied with reading books only on spiritual matters. How spiritual awareness is translated into the "affairs of the world" – the daily realities of the average person – as presented by philosophers, historians, economists and the like, while perhaps not being entirely "enlightened" are worth reading, contemplating, discussing. At the least, they can take us out of the ivory towers of spiritual refinement and put us back in the trenches with the nitty gritty realities of *samsara*, giving us some grist for the mill so that we can test our awakening hearts and minds in the practical matters of the day. Along with the classics of antiquity and other distant times, there are any number of modern thinkers whose perspectives are worth considering, such as Marilyn Ferguson, Noam Chomsky, R.D. Laing, and even the political reflections of former presidents and world leaders.

Of course, we *can* always just focus on spiritual matters and on our own transformation – then step into the world wherever we like, raising the consciousness where we are. But, more than likely, we shall gravitate toward those figures whom we feel close to or identify with. The world as presented by great thinkers and visionaries may not be entirely complete or accurate, but it can offer us a wider context from which we can choose how and where to deploy our efforts. Even someone like His Holiness the Dalai Lama recognizes the necessity of this, which explains the often very political content of his writings.

Seeking refuge in the Sangha

Finally we come to refuge in sangha. Sangha is about community – forging a connection between us and those who exemplify what we are trying to accomplish in our lives or who, like ourselves, are also trying to figure out how to manifest conscious, engaged activism in their day-to-day lives. In Buddhist tradition, there is a distinction drawn between "noble" sangha and "ordinary" sangha. This distinction is worth looking at as it can clarify several issues, including jealousy, competitiveness, and personal disappointment.

For now I will focus exclusively on spiritual matters. As I have said at other times, regardless of whether our intentions are clear and pure and whether or not our actions are wise and skillful, we shall continue to breathe and act in this world. Thus until we have reached a state of enlightened awareness where our clarity and purity create only wholesome results in the world around us, we can expect mixed outcomes – some good, some not so good, even some bad – with the hope that the greater weight goes to what is good or at least not harmful. In other words, we should not be too surprised that things don't work out exactly as we envision them, and that there is some karmic fallout and kickback that lets us know that we are not as smart, or compassionate, or selfless as we would like to imagine.

At the same time, this does not mean that we should not strive over the course of our lives toward clarity and purity as the most noble of goals. In fact, one can argue that for some of us, a path that is more active and involved in the world is the fastest path to clearing things up for ourselves and others – providing we are given the tools, the time, the space, and ability to work with our mindfulness in the course of things.

I say this for pragmatic reasons because, generally speaking, few of us have either the luxury or inclination to devote all of our time and mental, physical, and spiritual energies toward a solely contemplative life in a monastery or cloistered retreat. But it would be erroneous for us not to value and appreciate those who *do* have such time and opportunity – who have a single-minded focus on spiritual matters and can create the energy and openness that not only contributes to their own awakening, but also creates an energy vortex that can inspire and create opportunity for others as well. This is the value of monasteries and the treasure of saints, hermits, and practitioners of faith who dedicate their lives and express their conscious, engaged activism in this particular manner.

There are many such men and women around the world, who most of us have never heard of. Of course, such an exclusively religious life may, for some, seem rarified, cloistered, impractical – a way of avoiding the big responsibilities of life. In some cases this may be true. Even the great Tibetan saint Milarepa once said that "A monastery is where driftwood gathers." At the same time, there are those whose abilities are best trained and honed in such environments. And to have the opportunity to retreat, to have a place to go to which is exclusively focused on deepening our understanding and experience of transforming the Three Poisons can be invaluable for everyone; such places are "pockets of light," and it is for these reasons that it is worthwhile supporting them and their practitioners.

And then there are those whose spiritual practices and lives as spiritual elders and guides lead them to up the moral and ethical standards in practical walks of life beyond "spiritual" ones alone. Such is the case with such spiritual adepts as Mother Teresa, the Dalai Lama, Gyalwa Karmapa, or Zalman Schacter, whose impact on wider world events should not be underestimated.

In more mundane matters, it is also true that there are

causes or issues we would like to spend more time or energy on, but are limited from doing so for any number of reasons. There are others, however, who have the inclination, time, resources, or a combination of all three, to devote their energies almost exclusively to worthy causes, to making a difference. We should celebrate and admire those who are willing to spend their time and energy in this way as they are often the ones who keep social movements and political action groups alive over time. For the rest of us, contributing our time, energy, or resources whenever we can keeps us connected and can demonstrate our commitment to such causes and issues.

Beyond the mutual support and benefits that are derived from supporting those dedicated activists who are "minding the fort," so to speak, it can be just as important, if not more so, for us to find those around us on a day to day basis who share a similar path. And by sharing a "path" I mean more than just an interest in particular causes or issues: even more important is to find those who are committed to *inner* as well as outer change, and can support our own commitment in this respect. Basically, we need to find others who are similarly interested in treading the path of a conscious, engaged activist.

To come across teachers and associates committed to such a path is rare in the normal course of our daily lives. These days, however, there are any number of spiritual groups, Dharma centers, psychotherapeutic groups, and so on; if they do not yet exist in your area, the chances are that there are other people also looking for them who would, if the opportunity arose, be willing to join together. That being said, it is not necessarily likely that such a support group, spiritual organization, center of activity, or gathering will be harmonious, blissful and nurturing in the same way one might expect a group of quilt or dog enthusiasts to be bonded together. This has to do with the very nature of such groups.

Generally speaking, what matters most in a "pocket of light" group or community is that all agree upon what it is important *to aspire to*. There needs to be a *shared intention*. This intention centers on each person's commitment to transforming their Three Poisons. With that in place and agreed upon, the complex and often messy entanglements of human interaction can then be played out and worked on, and each member's personal transformation is hopefully accelerated in the process. For in the process of committing to that intention, each person will be dragged backward into their own Three Poisons. Each person's personal commitment to work on transforming their Three Poisons is mirrored in their tolerance or intolerance, patience or impatience, compassion or lack of compassion for everyone else in the group. Naturally, everyone in the group will be at a different stage of inner growth, which is why such groups are complex and personally sometimes fraught. The aim of the group is for the whole to collectively help each individual member toward his or her goal.

While it may be true that our interaction with each and every being we meet will mirror what is going on inside of us, the people in a "pocket of light" community are *committed* to being mirrors. This is very different, and in a way trickier, than "normal" social discourse, where we try to cover for each other, turning a blind eye, if at all possible, to what we find embarrassing or awkward. Here, we refuse to turn away from one another. We tell it how we see it. And in being committed to openness in this way, of course, we also subject one another to the sum total of our own confusion and enlightenment. Our ultimate aspiration to benefit others, and our relative wisdom and ability to do so, are tested in a well-focused "loving-nature laboratory." This can make such groups at times feel quite claustrophobic and at other times quite liberating. A wide range of emotional responses needs to be

embraced and accepted if one is to harness and work successfully with the intensity of such groups. If any group member
begins to feel smug, or noticeable "in-crowds" or cliques start
to appear, it is a sign that partisanship is emerging and the
group is becoming a social club that needs to be shaken up.
This will inevitably happen, one way or another. The reifica-
tion and ossification of behaviors into personal styles and
mannerisms can stifle true growth. For this reason, *all* groups
need their heretics, or those who are willing to shake things
up, to redirect the group back to its original purpose: being a
pocket of light, for the benefit of all, not just a few.

Pockets of light and sources of inspiration may be found at
the types of group mentioned above, which we can contact,
be a part of, pay membership dues to, and so on. However, I
would suggest that we also need to be quite flexible in our
expectations of how a pocket of light might appear. Our
sources of inspiration and community can be an informal,
unorganized association of close friends from over the years,
people whom we occasionally talk with or email. However
such sources of refuge in our lives appear, it is valuable for us
to visualize them and try to manifest them. For without their
support, generating the enthusiasm, discipline, patience, focus,
and other qualities we need to be a light-bearer in a Dark Age
is far more daunting a task.

Recognizing the importance of these "jewels" for our lives and
our work as conscious, engaged activists demonstrates not
only our interdependent relationship with all those around
us. It is a sign of our spiritual maturity and understanding
that, in order to get things done – to muster a force more
powerful than our own person or personality – we don a
mantle of enduring inspiration, arm ourselves with the skill
and wisdom born of discriminating compassionate mindful-

ness, and step forward into action with force and the protection of all those who support our unabashed attempts at authentically being who we are: a conscious, engaged activist wishing to benefit all we can by our efforts.

Pockets of light bring together the refuges of sources of inspiration and methods to transform our own lives and the lives of those we touch, into a tangible social group or culture that we surround ourselves with. This powerful trinity of refuges constitutes a unity that is indispensable for true and lasting change, within and without. As we open up, surrender our sense of personal ego and advantage, and learn to trust and be reliant upon these sources of support, our field of action and effectiveness grows. Our refuges then also become bases, which foster and develop natural born leaders for future generations.

The Buddha at Peace

"We must be the change we wish to see in the world."

Mahatma Gandhi

In the first verses of the classical Buddhist text, the *Vimalakirti Nirdesa Sutra*, the historical Buddha, Shakyamuni, is sitting among countless disciples, bodhisattvas, goddesses, and gods, all experiencing in their own way the splendor of his field of enlightened energy – the "Buddhafield" that radiates from the enlightened being at its center.

All seemed so perfect. However, in Buddhist lore it is said that when beings are stuck or in need of further teaching, a Buddha will telepathically influence the mind of a disciple to pose a question. In this way, Shakyamuni prompted his disciple Shariputra to raise the following question about the Buddha's Buddhafield or enlightened realm: If an enlightened realm is a perfect, splendid place, why do some beings residing in it suffer? Why are there beings suffering in sickness, poverty, and warfare? For indeed, beyond the enclave of blissful gods and disciples, this is what Shariputra saw in the world outside.

To this the Buddha replied, "What do you think

Shariputra? Is it because the sun and moon are impure that those blind from birth do not see them?"[15] The Buddha was referring to the Three Poisons that blind us to the splendor of the world. To demonstrate beyond a shadow of a doubt the world's splendor, the Buddha touched his big toe to the ground. Everything was transformed into precious gems blazing dazzlingly beautiful light in all directions. Thus the Buddha revealed to Shariputra and every other being present the full splendor of his Buddhafield – the true nature of the world around us. And then, to show Shariputra once more what the world looks like under the influence of the Three Poisons, the Buddha removed his toe from the ground.

The message from the Buddha here is that, **on an ultimate level, everything is fine. There is, absolutely speaking, *nothing really* to worry about, because what we *do* worry about is *nothing that is real*.** What makes it seem real are the Three Poisons – our ignorance, our attachments, our aggression.

The Buddha's war against the Three Poisons does not require him to suit up for battle. In fact, it requires nothing of him at all. In his love, compassion, joy, and equanimity he effortlessly creates the context and the methods that can give beings the time, space, and opportunity to unravel the mystery for themselves. However, like all of those with common sense, the Buddha knows that "You can lead a horse to water, but…." He knows that for us to manifest our enlightened potentiality and become free, independent, conscious, and engaged activists requires work that is rooted in our own intention, our own motivation to change.

---

[15] *Vimalakirti Nirdesa Sutra*, translated by Robert Thurman. University of Pennsylvania, 1976, pp.6–7 (online version).

Beyond Hope and Fear

The Ven. Khenpo Karthar Rinpoche addressed this issue in a talk about the Medicine Buddha, a being we met in Chapter 6 (see page 108). The Rinpoche said that if all it took for us to become enlightened was grace – being blessed or blasted with *shakti* or fairydust by some divine being – then we would all have become enlightened a long time ago. But this is obviously not the case. If, however, we hold onto such a belief or faith, that grace is all that is needed, then it is easy to find ourselves caught in a cycle of hope and fear: hoping that it will happen to us, that things will just change by themselves and everything will be fine; or fearing that it won't happen at all, or that it doesn't matter what we do.

The late Venerable Chögyam Trungpa Rinpoche also warned against hope and fear. Hope, he argued, can make us lazy and cause us to lapse into inertia, believing that "the universe will provide," or some similar manifestation of pre-destination or a dualistic belief in some outside force or being coming to our rescue, making everything all right. Fear, on the other hand, causes inaction in a different way, by creating paralysis and a resistance to change – the groundwork for the devastating dualistic notion of nihilism, the belief that nothing is worth doing because nothing makes a difference. Whether we are too loose or too tight, in either case we lose the will to move forward and end up wallowing in self-absorbing indulgence, self-denigration, or apathy. But if things are to change for the better, move we must. And, **if we really want to change, we need to get behind ourselves in the moves that we do make.** We need to choose between extremes of looseness and tightness. We need to seek a middle way that allows us to thread our path around all the illusions that the web of the Three Poisons casts before us.

The Buddha's demeanor does not change in peace or war. Enlightened beings are always available to us. In their intimate connection to everything – having awoken to the illusion of separateness – they appear in accordance with our needs and perceptions. It is down to us, a reflection of our own needs, whether we perceive a peaceful or a wrathful Buddha. Thus the Buddha at War is also the Buddha at Peace. In either guise, he and other enlightened beings – of all traditions and times – are there to inspire us to use our resourcefulness to undo the Dark Age in which we suffer. For, like everything else, what is this Dark Age but an illusion?

In a similar fashion, the conscious, engaged activist may appear in any number of guises, and act in any number of ways, depending on the circumstances. In the course of history, even in the course of our own lives, we see that what we are called to do, what resources we draw on from within, do change. There is a slogan in Buddhist mind training: "Don't be consistent" (or "Don't rely on consistency"[16]). In a world that fears the truth of impermanence, such a slogan is illogical and threatening. Our social and cultural mores emphasize certain behaviors as being more acceptable than others. On the one hand this is reasonable, but only to a limited degree. For, in the long run, too strict a prescription of how we are supposed to be is stifling and can drive us away from trusting the wisdom inherent in our loving nature. As beings of the human realm, bound by the energies of our passions, awaiting transformation to their enlightened potential, we are not, nor can we ever really be, consistent. What is demanded of us to grow and act in the world, here and now, requires us to draw deeply from the limitless resources that are within each of us.

[16] Jamgon Kongtrul, *The Great Awakening*. Shambhala Books, Boston, 1987, p.31.

As we revolutionize our minds and come to an understanding that for one of us to be liberated, all must be liberated, we become more conscious, engage each situation with greater wisdom and clarity, and employ whatever skills or actions the situation before us demands. As love, compassion, joy, and equanimity become the motivating intentions upon which all of our actions are based, the peace and stillness of our minds – the mind of the Buddha at Peace – will not be disturbed by whatever action we are inspired to take. **It is said that the end point of Samurai training comes when the warrior moves through the day in a state of perfect peace and equanimity and then, as he lies down to sleep, notices that there is blood on the edge of his sword.**

In the End...

If we accept the truth that the Dark Age we currently face is the shared illusion that arises from our previous actions and emotional responses to all the dilemmas we have faced over the course of human history, then our future will be determined by how we respond to *today's* dilemmas. If our responses come out of anger, then we shall see the fruits of anger in the future. If we respond with despair, likewise.

The only option to consider if we truly want to start contributing to a better today and a brighter tomorrow is to commit ourselves to living and acting from our loving nature, doing whatever we can to minimize our reaction from our Three Poisons, and ultimately transforming them. We commit ourselves to acting compassionately with the clearest intention that we can muster.

If we want our world to look different, to see it as the Buddha sees it, we need to undertake the transformation of ourselves from within. This task is at least equal in importance to our external actions in the world. Otherwise, in the face of the sickness, poverty, and warfare that still rages within us, a lasting world peace is not possible. Whatever we do and whatever we create will be undone and, like a house of cards, is not worth betting on.

And even as more enlightened awareness grows and expands from the "pockets of light" that continue to shine, the work of making such awareness real and applying it practically to today's conflict and strife remains an immense task – a task that men and women of courage and virtue have wrestled with since the dawn of civilization. Even to focus on less ambitious goals intended to transform social and political policy, and to support more enlightened behaviors in the world will not be accomplished in a few short years. It would be foolhardy and downright naïve to assume that one or two election cycles, even in the most progressive, democratic nation can effect a transformation of deep-seated, historical patterns of greed and self-interest. Habitual patterns reinforced over generations do not easily fade; they easily resurface by the sheer weight that they carry, if the efforts to change them are not carried through with similar force and determination.

In this context I am reminded of a Tibetan teacher who presented us with a startling look at Tibetan culture. Tibetan belief includes a tradition of detecting and identifying great teachers from the past who have been newly reincarnated. Once recognized, usually at a very young age, these *tulkus* or *Rinpoches* ("Precious Ones") are often installed as heads of sects, monasteries, and so on, with full responsibility for, and access to, the material and spiritual treasures passed down through the ages, so that they can be used to benefit the world they currently live in. At the same time, Tibetan culture is clan- and family-oriented. So even if a child is identified as a high lama and is raised to hold a position of high ecclesiastical authority, they are still beholden to their family and clan, and those who head them. Consequently, if there are conflicts or problems in the community, these highly evolved and spiritually-oriented teachers are expected to go along with what the clan and family leaders tell them to do.

They may know better and yet, because they understand that "blood is thicker than water" and that the reinforced habitual patterns of families, clans, and the culture in general affect a number of beings all at once, they are very conscious of implementing or encouraging change in ways that do not disturb the overall beneficial functions that the family and clan may perform. This is very much in keeping with the Native American "seventh generation" principle – the principle that, before any action is taken by the clan, its implications not just for now but for the next *seven generations* must be considered. In our own instant, quick-fix cultural milieu, not only does such an attitude seem foreign. It seems painfully slow, and not *exciting* in the least. But that is the challenge we face if we want to steer our cultures, our civilization, our fellow humanity in the direction of embracing compassionate, enlightened principles in all it does.

What we ask of ourselves is no small thing. The enlightened ones who walk among us, the "peacocks" who manage to demonstrate skill and wisdom in creating change around us in whatever capacity they can, have not achieved their skills over a weekend, perhaps – in the Buddhist view – not even in one lifetime. Yet, because it is our birthright, we cannot help but strive toward this awakened state and act accordingly. Until then, we must accept the fact that unless we are an enlightened being and can act so flawlessly that there are only *intended* effects from what we do, in the present through to the future, our actions will lead to unintended and unwanted effects, even "collateral damage." No situation we walk into is clear-cut. A multitude of forces – positive, negative, and mixed intentions, and actions skillful or otherwise – come together to present us with the situation we want to make better. We can have the best intentions, act compassionately with the wisdom and skill derived from practices that focus our mind, and dedicate our efforts with the hope that something of lasting value will persist.

But as the endless moments keep coming, it is difficult to know what, of that which we have done, will endure. So while we may derive happiness or satisfaction from the victory of our cause – our candidate being elected, a policy changed for the better, our adversary vanquished – something new and different will always emerge. Our work in one sense may be done, but in the endlessness of time marching on, new work will be called for. We may not choose to address that work. The skills we employed to do what we just accomplished may not even be needed or called for in what needs to be addressed next. But we cannot ignore, or dissociate ourselves from, what follows in the wake of our actions by reveling only in what we have done up till now. To do so is to ossify our hearts and minds, to lapse into nostalgia and a very tenuous self-satisfaction. **Smugness is not an admirable trait in anyone and is especially inappropriate, and a gross miscalculation, for the conscious, engaged activist.**

For, long after we have influenced the course of any given event directly, we can learn about cause and effect, see the skill or error of our ways, by witnessing what has endured and what has fallen away. This deepens our spiritual awareness and places us in the position of sage – someone who has been there, knows the path and the pitfalls, and thus can contribute through passing on the wisdom of our age and experience to those who are now more keen or able to continue with the work that needs to be done.

It is sad if those of younger, more agile abilities do not seek out this wisdom. But when the wisdom-holders, or "elders," themselves choose not to stay engaged, then, the culture of sharing available wisdom is lost, and this is sadder still – and is, in fact, one of the causes of history repeating itself and of people needing to "reinvent the wheel" again and again. But as tedious and futile as it may seem repeatedly to bring about changes which in turn get undone for any number of reasons, it takes much longer to change consciousness than it does to change external events. As has been said earlier, it is in the consciousness of humanity where the fundamental changes need to occur before we can expect to see the external improvements that we may desperately fight for persist.

In the very end, whether we stay engaged or turn away from honestly looking at the fruits of our actions, on our deathbeds we shall look around and see that while we may have made a change to improve our world, things could be even better. We shall die with unfinished business. This unfinished business will, according to the principles of karma, be the cause for our return. Those capacities that we have developed in this current lifetime will continue in our next life, but so will any traces of our Three Poisons that remain untransformed. The circumstances that mirror what we have not transformed within us will manifest as the circumstances we show up to in our next life. As in the saying, "Wherever you go, there you are," **we never, ever get away**. Our sentience, our consciousness, and the desire to manifest our loving nature present us with perpetual moments of unfinished business, which are, at the same time, endless moments for awakening. From the Buddhist point of view, this awakening becomes less and less personal and more and more transpersonal and transuniversal. In the end, our enlightenment is not an "escape" from it all, but rather a total 100 percent immersion into the stream, radiating love and compassion overtly and in inexplicable ways to countless beings whose Three Poisons create the illusion of separation (which includes the illusion of escape) and are the causes and conditions for sickness, poverty, and warfare.

To be, live, and act in such a way is to be love incarnate. The Ven. Chögyam Trungpa Rinpoche, Lord Ösel Mukpo of Shambhala (see page 20), often said that being a warrior of Shambhala was to be a "darling of the world" – having a soft front and a hard back, a balance of wisdom and skill to care, to love. Thus, **love is who we are and love is what we are destined to do**. This is what being conscious and engaged is truly all about, and if we focus on this here and now, we implicitly understand the logic of both "getting our own house in order" and attending to our world as best we know how.

The roads that activists follow may look similar, contradictory, or in direct opposition to one another. Some will walk arm in arm. Some will take up arms against each other. This does not matter. For if each is working with the highest possible intent, based on a commitment to mindfulness, and dedicated to the betterment of all, regardless of the actions taken, there will be a confluence of pooled goodness that will reveal itself in a future possibly more glorious than any of its contributors could have imagined possible.

Even if we feel overwhelmed at times, when our wisdom fails to provide us the ultimate view of a world shining with possibility and we feel lacking in the skill to be able to make effective, lasting change, we should try to visualize and hold in our hearts the images of a world free of the Three Poisons and the sickness, poverty, and warfare they inevitably create. For if we focus solely on thoughts of gloom and doom, what is wrong, and how hard it all is, we shall be weighed down from within and never fully be able to claim the power, joy, and compassion that we truly are. To be an effective agent of social and political change, the conscious, engaged activist must train himself or herself to see through the pessimism, the illusion of solid darkness, and remain steadfast in a vision of light and promise.

Dark Ages do come to an end. In truth, they never were, are, or will be anything other than the illusion that conceals an unending light. In truth, each of us knows this to a greater or lesser extent. However, the conscious, engaged activist commits to putting an end to the illusion – no matter how long it takes.

"How to React as a Buddhist to the September 11th Tragedy"

A Statement Made by His Holiness the 14th Kunzig Shamar Rinpoche on September 24th, 2001

"During the past two weeks as I have traveled in the United States, many have asked me to explain the horrible acts of the terrorists on September 11th, and to suggest a course of action from the Buddhist perspective. I offer the following thoughts for guidance.

The terrorists who brought about this senseless tragedy are afflicted by ignorance and, consequently, can be deceived by a blind faith in a belief system that distorts the true spirit of Islam. They do not have the wisdom and proper sense of judgment to determine what is right or wrong. Because of their ignorance and blind faith, people with evil intentions have manipulated and misused them. Therefore, just as we should show compassion for the victims, we should also have compassion for the terrorists due to their ignorance.

When governments and individuals set a future course of action, their motivation or aim is the critical determinant to what is appropriate and morally correct. The seeking of revenge clearly is not acceptable in Buddhist terms. However, if a government or individual must take an action that has harmful effects, but is done for the purpose of preventing evil and benefiting the majority, then this is acceptable.

According to the Buddha's teachings on ethics, I believe there are four different combinations of aim and intention and action. Listed from the most evil to the most compassionate, they are:

Bad or evil aim with negative or hurtful action;
Bad aim with benign or positive action;
Good, realistic aim with destructive or harmful action;
Good or pure aim with benevolent action.

In order to counter terrorism, governments of the world and their leaders must pursue this goal only with the aim of benefiting everyone, including the ignorant terrorists themselves. If purely benevolent acts are inadequate to achieve this goal, then there is no choice but to engage in narrowly targeted acts designed to root out the evil of the terrorists while inflicting the least amount of harm to the innocent. This can be accomplished through the use of wisdom and compassion which we find through logical analysis that is a part of human wisdom. It is important not to make decisions based on our obscured emotions.

On a personal level, we should not dwell in our sadness or fear over this tragedy. Instead, we should use it as an inspiration to develop our compassion. We should make wishing prayers for the victims, but also expand our wishes to include all beings who have suffered throughout the world. This tragedy must inspire us to achieve a vast compassion for all beings."

Shamarpa.

Postscript on an American Election, November 3rd, 2004

In the spring of 2004, I had a dream where I was with Senator John Kerry. He had already won most of the Democratic primaries, as I had predicted. I wasn't particularly enamored of him as a candidate. It was just that he was the most "presidential" of the pack.

In my dream I yelled to Senator Kerry that he was going to win in a landslide. He looked shocked by my bold exclamation and promptly exited my dream. When I awoke in the morning, I emailed the Kerry campaign and wrote, "Visualize Kerry in a Landslide." It became a mantra on the internet and the newly formed Air America. As the election drew near and I listened to gleeful shouts of "Kerry in a Landslide," I began to wonder. For in truth, every time my mouth tried to proclaim these words forcefully and with certainty, my gut tightened and I felt an air of uncertainty close in around me. I've had prophetic dreams, but I've also had the usual and common flights of fantasy and unresolved emotional dreams. Sometimes it can be hard to tell the difference. My stomach tightening was telling me at a visceral level the true nature of my dream. But I so wanted to believe...

It's not that I believed that the victory of John Kerry was going to change the political or social landscape all that dramatically. This I was willing to concede. I did not see him unilaterally pulling out of Iraq as some of my leftist and pacifist friends wanted. Clearly, in the quagmire that the neoconservative Bush administration had created in Iraq, to do so would cause more harm than good. I did not see him solving the outsourcing problem. As a capitalist economy with global access, to think that this trend won't increase is naïve. I did not believe that whatever health care reforms a Kerry administration was promising would really break the backs of the pharmaceutical and insurance interests or provide better health care. The allopathic medical model is just too flawed to begin with and nobody in the dialogue on health care is seriously considering prevention. And, even if Kerry *was* swept in, a House and Senate on the other side of the political fence ensured gridlock.

But what I was hoping for in this election was a change of heart in public dialogue. I wanted to see an administration capable of explaining to people in plain terms the complexities and interconnectedness of the world we now live in. I wanted to see more compassion, sensitivity, and thoughtfulness in political and diplomatic discourse. I wanted to see an awareness of the light, even if we could not raise ourselves out of the darkness of the times.

In uncertain times, a message that reminds people of their responsibility to those around them appeals far less than a message that tries to soothe the fear and despair in people's hearts. Even though the Bush administration had led the country into a war under false pretenses, even though the wealthy and corporate interests had been the only ones reaping the riches of a supposed economy on the mend, even though every campaign promise of 2000 had been left behind untouched, George W. Bush's message of "Stand with me" was what the majority of people in this country wanted to hear.

The media pundits called a vote for George W. Bush the "moral" vote. Some went so far as to more clearly identify these voters as evangelicals and those who were a part of, or leaning toward, the religious right. In the light of Kalachakra predictions of a Western and Eastern form of fundamentalism being the source for 300 years of conflict, it would seem that even though this country is clearly divided, the current administration will take its marginal victory as an overwhelming mandate and continue to pursue policies that will continue to force their will on the world. And some in the world who feel that their way of life and beliefs are being challenged and disregarded will push and fight back with whatever means they have available. The US will blithely talk of "collateral damage" and bomb from the air and in the safety of tanks in the name of "defending freedom," while accusing those who use hand-to-hand and more personal tactics of suicide bombings and beheadings as being nothing more than barbaric terrorists.

In the elections of 1800, it has been said that there were papers that warned that if Thomas Jefferson was elected, God would be angry and would send a rain of fire down to destroy people's homes. Jefferson won and it didn't happen. Like the other Founding Fathers of this nation, Jefferson saw how people with limited access to education and simplistic belief systems could be easily manipulated. This is what had kept the pompous aristocracies of Europe in power for generations, which no doubt is why Jefferson and several other revolutionary fathers had little tolerance for these aristocracies or for the emerging wealthy landed gentry in a young America who wanted to create their own American royalty. Of course, Jefferson's real solution, and the solution that the Founding Fathers agreed upon, was far less radical – at least on the surface. *Education*, they said, was the key. An intelligent, informed electorate was, and is, the greatest insurance that there would be responsible government.

In 1996, my wife and I and two of our children drove across America. Once off the coast of California we saw the wide open corn fields, the feed lots, the large crosses, and the endless miles between urban centers. We drove into small towns and mid-sized cities that had once been the teeming thoroughfares of commerce and activity for miles around. Interstates had replaced the small state routes, railroads, and river transportation. Agri-business had swallowed up the small farms. For the most part we saw people who looked like shadows of their former selves and of the strapping farming folk who once proudly inhabited the plains. Rural America is not thriving and the churches are the common places where people get together to feel a sense of community and purpose. And the plain-spoken commentary of a Fox media network, and right-wing and evangelical programming and news is what they are fed, day in and day out.

In many respects, what they are hearing from the media and their preachers is not that dissimilar from what is taught in the *madrasas* (religious schools) of Pakistan and the Middle East. That these people voted the way they did in this election should come as no surprise. And that those living on the East or West coasts and in the more progressive cities of the Midwest expected people to vote differently because of the sheer volume of lies exposed over time, just demonstrates to me that while they may claim to be progressive, they do not fully comprehend the power of fear and ignorance. Then again, perhaps they just couldn't imagine the magnitude of the problem.

But now, stung twice in two successive elections, people are more awake. They are looking at local, national, and international issues with greater discernment. And they are more aware of power and how it is wielded. In truth, my biggest concern for this election was that if Kerry had actually won, even by the slightest of margins, many of those who had fought for change would have gone back to sleep, lulled into the security of thinking that all would be made right. Of course, having lost, I am equally concerned that those who fought so hard will now believe that all is lost and that there is no point in carrying on, or will be so bitter in their discourse as to become as vicious and dismissive as those whose tactics they have denounced.

As I have said, no effort is ever wasted. Dark Ages dissolve in the face of awakening, just as the sun – which is always there – gradually begins to dissolve the clouds that obscure it. Hopefully, there are enough mature souls putting their efforts into these four years who understand that the fight that was waged for this one election could not, nor could it ever, change all of the wrongs that we as humans have perpetrated against ourselves, for generation after generation. Once aroused from our slumber, once we have become sufficiently conscious and engaged, there is no ethical or moral way to turn back, to turn a blind eye.

We now have more work to do. Or rather, we have the same work to do – only with a greater sense of urgency.

The Buddha is still at war.

Robert Sachs.

BIBLIOGRAPHY

Chödrön, Pema. *The Wisdom of No Escape.* Shambhala Books, Boston, 1991.

Chögyam Trungpa Rinpoche. *Great Eastern Sun: The Wisdom of Shambhala.* Shambhala Books, Boston, 1999.

Dalai Lama, H.H. the 14th. *A Policy of Kindness.* Snow Lion Publications, Ithaca, NY, 1990.

Dalai Lama, H.H. the 14th. *The Little Book of Wisdom.* Rider, London, Sydney, Auckland, Johannesburg, 1997.

Dharmarakshita. *The Wheel of Sharp Weapons.* Library of Tibetan Works and Archives, Dharamsala, India, 1981.

Ellis, Joseph J. *Founding Brothers: The Revolutionary Generation.* Vintage/Random House, Inc., New York, 2000.

Gyalwa Karmapa, H.H. the 16th. *Dzalendara and Sakarchupa.* Karma Drubgyud Darjay Ling, Eskdalemuir, Scotland, 1981.

Gilbert, Gustav. *Nuremburg Diary.* Farrar, Strauss and Co., 1947.

Kongtrul, Jamgon. *The Great Awakening.* Shambhala Books, Boston, 1987.

Kunsang, Erik Pema. *A Tibetan Buddhist Companion.* Shambhala Books, Boston, 2003.

Sachs, Robert. *Perfect Endings: A Conscious Approach to Dying and Death.* Inner Traditions, Rochester, Vermont, 1998.

Sachs, Robert. *The Passionate Buddha: Wisdom on Intimacy and Enduring Love.* Inner Traditions, Bear and Co., Rochester, Vermont, 2002.

Tarthang Tulku Rinpoche. *Skillful Means.* Dharma
  Publishing, Berkeley, California, 1978.

Zopa, Lama. *Ultimate Healing: The Power of Compassion.*
  Wisdom Publications, Boston, 2001.

INDEX